Burton, Jeffrey B.
The chessman

AF
Burt

	DATE DUE		
70¢ 8/30/17	9/9/12		

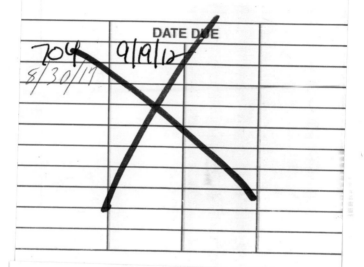

8/12

The Chessman

A novel by Jeffrey B. Burton

The Chessman

A novel by Jeffrey B. Burton

MACADAM CAGE

MacAdam/Cage Publishing
155 Sansome Street, Suite 550
San Francisco, CA 94104

www.MacAdamCage.com

Library of Congress Cataloging-in-Publication Data

Burton, Jeffrey B.
The chessman / by Jeffrey B. Burton.
p. cm.
ISBN 978-1-59692-370-6 (hardcover)
1. Serial murder investigation—Fiction. I. Title.
PS3602.U76977C47 2012
813'.6—dc23
2012013111

Publisher's Note: This is a work of fiction. Names, characters, places, and incidents either are the product of the author's imagination or are used fictitiously. Any resemblance to actual events, locales, or persons, living or dead, is entirely coincidental.

Designed by Dorothy Carico Smith

Printed in the United States of America

1 2 3 4 5 6 7 8 9 10

"Of all ghosts, the ghosts of our old loves are the worst."

—*Sir Arthur Conan Doyle*

Prologue

The special agent flipped open his ID for the two policemen hovering about the front entrance to what was now Washington, D.C.'s most recent crime scene. Judging from the two news vans being held at bay down the street, it would also be tomorrow morning's lead story.

Actually, the special agent silently corrected himself as he inspected the security system a few paces inside the residence's entryway, it would be *this* morning's lead story and it would appear on all network and cable news shows, a lead story that would rock this old town to its marrow. The agent slipped elasticized shoe covers over his black Florsheims and headed toward the stairs. The coffee that had singed his esophagus as he double-timed it to the crime scene had done little to banish his grogginess. He was getting too old for these midnight calls, and could easily have curled up on one of the circular staircase's marble steps and grabbed another five hours of shuteye. Of course, that might not play too well in his upcoming review.

The Brink's Home Security System had been comprehensive, top of the line by any standards. And if the victim himself hadn't shut off Brink's, that meant *Oh Shit!* As in *Oh Shit* the unknown subject—the UNSUB—had an IQ. Two calls on the way over informed him that the housemaid was visiting a sick sister in Seattle. The chauffeur, who was safely tucked in at his home in Alexandria, had dropped his employer off at his Georgetown abode after a late dinner with a group of senior senators, with strict orders to pick him up at ten o'clock sharp the following morning.

The special agent hit the top of the stairs and walked down a long hallway, toward an open room and the muffled voices of the team of investigators. He looked down at his wrist. Three a.m. Likely scenario: the victim comes home, taps in his security code, goes upstairs, hangs his tie and suit jacket in the walk-in off the bedroom, sheds his Ferragamos, enters the master bath for a quick brush of the ivories, and enters the master to find the shooter sitting on his bed. No sign of a struggle, perhaps he knew the UNSUB, perhaps he let him—or her, it was D.C., for Christ's sake—into the house right after the chauffeur vamoosed. Either way, no sign of a struggle, and the man recently designated by the president and soon-to-be chairman of the United States Securities and Exchange Commission gets one smack dead center in the forehead.

But that was only half the reason why the agent had to forfeit a night's Z's and haul ass across town. The other half was something he had to see for himself—get an actual visual—before they took the SEC commissioner's body away for a formal autopsy.

The special agent spotted Detective Howell and headed toward him. He'd met Howell a time or two in the past year.

Howell watched as he approached, then nodded. "The shooter must have dialed 911 from the phone by the bed on his way out."

The agent watched as another detective dusted the bed phone for fingerprints. "What a sport."

"I heard the tape. No sound whatsoever so dispatch sends a squad and an ambulance." Detective Howell looked at the FBI agent. "Does that tell you anything?"

The agent shrugged. "Did you put in the call?"

"Yes."

"Why?"

"Talk to them," Howell said, tossing a thumb over his shoulder.

The special agent walked over to the body and knelt down. Two medical examiners were on the floor, one dictating measurements into a handheld recorder. A forensic team worked the master bedroom, a couple more moving about in the bathroom. The agent got a bad feeling. He doubted that they would find anything of much use.

C. Kenneth Gottlieb II, seventy-year-old widower, lay on his back in a sea of off-white Berber with a fist-sized hole punched out the back of his head. Exit wounds tended to have that effect.

"What have you got?" the agent asked.

The examiner with the recorder stopped dictating and looked up at him through Coke-bottle lenses. "Forty-five cartridge, maybe."

The agent inspected the victim's forehead, the entry wound, and began to think that he'd only have to follow this case from a distance, through the newspapers, and that he might actually get some more shuteye tonight instead of spending the rest of it in a drafty conference room.

"Anything else?"

"Craziest thing I've seen in eight years on the job." The ME held up a small baggy and the special agent realized instantly that sleep was out of the question. The baggy held a single chess piece: a crimson-covered glass queen. "This was inserted nearly half an inch into the entry wound. Wedged so tight I used a needle-nose to pull it out after the photographers were done."

The agent stood, typed a number into his cell phone as he walked from the room. The call was answered on the first ring.

"He's back."

Book One

Opening Moves

Chapter 1

It had been a harried day. And it didn't seem likely to let up anytime soon.

Retired Special Agent Drew Cady thought he'd left his former life far behind, and immediately kicked himself for picking up the phone, even though he'd recognized via caller ID that the call came from Quantico—from a certain academy located on the United States Marine Corps Base in the green hills of Virginia.

Hard to believe that a mere six hours earlier Cady had been in his home study, sipping a glass of freshly squeezed orange juice, and about to drop a lowball in an online auction for a 1918 Abraham Lincoln half dollar. American numismatics had become an addictive hobby after his *early* retirement. Cady had done a little consulting on the side, mostly helping hotel chains bring their security systems into the twenty-first century, but to be honest, coin collecting had become an encompassing pastime. And this little gem was in superb condition, a blush of rose patina splashed across the coin for flavor.

Nope, Cady never should have answered that phone call.

Although no specifics were mentioned, Roland Jund, his old boss and currently one of the bureau's assistant directors, had cajoled, persuaded, sweet-talked, and all but blackmailed Cady into dropping everything, heading straight to the airport—a car would be arriving at Cady's door in mere minutes—and flying from his home in Canton, Ohio, to the nation's capital. And then making haste to the J. Edgar Hoover Building—the bureau's headquarters—on Pennsylvania Avenue in the District, where Jund would connect with him as soon as possible.

Once past security, Cady had been ushered into an empty conference room by an overly somber secretary and informed that the "other agents" would be joining him momentarily. *Which part of "retired" do they not quite grasp?* Cady wondered to himself. Fortunately, they'd passed a coffee station during the trek to the meeting room and Cady was able to score an unoffered cup of java while Miss Somber stood off to the side, scowling at him. The cup—too sweet, as though Cady had subconsciously spooned in extra sugar to counter whatever harsh medicine lay before him—sat nearly empty on the conference table next to his unblemished yellow pad. *Good thing I rushed here to sit waiting, twiddling my thumbs*—an action never gracefully completed since the loss of fifty percent use of his right hand.

And exactly why am I here? Cady wondered. *Three years is a lifetime in this business.* What urgent help could he possibly provide? Today's news cycle had focused solely on the murder—no, make that assassination—of SEC Commissioner C. Kenneth Gottlieb. Cady didn't know Gottlieb, would have had trouble picking the old gent out of a police lineup. Gottlieb had been one of five commissioners sitting on the Securities and Exchange Commission. He had been selected by the president to replace the SEC chairman, who had recently resigned under a bipartisan storm cloud of disapproval over the continuing loss of public trust in the financial markets. And with Gottlieb's ascension, word on Wall Street had it that the times they were a-changin'. But that was so much inside baseball, and to Cady, Gottlieb was just another bureaucrat in a town chock full of them.

Jund refused to say anything over the phone, very hush-hush, which frightened Cady and was in itself an answer.

There could be no other explanation.

Cady's head snapped toward the door as Jund entered the room, briefcase in hand, followed on a short leash by Elizabeth Preston, Jund's administrative mini-me. Trailing them was a young black man that Cady couldn't place. All wore the same grim expression. Cady stood and held his gimp hand toward his old boss.

"Drew!" Jund faked a toothy grin and pumped Cady's hand, pretending not to notice Cady's less-than-powerful grip. "Great to see you. You remember Liz, of course?"

"Of course I do," Cady said, nodding at Preston and noting the additional gray in her salt-and-pepper, shoulder-length cut. She shot Cady her Mona Lisa smirk and he considered himself lucky. They'd locked horns in the past. He bore Preston no ill will, but she remained all but impossible to read.

"And this is Special Agent Fennell Evans. He's our boy genius at FSRTC."

"Please call me Fen."

Cady reached across the table and shook Agent Evans' hand. FSRTC was the Forensic Science Research and Training Center at the Academy.

"So how's the stamp collection coming along?" Jund needled him.

"I collect coins, sir. In fact, this trip of yours is costing me a little something that I've been tracking for three months."

"Let me get dinner tonight. I'll let you sort through the change I get back from the cashier."

"Good one."

Cady suddenly remembered why he both loved and hated the assistant director. The polished marble charisma not only allowed Jund to navigate smoothly in the tumultuous waters of the bureau, but to rise to a position of such power in a relatively short timeframe. Cady had also seen Jund's rough edges, sandy and jagged, where all polish had worn thin. He'd hoped not to see those edges again.

"My poison's golf, Drew. Can't play it nearly enough." And with a hushed cough, Jund sat down, signifying that the witty banter segment of the meeting had ended. He opened his case and took out a manila file folder and pen. "I sincerely apologize for rattling your cage and making you fly out here, Drew, but I think you'll soon understand the reason, as well as why all the cloak-and-dagger." Jund flipped open the folder and scanned the summary page, leaving small checkmarks in the margins as he cruised past each paragraph.

"As you are no doubt aware, late last night a commissioner on the Securities and Exchange Commission, C. Kenneth Gottlieb, was found murdered in the master bedroom of his own residence. Shot once in the center of his forehead. Due to Gottlieb's stature, this case is political dynamite."

"CNN was sketchy at the airport. Any suspects or arrests at this time?"

"No arrests, but let me take a moment before we discuss suspects." The assistant director leaned forward in his chair. "The crime scene was immaculate, no sign of a struggle, no sign of burglary or vandalism; frankly, nothing appears to have been taken, though his home contained jewelry, high-value artwork on the walls, and a safe or two."

"Perhaps Gottlieb got less from an escort service than he bargained for and the hookup went sour."

"Of course we're looking at all scenarios, but in light of what I'm about to tell you, a sex crime appears highly unlikely. You see, although nothing seems to have been taken, Drew, something was left behind—something left specifically for us to find." Jund prompted the forensics expert: "Fen."

"A chess piece was inserted into the killing wound in—"

"Jesus." Cady looked down at the scars crisscrossing the top of his right hand.

"I second that emotion," Jund said.

Three years earlier Cady had spent the aftermath of the Chessman case in a hospital undergoing a string of surgeries, and then another month at home tapering off the opiates. "What type of chess piece was it, Agent Evans?"

"A clear glass queen. The same make that the Chessman utilized in the previous homicides."

"If the Chessman is not dead," Cady said, thinking aloud, "and a new game is beginning, everything we thought we knew about the original case needs to be reexamined in a new light."

"Look, anyone who only follows the headlines will recall all that ugliness from back then." The assistant director continued, "It wouldn't take a rocket scientist to steal his M.O. Gottlieb's a copycat killing."

"We went 'no comment' on the chess pieces."

"We did, Drew, but this town's a sieve. You know that. Rich and famous cadavers tend to have that effect. And once the leaking began it turned into a three-ring media circus. The press ran all sorts of bullshit back then."

"I remember."

"A double lobotomy appears a pre-req for J-school these days. We did the best we could to keep our trump card silent. But everything came out eventually. Hacks wrote books."

"Remember that discussion we had, sir? Back when I left the bureau?"

Jund nodded. "That's one of the reasons you're here, Drew. Your *nightmare scenario*. How it ended too tidily and all that…but let's not jump ahead of ourselves."

"What's for me to jump ahead of, sir? I'm retired."

The room sat in silence for several seconds.

"With your experience on the original case," Liz Preston spoke for the first time, "we were hoping to utilize your services on a strictly consulting basis."

Cady laughed out loud. "You've got to be putting me on, right?"

"We could use your *unique* insight."

"You've got agents far brighter than me lining up around the block."

"No one knows the Chessman case better than you, Drew. You lived it. For better or worse, you're our SME—subject matter expert. Help us prove it's a copycat."

"But what if it's not a copycat killing?"

"Well, if he's truly alive—and that's a pretty big *if* at this point— you got within kissing distance of the bastard once before."

"If I did so well, sir, how come his last victim's brains wound up all over my suit jacket?"

"You put us on the right track from your hospital bed."

"That was a process of elimination." Cady looked at the assistant director. "And from what you've just shared with me, I likely screwed that up as well."

"I don't buy that," the AD said softly. "Occam's Razor—think horses, not zebras."

"With all due respect, sir, when it came to the Chessman, the simple solution was never the best."

"The Chessman is dead." Jund began counting his fingers. "We got his body, for Christ's sake; we've got a body of evidence—finger-prints, the murder weapon, even the leftover chess pieces; and we've got motive and opportunity. It was a slam dunk. Now, until we get hard proof to suggest otherwise, Gottlieb's murder is a copycat."

"But if it's not a copycat, if it turns out to be the Chessman—why should he return?" Cady asked. "He achieved the perfect checkmate, did it in such a manner that guaranteed we end the manhunt, because you and I would have moved heaven and earth to find him. So why should he return now?"

"Arrogance," said Jund.

"Perhaps he wants back in the limelight. An encore performance. You know these sadists never get enough," volunteered Agent Preston.

"He's anything but your garden variety sadist. The SOB was playing three-dimensional chess while we were playing checkers."

"Perhaps the game never really ended," Agent Evans hypothesized. "You said yourself that everything from the original case must be reexamined."

Cady nodded, lost in thought.

"I'm confused, Drew," Preston spoke again. "According to your nightmare scenario, the Chessman tricked us all into believing that he was dead. So even if we assume he's still alive somewhere out there, you refuse to credit him with Gottlieb's murder?"

"I have no idea what to think right now. All I'm saying is that if he went to such great lengths to stage his own death, to throw us off the scent, then his resurfacing doesn't make any sense."

"Then help us prove it's a copycat, and then you can be on your merry way," Jund said, a pleading look in his eyes. "But if your nightmare scenario turns out to be the case, Drew, we'll need you to smoke him out."

"Quite frankly, sir, you should have fired me three years ago."

"Admittedly, the investigation went dramatically south. But we're neck deep in a situation here and we need your help to—"

"No."

"What?"

"I said no."

Assistant Director Jund dropped his pen onto the open folder. "Liz, could you and Agent Evans be so kind as to take a fiver?"

It was impossible to tell which agent made more haste to exit the conference room, leaving the two men alone to gawk at each other.

"What's the matter with you, *Agent Cady*?" The job title slid thickly off the assistant director's tongue, as though addressing Cady like he was still with the bureau would make it true. "You used to be my prize bloodhound. Tough as nails."

"I was never tough as nails, sir."

"The hell you weren't."

"Senator Farris came to see me that first night in the hospital… at George Washington."

"That so?" Jund replied. "The good senator was all over my ass that week, calling for my resignation. Had an 'off the record' with him to make it stop. Never knew he visited you in the hospital."

"Visit might not be the right word. I had my hand elevated, my jaw wired shut, a Grade 1 concussion, and a knee the size of Mount St. Helens, and even with the morphine drip, my head throbbed. I felt like I'd been hit by a Mack truck and I couldn't sleep a wink."

"I've seen road kill look more chipper than you did that night."

"About four a.m. there's a commotion outside in the hallway. A second later Arlen Farris storms in, glares at me for an eternity and says, 'I wish to hell it were you down there in the morgue instead.'"

"Senator Arlen Farris is a bully and a jackass."

"I'd gotten his son killed."

"No you didn't, Drew." The assistant director took a thicker file from his briefcase and placed it on top of the open folder in front of him. "The only reason you were at Patrick Farris's home that night was because of their bullshit."

"However deceptive the senator and congressman were, I should have seen through the smokescreen."

"Clairvoyance is not part of the job description."

"Remember, sir, they came to us for help."

Jund looked at the file he had just set on the tabletop and then abruptly switched subjects. "How's Laura? You two work through it?"

"I guess," Cady said. "She got remarried in June. Some guy who owns a car dealership in Akron."

"I hadn't heard." Jund's face reddened. "I'm sorry."

"A mutual friend set them up on a blind date. I guess they clicked."

The assistant director looked at Cady's left hand. "You're still wearing the ring."

"Guess I'm living the lie." Cady paused, searching for the right words, and then said, "Look, sir, I don't want to waste anyone's time. I appreciate your confidence in me, I truly do, but I'm not cut out for this. Not anymore. If anyone wants to pick my brain on what happened back then, I'm a phone call away."

"I'm beyond spent, Agent Cady. I've not slept in nearly thirty hours, so please forgive me if I give you the Cliff Notes version of the pep talk. You're like a broken pop machine, son, with an 'Out of Order' sign hung on the front."

"Or perhaps all I want is to be left alone."

"The pointy heads in Behavioral would mumble something about you being in *dire* need of redemption. And closure."

Cady began shaking his head.

"Hear me out," Jund said, leaning back. "I was raised by a couple of atheists and I imagine my soul is flapping in the breeze like a busted box kite, so I can't speak for redemption. However, Agent Cady, I can speak fully to the closure I suspect you crave. It's private and personal—different flavors for everyone—but for me closure is when I sit behind the defendant in the courtroom and burn a hole in the back of their head with my eyes. After a while, they'll sense it and turn around. They always do. And that's when I give them my best Stan Laurel impersonation."

"From Laurel and Hardy?" Cady asked, confused.

"I do a picture perfect Stan Laurel, Agent Cady. Picture perfect. It tells them that they got caught by someone with the IQ of a dead hamster. Remember the Dog Kennel Killer from ten years ago? At the trial he kept looking back at me, could not believe his eyes. I even let my mouth hang open for the complete village idiot look. When they brought him back to his cell that afternoon, he tried to chew through the veins in his wrist. I like to think that was on me. I realize that may sound certifiable to most, Agent Cady, but that's how I get my closure. That's how I sleep at night."

Cady digested what the assistant director had said, certain the man was joking, and shook his head again. "It's not about closure, sir."

"It has everything to do with closure." The AD leaned forward and slapped the new file folder for emphasis. "You told me more than once that you thought he'd slipped away, that the final act had been staged like some Off-Broadway production. That's three years of second guesses and hesitations percolating beneath the surface— driving you round the bend. If it turns out not to be a copycat, then you can help us nail the bastard's hide to my wall, Agent Cady, and that will give you all the closure that you will ever need to move on with your life."

"Sir—"

"No, Agent Cady. Please let me finish. I'm not asking you to be the SAC. You will not be leading this investigation. That's Preston, for now anyway. This is backseat only. You won't be near the headlines."

"What would you have me do?"

"Some light lifting. Liaison with Liz and review the Gottlieb file.

It won't take long, as it's about the size of your fingernail. See if it screams copycat."

"Somehow I don't think you flew me out here for that."

"I need you to cover home plate."

"What does that mean?"

"If it's not a copycat—if the Chessman is genuinely alive and hiding in the weeds after having fucked us over big time—nobody knows more about what happened three years ago than you do. So I need you to travel back in time and find me a loose thread. Then I want you to bring me that loose thread so we can both yank on that son of a bitch for all its worth, right on up to his lethal injection."

"You want me to cold case the original investigation?"

"Everything came to an abrupt end after Patrick Farris. The Chessman was dead, so for all practical purposes the investigation ceased in its tracks. But if we were wrong…if we were wrong…" The AD let silence fill the void.

"A cold case," Cady said, chewing it over in his mind.

Jund stood, picking up the FBI file. "Solve the case in the past and we can catch the murdering prick in the present."

Assistant Director Jund held out the Chessman folder.

Cady took it from him.

Jund didn't get a chance to respond before there was a light knock and the door opened to reveal Miss Somber.

"Sorry to disturb you, Director, but the *Washington Post* has connected Gottlieb's death to the Chessman. One of their reporters is calling for a comment."

Chapter 2

Cady sat at the chair in his Embassy Suites hotel room and continued to marvel at how Assistant Director Jund could play him like a cheap toy out of a kid's meal box. Within seconds of tap dancing the Woodward wannabe off the line empty-handed, Jund had Cady signing a contractor agreement, multiple confidentiality forms, and then had pawned him off on a blonde Admin named Penny Decker, who made quick work of providing him with proper ID and computer access to the bureau's network so he could send Jund his status reports.

A cubicle the size of a postage stamp was made available for when Cady was in the office. Cady had sat in the cube and read through the Gottlieb file. The clear glass queen tied Gottlieb to the earlier deaths, and burglary appeared not to be a motive—also the case in the earlier deaths. But the AD had been correct; there wasn't much to prove or disprove the existence of a copycat killer. Cady sent Agent Preston an e-mail stating as much and headed out for the day. When Cady checked into the hotel, the receptionist informed him that his week-long reservation had been made the night before.

Cady thought about Roland Jund and shook his head. A kid's meal toy.

—

The Chessman file waited on the coffee table in front of him. He remembered that first morning, the grim scene at the law offices of Sanfield & Fine. Cady had been there merely as an observer, ignorant of the chain of events about to unfold…and the toll on body and soul that they would exact.

Cady closed his eyes, inhaled deeply, and tried to force himself back into the zone. On the count of three he opened both his eyes and the file folder.

On top was the CE, the chronicle of events form that he'd personally typed up three years earlier. It was followed by a separate folder containing a copy of the D.C. Metropolitan Police Department's investigation into the slaying of K. Barrett "Barry" Sanfield. The detectives at MPD had done a meticulous job, but were quite content to share the hot potato with the Fibbies after the Zalentine twin killings connected the M.O. It was political dynamite and MPD was more than happy to ride shotgun, even if it only spun them an inch or two away from the harsh glare of the media magnifying glass.

Cady could hardly blame them.

The MPD's homicide report on Sanfield began with pictures of the power attorney from better days, a couple of obvious professional shots that the litigator had taken for promotional purposes, such as those appearing on his firm's web site, in articles or legal journals, or at conferences that he might keynote. The pictures of Sanfield that came after these would never appear in a legal journal or be distributed at a keynote speech. These pics were the ones snapped by a forensic photographer.

K. Barrett Sanfield was the D.C. power attorney—the Magician, as he was known among the inner circles—that the politicians with the thickest billfolds rushed to in order to make certain *situations* disappear. Sanfield had been one of a handful advising President Clinton on the Lewinsky matter, before the blue dress came to light and made all else a moot point. Sanfield had been behind-the-scenes for Gore during the chaos in Florida. Those two *situations* hadn't broken his way, unlike the vast majority of Sanfield's cases—the ones you didn't see on the evening news—which was exactly why his anxious clients didn't blink an eye at his billing rate.

Sanfield had been Arlen Farris's campaign manager in 1976, the win that sent Farris to the United States Senate as the Junior Senator from Delaware. Farris had ridden in on Jimmy Carter's coattails but stayed a few decades longer. Sanfield had followed Farris to D.C. after the election and set up shop—said shop being Sanfield & Fine, Attorneys at Law. Very blue chip. Business thrived and, in the early 1990s, Sanfield's effectively connected law firm was able to command a corner wing on the twelfth floor of One Franklin Square, a posh high-rise commercial office building on K Street.

Sanfield, long divorced with no children of his own, had not been found until the following morning. Stephen Fine, son of Gerald Fine—Sanfield's partner and confidant—and a junior partner workaholic his own self, had arrived for work at his usual 5:30 in the a.m., seen Sanfield's door was shut, was amazed that anyone, much less his godfather Barry, had beat him in that morning, and, after brewing a double bag of leaded, peeked his head into Sanfield's office to say hi. And what the junior partner saw caused him to drop his cup of java, scamper out to the foyer as though the devil himself were in hot pursuit, smack the down button a couple dozen times, and call 911 on his cell phone in the elevator as he fled to the safety of the guard station on the first floor.

Cady had been at the scene within hours of the discovery of Sanfield's body. His presence there was twofold: ostensibly to lend a helping hand to the local gendarmes, as well as facilitate the use of the FBI Crime Lab in the collection and analysis of crime scene data. But the ulterior motive for Cady's loitering was to keep Assistant

Director Jund apprised, firsthand and in real time, of any new developments in the Sanfield slaying. Cady imagined that even at this early a stage in the investigation, a flock of politicos was already lining up to breathe down the assistant director's neck.

"I thought Barry's killer was still in the office," Stephen Fine said when Cady had initially interviewed him for the bureau. Looking at the forensic photographs of K. Barrett Sanfield, Cady wondered if Fine was still the early bird of the office.

MPD determined, and Cady concurred, that the scene had played out this way. Sanfield had stood up, likely in an effort to defend himself from the attacker or attackers. It had been a short struggle, no defensive cuts on Sanfield's hands, but the blade had entered upward underneath the solar plexus and breastbone, through the pericardium, puncturing the right atrium of Sanfield's heart. Death was almost instantaneous. MPD's initial line of thought was that Sanfield hadn't sensed danger until the last possible instant, and that perhaps Sanfield knew his killer.

The most they could glean from the entry wound was that the killer was likely right-handed. The knife was likely a type of OTF stiletto—a stabbing weapon—the kind outlawed in the late 1950s. Aside from the fact that the killer wasn't considerate enough to leave the spring-release blade at the scene, the medical examiner noted from the entry wound and internal damage that the blade had been twisted, rotated back and forth repeatedly, in order to router a wider opening. Some might call that overkill, but not in the manner that domestic crimes of passion involving all manner of kitchen cutlery are overkill. Here the ME realized that, however bent, there was an iota of logic involved. After Sanfield had sunk back down in his chair, and a minute of bloodletting had passed, the killer pressed the chess piece—a glass queen—crown first into the gap he'd created beneath attorney's solar plexus. Not something you saw every day.

MPD's crime scene investigators took fingerprints from every conceivable surface in Sanfield's executive office, all door handles, his aged mahogany desk, his credenza and matching wall-length bookcase, his two-tone leather couch, his Herman Miller Aeron chair, his liquor cabinet, the Scotch bottles—you name it. MPD was able to quietly, and impressively, match all prints against clients, staff members, and janitors. Clients and colleagues in Sanfield's orbit were okay with this effort at ruling out the known prints on the agreement that none of the prints would be sent to any database. Unfortunately in this case, once elimination printing was finished, MPD was left with no remaining unknown prints.

In terms of building security, tenants could opt to go with the corporate security firm contracted by One Franklin Square, Cadence Security, or negotiate with another company of their own choosing. Sanfield & Fine chose to stick with Cadence Security and had them set up the access control system for S&F's office facilities. Cadence's single card solution for parking and office entry, as well as building and elevator access during afterhours, appeared to be a no-brainer. Each S&F employee was issued one proximity ID card—a prox card—that they wouldn't even have to remove from their wallet, purse or badge holder as they waved it in front of the card reader and let the radio frequency identification technology, a transponder chip in the prox card, take care of the rest. If you were authorized to enter, the door would unlock. If not, well, good luck with all that.

An initial break came when the electronic surveillance report provided by Cadence Security indicated that Debbie Varner, one of the newer paralegals, had entered the offices through the reception door at 8:42 that evening, a time that the ME was able to establish as the general time of death based on internal temperature readings of Sanfield's body.

Upon immediate face-to-face questioning, a hysterical Ms.

Varner informed the detectives that she'd misplaced her security badge, which she normally kept in the armrest compartment of her Subaru, thought she'd accidentally left it at home, had piggybacked in that morning with Peg Maynard, another fresh-faced Sanfield & Fine paralegal, and fully planned on reporting it if her badge didn't appear in another day or two. Her alibi for that night had checked out, as Ms. Varner and her roommate/partner had been at dog obedience training across town from 7:30 to 9:00 p.m., surrounded by many witnesses—and not just the four-legged variety.

Cady remembered thinking at the time that no matter how the case turned out, these two new paralegals weren't long for Sanfield & Fine.

Ms. Varner's badge had also been used to activate the elevator at 8:58 p.m. From the front reception area, it took less than a minute to wind through the hallways to Sanfield's corner office suite. Then a little extra time to return to the elevator foyer and summon a lift— assuming the killer didn't sprint. That gave the killer about fourteen minutes to stab Sanfield, insert the glass queen, and get back to the elevator. But the real question for Cady was, why did it take so long? Every additional second on the scene could spell the perpetrator's downfall. Did the killer know Sanfield? Was that why there weren't defensive wounds about Sanfield's hands? Or was he there for the hit, but also searching for something? Too many questions.

A secondary break came when MPD's Detective Bruce Pearl worked with the red-faced and major-league pissed off head of Cadence Security—Dick Heath, an ex-FBI man himself—to review the night's digital surveillance recordings from the closed-circuit television surveillance cameras strategically placed at all the entrances and exits of the block-long high rise. Video from each security camera was transmitted to the monitors at the corresponding guard station covering that particular access point.

Heath, Pearl, and a team of Cadence guards reviewed the digital recordings from the prior evening. The building was for the most part emptied out by that time of night, with only an occasional workaholic sneaking out into the darkening skies. Heath got a hit on the monitor he was glaring at, with a time log reading in the bottom right corner of the video of 9:01 p.m., a time that fit hand in glove with the digital timeline established per Ms. Varner's prox card. A hunched figure with a baseball cap, carrying something indecipherable in his right hand, was shown leaving through the northeast exit. Suddenly, he materialized on Heath's display monitor as if out of nowhere, as though he'd figured out a way to slide through One Franklin and only get detected on this single surveillance camera. His face was aimed downward, away from the camera, off in the shadows to the side. But one thing was starkly evident; the figure had a pronounced limp.

Heath called Detective Pearl and the other Cadence guards over, scanned back the video recording, and let the others view this misshapen figure as he made his exit.

"Ah, hell," one of the night watchmen spoke up. "That's just the kid."

Cady flipped a page ahead to the most interesting part in this section of the case file, the transcript of Detective Pearl questioning the Cadence security guard, a bodybuilder type named Ritter, who knew *the kid.*

"How long has this person been hanging around One Franklin Square?" asked Detective Pearl.

"He began showing up a month, maybe six weeks back. He had that club foot or something and a crippled-up claw of a hand that always held a juice box, the kind my kids get in those Oscar Mayer Lunchables."

"Did you ever talk to him?"

"Absolutely. The first night I saw him limping back and forth by the main entry, I went over to see if he needed help."

"What did he have to say?"

"Look, Detective, I'm not up on the medical conditions for the mildly retarded, so in the back of my mind I'm assuming he's got cerebral palsy or something. Anyway, he was a real happy guy, nodded at everything, and there was a bit of spittle problem. I remember taking a step backwards. He stuttered something about the Metro bus, and I figured the kid was waiting for the 9:05. The kid was here about every other night for an hour."

"You keep calling him *the kid*. How old do you think he was?"

"He wasn't really a kid. I guess I just thought of him that way, just like I think of them as kids in the Special Olympics. You know, both that and him sucking down those juice boxes. Hard to tell, but I'd say he could be anywhere between early 20s and a youngish 40."

"What did he look like?"

"Obviously Caucasian," Ritter said. "I'm five-ten, and he was taller than me even though he was scrunched up, so maybe six-one if he stood up straight. Greasy complexion, always looked like he'd recently washed his face with fried chicken or something. Black hair. And he always wore a Nationals' baseball cap all crooked on his head, rain or shine. Plus, he wore one of those hairnets underneath."

"He wore a hairnet?"

"I figured one of the restaurants down the block had him making onion rings or something easy, and that he came here to kill some time before the bus picked him up."

"Did you talk to him often?"

"Just that one time, Detective. To be honest, he wasn't hurting anyone and I didn't want to get any more spittle on me, so whenever I saw him across the lobby or outside by the windows looking in or when he'd play by the elevators, I just gave him a nod. I think the other guys did the same. We all kind of felt sorry for him, you know."

"He played by the elevators?"

"I saw him there. Once or twice. Just farting around. You know, pressing the buttons and going in and out. Didn't hurt anything because at this time of night, he'd need an ID card to make them actually run."

Heath and Detective Pearl were able to hunt down and account for the handful of other figures caught on the video cameras that evening, but the kid never came back. The Metro bus drivers on One Franklin Square and the other nearby routes had no recollection of a mentally handicapped man sporting a limp and a Nationals' cap. Pearl had his people check with all restaurants within six city blocks, but none of those establishments had anyone fitting the kid's description slinging French fries or bussing tables.

Cady leaned back in his hotel chair, closed his eyes, and pictured Sanfield: alone in his office that evening, maybe all of ten minutes from packing it in for the night, when he hears an odd voice coming from the hallway. He looks up and sees what appears to be a mentally handicapped young man standing in his doorway with a Nationals' baseball cap all catawampus atop his head. The guy is wearing some old-time latex medical gloves—the ME had found traces of corn-starch powder in the blood on Sanfield's dress shirt and around his chest wound—and probably mumbles something incomprehensible about Sanfield's trash can. A confused Sanfield likely tells the fellow that the janitors had already come and gone an hour earlier. But the kid limps towards Sanfield's desk to double-check for himself. Sanfield isn't frightened at this point; like most people, he's uncomfortable interacting with the mentally challenged but isn't afraid of them. Then the kid passes by Sanfield's rubbish basket, suddenly the limp has disappeared and now the simpleton has some kind of dagger in his hand. At this point Sanfield stands to defend himself against the intruder—but it's too late. Much too late for Sanfield. Perhaps the attorney's last thought was *My God, I'm being murdered by the guy from Flowers for Algernon.*

Cady scribbled a note on his yellow pad, a reminder to contact Detective Pearl, a diminutive man, possibly all of 5'4", with a weed crop of gray hair. What he lacked in height Pearl more than made up for in intellect, and Cady still remembered their last conversation from three years back.

"He's going to be a bitch to catch," the homicide investigator had told Cady.

"Why is that?"

"It's a locked room mystery that rivals anything by Poe, but if I wanted to snuff a high profile in a secured building with guards buzzing about like wasps," Pearl said, his dark eyes unblinking, *"I'd have done it damn near identically."*

Chapter 3

The first e-mail from Richard Gere was expelled straight into Stouder's Deleted Items folder with the rest of the nonsense and other spam. The subject line read simply *I Know Your Secret*, but the body of the e-mail was blank. Stouder noticed how they had faked the movie star's name in the Yahoo address by adding an extra "A" to the first name; then he tapped the Del key and sent the e-mail to join its colleagues of Viagra and Pharmaceutical ads in delete purgatory.

The second e-mail from Richard Gere—nay, make that Richaard Gere—added a minor twist to the subject line. However, the minor twist added to that second e-mail rated a ten on Stouder's personal Richter scale and sent tremors down his spine. The subject line of the new e-mail read *I Know Stouder's Secret*, and the message was an ominous *We'll Talk Soon.*

Though safely enshrined in his luxury condo in the gated community of Bedford Village, Stouder snapped his head around as though trying to catch someone reading over his shoulder. He walked down to verify that his front door was locked and bolted, with the privacy brace jammed hard under the doorknob. He made sure all window shades were tightly drawn and then walked into the kitchen. Stouder poured himself a second glass of Merlot. He squeezed his fingers into tight little fists to help cease the quivering.

I Know Stouder's Secret... We'll Talk Soon.

The thing that turned his blood to ice water was that he wasn't viewing e-mail through his home account. He could understand his name appearing in his formal e-mail set up through Outlook, as his name was part of the address—not hard for the cyber marketing jerksticks to customize via that avenue. But Stouder was reading from his strictly *hobby* AOL account. None of the data Stouder entered as he set up this bogus AOL account was accurate—not the name, address, phone number—absolutely nothing. Plus, he'd just set up this new AOL account since the *incident...* and the incident had only occurred last Saturday, for Christ's sake.

So a fake Yahoo account was sending Stouder's bogus AOL account a message claiming to know his secret. It was bad enough seeing this *unknown other* use his name in the subject line, but what really gave him pause and sent him seeking more of the Merlot was the purported knowledge of his secret. Everyone, of course, had secrets. The odd skeleton withering away in the closet that they'd just as soon not have waltzed out into the bright light of day.

And Stouder did indeed have a secret.

But it was nobody's business but his own. It wasn't as though anybody got hurt. Stouder simply went to matinee movies. Disney movies. Opening weekends in Fairfield County movie theaters—many, many miles from his home. A baseball cap and a fuzzy black Halloween moustache were his wardrobe. And if any young boy would happen to make his way, alone, to a nearby restroom, Stouder would follow. Side by side at the urinals, Stouder'd take a quick peek down when no other adults were present. And when the unknowing little tyke finished his business—more often than not forgetting to wash his hands before scampering back to the movie—and Stouder had finished himself off in a stall, he'd head out through the nearest

exit. No one would be the wiser. No harm, no foul. The very defini-
tion of a victimless crime.

I Know Stouder's Secret…We'll Talk Soon.

The Internet had opened many doors for Stouder, hence his various hobby e-mail accounts. He downloaded nothing, and even, for
the most part, avoided the legal pornography sites. But his downfall
was the chat rooms—those damnable enticing chat rooms—where
you could say anything you wanted, where you could be anything
you wished. Stouder's fingers began quivering again. Could this
unknown other know about the incident?

But the incident was never really Stouder's incident to begin with.
Those damnable, damnable chat rooms. Stouder spent his nights
surfing the bulletins, reading mostly, posting the odd comment here
and there. And that was enough, but the requests for *private* chats in
Stouder's *hobby area* were all but impossible to ignore. It was hyp-
notic, unavoidable, like metal shavings toward a magnetic field. Of
course he used a fake logon name, just like the rest of them, and he
watched his language. If anything, Stouder came across like a counselor or schooled mentor, as someone attempting to lend a hand
to these *younger* ones, helping them turn away from this *delinquent*
choice of lifestyle.

But Ricky was a siren song, their nightly chats provocative,
enchanting…fulfilling. Ricky kept requesting that they meet, as he
was almost fourteen and his parents—rich and distant—were away
in Europe for the month. Ricky's sister was at AU during the day, so
Stouder could name a time. Stouder knew he was playing with fire,
knew about sting operations, and knew that Ricky was quite likely a
group of frat boys gulping suds and giggling at a computer keyboard
in Madison, Wisconsin, or some other godforsaken place.

But the tiny chance that Ricky was truly on the up-and-up literally consumed Stouder, ate away at his soul, denied him sleep,

haunted his waking hours, until finally one evening he sped home, logged into the site, and grew an ulcer waiting for Ricky to arrive. When Ricky finally turned up, they set a meeting for the next afternoon at one o'clock. Stouder then jumped in his red Mini Cooper and set off on a giddy road trip to the Greens Farms neighborhood of Westport that evening and drove past the address on Nash Street, just for a quick look-see. Nice spread, tan stucco with arches, exactly how Ricky had described it.

As ever, Stouder was a careful man. Early the next morning he borrowed his aging mother's poodle, something he never did, telling the old bitch he was thinking of getting a dog and wanted to see how it would be. Then he combed in gray and slicked his thinning hair back, popped on obnoxious sunglasses, the fake Halloween moustache, the baggy sweats that made him look ten pounds frumpier, and even placed some orange peels in his cheeks to alter his facial shape as he'd read about once in a thriller. By ten o'clock he was walking slowly up Nash. He'd parked three blocks down and two over. Tanzy, or whatever the goddamned poodle's name was, seemed to be enjoying the sun and Stouder had yet to pick up any of her droppings.

This area of Westport had that nouveau riche look and feel. Stouder was able to eye the house on Nichols as he walked steadily past, just a neighbor out on a casual midmorning stroll. The house looked more impressive during the light of day, hiding Ricky's tragic loneliness inside. Stouder continued up another block, didn't want to make anything look too obvious. He toyed with showing up early. Spit out the orange peels and simply knock on Ricky's door. He was in the act of crossing the walk toward Ricky's side of the street when he spotted the clunker pull up in front of Ricky's house. A man with shoulder-length hair leapt out and jogged up the drive. Stouder let Tanzy sniff at a bush and pondered this odd turn of events.

Another man. Jealousy spiked at Stouder's heart. Unless…could it be Ricky's father, back from Europe two weeks early? The man looked at least a decade too young to be the boy's father. And the clunker looked wrong for a rich daddy. He pictured Ricky's father in a Lexus. Perhaps it was Ricky's sister's college boyfriend. That would explain why the young man was in such a rush. A groggy college student getting a late start and about to catch seven kinds of hell from his girlfriend. That had merit. Stouder pulled on the leash as he and Tanzy began meandering back toward Ricky's house.

Suddenly, a door slammed. The young man Stouder had observed heading up Ricky's drive minutes earlier came bolting down the lawn toward his car. He almost made the beat-up Nova before two of the half-dozen police officers, who unexpectedly poured out of nowhere Stouder could detect, wrestled the greasy-haired young man to the sidewalk. Stouder's heart almost gave out on the spot as the incident unfolded right before his eyes, as though he had a front row seat at some poorly produced Theater of the Absurd performance. Tanzy began barking and for a brief moment all eyes switched to him. He struggled with the leash, dragging the damned dog across the street, away from the high drama. An NBC truck had materialized in the center of the street; cameramen with shoulder units were filming the perp's take down. The light bulb went on in Stouder's head. Ricky wasn't a troubled youth questioning his budding sexuality. Not at all. Ricky was a goddamned Dateline NBC sting operation.

As Stouder yanked the forever-barking poodle across the street, he couldn't help but keep his eyes glued to the greasy-haired man being cuffed on the walkway. Saliva hung from the poor schmuck's mouth, his face a blur of tears. They made brief eye contact. Stouder mouthed a silent prayer as he reached the opposite side of the lane to the continual shrieks of "I didn't do anything! I didn't do anything!"

Yes, P. Campton Stouder certainly dodged the proverbial bullet that particular morning. In his mind's eye he pictured himself being forced to the ground by the local authorities as he attempted to flee the scene of his entrapment, while a news crew filmed everything in its full excruciating, humiliating detail. Hardly an ordeal befitting the Executive Deputy Attorney General for Economic Justice in the great state of New York.

And now someone knew his secret.

Chapter 4

It was after 11:00 p.m., so Cady ran down to the Embassy Suites bar and ordered a Reuben sandwich and chips to take back to his room. Cady hesitated when the bartender asked if he wanted anything to drink. Frankly, he'd kill for a Guinness, but it was going to be a long night. Cady had the very peculiar case of Adrien and Alain Zalentine—the Zalentine twins—to review before nodding off, so he ordered a large coffee instead.

Zalentine Jewelers—of the *Zalentine, It Rhymes with Valentine* slogan—was founded in 1928 in a San Francisco watch repair shop owned by Lionel Zalentine. Lionel's philosophy was to sell the finest quality jewelry at the finest prices. By 1942, the year that Lionel gulped a huge glass of ice tea on one scorcher of a day and then sat down on a bench outside his shop and died, there were sixteen stores across California and Arizona. Lionel's only son, Lansing Zalentine, had three favorite words, words he parroted in every meeting or company event. Lansing's three words were *Expand, Expand, Expand,* and by his death in 1985, Zalentine Jewelers had expanded to over five hundred locations in the United States and Puerto Rico. Lansing's oldest son, Vance Zalentine—the current Zalentine Diamond King—nearly doubled his father's success by peppering shops in suburban retail malls across the United States and Canada. He had also moved the headquarters of the diamond franchise from San Francisco to Los Angeles. Vance married Amanda Whitaker, a former Miss Sacramento, in the late 1970s, and within a year she gave birth to a pair of identical twins—Adrien and Alain Zalentine.

Cady recalled flying to Los Angeles three years earlier on a hasty one-day trip to interview the parents. Assistant Director Jund had made it abundantly clear that, due to the family's stature in the community, he wanted his Special Agent in Charge to meet with both the diamond patriarch and his wife. Pure and simple politics: show the Zalentines that their sons' murders would be receiving attention at the highest of levels.

The one-time beauty pageant queen had been face-lifted and botoxed beyond anything this side of E.T. Amanda Zalentine sat still in the library, staring out the windows, off into the open space of the front garden. Mrs. Zalentine was a basket case and, if not for the melancholy look in her eyes, Cady would have thought her to be in a coma. Both her boys had been murdered, and so she sat, alone in the library, staring off into another time and place, most of her emotions medicated away.

Her husband, Vance Zalentine, however, was a different cup of tea. "Those deviant little shits were nothing but trouble since they were five years old. They had this bond, were somehow hardwired into each other—one entity, almost—and eerie like a *Twilight Zone*."

The Zalentine mansion sat on a hillside in 90210, thirty acres screaming money, and the kind of place where if they refused to let you in, you'd need Eisenhower to plot the invasion. Mrs. Zalentine hadn't been much help, nodding her head like a tilting bird to all of Cady's questions. He switched gears and went into Zalentine's workout room, the size of an airport runway, as Mr. Zalentine huffed and puffed on the Stairmaster.

"It's my fault, really," Zalentine said, pointing a dripping arm toward the library from which Cady had just left Mrs. Zalentine. "I was so goddamned busy twenty-four-seven, I let the alky raise them. But I'll never forget coming home early from a business trip one Friday afternoon, parking the Bentley, and then hearing a string of pops, like tires backfiring, coming from behind the pool house. I snuck around the gardener's shed to see what was going on and I caught the little sociopaths red-handed." Zalentine took deep gulps from his bottle of Evian and continued, "The twins had bought a dozen hamsters from some pet store, and here they were ramming these M-80 firecrackers up a hamster's ass or sticking them down the poor thing's throat and then lighting them off, one after another. Boom! Boom! Boom! Dead hamster parts all over the fucking lawn, a bloody mess. They were ten years old back then. I should have caned the living shit out of little twerps—you know, like they do in Singapore—then they might still be alive."

"Why did they stay out east after college?" Cady asked. "Why not come back home?"

"That was my doing. I was hoping they might mature with time. So I trust-funded them with a generous monthly allowance in order to keep them fat and happy and the hell away from me. A couple of sports cars here, some half-baked investment over there—chump change." Zalentine wiped his brow with his forearm. "You do know they never finished Princeton?"

"I'd heard."

"Turned out they were paying a couple brainy nerds to take their classes and do their assignments. Some kid heard about it and ran to a professor. Three years of tuition and two hundred grand in legacy donations flushed down the shitter."

"Do you know of anyone who would want to harm your sons?"

"You may want to check into where they bought their club drugs from, you know, designer pharmaceuticals—Vicodin, ecstasy, whatever's the current craze."

"There was some high-grade cannabis found onboard their sailboat. We're pressing that angle, but it seems unlikely for a dealer to go to this degree of trouble over recreational drugs."

"Isn't that what these things always turn out to be? Bang-bang over the dope?"

"That's often the case, but your boys had access to no small amount of funds, Mr. Zalentine. Hard to imagine they'd stiff drug dealers to the point of a double homicide."

"To be frank, I can't begin to imagine the predicaments those two might have burrowed themselves into." Zalentine took another gulp from the water bottle. "Pains me to say this, but there could be some oddball sex angle. I'd heard some rumors about the weird stuff they'd get into with girlfriends. It didn't sound pretty, and that was a few years back."

"You didn't want your sons around here. Why is that?"

"I sell diamond rings, Agent Cady. Lots of them. I know what makes people tick. For example, I can tell by your look that you're silently judging me—as a father and a human being—and finding me wanting."

"Sir, I'm just here to ask—"

"Fuck it, doesn't matter," Zalentine said, waving his hand. "I can size up a couple that walks inside any of my jewelry stores within thirty seconds, can tell you exactly what engagement set they'll buy, whether they'll still be married in five years, which one will be the first to cheat—you name it and I can tell you all of that within thirty seconds. So imagine how I could size up my sons. I know it's not the most glowing endorsement of my own flesh and blood, Agent Cady, but do you remember those Menendez brothers—Lyle and Erik—remember them?"

Cady nodded.

"So the reason that I made damn sure they didn't live here after the great hamster detonations, Agent Cady, the reason I sent them off to any boarding school in the country that would take them, and then off to a college on the East Coast, was quite simple. I didn't want to wake suddenly one night to find Adrien and Alain at the foot of the king-size, naked, with scalpels, prepared to take their tricks to an entirely new level."

So it may not have come as an earth-shattering surprise to Vance Zalentine when he received the news that his boy, Alain, had been shot to death at a rest area off U.S. Highway 50, outside of Queenstown, Maryland. Alain Zalentine, out tooling around in his Porsche Carrera GT, had pulled into a rest stop and gone inside to use a bathroom stall. Unbeknownst to Alain, someone had followed him in, given him a minute or two to get settled, then kicked in the stall door and shot Alain dead center in the forehead.

It was not a robbery. Alain's eel-skin wallet, stuffed with six hundred dollars cash and six credit cards, and the keys to his Carrera remained in the pockets of his Dolce & Gabbanas, scrunched down about his ankles in the puddle of blood. Rather the opposite of robbery, and the reason the case immediately drew in the bureau, was that something had been left behind. In this case, a glass bishop had been inserted straight into the entry wound in the middle of Alain's forehead.

Another oddity left at the murder scene was on the men's restroom door. An OUT OF ORDER sign had been duct-taped to the entrance. The cleaning crew from Queenstown had been confused about that sign as well as how it had gotten there. The sign, which looked like something you could pick up at a dollar store, was not one of theirs. Their records did not indicate that any facility at the rest area was not in working condition. The crew went inside, immediately noticing a set of legs extending beneath the stall. They might have thought something else was happening if not for the blood… and the smell. Evidently death was the ultimate laxative. Queenstown PD took the call, but when the chess piece went over the wire, a handful of FBI special agents, led back then by Cady, swarmed to the death site.

The chess piece linked Alain Zalentine's murder directly to the Sanfield case. The related murders had crossed state lines, or, more accurately, crossed from the District of Columbia into Maryland, as D.C. was not part of any U.S. state. As such, the crimes entered FBI jurisdiction and Cady found himself building a task force on the fly in order to work closely with state and local authorities because, contrary to popular belief and Hollywood depictions, the bureau did not swoop in and take over cases from the powers that be.

Queenstown PD had already contacted Beverly Hills PD. A squad car with a grief counselor was en route to the Zalentine mansion to notify Alain's parents. Queenstown had also networked with the Cambridge, Maryland Police Department. They had so far been unable to contact Brother Adrien via his home or cell phone, numbers which had immediately been provided by Verizon-Maryland. Cambridge was sending a squad over to the Dorchester Towers, where the Zalentine twins each owned a luxury condo, to see if they could rustle up the missing Zalentine sibling.

Unlike the hustle and bustle of an identically named city in Massachusetts, Cambridge, Maryland was laid back, quiet and tranquil… or it had been. The Cambridge DA had been alerted. The victim, an heir to Zalentine Diamonds, would make this a high-profile case, and every move taken would have to be done per protocol—by the proverbial book—for it to be solid in court. Agent Cady immediately realized why they were taking these precautions. Brother Adrien was off the radar and the detectives were considering the potential of this being a Bubba Bump, as most murders are committed by someone the victim knew, very likely a family member. Adrien, for the time being, was a prime suspect—think Paris Hilton as a psycho killer. If that proved to be the case, a courtroom media circus would most certainly be on the horizon. A celebrity killing on the docket in the Queenstown courthouse. Cady could see the promo: *Cain and Abel Slaying Rocks Sleepy Berg*, news at eleven. Yes, the district attorneys in both Queenstown and Cambridge were going to be involved every step of the way.

But first they had to find Brother Adrien.

Referring to them as luxury condos was the understatement of the year. Alain and Adrien owned the top floor of the Dorchester Towers, off Washington Street, near the city center. Both had sizable three-bedroom condos, but the rest of the floor was dedicated to a gymnasium that would make high-end fitness clubs flip cartwheels in envy, a movie theater that could seat one hundred people, and a game room the size of Fort Knox, containing everything from classic pinball machines to Donkey Kong and Pac-Man to multiple Game-box, PlayStation, and Wii setups. Yet another section contained a fully-stocked bar in the model of Disney World meets Disco. Cady had walked the floor to get a sense of how Alain lived. All in all, it was a sixteen-year-old male's wet dream.

Alain, in better days, had been wiry—thin but muscular—six-even, with a model's head of blond hair parted to the right. Ditto identical twin Adrien, Cady noted from pictures lining the hallway walls of Alain's condo. Except Adrien's hair was parted on the left, which made for an interesting face-on picture that Cady noticed in the Disney Bar. The boys were certainly in love with their own images.

And speaking of Adrien, he and his blond locks were still

nowhere to be found. Not in his condo, nor in his top floor play palace. Adrien continued to be inaccessible via his cell phone no matter how many urgent messages had been left for him. This was a major red flag. Cady began to believe that Alain might just turn out to be a Bubba Bump after all; some messed-up domestic that resulted in homicide. Perhaps Alain hadn't given Adrien his fair share of turns on Nintendo or whatever in hell other games they had in that home arcade. Cady wondered about the chess pieces. How had Sanfield been dragged into this fray? Did Sanfield know the twins? Had he represented one of them in a dispute?

With the help of the condo's management, Cady was able to make a quick tally of the five sport cars the Zalentine twins owned. Minus Alain's Porsche from his fatal stop at the Highway 50 rest area, there was a Jaguar XKR missing. Within six hours an APB went out listing Adrien Zalentine as a person of interest wanted for questioning and describing the missing Jag—an ebony convertible.

Officers of the Cambridge PD began knocking on doors and interviewing neighbors on lower floors of the Dorchester Towers. Reports came back painting the twins as elusive, a bit elitist, snobbish; they wouldn't speak, say "Hi," or smile if you saw them in the elevator, just awkward silence until the doors slid open and you were gratefully able to depart. The Zalentine twins didn't partake in any reindeer games or get-togethers the condominium association planned.

One tenant, an attractive and single blond attorney on the eighth floor, reported that one of the twins, she could never tell them apart, always asked her to go sailing with him on his boat sometime whenever they bumped into each other. The woman told the officer, "He was good-looking, almost pretty, and I knew the Zalentines, obviously, were big-time loaded, but I always came up with an excuse, any excuse, to put off a sailing date, because my Creep-o-Meter alarm went off whenever he came around."

So the Zalentines owned a sailboat.

A little more digging and Cady had discovered that the twins owned a Sydney 36CR, a thirty-six-footer, and had a boat slip at Bachelors Point Marina in Oxford, Maryland, no more than forty minutes from Cambridge. The Bachelors Point Marina had excellent access to Chesapeake Bay.

Cady called the marina, got a pleasant enough manager on the horn, and asked the gentleman if he'd seen Adrien Zalentine that day.

"Haven't seen either of them," the marina manager told Cady, "but those two boys come and go like ghosts. Let me send a guy out to check the dock."

Five minutes later the manager told Cady the Zalentine slip was empty. Forty-five minutes later Cady was talking to the now-nervous marina manager in person. On the way into the club house the agents had noticed Adrien's black Jag in the corner of the marina's parking lot, parked at a slanted angle to keep other cars away.

There continued to be no answer on Adrien's cell phone. The marina couldn't raise *The She-Killer*—the name of the Zalentines' sail boat—on the VHF marine band. At that point Cady brought the Fifth Coast Guard District into the mix. The Guard immediately sent out helicopters in search of *The She-Killer*, in hopes of locating the lost Zalentine.

It appeared that the twins were about as introverted at Bachelors Point as they were at their condo building—no close sailing chums—but one of the yachtsmen had a strong opinion about the Brothers Zalentine. "Don't think they ever sailed much if at all," the man said. "Mostly saw them motoring about using that Yanmar diesel they had. A real shame because that Sydney was built for racing. Over a quarter-million dollars to use it as a speedboat, what a waste."

In fact, the consensus around Bachelors Point was that the

Zalentines were not real sailing enthusiasts and just had the boat as a status symbol. Something to show off to the girls. Aside from Adrien's Tuesday morning jaunts, several members remembered catching a glimpse of them taking various dates or girlfriends out for a nighttime cruise. One great wit said he'd taken to calling the Zalentines' Sydney 36CR *The Love Boat*.

The manager mentioned that the handful of times he saw Adrien on his Tuesday morning junkets, that Adrien was here and gone before noon. He thought it quite odd that Adrien would be out overnight.

At this point, Cambridge PD had picked up a search warrant in order to enter Adrien's condo, across the hall from Alain's, so Cady headed back to the Dorchester Towers. At 5:00 p.m. that Wednesday, almost an entire day since the Queenstown cleaning crew found Alain in the restroom stall, the Coast Guard contacted Cady.

Brother Adrien had been found.

Chapter 5

Cady lay on the still-made bed, rested his eyes, and spent ten minutes working the squeeze ball, something he did six times a day in hopes of increasing the muscle strength in his right hand. He never left home without the foam ball.

When he'd completed the exercise, Cady returned to the hotel room table and dove back into the case file.

A Coast Guard helicopter had spotted the sailboat, *The She-Killer* stenciled in bold lettering on the stern. When they flew over it they saw something troubling and radioed the patrol boat in for a closer check.

Ten minutes later Cady got the call. Adrien Zalentine had indeed been found, alone, onboard his craft, a bullet through the center of his forehead, and a glass bishop shoved deep into the entry wound. The identical twins that came into the world together went out on the same day and in the same precise manner.

Twins in life, as well as in death.

Cady knew little about sailing, but the yachtsmen at Bachelors Point Marina had done enough oohing and aahing about the Sydney 36CR that Cady knew the craft was about as slick as could be. What remained of Adrien Zalentine was nothing for the weak of stomach, which came with the territory of having a baseball-sized chunk missing from the back of your head. His body lay diagonally across the stern, feet upright beneath the steering wheel. Adrien's blood had settled, his face a ghastly sight, and two days in the scorching sun had been anything but kind.

Chesapeake Bay was shallow for the most part, and the spot where the Zalentine twin had anchored was about twenty-five feet deep. Cady had it explained to him that Adrien had, evidently, diesel dropped the kedge from the bow, laid out the rode and reversed the engine until the kedge dug into the bottom. Zalentine did it windward so the boat wouldn't swing in the breeze. The boat wasn't close to shore so he hadn't needed to anchor, could have just slowly drifted, but perhaps he fancied a swim or just wanted to enjoy this particular patch of blue. The past several days had been relatively calm, sunny, with a pleasant breeze for relaxed sailing. Cady thought about the shooter. Had the two known each other? Or had the UNSUB followed Zalentine out to this *patch of blue*, rafted up alongside the 36CR, all full of smiles and misdirection long enough to pull the gun and blow Adrien Zalentine's brains out into the bay, and insert a certain chess piece into the killing wound?

Cady left Adrien for the forensics crew and stepped below deck. It seemed as if he'd passed into an optical illusion, as it appeared far more spacious than what he'd seen at the surface as he watched the Coast Guard tow the sailboat back to their LeCompte Bay station. With over six feet of headroom, Cady could stand straight up and look about the cabin. He saw a large refrigerator below what one Coast Guard officer had called the nav station. Opposite the galley was a sink, as well as a propane stove and oven. Double quarter berths appeared on each side of the companionway steps. Port and aft of the V-berth was the head and shower.

Cady walked over to the 12-volt refrigerator and used a handkerchief to open the door. Several things of interest. A variety of imported cheeses, with names like Fourme d'Ambert and Camembert, and a box of Mini Toasts and Water Crackers stared neatly back at him. There was a half bottle of black wine labeled Chateau Margaux that probably cost more than a ride on the space shuttle. The cork had been pressed back in place. Cady wondered if opened wine should be stored in a refrigerator. But behind the wine and cheese and boxes of crackers was something that really caught Cady's eye: a sandwich bag of what appeared to be marijuana, later determined by the lab to be Ice Hash. And when the forensics crew combed through the cabin and itemized their findings, a couple of water pipes had been found in one of the Sydney's side drawers.

Evidently, Adrien Zalentine's Tuesday morning excursions involved more than a deep love of the nautical life. Other items on the list of cabin belongings included a mountain-sized box of Oreo cookies, a twelve-pack of bottled water, a plastic container of instant Kool-Aid mix, and a half-eaten bag of Fritos. It looked like Adrien had the munchies issue fully addressed. But something had occurred then, before Adrien got out his water bong, something that put Zalentine's Ice Hash days permanently behind him.

Also found in various compartments were a twelve-pack of Trojan Magnum Twisters, several bottles of suntan lotion, a large tube of half empty K-Y Jelly, three-strand twisted marine rope, extra swimsuits—including a couple of female suits the size of dental floss—and almost two hundred pounds in barbell weights, the kind with a donut hole in the middle. Cady pictured the twins entertaining some female companions, slipping into the cabin to change into a bathing suit, and doing ten quick arm curls to pump up their biceps before returning to deck.

Adrien's condo confirmed that both of the Zalentine twins were tidy, exceedingly so in Cady's opinion, as dirty laundry in hampers was folded neatly, no dirty dishes sat in their black granite sinks or remained in their brushed nickel dishwashers, and, despite the lack of a hired cleaning service, there was nary a dust bunny to be found.

Previous girlfriends were questioned. From what Cady could tell, neither of the Zalentine twins practiced long-term relationships. Anything more than three weeks appeared a major commitment. Evidently, Vance Zalentine was correct. His boys could be quite captivating—of course, being absurdly well off didn't hurt—but neither twin played nice in the sandbox. Stories trickled in of how Adrien or Alain would wine and dine a new girl, a virtual shock-and-awe of charm, until one brother got his date between the sheets, and then he'd trade his conquest off for the sexual pleasure of the other brother. That is, Adrien would begin posing as Alain—and vice versa—until both twins had gotten to know each of their girlfriends in the biblical sense. Then, after nonchalantly informing the unsuspecting female of their sexual betrayal, the twins would sit side by side on the leather couch in order to soak in the woman's reaction and heartbreak, both brothers' blue eyes wide as saucers as though witnessing the Aurora Borealis for the first time.

One recent ex summed it up quite succinctly: "They had voids where their hearts should be—a couple of turds in search of a punchbowl."

Alibis of these girlfriends withstood double scrutiny.

Special Agent Dan Kurtz, the bureau's Yoda of firearm examiners, felt fairly certain that the flattened bullet—determined to be a .45 ACP cartridge, which had passed through the center of Alain Zalentine's forehead and out the back of his skull, then smashed through the wall tile and lodged into the sheetrock behind—most likely came from a Sig Sauer P220. Hell, Cady thought, some FBI agents still carried their Sigs for old times' sake. Enough juice to make a noticeable entry wound and a god-awful exit. The P220 was likely the same gun the UNSUB used to kill Adrien Zalentine on the sailboat.

Kurtz, genius that he was, even passed a digital image of the bullet through the IBIS database—the Integrated Ballistics Identification System—to see if he could link the Sig Sauer P220 that fired the bullet that killed Alain Zalentine to other crimes used by the same gun. Unfortunately, no matches came back. Cady figured the odds of his ever finding the actual Sig Sauer for Kurtz to positively match striations was right up there with his collaring sasquatch or stumbling across the Holy Grail. The shooter would have been a fool not to toss the Sig Sauer into Chesapeake Bay on the return trip from his tête-à-tête with Adrien Zalentine.

Cady closed the Zalentine file. He looked at his uneaten Reuben and then at the digital clock by the hotel room's double bed. Almost two o'clock in the morning. Cady was exhausted, mentally and physically, but he wondered how well he'd sleep with thoughts of the Zalentine twins dancing in his head. Cady walked into the bathroom, splashed water on his face, and asked himself repeatedly why he'd agreed to cold-case this for Jund.

Then he returned to the Zalentine files.

Cambridge PD traced the Ice Hash back to some small-time yuppie dealer named Courtenay LaMotte, a man who expanded his client list by fluttering about the upper-crust watering holes in Cambridge and neighboring communities. Turned out Courtenay LaMotte's real name was Jim Webber. Webber was able to minimize his overhead on account of living out of his mother's basement. He was twenty-six but looked all of fourteen, a tall twig of a boy who hadn't yet begun to shave.

A black Cambridge detective named Allan Sears picked Webber

up, brought him back to the station, tossed him in an empty inter-rogation room for three hours—no chairs, no table, no potty breaks—then came back in, Mirandized him, and informed Webber he was going down hard for the two Zalentine killings. Webber, sob-bing like a baby, walked Sears through every dime bag he'd ever sold since junior high. The Zalentines were his best customers, always paid upfront in cash, even tipped him and placed future orders. He had absolutely no motive to kill Alain or Adrien. Unfortunately, burger and gas station receipts corroborated Webber's alibi that he'd been in Virginia, buying ecstasy tablets from his source, when Alain and Adrien had been murdered.

Detective Sears came to Adrien's condo to let Agent Cady know the results of the Ice Hash connection, walked in, saw Cady standing in the kitchen, looked at the island, then turned and left. A minute later Sears came back in and said, "Have you checked his hidey-hole?"

"What do you mean?" Cady asked.

"In Alain's kitchen space, the island is *Better Homes & Gardens.* Open cupboards below the tabletop to stack the fancy pots and pans they never used. But Adrien has his island space walled off, looks okay with the wooden doors on one side, but that's how it looks in, say, my house. Certainly not *Better Homes & Gardens.*"

Cady squatted down. "You're right. Both condos mirror each other, except for this. Why would the designer go pedestrian in one condo and high class in the other?"

"More likely Adrien did some remodeling," Sears said. "When I worked in Baltimore, we had this child pornographer dead to rights, a real sick piece of work. He wasn't downloading, he was distribut-ing. We warranted his house, found his cameras and picture rooms, but no pictures, not even digitals in the various cameras. So we sledge-hammered the island and hit the mother lode. Eight cameras full of the most disturbing shit you can imagine, and about twenty pounds of hard copies. He's doing life in Hagerstown—that is, if the other inmates let him."

Cady began knocking on the wooden panel of the island. "So we should bust this open?"

"Well," Sears said, stooping over and joining Cady, "we found out after the sledgehammer that there was a trick latch."

Sears got under the countertop, ran his hands across the wood, felt a seam, and then checked up and down the side panel. An idea occurred to him and he backed up six inches. He began running his fingers underneath the countertop.

"Yup," Detective Sears said. He pressed some latch under the lip and a section of siding popped open an inch. "Tree house cool."

Cady looked at Sears. "I'm getting you a job application."

Sears had a baritone laugh. "No thanks. I came here from Baltimore to lower my blood pressure."

Cady swung back the partition. A Gardall wall safe with some kind of push button electronic lock faced him and Sears. "I'll be damned."

"What do you think is in there?" Sears asked.

"Remember, these are Zalentines, so my guess would be upper-end diamond jewelry—rings, watches—the type that costs more than we make in a year. Maybe some rec drugs. Maybe a wad of cash."

"Your team come across any combo numbers?"

"No," Cady said. "We'll call the parents; see if they know anything about it. Otherwise we'll get a driller."

Cady's guess at the wall safe's contents proved incorrect. And the next morning—when the Gardall was drilled open—everything changed.

Chapter 6

"Shakespeare got it almost right: 'The first thing we do, let's kill all the lawyers.' But he left out the most important part—how we should first hang 'em upside down from trees and pour boiling olive oil down their assholes."

Stouder nodded quick agreement to the Goliath-sized rummy sitting next to him at the bar and wished the bartender, who at first glance appeared to be the only other person in the Brass Rail at 10:00 a.m. on a Tuesday morning, hadn't immediately deserted him after pouring Stouder a glass of the House wine. Well, calling it the House wine might be a bit of hyperbole, as Stouder's glass of Merlot tasted like something a skunk might utilize to defend itself. Of course the taste might have something to do with the predicament Stouder found himself in.

It hadn't helped when Stouder turned about on the bar stool to unexpectedly discover this barfly on the seat to his left, invading Stouder's personal proximity, the drunkard's face all but ten inches from his. The stranger looked like Mr. Clean, white t-shirt, all bald with white eyebrows, but sans the earring. And what kept Stouder nodding like a bobble-head was not the man's bread-loaf-sized biceps or the way his knuckles looked like tree roots, the kind you'd spend half a day chopping at in your garden, or the Canadian Club

Mr. Clean kept pouring into a shot glass and from there straight down his gullet, one shot glass after another—but rather the manner in which Mr. Clean vocalized his passionate disdain for the legal profession.

"At least when a plumber gouges you, you get a working shitter out of the deal. But these fucking lawyers have no sense of *proportional* value. No sense whatsoever. You pay 'em to review that boilerplate bullshit whenever you buy a house, right? You know that small print they pretend to read at their desk in front of you?"

Stouder nodded again, repeatedly.

"Then the fuckers turn around and bill as though they'd just litigated the Scopes-Monkey trial. Un-fucking-real."

Stouder had gotten another correspondence from Richaard Gere the previous night. It had merely stated *The Brass Rail, 29th and Lex, 10:00 a.m. Tuesday.* Stouder had been up all night wondering if he should bring the authorities into the situation, especially since he *was* part of *the authorities.* These hooligans could find themselves on the receiving side of some serious time for attempting to blackmail a New York State Deputy Attorney General. But there was, after all, the matter regarding his *little secret* for him to consider. What did these people know and what could they show? He'd rescheduled his morning with a hasty excuse about illness and a fabricated doctor's appointment and scampered out before he'd have to deepen the fib.

"The cocksucker that handled my divorce, for instance, charged me $800 every time he walked across the room to pick up a paperclip. In fact, the only guy who ever got his money's worth out of any attorney was O.J. Simpson."

Mr. Clean certainly had some heartfelt convictions.

And so, against his better judgment, Stouder sat still and periodically nodded his complete agreement with Mr. Clean and wondered how much longer he should give it before he scampered the hell out of The Brass Rail.

"Truth be told, I'd done some things—things that in the light of day I ain't proud of—that killed the marriage. I'm big enough to own that. Now my ex ain't necessarily over it, but we get along. Hell, I stopped by her apartment last month for some drinks and got the balls licked. But that's not my point. My point is the bills this fucker kept serving at me were unconscionable. Talk about kicking a fellow when he's down."

Stouder nodded, deeply wishing to the core of his existence that he were anyplace but here.

"And that really *irked* me," the drunk continued. "That's a word you don't hear much anymore, but it irked the living shit out of me. Every time I cut him a new check, it was like twisting corkscrews into my eyeballs. But I kept a stiff upper lip, patted him on the back when the papers finally came through. I even bought him a drink— he even ordered some of that red piss you're drinking—when I cut him his final check at a tavern not unlike this one. All amiable and ain't you just done me the biggest fucking favor in the world and all that kind of shit because you've got to do things right and let a little time go by. You know what I mean?"

Stouder nodded by rote.

"I even passed along some business referrals. You know, to dicks I could care less about. I even sent the shyster a Happy Holidays card that first Christmas after the divorce. All happy times are here again and bullshit. But, you see, I didn't forget his gouging. I just couldn't move on, I guess. So after a proper amount of time had passed, I came to visit him late one night, and woke his ass out of bed with an invoice of my own, know what I mean?"

Stouder started to nod, but paused and stared at Mr. Clean.

"A little something that needed to be paid in full, an account that needed settling. You should've seen that fucker's pale face.

Sonofabitch—that's right!" Mr. Clean got excited, dug something out of his pocket and slapped it on the top of the bar, right next to Stouder's glass of Merlot. "That's how I came about this little coin purse."

Stouder looked at the poor excuse for a coin purse sitting on the counter in front of him. Oddly shaped, the slit down the middle warped open, and looking more like one of those rawhide pig ears his mother bought for Tanzy, the poodle, than any coin purse Stouder had ever seen before.

"That's one hundred percent yam sac, that is," Mr. Clean said. "One hundred percent."

Stouder felt the bile rise in the back of his throat and struggled to keep it down.

"You're going to want to head into the back parlor, beyond the pool tables." Mr. Clean now sounded sober. "They're ready for you."

Stouder stood still in the parlor's entryway, trying to recoup from an overly invasive frisk by Mr. Clean. Not a big room, certainly nothing to host any type of event Stouder could think of outside a biker gangbang. A single circular table sat in the middle of the room. It was covered with a lime-green tablecloth that may have been new during the Kennedy Administration. A speakerphone sat atop the table. Next to it an inch-thick manila folder labeled with Stouder's name. One wooden chair sat in front of the table. It appeared fairly obvious where he was meant to be seated.

"Do come in, Deputy Attorney General Stouder. Please, sir, make yourself at home." A voice emanated from the conference phone. "It's a pleasure to finally meet you in the flesh."

Stouder took three steps into the room when the door to the back parlor slammed shut. He almost hit the ceiling, and twisted about to see if there was anyone in the room with him. Completely empty.

"Sorry about that, sir, but we need to have a little pow-wow and it just wouldn't do for anyone to listen in, wouldn't you agree?"

Stouder remained standing. He bit his lower lip, tried not to tremble, and recited the lines he'd rehearsed on the drive over. "If you think you can intimidate a New York State Executive Deputy Attorney General with these juvenile antics, you are sadly mistaken. If I don't call my secretary in fifteen minutes, she's to turn over an envelope to my team of prosecutors containing our correspondences, my thoughts on the issue, as well as the address of this..." Stouder looked around the room disdainfully and continued, "... establishment."

"By all means, Deputy Attorney General, by all means you'll be able to call your secretary. I'm afraid we've gotten off on the wrong foot." The voice sounded impossibly mellow, like a midnight deejay on a jazz station telling the audience about the mild night temp before putting on another track of Miles Davis. "And we probably shouldn't have used St. Nick as a greeter."

St. Nick must be Mr. Clean, Stouder thought. "Your man is a drunkard!"

"Now, now, Deputy Attorney General Stouder, before we go casting aspersions at St. Nick—who truly does play Santa Claus for the kiddies in December—did you know that Ulysses S. Grant ordered a barrel of whiskey to always be on hand for his beck and call? The good general would dip his cup into it to quench his thirst. Shall we discuss how Winston Churchill drank a bottle of wine with breakfast?"

Stouder stared at his fingernails. "And your point is?"

"St. Nick has special talents, sir. Let's just say he gets the sausage made and leave it at that. Give me a handful of functional alcoholics like St. Nick and I can rule the world." The voice on the speakerphone sounded more and more like one of those neutered hosts on NPR, no longer a late-night jazz deejay. "Deputy Attorney General, you've heard of the carrot and stick approach? You know, for rewarding good behavior and punishing bad?"

"Yes."

"That's good, sir, because, and I hate to brag, but the file in front of you is one hell of a big stick. By all means page through it if you don't believe me."

"If you've done your homework, you will know that nothing concerns me more than the health and welfare of children. I have been a child advocate for years, well before I was appointed to my current position. I've donated thousands to child shelters across the United States."

"Of course you have, Deputy Attorney General," the NPR jazz deejay voice said slowly, as though signing off for the night. "Of course you have."

"Then let's dispense with this ridiculous masquerade. I've been researching how sexual predators utilize the Internet to prey on unsuspecting children. I will shortly be announcing the formation of a task force to tackle this very issue. I have respected colleagues by the dozens who know about my advocacy in this area." Stouder had hit upon most of his rehearsal points. "Nothing in that folder will mean a thing to anyone."

"Humor me, Deputy Attorney General Stouder. You really don't want St. Nick to walk through these pages with you, do you, sir? I have a queasy stomach."

At the mention of St. Nick/Mr. Clean, Stouder opened the folder and paged quickly through the first section, which contained transcripts of his chat room talks with Ricky and the others.

"Meaningless." Stouder threw up a hand. "And very likely doctored."

"Page on, Deputy Attorney General Stouder," the NPR speaker

voice pushed.

The next section contained side-by-side pictures of him, both in and out of his costume. Stouder turned white. But that wasn't what sent him into shock. What nearly sent Executive Deputy Attorney General P. Campton Stouder into a state of anaphylactic seizure was that the pictures had been taken of him in his master bathroom. The bastards had been in his house.

"Amazing what those Nanny Cams can pick up, isn't it, sir?"

Stouder felt his hands begin to quake, but he did his best to stay in character. "You've just tacked on several more felony counts to your blackmail scheme."

"Once you see a pattern, Deputy Attorney General Stouder, everything else is a cakewalk." The NPR voice no longer sounded casually ironic.

Stouder ceased speaking as he paged through the remainder of the folder. Pictures of him on the prowl, outside Ricky's house, at a theatre restroom, next to a boy at a urinal.

"If you see any you'd want for holiday cards, I can get you a discount at Proex," the NPR voice remarked.

Stouder continued to page through the photos, one after another after another. The last were a series of pictures of the boy who had been next to him at the urinal. The last document was taken from that morning's paper, which had a picture of this same boy, who had been missing since Tuesday, since he'd gone out to play with the local kids and never returned. Nor had any of the neighborhood kids seen him that day.

"It does seem odd to call it an AMBER Alert when there's a little boy involved, doesn't it?"

"You son of a bitch."

"Now, now, Deputy Attorney General Stouder, don't say things to which I could take offense. That little Connelly boy is in no real danger. Certainly not from the likes of you. He's currently in a South American country—what the heck, for the sake of our chat, let's say Guatemala—working in a sweatshop that makes Nike knockoffs."

"Bring him home now," Stouder mumbled.

"No need for the long face, sir. Consider it summer camp. He's learning a trade, and the guards have been instructed to give him extra rice and beans."

All pretenses were gone; all the wind out of his sails. He was screwed, stewed, and tattooed. He knew exactly how this would play out. He'd be jailed as the lowest of the low. Stouder wilted like overcooked spaghetti flung on the wall, began to shake as if he were seated bare-assed in a drafty igloo.

"All you have to do, Deputy Attorney General Stouder, is a little favor, for me and St. Nick and the handful of other fellows who have come to know you so intimately this past week or so, and the Connelly boy will be dropped off at the library near his house with an amazing tale to tell. But before the Connelly boy left for South America, he played a little game of hide and seek with the fellows in your house. You know, some hair here, some fingerprints there. St. Nick tells me the Connelly boy may have even pricked his finger and touched a few items before the bleeding stopped. But don't worry about the mess, sir. St. Nick said it'd take one of those CSI lights for anyone to even notice anything amiss. So tell me, Deputy Attorney General Stouder—as a legal scholar—if that file were sent to the investigating detectives, would that be enough to merit a search warrant?"

"What is it…you want from me?" Stouder whispered, barely audible.

"Just a little favor, Deputy Attorney General. We need an extra set of eyes and ears. That's all. Just an extra set of eyes and ears."

Executive Deputy Attorney General P. Campton Stouder then

did something he'd not done in over forty years, not since he was the Connelly boy's age.

Stouder began to weep.

Washington, D.C.

Three Years Earlier

Chapter 7

"Let me see if I am able to wrap my wee little mind around this," a red-faced Assistant Director Roland Jund said to a conference room full of special agents. "Alain Zalentine had the great misfortune of getting his brains blown out the back of his skull in a truck stop restroom."

"A rest area restroom, sir."

"Yes, Agent Cady, thanks for sharing your grasp of the finer nuances of outhouse semantics," Jund said, sighing. "Then, the following day we find his twin brother, Adrien Zalentine, dead on his sailboat with his brains blown into the Chesapeake. Now these two boys are not just Leo and Schmuck Pimpledwarf from Dogpatch Lane—no, of course not. These two young lads are the heirs to the biggest fortune in North America this side of Bill Gates. And damned if both of the boys don't have these glass chess pieces jammed deep into their wounds." The AD tossed a stack of 8x10s down the conference room table. No one reached for a copy. They all had the same graphic pictures inside their own folders, the folders Cady had distributed to everyone before the AD's arrival.

"Then we have K. Barrett Sanfield, D.C.'s uber lawyer—*the Magician* for Christ's sake—stabbed to death in his own office some five weeks back, to wit a case that has yet to move forward one square inch. But finally we have a clue, a link actually, and a none-too-subtle link at that, on account of a glass chess piece having been pried out of Sanfield's solar plexus."

Jund looked around the table and then continued, "And now we discover, upon opening some kind of hidden wall safe in Adrien Zalentine's kitchen, which sounds like something right out of the Hardy Boys by the way, we discover that the Zalentine twins—of the *Zalentine, It Rhymes with Valentine* dynasty—that these two degenerates may just be the biggest serial killers to hit the East Coast since the Boston-Fucking-Strangler!"

There was a hushed silence. Cady knew that Jund took the deaths of women and children hard, and personally, but he had never seen the AD this intense before and suspected none of the other attendees had either. He glanced quickly around the table. There was Elizabeth Preston paging through her packet of materials as if in search of a miracle; to her right was Special Agent Tom Hiraldi. Hiraldi was young, fairly green, and involved in the Chessman investigation due to his having taken state in high school chess club two years in a row—the bureau's resident chess expert. Before Jund had arrived, Hiraldi had been theorizing about what the queen and bishops meant, what chess moves they might signify, what clues they might provide. His dissertation on the King's Gambit came to an abrupt end once Jund stormed into the meeting and sat down.

Across the table sat Bryce Drommerhausen, a top profiler yanked hastily from his BAU at NCAVC—his Behavioral Analysis Unit at the National Center for the Analysis of Violent Crime—to help the agents get a bead on the Chessman's motivations. Drommerhausen had previously submitted the Chessman's modus operandi into the Violent Criminal Apprehension Program's database for comparison, but, not surprisingly, ViCAP had come up snake eyes—that is, no pattern was found. Drommerhausen stared fixedly at Jund.

Special Agents Arty Gonzalez and Maggie Fitzwilliams, the forensic specialists who had examined both Zalentine crime scenes, looked white, stricken. Special Agent Dan Kurtz, likely quite happy not to be there in person, was on speaker phone from Quantico. Cady had brought Allan Sears, the Cambridge detective who had been so helpful at the Dorchester Towers, along for what appeared to be a turbulent ride. So much for Sears' blood pressure.

"Sir," Cady began, "the fireproof wall safe hidden in the island of Adrien Zalentine's kitchen contained six female purses. One belonging to a Sarah Glover of Wilmington, Delaware. Sadly, Ms. Glover's body had been found in a shallow grave in a wooded area on a side road off 270 near Rockville. Her murder has remained an ongoing investigation and, quite frankly, more of a cold case for nearly three years now."

"Well, Agent Cady, I don't imagine the Glover strangling remains a cold case any longer."

"No, sir." Cady realized the AD had read the file. "Originally, the detectives investigating the Sarah Glover slaying believed she'd been kidnapped and raped repeatedly by the same UNSUB. However, lab results now indicate that the semen taken from her vagina and anus matches DNA from the Zalentine brothers."

"Which one, Alain or Adrien?"

"Quite likely both, sir." Cady looked down at his notes in front of him. "When a single fertilized egg splits in two, the two embryos develop into identical—or monozygotic—twins. Since these twins come from the same egg and sperm, they have shared DNA, their genetic makeup is a match, thus indistinguishable to a *standard* DNA analysis. In some cases they use fingerprints to tell identical twins apart."

"That so?"

"Yes, sir, and here's where it gets interesting. Sarah Glover's body was found by a trucker hauling plasma screens to Frederick. He got off 270 to check a tire, got that sorted out, then ducked behind the tree line to take a leak and noticed a pale hand sticking up out of the dirt. Said he made a mess of himself sprinting back to the truck for his phone. At that point Sarah Glover had been missing for three weeks. She'd been hitchhiking to Catonsville to catch some grunge band in concert and hadn't been heard from since." Cady pointed at the Cambridge investigator and continued, "Detective Sears and I have created a Glover-Zalentine timeline. It's labeled A-7 in your packet. We believe the Zalentine twins panicked. They'd badly botched a shallow grave, caught the story about Glover's body being found when it broke in the news and, that very next day, traded in their three-month old Mercedes-Benz CL600 for a Ferrari 575 M Maranello."

Cady felt his cell phone vibrate in his front pocket, knew it was his wife Laura calling about tonight's plans, and knew he would disappoint her once again.

"Glover had been in the Mercedes?"

"The CL600 was the only sports car the Zalentines owned that had *sufficient* trunk space. They'd probably seen enough CSI episodes to know how screwed they were if they'd transported Sarah Glover in the trunk to the burial spot off 270. Then, the day after trading in the Mercedes, the twins are on an Airbus to France."

"They knew they messed up so they put an ocean between themselves and the investigation," Detective Sears said.

"Exactly," Cady replied. "The twins follow the news of the investigation over the Internet from some five-star in Paris. The management company at the Dorchester Towers held their mail. The woman in the Dorchester office mentioned that the only time she'd ever spoken in-depth with the Zalentines was that month they were in Paris, when they kept calling her every other day to remind her about the mail. Of course they were feeling her out, trying to see if anyone had been poking around their home front. Phone records indicate that they kept calling their own answering services during that timeframe, checking daily to see if any police investigators were trying to contact them."

"After about five weeks of seeing and hearing nothing," Detective Sears said, picking up the narration, "they wiped the sweat off their brows and returned home. Probably peeked around every corner before stepping back into the Dorchester Towers. After another couple of weeks pass, they get an idea, something a little brighter to *facilitate* their new hobby. A sailboat."

"That's how they got rid of the other five, isn't it, the ones that haven't been found?" Agent Preston asked quietly.

Cady nodded his head. "A-12 in your packet is a list of the items found aboard their boat, *The She-Killer.*"

"Brazen name."

"Yes, it is," Cady responded. "Note on A-12 the barbell weights. Also note the forty feet of three-strand marine rope."

"It's a giant bay, Agent Cady," the AD said. "Will we be able to find the remains of the five missing females?"

"Let me bring you up to date on that, sir. Their boat had one of those depth finders, the kind fishermen use." Cady looked again at his notes. "A Humminbird Matrix 97 Combo, a high-end jobbie that has the capability of hitting depths of several hundred feet. However, I don't suspect they used the unit for fishing. The Zalentines had no fishing gear, poles or tackle, stored onboard or at their condominiums. Neither Zalentine twin has ever purchased a fishing license in their lives, and, after a painfully awkward call with Vance Zalentine, I learned they never went fishing as children."

"The Humminbird had a dual purpose. They were fishing all right, but for the perfect watery grave."

"Exactly, sir," Cady responded. "And here's where we got lucky. The Nav station onboard *The She-Killer* held a wireless Bluetooth GPS for electronic charting—fishermen can set coordinates so they can return to a successful spot at a later date. We believe the Zalentine twins used it to get a navigation fix, a waypoint if you will, on a couple of desired *deep* spots in Chesapeake Bay."

"What's being done with the GPS coordinates?"

"Bear in mind the Chesapeake averages about twenty-one feet of depth. That's just the average, there are much deeper spots. The Zalentines had two waypoints programmed into their Bluetooth. Unfortunately, one of the waypoints is in the deepest part of the bay, off Bloody Point near Annapolis. It's called The Hole and it's 174 feet below sea level. Searching The Hole will be a bit more problematic, more time-consuming. However, the other waypoint is about sixty feet down. The Coast Guard currently has divers sifting that area." Cady turned to Detective Sears. "Allan and I received a call from the officer in charge of the dive right before this meeting."

Sears cleared his throat. "Coast Guard divers just discovered two female bodies at this GPS setting. The preliminaries indicate that both are without clothes and are wrapped in some kind of camping tarp, wrapped tightly with the exact same brand of three-strand rope found onboard the Zalentine boat. The rope was threaded through 160 pounds of barbell weights; again, the exact same type of barbell weights found in a compartment onboard *The She-Killer*. The Guard is expanding the perimeter of their search at this dive site, but I suspect the other three victims are in or near the other set of GPS coordinates—The Hole."

"What about all of these other women the Zalentines took sailing on their *death boat*," Agent Preston asked. "Why were they permitted to live?"

"My thought," Detective Sears addressed the FBI agent's question, "is that these were for appearances. Diversionary dates paraded across that marina so nothing would stand out in any of the other boaters' minds. The brothers likely got their rocks off drinking wine and eating cheese and crackers with these *for appearance* dates, knowing full well what they'd been doing aboard *The She-Killer*."

"Plus," Cady added, "these *for appearance* dates were linked to the brothers and would be easy trace-backs if one disappeared. Of the five missing females with their purses in the Zalentines' souvenir chest, Claire Townley and Jenny Granger were teenage hitchhikers, Meagan Wright was picked up in a crowded nightclub in Virginia Beach, and Dayna St. Claire was a prostitute who worked out of Richmond, Virginia."

"Based on the mileage put on the twins' sports cars," Sears said, "I suspect Alain and Adrien spent time cruising the interstate, looking for lone female hitchhikers, young women they could charm into a meal and some drinks, perhaps a place to stay for a night or two, and then possibly, if they'd like, a pleasant night ride on their sailboat. A-1 in your packet lists the names, ages, and home addresses of the victims. Meagan Wright, the pick-up at the meat market in Virginia Beach, was the oldest. She was twenty-three. Jenny Granger, the youngest at age sixteen, was likely picked up off Highway 81 near Scranton, Pennsylvania. You can see how the Zalentines put miles on their cars so the disappearances wouldn't all occur in a concentrated area."

Agent Preston looked at the assistant director. "So when we catch the Chessman, do we arrest him or give him a gold medal?"

"I'll make damn sure he gets two desserts before his injection," Jund told Preston and turned to Cady. "How exactly does the Chessman intersect with these Zalentine thrill killings?"

"Agents have been interviewing the families of the six victims. At this point there is no evidence that the Chessman was involved with the Zalentine thrill-kills. Boaters at the marina never saw any males on *The She-Killer* besides the twins. Fingerprints on the souvenir purses are heavy on Alain and Adrien with smeared prints from the various victims."

"Do the fingerprints tell us anything else?"

"Agents interviewing the victims' families have been meticulous in lifting prints off old yearbooks or photo albums or CDs to help us eliminate the fingerprints on the purses and various IDs, credit cards, and keys inside the Zalentines' trophy safe. After eliminating the victims' prints, there are the periodic prints here and there, consistent with a gas station clerk or cashier swiping a debit card. However, Alain and Adrien's fingerprints are everywhere. The two must have taken these purses out frequently to look at the wallets, driver's licenses, cosmetic cases, you name it."

The room sat in silence, which Jund eventually broke.

"I know we've named him the Chessman—a singular individual—based on the surveillance recording at the Sanfield killing, but the twins...this homicide double-header indicates meticulous planning. Any thoughts on the Chessman being more than one person?"

"Two things, sir. First, Adrien was dead within two hours of taking his boat out that morning. By 10:00 a.m. There'd be no difficulty for a single shooter to be back at Dorchester Towers to tail Alain by noon. Second," Cady continued, "it had been five weeks since Sanfield's death. A lot of time to shadow the twins, memorize their routines, set them up. Whereas if you've got a team of killers, why not hit both condos at night? Stormtrooper it. Hell of a lot easier."

"With the precision and intricate plotting involved in these three murders," Bryce Drommerhausen spoke for the first time, "as well as having—forgive me, Elizabeth—the *cojones* to pull it off, I would suggest that the UNSUB has a military background. Ex-Special Forces, ex-Navy SEAL, you know, that type."

"An interesting point, Bryce," the AD said. "Something to keep in the back of our minds as the investigation proceeds."

Heads nodded around the conference table.

"Another thing, we need to bang on the Chessman's M.O. like a drum. Find out how Sanfield intersects with the Zalentines."

"Interestingly, something of a connection exists," Cady said. "Sanfield & Fine represented Alain Zalentine on a couple of speeding tickets. Rainmaker Sanfield brought Alain into the firm, but handed him off to Stephen Fine to make the tickets go bye-bye. By the way, Stephen Fine is suffering anxiety attacks and heading to an undisclosed spot in Bermuda for an extended stay."

Detective Sears began laughing and rubbed a knuckle against the corner of his eye. "I apologize for being inappropriate, but I just remembered that my wife's wedding ring is a Zalentine. I think they're going to have to change their tagline."

"Zalentine," Agent Kurtz piped in from the speakerphone, "It Rhymes with Frankenstein."

Detective Sears struggled to keep from laughing. "Next quarter's earnings may be a bit in the red."

"Thanks for the levity, gentlemen," Jund said curtly, bringing the meeting back into focus. "We need to bang on the Sanfield-Zalentine connection. I guarantee there's more to that relationship than a handful of speeding tickets." The AD frowned. "Anything more on the significance of the chess pieces?"

"The UNSUB bypassed any low-level pawns, dove straight into the deep end by taking out the queen, first, and then the bishops. The queen is the most powerful piece on the board, can move in any direction, so the UNSUB considered Sanfield to be some kind of Grand Poobah." Agent Tom Hiraldi had been ready for Jund's question. "Though not as powerful as the queen, obviously, or even the rooks, bishops are effective in their own right and can move diagonally across the board. They are considered, strategy-wise, about on par with the knights. Each game begins with two bishops. The UNSUB equated the Zalentine twins with bishops and has taken them off the board."

"So what does that mean?"

"It means the UNSUB is methodically stripping away the king's defenses."

"That makes it crystal clear that this thing's not over," Jund said, "because the king is still on the table."

There was only one thing crystal clear in Cady's mind at this point. And that was that Vance Zalentine certainly knew his twin boys.

Chapter 8

"Good morning, Senator Farris." Cady stood in the entryway of Farris's private chambers in the Dirksen Senate Office Building and shook hands with the senior senator from the great state of Delaware. The senator had a grip like a wood vice and a smile that said "crowns."

"Thanks you for meeting us on such short notice, Agent Cady," Senator Arlen Farris said, patting the agent on the back and leading him over to his desk. "Have you met my son, Patrick?"

"I've not had the pleasure, sir," Cady said. "Good morning, Congressman."

The congressman stood up from the guest armchair and shook Cady's hand. "Pleasure's all mine, Agent Cady. Please call me Patrick."

Cady nodded. He remembered seeing both Farris men on the cover of *Newsweek* a couple years back when Patrick Farris had won the same seat in the United State House of Representatives that father Farris had vacated for his senate seat decades earlier. The story had talked about the Farris Dynasty in Delaware, with a wink toward the Kennedy and Bush families. It had been a puff piece, and two-thirds of the Farris Dynasty stood before Cady now. The third member of the dynasty, Arlen's brother Graham, a two-term governor of Delaware, had passed away of leukemia a few years back.

"Assistant Director Jund mentioned that you had some information regarding the Barrett Sanfield murder investigation."

"Terrible, terrible thing," Senator Farris said, shaking his head, before catching Cady's eyes. "Barry and I grew up together in Milford. The two of us, team captains, led the Muskets to state in football our senior year. Would've won the damned championship game except for a jackass holding call and a missed field goal on the last drive of the game—two plays I'll be cussing on my deathbed. Barry's been my wingman ever since. Loved the SOB."

"My condolences, sir. I knew you and Mr. Sanfield had been good friends."

"I appreciate your thoughts, Agent Cady." The senior Farris pressed a button on his phone. "Mavis, are there three servings of that delicious sponge cake left?"

"Yes, Senator," a disembodied voice replied through the speaker-phone.

"Would you be so kind as to bring us three pieces—ah, hell, Mavis. Bring in whatever remains of it and three cups of Joe."

"Can do, Arlen," Mavis said through the phone.

"Senator, there's no need—"

"One spoonful and you'll be pulling your gun to get her recipe. Now stop calling me senator. My name's Arlen."

Senator Farris put his arm on Cady's elbow as though they were old pals and led the agent across the room to a seat on the couch. Cady could tell that Farris was born for politics, all sweetness and molasses, about to discuss Washington's most mysterious death since Vince Foster as though he were discussing a prize heifer at the Delaware county fair. Mavis, hair in a silvery bouffant with black glasses hanging from a chain around her neck, pushed in a cart containing cups of coffee and three helpings of her apparently famous sponge cake. On her way out she shut the door behind her.

"Well?" The senator eyed Cady as he tasted his first bite.

"Quite good."

"Tell her that on the way out. Mavis lives for praise of her pastries. Yesterday was this cinnamon streusel I'm going to legislate be mandatory in all bakeries." Farris shoveled a spoonful into his mouth. "I'd be eight hundred pounds if I didn't pan her yummies off on visitors."

Cady could easily see how Arlen Farris got reelected in Delaware landslides every six years. He had that homespun, good-old-boy schmooze down pat. But Cady sensed something lurking behind the senator's green eyes. Perhaps a glint of *don't fuck with me*, which was something *General Earmarks*, as some on the right side of the aisle had taken to calling Farris, would need to push through a wealth of pet projects benefitting Delaware—bridges hither and yon, wind-power construction, pre-kindergarten programs, Delaware National Guard's counter-drug program, the new Farris Cancer Center at the U of D's Medical Center, research and development of a Delaware Bay regional computer, mass-transit initiatives, you name it. All of which put smiles on a variety of grateful voting blocs come November. Farris couldn't be accused of not bringing home the bacon.

"Now, the reason I called Roland last night," Farris said—the senator seemed to be on a first-name basis with everyone north of the equator—"was to follow up on some questions he'd asked of me back at the time of Barry's murder. Sad to say that I wasn't much help. And that pained me." The senator put his coffee cup down and held out his hands. "Because when you find out who pig-stuck my best friend, Agent Cady, I'd like to strangle them with their own entrails. Hell yes, Barry had enemies, many political if you follow the news. This is Washington, D.C. for Christ's sake, but all's fair in love and war, shake hands, give a great concession speech, and live to fight another day. I told Roland at the time that it had to be some petty theft run amok and that Barry happened to be in the wrong place at the wrong time."

"But something has since come to mind?"

"Actually, it's more my son's insight that clicked the light bulb on over my head. It may mean something, but it may also mean absolutely nothing." The senator looked at his congressman son. "Patrick, tell the agent about the shitbirds at the Ivy."

"I knew Alain and Adrien Zalentine at Princeton."

Cady reached into his breast pocket and took out a notebook. "How well?"

"Kinda-sorta." The congressman tilted his hand back and forth. "I was a year or two older, but we were in the same eating club. T.I.— Tiger Inn."

"What's an eating club? A frat house?" Cady asked. He'd gone to Ohio State and eaten dorm food.

"No. Fraternities had been banned from Princeton until the 1980s, so these eating clubs cropped up for dinner and socializing. Great fun on a Saturday night."

"Have you kept in contact with them?"

"I know what you're thinking. Farris is a politician up for re-election every other year; of course he's going to mine the Zalentines for campaign donations," Patrick said, flashing a broad grin. "He'd be daft not to. That would make sense, right?"

Cady nodded.

"I never approached either for funding. Not once. Haven't kept in touch, either. Quite frankly, they were odd ducks to be around, even back in the T.I. days."

"How so?"

"For one thing, I don't remember ever seeing either of them alone, separately that is, without the other twin an arm's length away. Another thing, they always had this peculiar manner of examining things. I swear you could drop a cup full of Jell-O right in front of the two of them, and they'd both stare at it for several seconds, inquisitively, as though dissecting it, before glancing at each other for verification or something. Once I was heading out of T.I. after lunch and…you know the feeling you get when you realize someone is watching you?"

Cady nodded again.

"Well, I had that feeling to the power of ten. I actually got goose bumps. At the door I turned around. Sure enough, the twins were sitting there, side by side, staring at me."

"Did the Zalentines have any close friends at Tiger Inn?"

"Not that I recall. T.I.'s a bit exclusive in that you have to go through this pain-in-the-ass *bicker* process to get in. Interviews, bullshit games, that kind of stuff. The Zalentines never really had that camaraderie thing going. They were all but impossible to bond with, seemed to live on a different plane of reality, so I assumed they greased some palms here and there."

"Tell Agent Cady about the party," Senator Farris said, moving it along.

"Yes." The congressman folded his hands and looked off into the corner of the room, collecting his thoughts. "Dane Schaeffer's family owned a lake house near Hillsdale in Bergen County, on Snow Goose Lake. Dane's a fellow Princeton alum and an old T.I. chum of mine. His father did a lot of business in Italy, industrial laser systems or something. Anyway, Dane's father would periodically need to zip off to Milan or Naples for weeks on end, and he'd take with him whoever his girlfriend was at the moment. That freed up the lake house and Dane would throw these wild Friday-to-Sunday parties. Fully catered, booze around every corner, single malts, Dom Perignon, imported ales." Patrick flashed the Tom Cruise grin again. "And you'd better knock before entering any room. Think Gatsby with condoms. If you couldn't get laid at one of Dane's to-dos, there must be something seriously wrong with you. Everyone was invited, and everyone had a wonderful time…until the final bash."

"What happened?"

Patrick lost the movie-star grin. "A girl died, Agent Cady. She drowned in Snow Goose Lake. She and her boyfriend were down near the boathouse and, evidently, they went skinny-dipping. Not too uncommon a site at one of Dane's parties, but it was well after midnight. Dark outside. I imagine they were both drunk and the poor girl drifted away and drowned."

"You were at the party?"

"Not for long. I had a paper due that Monday morning that I hadn't begun…and a certain someone who shall remain nameless was having conniptions, grand mal seizures actually, over a certain dip in my GPA."

Senator Farris chuckled. "I wasn't paying for Cs."

"Some of my father's constituents wish he'd be just as frugal with the taxpayers' dime."

The senator chuckled again.

"Anyway, I drove up Friday afternoon, sipped some Laphroaig and ate two servings of roast hen or whatever Dane had brought in for that soiree. Then I pounded a few cappuccinos and snuck out before Dane could give me any shit about leaving."

"But the Zalentine twins were at the party?"

"Yes. They'd arrived just as I was leaving, maybe nine o'clock. Everyone used to park in this field across the gravel road from the Schaeffer lake house. Alain had recently picked up an Alfa Romeo, a Spider I think. So I mooned over it before I left."

Cady scribbled in his notebook. "What was the girl's name?"

"Marly something or other. She was fairly attractive, if I remember correctly. May have had her in a class or two, but I only knew her enough to nod or say hello in the hallway. I can get you her name. Or Google may have newspaper articles from ten years back."

"I can find that out. How about the boyfriend, do you know his name?"

"Sorry. I don't think I ever knew the gentleman."

"But you believe the Zalentines had something to do with this girl's death?"

"After hearing the news about Alain and Adrien this past week, what they'd been doing to those poor women, I really don't know what to believe."

"Tell him what the shitbirds wanted," Senator Farris said.

"Dad and I were hitting eighteen at Chevy yesterday afternoon and talking about Uncle Barry. I still can't believe he's dead. The newspapers have hinted that his death and the Zalentine homicides are somehow connected. Same M.O. or something, right?"

"I'm not at liberty to discuss the investigation."

"Understood," the congressman replied. "Anyway, I mentioned to Dad that I'd referred the twins to Uncle Barry over a legal matter they had some concerns about."

Cady's head perked up. "This was back then, at Princeton?"

"Yes. In fact, it was that following Monday morning, the Monday after the accident at Dane's party. I'd had about three hours of sleep after finally finishing that term paper for Poly Sci before Alain and Adrien woke me by banging on my door at about seven o'clock that morning. I knew they weren't early risers and they'd never been to my apartment before. It was odd, but they knew who my father was and thought I'd be able to refer them to a good trial attorney. They wanted a real street fighter and thought I might know someone."

"This wasn't for speeding tickets or driving under the influence, was it?"

"No." The younger Farris shook his head. "This was something big. They never told me what it was about, but I got the distinct impression that it had to do with the family business, that they felt their father was screwing them over financially, denying their birthright or whatever. I assumed there was going to be legal Armageddon over the diamonds, so I referred them to Uncle Barry. I figured if it turned into a cash cow, maybe I'd get a commission."

"Did they meet with Mr. Sanfield?"

"I assume so. I left a message at Barry's office. He called me back while we were finishing our coffee. I made an introduction, then handed the phone to Alain and went off to brush my teeth and throw on some sneakers. When I got back to the kitchen Alain said something about having set an appointment."

"The Sanfield & Fine records only indicate having represented the Zalentines over a string of relatively recent speeding tickets." Cady looked from the congressman to the senator.

Senator Farris nodded once. "I think we all know about Bar's reputation. There were certain things Barry worked on that were better left unspoken and without a paper trail. You scratch my back and I'll scratch yours, that type of shit." The senator's eyes were moist. "But I'll tell you one thing you can take to the bank, Agent Cady. Barry sure as hell never covered up any girl's death, not for those two shitbirds."

Chapter 9

"**D**amn it, Agent Cady, I dotted every i at the inquiry. Crossed every t. There was no reason to suspect foul play."

"I have no doubt, Sheriff Littman." Cady had the Bergen County Sheriff on speakerphone in his cramped two-chair office at the Hoover Building.

"Situations like this, a family's wealth works against them. The Schaeffers may have money growing on trees, but that itself guaranteed no preferential treatment. If anything, that inquiry took the long way around the pond."

"Thanks again for faxing me the findings summary and pathologist's report. I've got one or two remaining questions."

"Fire away."

"The ME placed Marly Kelch's blood alcohol content at .058. That's under the legal limit."

"I wouldn't advise anyone to drive a car with that BAC level, but what's your point? We didn't pull her out of a car wreck. We pulled her out of a lake."

"My point," Cady said to the Bergen County Sheriff, "is here's a very athletic young woman, a hotshot on the Princeton women's tennis team—who, by most accounts, isn't much of a social drinker. And she goes for a quick swim off the dock by Schaeffer's boathouse and manages to get herself drowned."

"Now there you go again, implying I don't know how to do my job. I had Bev send you those materials yesterday, I just walked you through the case step-by-step, and here you go again second-guessing me."

"Look, Sheriff, I'm only playing devil's advocate, probing for weak spots, to find if there are any holes in what happened that night at Schaeffer's mansion."

"Holes?" Sheriff Littman said. "What the hell are you investigating ten years down the pike that circles back to this poor girl's death?"

"I'll tell you what little I know, sir, but I don't want to taint your answers at this point."

"I'll bounce your ball for another minute, Cady. First off, as you said, Marly Kelch didn't drink much, so Schaeffer's shindig, with hooch bussed in by the truckload, had to be a novel concept for her. And Kelch weighed all of, let me see, I've got the full report here in front of me." Cady heard papers rustling through his office phone. "Kelch weighed 115 pounds. Second, several witnesses at the party saw Kelch drinking wine that night, walking around with a glass of Merlot. Golly, Agent Cady, a skinny young woman who doesn't know how to handle her liquor...someone get me the president on the phone."

"Good one," Cady said.

"Third point, that *very athletic* girl has just come off a round or two of *very athletic* sex with her boyfriend, and then they get the bright idea to take a naked dip in the dark and cold waters of Snow Goose at two in the morning. Kelch likely gets a cramp or becomes disoriented or begins inhaling water. The boyfriend, who blew a .11 when we arrived on the scene, was completely worthless. He dogpaddled to shore, passed out for an hour, then woke up and wondered where his date went."

"Bret Ingram was not Kelch's boyfriend. I talked to Dorsey Kelch, her mother, and several of her old tennis mates. They said she hadn't been seeing anyone on a steady basis."

"Well, if her mother says so, I guess that's that, then. Now, actual witnesses at Schaeffer's party made noises about those two acting awfully friendly before they both disappeared down to that boat-house around midnight together. Do you understand the very nature of the parties that the Schaeffer boy threw? Booze drains inhibitions, couples pairing off left and right as the sun goes down, switching pards the next day—young people in heat, going at it like rabbits. What's that term that's so endearing amongst today's youth—*fuck buddies.* You know, the Schaeffer boy's basically a good kid. I heard he spent all Saturday in his pontoon boat circling Snow Goose, checking the banks and docks to see if Kelch had made it ashore and passed out. Anyway, I took the Schaeffer kid aside, before the body was pulled out of the lake, and told him in no uncertain terms *no more.* The parties end."

"No further problems at the lake house?"

"None, but I don't think the Schaeffer boy ever stayed there again after that weekend. Bad memories. His father got remarried last year and I saw the kid at the reception."

"You were invited?"

"Don't go there, Cady. It was a huge event in Hillsdale and the old man sent me a courtesy invite to the reception. I'd much rather stay home and watch the ball game, but I am an *elected* official, and knowing the folks in Schaeffer's circle, I knew it wouldn't be too bright of me not to attend."

"What's the Schaeffer boy doing now?"

"A bit of a recluse. He's a financial wizard and manages the fam-ily's portfolio from some cabin out in the sticks near Chester. The boy's hair is gray now. Completely gray."

"That night changed a lot of lives."

"It certainly did."

"Your team used sonar to find Kelch?"

"Yup. Got a dive team in with the side scan sonar. They don't even have to get wet until they find the body. We didn't want a floater showing up on Snow Goose. You ever see a floater, Agent Cady?"

"Yes," Cady said, and did his best to shove the image from his mind. After drowning, a body eventually floated to the surface, after it became bloated and full of noxious gas. The remains of a drowning victim were not a pretty sight. Fish often fed on any exposed flesh, accelerating the decomposition process.

"Well, then you know," Littman replied. "The divers found her the next evening. Sunday night. Not as bad as a floater, but not good."

"I see in the pathologist's report that there were a couple of nicks and scratches."

"Very minor lesions. No bruising about the face or choking marks around the neck. No tissue under the fingernails. Nothing to indicate that a struggle or rape had occurred prior to death."

"Unless there's a witness or the victim is badly bruised," Cady said, thinking aloud, "proving a drowning as murder is all but impossible."

"The ME felt that Kelch was your standard drowning victim. Water in the lungs indicated that she was still alive at the point of submersion. The evidence backed up the Ingram boy's statement. And it wasn't as though Ingram himself came across as Prince Charming."

"Did you get Ingram's statement at the scene?"

"The kid was a slobbering, sobbing heap. He had to have been blottoed six hours earlier. No way would he have been in any shape to sexually assault Ms. Kelch. Nope, it was most likely some old-fashioned drunken screwing, not exactly what they advertise in the Princeton brochures, but there you have it. Consensual sex."

"I see in the report that there was semen in her vagina. Was that ever tested against Bret Ingram?"

"Again, there was no indication of foul play. No sign of a struggle, the inquiry substantiated the boy's story. He admitted to having sexual intercourse with Marly Kelch on two occasions prior to the skinny dip. Quite frankly, Cady, at one of the Schaeffer boy's parties, there's probably more mixed semen in more places than at Hef's mansion. Hell, even Kelch's clothes were folded neatly in the boat house."

Cady remember the dirty laundry folded neatly in the hampers at the Zalentines' condominiums. "Folded neatly before *some old-fashioned drunken screwing?*"

"You're pissing me off again, Cady," Sheriff Littman said. "So Kelch was a tidy person, took good care of her stuff. So what?"

"Just following a train of thought. When did Ingram give his formal statement?"

"That afternoon. Tossed him in detox until two to get him sobered up."

"Did he have counsel?"

"Of course. I think a couple of his friends got the mouthpiece, as Ingram was in no condition to make phone calls."

"Do you remember his lawyer?"

"Local defense attorney named Leon Grotsworth. Good enough fellow—well, except for his chosen profession. But Ingram answered every question, repeatedly, and nothing had changed from his drunken babblings of that morning. Simple story, really—*got tanked, had sex, went swimming, passed out, got up to piss and puke, couldn't find honey-bunny but her clothes were still there, stumbled about looking for her, then went into panic mode and woke everyone up trying to find her."*

"Did Schaeffer set him up with Grotsworth?"

"Like I said, Schaeffer immediately tore off in his boat searching for Kelch right after we interviewed him. Don't think Bret Ingram was even in his vocabulary at that point in time. These were all a bunch of spoiled rich kids, so someone got him lined up."

"Ingram wasn't rich. He got into Princeton on grades and grants. Worked full time plus in the school library to make ends meet."

"Look, Agent Cady, I've been a good boy and bounced your ball. I've got a meeting with my executive staff in less than five minutes. Can we wrap this up?"

"You've been more than helpful, Sheriff. Just one last question. You mentioned Ingram had a *couple of his friends* that likely set him up with Grotsworth. Do you remember any of them?"

"There were a few people milling around trying to comfort the kid. Couple of brothers were..." the sheriff stopped mid-sentence. "Son of a bitch!"

"Sheriff?"

"Son of a bitch!" the sheriff repeated. "You're working the Zalentine case, aren't you?"

"Yes, sir. I am."

"I sent you the summary and the pathology report, but I've got the entire Kelch folder right here. We interviewed everyone at Schaeffer's party. Let me find the list." Cady heard more paper rustling. "Son of a bitch! That was them!"

"I already knew the Zalentines were at Schaeffer's party that night, Sheriff."

"I remember these goddamned twins sitting on the dock with Ingram, rubbing his shoulder, fetching him coffee, consoling him. But what those fuckers were really doing was getting the story straight. A hundred bucks says they're the ones who got Ingram lawyered up."

Cady said nothing. A dead silence ensued.

"I am so sorry, Agent Cady. It seemed like such a tragedy at the time. It never occurred to me to hit Ingram with some hard curves," Sheriff Littman said quietly. "Turns out I didn't dot every i."

"No one knew about the Zalentines back then, Sheriff."

"I'll tell you what, Agent Cady. I'm going to get Bret Ingram in here pronto. No beanbag this time. I'll find out exactly what happened at Snow Goose."

"It's too late, Sheriff."

"What do you mean?"

"Ingram's dead."

Chapter 10

After receiving the findings summary from Bergen County, Cady had sicced Agent Preston on discovering all she could about Bret Michael Ingram, where he was from, any other run-ins with the law, what he was currently doing, etcetera, etcetera. Cady also instructed Preston to do the same for Marly Kelch's surviving family members—to find out if there might be any father or brother acting as an avenging angel.

Less than half an hour later Agent Preston had stood in Cady's door.

"He's dead."

"You're kidding me." The statement was more rhetorical. Cady very rarely joked, but next to Liz Preston he was Henny Youngman.

Her upper lip curled. "Not unless there are two Bret Michael Ingrams with the same SS number and date of birth who attended Princeton during that timeframe."

"Murdered?"

"No. He died in a fire in Northern Minnesota, almost a year ago."

"Minnesota?"

"Yes."

"Get me everything."

It turned out Ingram limped along at Princeton for another

month after the "accident," sort of attending classes, before packing it in and pulling the plug on higher education. Cady could easily understand how the incident at Snow Goose could cause a young man to re-examine his life, but where Ingram wound up next took Cady aback.

"After dropping out of Princeton, he spent three months at the Copacabana Palace Hotel in Rio de Janeiro, right on the beach."

"Geez, Liz, and here I thought most dropouts moved back home with Mommy and Daddy and worked at Blockbuster."

Preston shrugged. "Then, after Rio, Ingram resurfaces to close on a lakefront real estate deal in Cohasset, Minnesota, of all places. Actually, he purchased a resort. A place called Sundown Point."

Cady thought for a second. "We know now why they called Sanfield *the Magician*."

Cady's phone rang. He caught it on the first ring. The pathologist had just completed the autopsies on the five female victims pulled from the bottom of Chesapeake Bay.

Cady pulled up behind the D.C. MPD squad car.

He'd been played. The congressman and senator were frightened. Frightened enough, that is, to give the FBI a minor shove in the right direction. Frightened enough to beef up security for Patrick Farris. But not frightened enough to be truthful.

Senator Farris was at a fundraiser in Dover, Delaware, a black-tie event to help fill the campaign coffers. Having the elder Farris two hours away worked to Cady's advantage. His instinct told him that Patrick Farris would never stray off the established template if his senator-father was in the room running interference. With that in mind, Cady called the congressman on the drive over to his house, apologized for the lateness of the hour, and downplayed how he had some questions about other students the Zalentines had known back in their Princeton days. Cady also lied about how it would only take a minute or two of the congressman's valuable time.

Surprisingly, Patrick Farris had been pleasantly agreeable.

Cady walked over to the driver's side of the squad car and ID'd himself.

"We've been instructed to swing by every hour," the officer behind the wheel said. "Do you know what this is all about?"

Cady shrugged. "Preventative measures."

"I hear the Service carts him to and from Rayburn," the officer in the passenger seat said. "It's the Chessman, isn't it?"

Cady cursed silently. Too many cooks involved in an ever-widening investigation made it all but impossible to keep the lid on anything. "The congressman knew both Sanfield and the Zalentines. Keep that to yourself, though. Like I said, preventative measures."

"He expecting you this late?"

Cady looked at his wristwatch. Almost eleven.

"Yes."

Chapter 11

Patrick Farris answered the door to his three-story row house, a brownstone in Woodley Park—a couple of rock-throws off Connecticut Avenue. Farris looked drained.

"Agent Cady," the house rep said, standing aside to let the federal agent come in. "Welcome to my humble abode."

"I apologize, Congressman, for keeping you and Mrs. Farris up so late."

"No worries. My wife is in Florida and I'm a night owl."

"You look exhausted."

"Long day." Farris led Cady up a short set of stairs to a living room the size of a basketball court with a cappuccino leather sectional curving across the hardwood floor at mid-arena. Two matching ottomans sat atop a sheep pile throw rug in front of the elongated sofa. A couple of Italian leather armchairs sat on opposite ends of the sectional, tilting inward. Seating accommodations had been arranged to allow guests a perfect viewing of something that immediately captured Cady's eye as he ascended the final steps. The Farrises had an aquarium the size one normally finds in a doctor's waiting room. If the three-story had a room for entertaining, this was certainly it.

"Alternative fuels are indeed the wave of the future," Farris continued, "but you can only read so many House bills on biofuel, wind power, and electric cars before all life is sucked from your marrow and you crave to toss yourself into the Potomac."

"So you're on that House Select Committee?"

"Idiot me thought I'd hit a grand slam when I first got assigned to it."

Cady walked along the front of the tank, looking at Farris's assortment of exotic fish. The aquarium sat on an oak base and had to be six feet long by four high. Various decorations lay on the light blue gravel at the bottom of the tank: a sunken pirate ship snapped in two, a half-buried treasure chest, and a yellow submarine with pictures of the Fab Four staring back at Cady from each of the submarine's four portholes. A couple starfish sat motionless, a variety of multicolored aquatic plants stretched upward, and rocks, coral, shale step ledges, and driftwood were also strewn about the colored gravel.

"Fortunately, we've got a service that checks the filter system and temperature," Farris said. "The fish were my wife's idea. The Fab Four and the topless mermaid on the swing set were my two cents."

"I bet." Cady peeked at the mermaid, and then began checking out the fish. "What's this one with the red tail?"

"That critter's a Tinfoil Barb. It's still got a bit to grow. Many in there are rainbow fish and a variety of Gouramies. There's also a Blue Dempsey and a Bala shark, and an eel lurking near the pirate ship."

"Interesting." Cady turned and looked across the room. Open doors on the back wall led out to a second-story terrace.

"Can I get you something to drink?"

"No thanks."

"Mind if I finish my Glenfiddich?" Farris picked up his glass and raised it to Cady.

Cady shook his head.

"Never thought I'd become a Glenfiddich man like my father." Farris finished his drink in one swallow. "Hell, Scotch might even work as a biofuel."

"I found out today that the friend of Marly Kelch—the girl who drowned at Schaeffer's party—a guy named Ingram, died in a fire last year."

Farris walked over to a cart in the corner stacked with bottles, picked up the open bottle of Glenfiddich 15 and refilled his glass. "I guess they're all dead now."

"You don't seem surprised."

"I'm sorry to hear about Bret, Agent Cady."

"You said you didn't know him."

"What?"

"In your father's office, you said you didn't know Marly's boyfriend, but you just said you were sorry to hear about Bret. I never mentioned Ingram's first name."

Farris looked out the open doors of his terrace. "I became curious and Googled old articles after we spoke."

"Bret Ingram was never charged with any crime, Congressman. I read through all the news accounts as well. The articles, brief as they were, focused on Marly Kelch's *accidental drowning* on Snow Goose Lake. It was treated as a tragedy. They didn't itemize the minutiae of who was partying with whom, perhaps out of respect for the Kelch family. Or fear of the Schaeffers."

Farris walked out to the edge of his terrace, drink in one hand.

Cady followed.

"What happened that night at the lake, Congressman?"

Farris took another long sip from his glass and stared across the alleyway. "The Robillards are home early."

Cady glanced across the way, a dim light from a back hallway clicked off in the neighboring condo.

"They've got a timeshare in Venice." Farris turned to look at Cady. "When they're not in Italy, Gretchen and Phil often have me over for one of Gretch's home-cooked meals. They've been married nearly sixty years, Agent Cady. You've heard of love at first sight? With the Robillards, it's love at every sight. I've seen it up close. Whenever Gretchen enters the room, Phil's eyes light up and the two are like kids again. Makes me feel like I should excuse myself and grant them some privacy." Farris turned back toward his neighbors' home. "That's the way it should be, right?"

Cady said nothing.

"It's going to break their hearts when they hear about me and Emma."

"Emma?"

"My wife and I are separated. Long time coming. Emma's a real trooper, though; she'll be there for the next election…then a quiet divorce decree, and separate ways." Farris took another mouthful of Scotch. "I see you're wearing a ring, Agent Cady. Did you hit the lottery? Have you got what Phil and Gretchen possess?"

Cady said nothing. Laura had been in her fifth month of pregnancy when she'd miscarried last December. Cady had been in Detroit tracking down rumors of Al-Qaeda connections at one of the Islamic centers—comments by a cleric had raised eyebrows but ultimately were editorial in nature. Cady flew home, took weeks off, but something had broken—had been years in the breaking, according to Laura—and all the king's horses and all the king's men were having a devil of a time putting it together again. Cady planned on taking an extended leave of absence once the Chessman case was resolved.

"Your silence is most telling," Farris said, toasting the agent with his drink glass. "I welcome you to the club."

"What happened at the lake, Congressman?"

Farris began to giggle and Cady realized that the man was on more than his second Scotch. He was getting the distinct impression that the congressman's imbibing might be a nightly occurrence.

"What happens at Snow Goose stays at Snow Goose."

"I don't see the humor."

"In that we are in perfect accord, Agent Cady."

He tried a new approach. "You knew Marly Kelch more than you let on, didn't you? Marly was more to you than someone to nod at in the hallway."

"Forgive me for butchering Faulkner, my friend, but the past is not dead." Farris polished off his glass and then chewed an ice cube. "In fact, it's not even past."

"What am I to make of that?"

It was Farris's turn to say nothing.

"What's with all the security, then? Secret Service chauffeurs, MPD cruising the neighborhood?"

Farris remained silent.

"I don't get it." Cady walked back inside the row house, went to look at the rainbow fish. "I came here tonight to tell you about the pathologist results on the five Chesapeake Bay victims. The ones Alain and Adrien took out on their sailboat. All five of the women had been drowned, stabbed repeatedly after death, then wrapped in tarp, weighted down, and tossed in the bay."

"Stabbed after death?" Farris asked.

"Keeps the gas from ballooning, an added insurance policy against the women ever floating to the top of the bay. I didn't envy the medical examiner working with the decomposing remains of these five young women, but he was able to enlighten us on one other point. All the victims had laceration marks around their waists, Congressman." Cady turned to look at the house rep. "Rope burns."

Farris had remained by the terrace balcony, back to Cady, staring off in the general direction of the Robillards and the elusive nature of true love, but Cady saw the man's shoulders quiver.

"You see, after the victims had been repeatedly raped by Alain and Adrien, they'd been tossed overboard, a rope tied around their stomachs, kind of like a monkey on a string, Congressman. The women were made to drown for hours for the Zalentines' amusement."

"Fucking psychopaths." Farris put his empty glass down on the stone railing.

"Any time a girl would give up and let herself go, the twins would pull her up, let her rest a moment or two, and begin the torture anew. I imagine this made their jollies last longer. What do you think—"

"Stop it," the congressman whispered.

"What do you think triggered the Zalentines' bloodlust, Farris?" Cady asked, probing deeper. "What really happened that night at the lake?"

The silence between the two men could be stirred with a boat oar. Cady turned to the aquarium, looking for the eel in the pirate ship, when something else caught his eye. His blood froze. The top half of a single chess piece stuck out from the colored pebbles behind a piece of coral. A clear glass king. Cady bent for a closer examination. It looked identical in shape and size to the kings in the chess set the crime lab had tracked down, the chess set with clear glass pieces that matched the ones inserted into the killing wounds in both Sanfield and the Zalentine twins. The chess pieces came from a fourteen-inch glass chess set, one that went for under $20 and could be found at any game or toy shop at any mall or department store from coast to coast—making it impossible to track a purchase. Cady had juggled a similar glass king as he contemplated what statement the killer was trying to make.

And now to find this piece hidden in Farris's fish tank, like a prize inside a Cracker Jack box, broke reality.

"Turns out I misled you." Farris slurred his words to the night. "Misled myself, too, Agent Cady. Once upon a time, long ago, I knew exactly how it felt—Phil Robillard's affection toward his wife. Cuts deep and endless. Alas...unrequited."

His mind spinning like a merry-go-round, Cady withdrew his Glock 22 from his shoulder holster. Farris was the Chessman? He'd known Marly Kelch? Loved her? Had discovered what the Zalentines had done to her that night, how Sanfield had helped them cover their tracks—and set about taking his vengeance? He'd hidden the glass king in the aquarium as some kind of sick keepsake?

"Turn around very slowly, Congressman Farris." Cady aimed at center mass, reminding himself what the Chessman had done to the Zalentines and Sanfield. "Place your hands in the air where I can see them."

Farris turned around, a questioning look on his brow.

"Walk slowly into the room, Congressman. No sudden moves." Cady cursed himself. He'd left a set of flex-cuffs in the car.

"I guess this ends it, then." Farris walked into the living room toward Cady, palms in the air. "Every last one of us. But," Farris said, squinting at Cady, "who are you?"

Cady squinted back, trying to digest Farris's peculiar comment when thunder clapped and the top half of the congressman's face blew apart, showering Cady in a mist of brain tissue, blood, and skull matter.

Cady dropped to the floor in a blink, his side against the sectional. A blink later Cady put two rounds into the ceiling fixture, showering the room with glass and darkness. The only light came from the aquarium and the half moon shining from the open terrace. Cady crab-crawled backwards until he was up against the whiskey cart. He could make out the dark lump in the middle of the room that had seconds previously been Congressman Farris. The man was dead, no ifs, ands, or buts.

The Robillards are home early flashed through the agent's mind. *They've got a timeshare in Venice.* Cady suddenly knew it had not been Phil or Gretchen Robillard—the Antony and Cleopatra from across the way—who had flicked off the back light in the neighboring condo.

Cady wrenched a faux antique phone from the whiskey cart, knocking over and shattering Farris's near-empty bottle of Glenfiddich. He tossed the handset onto the hardwood floor and punched in 911. Cady crouched, worked his way silently against the terrace door and listened. Nothing. Then footsteps. He closed his eyes, remembered the cement patio beneath the terrace. Cady took off, covered the terrace in an all-out sprint. Left hand on the balcony, he hurtled over, landed fifteen feet below and went down hard into a gravel bed, and knew immediately that something was seriously wrong with his right knee.

Cady pushed himself up and hobbled to the wooden privacy gate that led out to the alleyway. He made out the padlock in the moonlight, and then sent a side kick with all his might at handle level. The pain seared up and down his right side. He bit down hard, twisted about and repeated a side kick, this time with his left foot. The gate burst open and Cady pushed through, weight on his left side, Glock sweeping the path in front of him. He held his breath and listened for something to tell him which way to go. Nothing.

Cady took a step down the alleyway, knew if the shooter made it to Connecticut Avenue, he'd be quickly lost amongst the restaurants and nightclubs near Woodley Park Metro. Cady hobbled toward Connecticut. Suddenly a shadow in his periphery—then a sledgehammer cracked into the side of his face. Cady dropped like a bag of cement, handgun skittering across the way. Dazed, on his stomach, he swam after his Glock when a jackhammer of darkness smashed down upon his right hand, shattering bones and tissue, his palm a washcloth of crimson.

Cady screamed. He screamed to stay conscious. Something was wrong with his mouth as his scream came out a low guttural echo, hardly audible. He tasted blood and teeth and looked up. A figure flew across the shadows, nearing the end of the alleyway, long coat flowing behind him like a cape, a dark case in one hand, suddenly slowing, turning the corner...escaping.

Cady heard the sirens as he pulled himself back to the entrance to Farris's patio, vomited, and passed out.

Chapter 12

Two days later, on a lead provided between surgeries by a bedridden Agent Cady at George Washington University Hospital, FBI agents tried unsuccessfully to contact Dane Schaeffer at his cabin home outside Chester, New Jersey. The following day Agent Preston and her team returned with a warrant, but Schaeffer's house was deserted. No car in the attached garage and black bananas sat on a lonely kitchen countertop. The only thing of interest was when Agent Preston nudged Schaeffer's mouse on the pad in his office and the monitor blinked awake. Two short sentences in a Word document displayed on the screen in size twenty-six Times New Roman.

Forgive me, Father. Please forgive me…

A week later some hikers from Mason Neck State Park found a Lexus RX Hybrid on a dirt road down near the river—abandoned in a place where no vehicles should be. The hikers figured teenagers, a stolen car, and a joy ride, and called the police. The Lexus RX turned out to belong to Dane Schaeffer. Agents were present to discover a handful of glass chess pieces stuffed inside a brown envelope in Schaeffer's glove compartment, as well as a smashed trombone case hidden in the car's trunk. After popping out both the Kohlert TB524 and the high pile plush lining, the federal agents found something doubly interesting: a Remington 700 LTR 308, a light tactical rifle.

A day after finding Schaeffer's abandoned Lexus, Special Agent Dan Kurtz was able to match the round that killed Congressman Patrick Farris—a .308 Win—to the Remington 700. They were also able to determine that it had been vigorous strikes from the hard-shell Kohlert trombone case that had shattered Agent Cady's jaw, broken both his nose and left cheekbone, and turned his right hand to mush.

A week after this discovery they pulled a floater out of the Potomac River. Dane Schaeffer was not a pretty sight.

Book Two

Middlegame

Chapter 13

Present Day

Elaine Kellervick's husband was at the Chem-Eng conference in Denver until Friday evening, which translated fluently into her eating that last slice—allegedly Steve's slice—of the two extra tiramisu cheesecake slices she'd brought home after her dinner with The Dames, as her gang of lady chums referred to themselves, at the Prudential Center the night before. She'd not mentioned the cheesecake to Steve on the phone this morning and, although both had made the same New Year's resolution to shed those extra pounds around their centers and both had been kickboxing religiously at the gym all year, Elaine reckoned that Steve need be none the wiser. Besides, she had something potentially big to celebrate this evening, and to heck with what The Cheesecake Factory may or may not be doing to her middle-aged thighs.

Elaine had been tasked by her walrus-stached, content-free pantload of a boss, Albert Banning, to reverse-engineer a competitor's trading strategy and revenue stream so that their Boston investment firm, Koye & Plagans Financials, could replicate *Mr. Schmooze*'s money-making results. She had met and mingled with Mr. Schmooze at a variety of events in the financial industry over the past decade and had been surprised and touched to have received a handwritten letter from Mr. Schmooze himself in response to a résumé she'd sent his firm after a particularly trying Albert Banning week a half-year back. Although they had no openings for her skill set at that time, his note had read, he "remembered" Elaine "fondly" and wished her "all the best." The note went on to say that she "would skip to the top of the list should anything arise" and that she should "definitely keep in touch."

Although it was something that didn't make it into the corporate literature or promotional brochures, it wasn't *uncommon* in the financial industry to data model the competition. When that boob Banning had given her this assignment, in a continuing effort to keep her name at the top of Mr. Schmooze's list, she'd sent Mr. Schmooze a teasing e-mail about how she'd been charged with discovering the secrets of his success, with a smiley emoticon winking at the end of the final sentence.

Every time she met with Banning or talked to the clown on the telephone or received one of his spell-check-free e-mails or even passed the nincompoop in the hallway, Elaine became completely and utterly flabbergasted. Utterly flabbergasted that Albert Banning was the Chief Investment Officer at K&P. Utterly flabbergasted that this Ted Baxter had Peter-Principled his way up to a position where he could inflict maximum damage to the firm on a day-in-day-out basis. Although, in retrospect, there'd been some foreshadowing miscommunications throughout the interview process, Elaine had been utterly flabbergasted since her second day on the job, two years previously, when it became abundantly clear that his pompous vacuousness did not conceal any redeemable brilliance. Utterly flabbergasted that Banning was able to locate his corner office each and every morning and didn't wind up stumble-bumbling about in a neighboring high rise looking for his chair.

Dear hubby Steve lived for her stories about Albert Banning, about how annual reviews were not unlike the old Bob Newhart comedic monologues; how if someone else were presenting in a meeting, you could wind your watch by how soon Banning would pick his nose and wipe any findings on the underside of the conference table; how he'd steal a second and even third bismark every time someone on staff—although never Banning himself—brought donuts in to share with the gang; how Banning's eyes faithfully returned, like a magnet to metal, to even the slightest hint of exposed cleavage. But then again, Steve could afford to enjoy these stories because he didn't have to report to the asshat on a weekly basis.

Banning certainly looked the role: dark wool suits and white dress shirts all properly tailored and dry-cleaned, and somewhere along the line he'd miraculously mastered cufflinks. He carried around a calfskin briefcase—which she strongly suspected contained his stash of Gummi bears and malted milk balls rather than any work—as his constant companion. After Elaine's first month as an investment strategist at K&P, Steve had to dissuade her from hiring a P.I. to determine if Banning's Yale MBA was truly on the up-and-up. Steve told her that "forging a résumé would indicate a certain creative spark" that they both knew Banning thoroughly lacked, and that "frankly, Elaine, a third of the graduates pooped out of these Ivys couldn't find their ass with a funnel, and Albert Banning wouldn't have the foggiest how to even *spell* funnel."

But Elaine knew her days at K&P Financials were numbered a couple of months back when Banning had e-mailed her and a few of the firm's other market analysts some generic economic questions requesting their answers, input, or comments. The queries had actually piqued Elaine's interest, and she'd jotted down a few paragraphs of thought on the current state of stock volatility and the P/E ratio to which she received no acknowledgement or note of thanks or any type of reply at all from the buffoon. So imagine Elaine's surprise when she noticed her insight quoted word-for-word in the *Fidelity Investor* newsletter in a short interview with you-know-who. So angry that she could have blasted straight into orbit, Elaine had marched into Banning's office waving a copy of the newsletter, only to see that he'd already had an issue framed and hung on the wall behind his black executive desk, situated between his MBA and an eight-by-ten of him standing next to an obviously put-upon Alan Greenspan at some long-forgotten conference.

"I told the editor that those conclusions came from our brilliant team here at K&P," a startled and placating Banning had mumbled. "I even sent them your names, but I guess they didn't have room in such a short piece."

Elaine stormed out of the swine's office in order to refrain from shattering his newly framed article with a pitch of the weighted tape dispenser sitting atop the corner of his desk. The all-star ignoramus had been hang-dog around her for a week—all *Please let me get the door* and *How are we doing today?* faux sweetness. But as if to rub salt in her wound, her quote, attributed to the bumblefuck, had been picked up and reprinted in the Business section of the *Boston Globe*. As far as Elaine was concerned, there was no God.

After two days of mathematical modeling of Mr. Schmooze, Elaine realized she'd bungled something up herself, that her data model was incorrect—tainted by Banning's involvement, no doubt— so she made a phone call to Mr. Schmooze's firm under the guise of a courtesy call, was fended off by a frosty and likely menopausal executive assistant. She tore through her desk drawer of clutter and found Mr. Schmooze's business card. Off went an e-mail request for additional information. Then Elaine scrapped her fouled-up model and began again in the interest of being overly meticulous—or, as Steve would attest, anal retentive. By the end of the next business day, with that blunderhead Banning asking her about her analysis every time they passed in the hallway, she'd wound up with the exact same results.

She scanned the summary spreadsheet, peeked at some numbers in the body of her market analysis, and then peeked again at her assumptions. A ghost of a pattern danced in the back of her mind, but then again, Elaine could ferret out a numerical pattern in some dice tosses. The data model was off, it had to be. Elaine set all of her files neatly—*neatly, Steve, not anal retentively*—on the table in front of her and began sorting through the materials. Although markets would yo-yo up and down, Mr. Schmooze—he whose client list stepped off the pages of *People Magazine*, starred in major movies, and won Oscars, Emmys, and Grammys by the boatload—had a performance line that for all practical purposes only scaled upward. Her figures had to be incorrect, as this was a statistical impossibility; only seven percent of Mr. Schmooze's months were down, with nearly uninterrupted investment gains averaging ten percent a year.

Elaine shook her head to vanquish any stray thoughts. She'd been working for the goofball way too long; his idiocy must be contagious. If she showed Banning her work, he'd laugh in her face and hold it over her every time she caught him making a doddering old fool of himself. She must be botching up Mr. Schmooze's *split-strike conversion strategy*, as that investment methodology was exceptionally complex to begin with, but would be where the magic, if there was any, lay.

Her phone rang. She recognized the New York area code and picked up the receiver. Serendipity—it was Mr. Schmooze himself. He mentioned that he didn't have much time, but wanted to get back to her before heading out to some "insufferable" dinner party with the Lieutenant Governor. They chatted about the sorry state of the industry and very, very gingerly Elaine brought up her data modeling.

"I suspected that's what your call was about," Mr. Schmooze said. "I wish it were seven, but we both know what that would mean… plus, I'm not Merlin the Magician. No, Elaine, the percent is closer to thirty, and even at that I've got clients heating up the tar and plucking the feathers."

"That's what I suspected," Elaine had said. "Garbage in-garbage out."

"If you can pop in to New York early next week and let me buy you lunch, we can discuss—very generically, of course—the firm's internals. In fact, Elaine," the Schmooze had said, "my true purpose for calling is that Paulette Glimski, my favorite data modeler, just gave birth to triplets—an in-vitro procedure that you hear so much about these days. Anyway, Paulette broke my heart earlier this week, although we saw it coming. She handed in her notice, said she's giving up Excel spreadsheets for diapers and pacifiers, so we're a little short-handed—in case you're still looking for an opportunity."

Thoughts of kicking Banning to the curb, leaving the breathing gaffe machine shorthanded, made her hot and she wished that Steve wasn't in Colorado, in more ways than one. She couldn't wait for their nightly call. In her mind, although playing hard to get of course, she'd already accepted the position. Mr. Schmooze had made it clear that there'd be no need to move, that the bulk of the work could be done remotely, telecommuting except for the odd meet-and-greet here or presentation there, and much of that could be done via web conferencing or net meetings. Yes, Elaine thought to herself, she'd be bringing a résumé on her day trip to New York next week.

Elaine snuck out early and on the drive home gave it serious thought. Telecommuting for Mr. Schmooze in New York City was exactly what the doctor ordered, a no-brainer; she'd get her sanity back. Elaine couldn't wait to tell Steve. He'd be ecstatic for her, even if he would miss out on the comic relief that Albert Banning's very existence provided. She'd already phrased a terse two-weeks' notice in her mind, which she would likely tamper down—no need to burn bridges—although it'd be nearly orgasmic to scrape the numbnuts off her shoe. Elaine began tapping the monthly code into the wall security unit when she realized the unit wasn't operating correctly.

"It might not be working anymore," a voice behind her whispered.

Elaine almost jumped out of her skin, but turned, landing in a classic karate defensive stance. The tall man in a black suit, a yard away, stared down at her. Elaine knew she'd never make the door. Her black belt training kicked in and she threw up a head kick.

The tall man drew back and patted her foot aside with the fingers of his left hand. The momentum threw Elaine off balance, but she adjusted and returned to the fighting stance. It was hard to tell, but the tall man appeared to be smiling. Elaine threw a throat strike, a quick towel snap to disable him while she cut for the door. But something went wrong and Elaine found herself pushed back against the wall. She hadn't felt the man's blow, but she couldn't seem to get her breath. Her face was pressed against the defective security unit.

The tall man looked into her eyes as the stiletto slid under her solar plexus and up into her heart. He rotated the knife handle, giving Elaine a final jolt right before she died. A final jolt to help the woman appreciate the irony of how worthless her years of strip mall karate had been. Using the stiletto as a handle, the tall man eased Elaine slowly to the floor of the entryway. He knelt down next to her and retracted the blade. He took out a glass pawn and pressed the tip of the chess piece into the knife wound. Then he stripped the surgical gloves off from the inside out, capturing the stiletto within the right-hand glove.

The tall man had gotten there early and fine-tooth combed the Kellervick residence, checking all the obvious and not-so-obvious places. It was clean. He searched the home PC for any files or e-mails created in the past week. Nothing of any consequence to anyone.

The tall man headed toward the back door but paused in front of the double-door refrigerator. He picked up a napkin and used it to open the appliance. He grabbed The Cheesecake Factory container.

The tall man loved tiramisu.

Chapter 14

Six Months Ago

L ucy would be home any minute.

He had to tell her. Drake Hartzell had put off telling Lucy the truth for as long as possible because of the heartache, pain, and cutting betrayal that would become her new reality. But he was running out of time. It would shatter her world—*their* world. Hartzell had to tell her tonight. There was no other way.

He stared out over the Hudson River through the floor-to-ceiling windows of his penthouse suite seventy-two flights above Manhattan. He wished with all his heart, or whatever chunk of spent charcoal passed for his heart, that he and Lucy were safe and sound back in England in their St. Leonards-on-Sea estate. The former NASDAQ chairman took another deep sip from his snifter and did mental gymnastics, attempting to figure out how much longer he could keep the balls in the air. They say that you can't cheat an honest man, but Hartzell knew firsthand that that was all bullshit. He had made an exceedingly lucrative living cheating honest men...and quite a few women, too.

Hartzell stumbled back to the living room, kicked over an empty cognac bottle, and sank deep into the leather sofa. *Good Christ,* he thought. *Good Christ.*

He'd come unimaginably far since his youth, that hellish hard-scrabble in Walton, and Hartzell didn't know what he missed less about that urban shit-hole in Liverpool: the way his family eked out a living on potatoes and gruel or the sting of his father's belt whenever the old bastard drank his unemployment check or—throughout Pop's briefer and briefer stints with industry—needed to let off steam after a particularly irritating shift at the dockyard. Hartzell never returned after holding a final palaver with the cruel son of a bitch, a meeting in which a fifteen-year-old Hartzell smashed his old man's teeth in, repeatedly, with a pipe wrench. He never once looked back; when the money began to pour in, he never sent any funds back to Walton, not even to help support his mother and three sisters. Never even crossed his mind. They were a part of Hartzell's life best relegated to the past. And after a stretch in the Royal Navy, he came to America in the late 1970s in order to reinvent himself in this the land of opportunity. And reinvent himself Hartzell did.

Highly regarded and highly sought after, Drake Hartzell made a most pleasant living as a money manager and investment guru. In addition, Hartzell, a renowned philanthropist, fundraised relentlessly for a lengthy buffet of charitable causes—trendy causes, causes that allowed him great access to the rich and the famous and the movie stars and the widows with buckets of money to burn. And they in turn were enthralled by Hartzell's cheery demeanor, his English accent and, now that he was nearing fifty, his distinguished mane of gray hair. Hartzell was the crowned prince at charming the glitterati and glamour crowds on both the east and west coasts of the *colonies*. They loved the stories of his luncheons with Tony Blair, his real estate dealings with Prince Charles, and his heartbreak over the death of Lady Di. Fascinating stories told with a smile on his face and a twinkle in his eye, and all met with looks of awe and hearty nods of instant friendship. Yes, Hartzell had reinvented himself all right, as a world-class schmoozer to the grotesquely and obscenely wealthy. So what if absolutely none of his stories from jolly ole England happened to be true?

Hell, most investors didn't even knowingly invest directly through him, but went through one of twenty hedge funds that, in turn, provided Hartzell with their assets to manage. Life was grand, exceptionally so. Hartzell's winning investment algorithm was a closely held secret; it had to be, in this era of corporate espionage and shady dealings. Truth be told, Hartzell himself had stolen his *winning investment algorithm* off an Italian immigrant from nearly a century ago…a chap by the name of Charlie Ponzi.

Hartzell's investment fraud flew quietly under the radar so as to not arouse suspicion. He promised clients modest gains and steady returns, when, actually, any funds redeemed by investors were taken out of the proceeds of more recent investors. Hartzell had even been able to survive the scrutiny that that blundering fuck Bernard Madoff had shined on the industry, thanks in no small part to greasing the palms of a variety of SEC officials, as well as the sheer byzantine nature of his various feeder funds. Hartzell was also a bright enough operator who dealt hefty political contributions to both sides of the aisle over the years, like a blackjack dealer flipping cards.

Hartzell's investment advisory firm, with him as broker-dealer, executed orders for his clients, on paper at least. Hartzell's exhaustive knowledge of electronic trading aided him immeasurably in removing a concrete paper trail and providing the *appearance* of transactions. In other words, the statements his investors received were falsified with deceptive history-related performance data, as well as related finance data inserted in place of the funds' true achievement. In still other words, a highly sophisticated cut-and-paste fraud. In reality, Hartzell's firm placed next to no trades. In order to obfuscate, to muddy the waters of any potential investigation,

Hartzell commingled his personal funds with the assets from his advisory business, along with his market-making finances—all quite contrary to regulation, and all increasingly siphoned off into numbered accounts set up in various ports around the world.

His idol, a Connecticutian named Phineas Taylor Barnum or, simpler yet, P.T. Barnum, was off by a mile. *There's not a sucker born every minute—try every second, and even that's a low-ball estimate.* Hartzell had a laundry list of rationales that allowed him to sleep like a baby each and every night. Witness the endless business executives riding their golden parachutes gently down to terra firma while their companies were left to crash and crater in the turbulence. Witness ambulance-chasing deep-pocket-picking shysters of every hue slobbering out of their cubby holes to win the legal lottery. Witness union knot-heads strangling the golden goose, destroying whole industries by squeezing compensation benefits completely out of whack with their members' education levels or skill sets. Witness skyrocketing tuition hikes, a thousand times the rate of inflation, with graduating seniors slowly coming to realize that they are both jobless and bankrupt. Witness the lobbyist parasites engulfing the body politic like a second skin. Witness Chicago trying to sell off a senate seat to the highest bidder. Witness an ex-Vice President, a Nobel Prize and Oscar winner—one whose home phone number Hartzell had listed in his personal Rolodex—doing the Chicken Little dance in order to rake in untold millions from carbon offsets, whatever the hell those damn things were. Witness 401(k)s wiped out on a colossal Chernobyl-style meltdown due to the fuckwits in D.C. raccooning into markets of which they knew naught. Witness a much larger Ponzi scheme referred to as the United States Social Security system. Witness the federal budget deficit, witness the burgeoning federal debt, witness endless bailouts to the incompetent and corrupt…and all arrears passed on to the unsuspecting newborns in each and every maternity ward across the land, sea to shining sea.

It was all malarkey—pure twaddle—a crock of the highest order.

So why on earth shouldn't Hartzell get his?

It would be criminal for him not to. If anything, Hartzell was performing a much-needed public service. He had spent over two decades shearing the frivolous rich, the malignant narcissists, the snobby twits and self-aggrandizing scatterbrains that were both loaded and pampered beyond any sense of reality, beyond any grounding on Planet Earth. Infantile temper tantrums at the drop of a hat, diva hysterics over lukewarm appetizers, any imagined slights or, God forbid, five minutes without a sycophant declaring their undying devotion—a pissier bunch you'd never meet. It was all he could do these days to remain in high spirits, witty and smiling, whilst mingling in the same room with these hoity-toity balls of curdled milk. And Hartzell only wished he could be around, a mere fly on the wall, when the news broke and it very slowly dawned on them that many of their investments weren't worth the paper they were printed on. If only he could catch a passing glimpse of their expressions as it sank in, or hear the collective sound, a sound of such magnitude as to register on the Richter scale, as tens of thousands of sphincters puckered up as the investors came to the realization that their golden years might not be as pleasant as heretofore anticipated.

All that said, Hartzell supposed himself a sociopath to no small degree, his sense of right and wrong beaten out of him as a child, but he had one slight chink in his suit of armor—an abiding love for a very special young woman, his daughter, which he imagined made him almost human. It was a paternal love that would very likely be his downfall, a deep caring that kept him from exiting, stage left, to a spanking new life in the West Indies or some other most hospitable place where he could live out the remainder of his life under a different name with a bottomless bank account to help ease all pain.

Hartzell's Achilles' heel was named Lucy, and she was a delightful brunette with aristocratic features, eternally searching brown eyes, and a quick tongue. Lucy was the byproduct of a short tryst he'd had with a minor English actress who'd had a minor part in a forgettable Broadway production of two decades past. Lucy's mother, Alison, had been an unbearable bore, but it had been pleasing to spend a little time with a beautiful woman from his side of the pond. After the show's short run, Alison had skirted back to Piccadilly to spoon-feed more nonsense to the unwashed masses. Hartzell was elated at her departure from New York City, even shuttled her to JFK International himself, but was absolutely infuriated ten days later when she called to inform him of *their* pregnancy.

Hartzell did his finest to dance Alison into having an abortion, but for once his charm fell flat. Alison was adamant—she was keeping the baby. Evidently, Hartzell assumed, she'd realized her income from him would be considerably more reliable than that from the London stage. Under the more-than-veiled threat of dragging Hartzell through the magistrates' court for child maintenance, completely unacceptable for a man of his position, he had agreed through his solicitor to set Alison up with overly generous monthly support allotments, as well as cutting the shrew a preliminary check for a quarter-million pounds sterling. It was a move that immediately turned the pouting wench into toothy smiles and, more importantly, would not imperil his reputation.

For Lucy's first five years of life, and more to polish his image, Hartzell had one of his secretaries mail the little one a weekly postcard from the Big Apple with a happy sentence or two from Daddy—all thoroughly forged on his behalf. Once a month the same secretary was instructed to pick out a children's gift and have it parceled off to his daughter. Hartzell didn't understand what all the talk was about—being a parent was a breeze. Once Lucy was able to talk, and after a glass or two of Dom Perignon, he began making the obligatory weekly phone call.

Yes, Lucy was the chink in his armor. Quite frankly, if Hartzell had to pinpoint the exact moment when this chink first materialized, it would be the first time that Lucy called him "Papa" over the telephone. He was up half the night thinking about his little girl and two weeks later, when he could finally pull away from work, he found himself in London, calling on Lucy in person.

By the time Lucy was six, she was spending the summers with Hartzell. *Brilliant*, he thought at the time, as he paraded Lucy—who could out-Shirley Shirley Temple—through an assortment of charity get-togethers and fundraisers, casting himself as the doting father. And the investments continued to roll in. By age ten, and another quarter-million sterling to a recently married Alison, Lucy came to live with Hartzell full time. Of course Lucy grew up with the finest nannies and the best tutors; she graduated from Trinity, and now was in her second year of studying dance at Juilliard.

But since the sharp decline of the U.S. Financial Industry, he'd been ill with worry. Not about the SEC or any federal investigation when he could no longer keep the balls in the air—because he'd always known that it was only a matter of time, that his days were surely numbered. And he had planned for that day all along. No, what kept Hartzell up into the wee hours of the night, what had caused him to lose twenty pounds in the past month, was how on earth he going to tell his daughter—the singular love of his life—the truth.

Hartzell heard the key in the lock. He heard the door swing open and shut in the foyer. He heard soft footsteps on the hardwood.

Lucy had arrived.

Chapter 15

Present Day

"Who killed my daughter, Agent Cady?"

Dorsey Kelch was Cady's first stop in his cold casing of the initial Chessman murders for Assistant Director Jund. He had contacted her that morning, asked if he could swing by her one-story rambler in the Wyomissing Borough of Reading, the seat of Berks County, Pennsylvania, and chat with her about her daughter, Marly. Mrs. Kelch had graciously welcomed Cady into her home; however, her toy dachshund, Rex, took an instant dislike to the agent and was quickly exiled to the backyard. After a short filibuster by the kitchen door, the dog marched over and sat under the picnic table. Mrs. Kelch served Cady a cup of green tea and oatmeal raisin cookies as Cady spent an hour paging through Marly's old high school yearbooks and photo albums, and scratching the names of old boyfriends onto his notepad.

"I hate to be obtuse, Mrs. Kelch, but it really is a fishing expedition regarding a current investigation. Double-checking facts, like I mentioned on the phone."

"How did my daughter really die, Agent Cady?"

"No hard evidence indicates that it was anything other than an accidental drowning. It would be unethical of me to feed you conjecture." Cady hated himself for stating it in this manner, for disturbing this poor woman's solitude by raking over coals of the past, but it was the truth at this point—the abridged version, anyway.

"Remember when you came by a few years ago, to ask about Marly's relationship, or lack of one, with Bret Ingram?"

"Yes."

"I called you at the number you gave me when the news broke that Dane Schaeffer had methodically gone about killing his old Princeton chums, but you weren't there. They said you were on medical leave."

Cady unconsciously squeezed the fingers of his right hand into a partial fist. "I spent several months in physical therapy."

Dorsey Kelch shot Cady a questioning look that went unanswered.

"Then I contacted Sheriff Littman in Bergen County. He recited what you just told me almost verbatim. No evidence exists to indicate...nothing conclusive—blah, blah, blah."

"After everything you've been through, the last thing I want is to turn your world upside down based on speculation. Quite frankly, Mrs. Kelch, it would sound like faulty assumptions and foolish guesswork."

"Blah, blah, blah," Dorsey Kelch repeated. "Thirteen years ago my only child dies in a god-awful accident at a god-awful party, but I put my faith in God and live with it. Ten years drag by and suddenly you appear asking if Marly was seeing this Ingram boy, if Marly knew the Zalentines. I'd never heard of Bret Ingram until the day the police informed me that my daughter was dead—the worst day of my life—and I'd never heard of the Zalentine twins until I read in the newspaper how they *drowned* all of those poor young women on that death boat of theirs. Turns out these same Zalentines were at Snow Goose Lake the night my daughter *accidently drowned*. But nothing is ever conclusive. Now, three years later, you're back in my living room jotting down the name of any guy Marly ever looked at. I'm asking you again, Agent Cady, who killed my daughter?"

"The evidence leads to Dane Schaeffer having taken it upon himself, for whatever reason, to kill the Zalentines, the Zalentines' attorney, and even to kill one of his best friends—Patrick Farris. Sadly, that's where the evidence ends. You have every right to be skeptical, Mrs. Kelch. Was Dane Schaeffer haunted by what happened to Marly, was he a part of it, or was it something else entirely? I don't know what made Schaeffer snap. And I don't know how your daughter died."

"But you don't buy that it was an accidental drowning?"

Cady realized he'd already dug a deep enough hole and said nothing.

Mrs. Kelch shrugged. "Will you promise me something, then, Agent Cady?"

Cady nodded.

"Will you promise to let me know what you find out, no matter what you think I've been through? One way or the other, I want to know the truth."

"Whatever I find out about Marly—good or not so good—I'll let you know. I promise."

"Very well." Dorsey Kelch dabbed a Kleenex to her eye. "You had some questions. How can I help?"

"First, was Dane Schaeffer at Marly's funeral?"

"He and his father were there."

"Did they have anything to say?"

"They were both extremely sorry. I don't remember much else, but I was taking Valium to get me through."

"Was Bret Ingram there?"

"Yes. The boy was so shook up he sobbed straight through the service. That's why it never occurred to me that it was anything but a tragic accident until you showed up a decade later."

"Do you remember if Ingram said anything?"

"The boy blubbered incoherently. I didn't have time for him. Not that day. I turned and walked away, left the boy mid-blubber."

"I have some questions about male friends Marly knew while growing up."

"I see you've jotted down Ted Thorsen, Marly's first boyfriend from back in junior high," Dorsey Kelch said, smiling. "Ted was all thumbs and left feet. He was so nervous around Marly, he'd visibly shake. Pete and I would go into the kitchen and cringe."

Dorsey Kelch had retired the previous year from teaching Honors English to college-bound seniors at Reading Central Catholic High School, where she had taught for thirty-five years. It was also where she had met her husband, Peter Kelch, who had been the music director and orchestra conductor until the Amyotrophic Lateral Sclerosis, also called ALS or Lou Gehrig's Disease, forced him into early retirement. Peter Kelch died from the resulting respiratory failure the summer of Marly's high school graduation, six years after the onset of symptoms.

"I see you've got Scott Dentinger, her counselor friend from church camp. They were real close, pen pals during the school year. Scott's a priest himself now. You've got her friends from Debate Club and the actors from the different plays she was in."

"Who's this young man?" Cady had a photo album opened to what must have been one of Marly's birthday parties in the Kelches' backyard. She was all teeth for the camera, couldn't have been more than fourteen. A little blond kid stood in the background by the swing set staring at her, his smile a mile wide.

Dorsey Kelch lit up. "That's little Jakey Westlow. God bless him. Marly babysat Jakey back when she was ten or so."

"What's Westlow doing now?"

"Another sad story. Jakey's mother, Lorraine, had Jakey pretty late in life and the father was never a part of their lives. One of those things."

"That can be rough."

"It was. So when Lorraine got kidney cancer, Jakey took care of her. She was all he had, and after she passed, Jakey broke apart." Dorsey Kelch dabbed at her eyes again with the Kleenex. "He committed suicide."

Cady finished his cup of green tea, slowly paging through the photo album, giving Mrs. Kelch a chance to compose herself. "That is a sad story."

"How's the tea?"

"It's excellent tea, ma'am."

"Please call me Dorsey."

Cady nodded again. "Who's this young man in the football jersey?"

"That's Eric Braun. They dated on and off in high school. In fact, Eric was Homecoming King to Marly's Homecoming Queen."

"What's he doing now?"

"The Brauns retired to Florida years ago, but Eric was at Marly's funeral. He was in the Marines at that point, I think, or some branch of the armed services, anyway."

Cady scribbled Braun's name into his notebook, along with the other names he was going to run checks on. He flipped through the remaining pages of the photo album, and then placed it gently on the coffee table.

"Your daughter was very beautiful, Dorsey."

"In more ways than one, Agent Cady," Mrs. Kelch said. "In more ways than one."

"B-R-A-U-N," Cady spoke into his cell phone on the drive back to D.C. "Eric Braun."

"Any others on the list military?" Agent Preston asked.

"Not positive, Liz. Life moved on and Mrs. Kelch doesn't know where several of Marly's old friends wound up. But if Braun is *Semper Fi*, that fits the profile. Braun would have capability, weapons knowledge, and motivation."

"I'll have Agent Schommer run the names."

"Thanks, Liz," Cady replied. "I feel good about this."

Chapter 16

Six Months Ago

"What's the matter, Papa?"

Drake Hartzell looked up at Lucy from the brown leather sofa. He could only begin to imagine the sight he must make, robe askew, hair a bird's nest, face moist and red, an empty Delamain bottle resting sideways on the Persian rug, an equally empty brandy snifter lying next to it, two paper shredders—one in front of each kneecap—and six overfed Hefty bags of white shreddings extending diagonally out from the couch.

"Hello, Slim." Hartzell wiped his face with the swipe of a forearm. "How was your night?"

"My god, Papa," Lucy said, sitting down in the chair across from Hartzell, concern written across her face. "What's going on here?"

Hartzell's nerve turned to pudding. "Nothing you need to worry about, Slim."

"Have you been to Dr. Hinderaker?"

"My health is fine." Hartzell almost snorted; he must really look a mess. "Never better."

"You've lost so much weight, Papa. Recently. And let's face it; you've been Mr. Mopey all month long." Lucy's eyes darted around the room, halting on the shredders sitting in front of him. "What aren't you telling me?"

"It's just these markets," Hartzell said. "These goddamned markets are crucifying me."

"The economy is *not* your fault, Papa. You didn't release the bear. Anyone with a brain the size of a pea knows that. It's like you've been telling everyone lately." Lucy leaned back and did an almost passable imitation of her father. "'*Buying low. Rock-bottom prices.*'"

Try as he might, Hartzell couldn't bring himself to smile.

"Papa?"

Hartzell stared at his daughter. He felt his lower lip begin to tremble.

"Papa, now you're scaring me. You have to tell me what's going on."

"I can't, Slim," Hartzell said softly, wishing he'd not had that final glass of cognac. "You'll hate me."

A silence hung over the two. Lucy stood, scooted around a shredder and sat on the sofa next to her father.

"Rubbish, Papa. I could never hate you, never in a billion years." Lucy cupped his left hand in both of her palms. "Now come on, out with it."

Unable to look her way, Hartzell told his daughter everything. He began with his origin, his real name, his childhood in Liverpool, his coming over to America. He gave her the short version of how the markets worked—the version he parroted to clients—but he then confessed to how he *worked* the markets, how the funds were diverted, how he cooked the books and had done so for many, many years, how with the financial meltdown his entire house of cards was soon to come tumbling down upon his head.

Hartzell felt her hands tighten at this point. Unable to meet her eyes, Hartzell continued speaking to the floor. He walked her through the grim reality of the situation, how they would likely consider him a flight risk and deny bail. How it would likely take a decade for the courts to sort it all out, and how no matter what dream team of attorneys he could assemble, the climate was such that he'd face the rest of his life in prison. He told her how he'd always known this day would come, no two ways about it, and how unlike Bernard Madoff he indeed had an exit strategy, and how he'd have vanished into the ether months ago, but he couldn't leave…because it would literally kill him to abandon her. He told her how it ripped him up inside to think that she might be made to pay for his sins by a frenzied media that smelled blood in the water or targeted for harassment by a fleet of angry investors whose nest eggs had abruptly evaporated. He ended by telling her how terribly sorry he was for ruining her life.

Hartzell felt a tear slide past his nose, followed by another. He repeated his apology again as her hands slipped away from his. Hartzell sat motionless and awaited judgment.

"Papa?"

"Yes."

"Look at me, Papa," Lucy said. "I need you to look me in the eye."

Hartzell's heart caught in his throat. He felt fear, a captured pirate walking the plank. Telling Lucy the truth was the hardest thing he'd done in his life. Hartzell turned his head toward the only person he'd ever loved. She'd been weeping in silence while listening to her father's confession, hearing her papa admit to being a fraud, feeling the rug slip out from under her feet. Hartzell watched as tears worked their way down Lucy's face. She made no attempt to wipe them away.

"Now listen to me carefully, Papa," Lucy began speaking, iron in her eyes. "You are not going to spend one second behind bars. Not now. Not ever. Furthermore, you are not going to give one penny back—not one red cent. Let them find us in the ether."

Hartzell felt a wave of shock pass slowly through him, and then a second wave of relief, and finally a tsunami of elation. He wanted to stand and cheer to the heavens, but another thought occurred to him that brought more tears to his eyes.

Lucy truly was his little girl.

Chapter 17

Cady squinted at the digital 3:33 a.m. on the clock beside his twin bed as the constant *Deet-Deet-Deet* of the alarm drummed slowly, annoyingly, into his consciousness. What the hell? Cady began arbitrarily pressing buttons and fumbling with switches, silently cursing the maid or room service joker that must have set the alarm as some kind of a middle-finger salute for a guest not leaving a tip. Cady got lucky and pressed something with his thumb that stifled the alarm. He rolled over and began drifting back into a doze.

"Thank you," a voice across the room whispered. "That was a tad annoying."

Cady sat upright, nerve endings taut as piano wire. Instinctively Cady reached for his sidearm, which, while traveling on FBI business, he kept holstered atop the bedside table at night. The Glock 22 was nowhere to be found. Cady then began reaching for the lamp.

"I'd really advise against that," the voice stated simply, as though ordering an extra side of coleslaw.

Cady stared at the shape in the chair near the window, shook off his drowsiness and willed himself to be observant. It was a shadowy figure, topped with what looked like a fedora, the kind worn in the old movies. Possibly a trench coat or long jacket, dark trousers.

"It's been a while, Agent Cady."

Cady froze, realizing he was a dead man. He knew who was sitting in the side chair of his Embassy Suites hotel room.

The Chessman.

"I'm no longer with the FBI."

"I'm sure that's been remedied," the voice replied, now an octave above a whisper. "Why else would you be in D.C.?"

Cady struggled to hear over his pounding heart. The Chessman's accent was noticeable for a lack of one, what the network news liked in their anchormen. Tom Brokaw-esque. The window chair was about two feet off the floor. At this angle, the man would be sitting upright, one foot in front of the other, his hat about even with the television. Cady took mental notes—*he's over six feet, possibly an inch taller than me.*

"We thought you were dead."

"Reports of my death have been greatly exaggerated."

So he was literate and quoted Mark Twain.

"Why did you kill Kenneth Gottlieb?"

"How's your right hand, Agent Cady?"

"Go to hell."

"A bit testy about that, are we?"

"What is it you want from me?"

"To see if you're the one. I can't just saddle up with any old partner for this here roundup, can I? I need someone with *gray matter.*"

"Partner? What the hell are you talking about?"

"Get with the program, Agent Cady. Someone started a whole new game."

"I wonder who that could possibly be."

"It's not my match."

"I don't believe you."

The Chessman tilted his head in the gloom as though to say *so what.*

"They never should have left my calling card," the hushed voice continued. "They won't like how I play the game."

"What is it you want from me?" Cady asked again.

The dark shape shifted. The Chessman's arm stretched toward him, something equally dark and lethal pointed at Cady's forehead.

"You have sixty seconds, Special Agent Cady, to prove your worth. Or I'll see what your gray matter looks like for myself."

"Sixty seconds?"

"Strike that. Fifty-five."

"What the hell?"

Silence.

"Gray matter?"

"Thirty seconds."

"But what does that mean?"

"It means twenty-five seconds left to live, Agent Cady."

Cady's mouth went dry. All he could focus on was the pistol in the Chessman's hand. He knew he somehow, very quickly, needed to impress the psychopath with his brilliance. Except Cady had no clue what to offer.

"Ten seconds."

Silence.

"Three seconds. Two seconds. One second. You lose—"

"Nothing you ever do, Braun, will bring Marly back."

Although the pistol remained centered on Cady's face, Cady caught an almost imperceptible twitch of the shadow figure's head.

"This entire charade, every twist and turn along the way, all crimes of passion."

"Hmm," the silhouette replied. "I am a romantic."

"Dane Schaeffer was a masterstroke. Perfect symmetry."

"Pray continue." Back to a Brokaw whisper.

"In Dane Schaeffer's death you were reborn, because Schaeffer became the Chessman and the game ended. Checkmate. Drugs were found in Schaeffer's system. We assumed he'd medicated himself to make his own drowning…softer, but really it made him easier for you to kill. Isn't that right, Braun? You held Schaeffer underwater until it was done, and then floated his body down the stream."

The dark shape sat motionless.

"What happened at Snow Goose that night?"

"I think you know."

"What did Patrick Farris and the Zalentines do to Marly Kelch?"

"A tale for another time, perhaps."

"You pounded the shit out of me and then smashed my hand as an insurance policy—so I couldn't get off a lucky shot." Cady voiced the million-dollar question, the one that had spun in his mind every day for the past three years: "Why didn't you kill me?"

"Another time, perhaps."

"You watched us from the Robillards. You were going to kill Farris that night, after I left, but you saw me notice the king in the aquarium. You knew what I was thinking. And you knew you couldn't get to him in custody."

"Mr. Gray Matter, I think this is the beginning of a beautiful friendship."

With that the Chessman was gone, out the suite's only door in an instant. All that remained was Cady's Glock 22 under an empty armchair. Cady grabbed the phone next to the bed and brought it to his ear. Dead. Two seconds later he opened the door to the room.

The hallway was empty.

Chapter 18

"He was in your room?"

Cady met Special Agent Evans on the street outside the Kellervick residence. It was a rush hour of local police, medical examiners, gawking neighbors, and a swarming hive of FBI agents. Cady led Evans to an untrampled section of the yard.

"Woke me out of a dead sleep, after three, about the time the old KGB used to come for dissidents."

"How did he know where you were staying?"

"Social engineering. Probably called the few hotels he assumed I'd be in until he got a hit."

"And they're checking the security cameras?"

"He took the east stairwell down and left through that side exit. He knew where the cameras were, so we've got a worthless overhead of someone dressed like Lamont Cranston as The Shadow."

"It confirms that he's alive."

"Very much so."

"It rules out a copycat."

"He denied killing Gottlieb."

"You believe him?"

"If the Chessman tells me to duck down, Agent Evans, I will leap as high into the air as I possibly can. The SOB is a house of mirrors, but we can use that against him."

"So you're staying onboard?"

"For the time being." Cady felt more at ease with the weight of the Glock 22—on loan from the assistant director—snug in his shoulder holster. It was a little past noon and he'd already had a full day. After an early morning debriefing at the Hoover, Jund had Cady double-time it to the airport for a flight to Boston and cab it to this address in Brookline to meet with Agent Evans. "What happened here?"

"Elaine Kellervick, thirty-eight-year-old Caucasian, was found stabbed to death in the entryway of her townhouse." Agent Evans nodded toward the door. "A neighbor the victim goes jogging with every morning stopped by. When no one answered the door, she peeked in the sidelights, saw the body, and called 911 from her cell."

"Kellervick live alone?"

"Her husband, Stephen Kellervick, was at an engineering confer-ence in Colorado. Mr. Kellervick's a managing director at Chem-Tel. He's also on a plane back as we speak. They tell me he sounded real shook up and he's been in Denver all week, so it's not an O.J. Although the autopsy will be more definitive, it doesn't appear to be a sex crime. The victim was fully clothed. The ME's initial best guess places her death between three and six p.m. yesterday."

"So we're here because…"

"A glass pawn was inserted into the victim's stab wound."

Cady nodded, anticipating this response. "The Chessman killed Barrett Sanfield with a switchblade—a stiletto to be exact. I'm bet-ting the autopsy will indicate that to be the case here as well. Where did Mrs. Kellervick work?"

"She was an investment strategist at Koye & Plagans Financials. Been there over two years."

"An investment strategist and the designated Chairman of the Securities and Exchange Commission. A pawn and a queen. He's got an interesting wingspan." Cady looked toward the front door. "Is Liz here?"

"She's inside," Evans replied. "Would you like a look?"

Cady nodded again. Both agents walked up the driveway and entered the townhouse.

Cady spotted Agent Preston huddled with an agent he didn't recognize in the living room. He sidestepped Agent Evans, who had knelt down with the criminologists around the lifeless body of Elaine Kellervick, and headed toward the Special Agent in Charge. As though in sync, Preston looked up and caught his eye.

"It couldn't have been Braun," Preston said and turned toward a tall blonde she'd been speaking to. "Have you met Special Agent Beth Schommer from the Washington Field Office?"

Cady shook his head and then Schommer's hand.

"Agent Schommer recently transferred in from Illinois."

"Go Bears."

"They're not going anywhere with that quarterback," Schommer said, then got to the subject at hand. "Eric Braun was processed out of the United States Marine Corps two years ago. He was piloting an AH-1W SuperCobra in Iraq—the Al Anbar province near Fallujah—when the Chessman killed Congressman Farris, Sanfield, and the psycho twins. Braun now lives in Hawaii. He makes a mint giving helicopter tours in Maui, flies tourists over waterfalls, that sort of stuff."

Cady nodded, but wasn't ready to give up. "If Braun has over a decade in the Corps, he'll have connections."

"We're culling through his known associates, mostly jarheads and other servicemen he was chummy with, but you know how that goes. It will take some time to rule any of them in or out." Agent Schommer glanced at Preston and then back at Cady. "Hard to believe Braun was pulling strings behind the scenes while flying missions in Al Anbar."

"We've had Braun under surveillance since we tracked him to Maui, after your call yesterday," Preston added. "No way was he your night visitor. Now that you've placed the Chessman in D.C. the morning after this," she motioned with one arm toward Agent Evans, still hunched over the body in the entryway, and continued, "I guess we now know that we're dealing with the real McCoy."

"Boston to D.C.?"

"We heard from an administrative assistant where Kellervick worked that she had cancelled a late afternoon meeting and left work at two o'clock yesterday. The admin said Kellervick appeared happy. So if he followed her home—or was waiting for her here—this could have been done by 3:30. Plenty of time to make it to D.C., even if the UNSUB drove. Remember, he took out the Zalentine twins on the same day."

"I called him 'Braun.' It was dark in the room, but that got a tic of his head. I read it as a tell. If he's not Eric Braun, I think he knows Braun. Any of the other names pan out?"

"No one else on the Kelch list served in the military," said Schommer. "To be honest, the remaining names are pretty farfetched. There's an accountant in Philly, Marly's summer camp boyfriend is a priest in Erie, and one of her old thespian friends owns a catering company in Allentown and still acts in community theater."

"He wore a smart disguise. Good costume for the cameras."

Agent Schommer didn't need to check her notes. "Her actor friend, Kurt Holt, is maybe five foot four inches tall and quite heavy. Kevin Costner he's not. Holt is also gay, which doesn't fit the profile, but we'll take another look."

"Beth is nearly done nailing down alibis," Preston said. "Frankly, Drew, it doesn't look promising. Ditto for Marly's male friends at Princeton."

"So much for my instincts, Liz," Cady said. "So much for that."

—

"Don't be a goddamn fool!"

Cady stood in front of the assistant director's desk, arms crossed. "If he wanted me dead, I'd be wearing a toe tag."

"But now that we know definitively that the Chessman is still alive—hell, now that you two are practically dating—we can use that to draw him out into the open."

"Using me as bait is a waste of everyone's time. It's not me he's after. And he'd be the *goddamn fool* if he tried another hotel room visit." Though not invited, Cady sat down in the guest chair in front of Jund's desk—the perks of being a consultant. "And we both know he's not a goddamn fool."

"Then at least I'm going to partner you up," Jund responded. "Do you know Agent Dave Merrill?"

"That's unnecessary where I'm going, sir."

"Where are you going?"

"You wanted me to find him in the past so we could catch him in the present, right?"

"Yes."

"Then I'm heading to northern Minnesota."

Chapter 19

Six Months Ago

"Will I ever see Mom again?" Lucy asked softly.

"We need to avoid England, but something can be finessed down the road." Hartzell looked at his daughter. "We can never return to the colonies, Slim."

He added red onions, sliced grape tomatoes, skim milk, and Provolone cheese to the frying pan as he scrambled the egg whites. Although it was nearly three in the morning and Hartzell had never been much of a chef, both of them were starving—larceny must make one hungry—plus it gave him something to do as they plotted potential futures. Neither one was ready for sleep after a night of difficult revelations.

"There are two options on the table. Option A is that we flee to a country that does not have an extradition treaty with the United States." Hartzell divvied up the scrambled eggs onto two china plates and then took the balled melon that Janice, their chirpy housemaid, had left for them from out of the refrigerator. "But I'm not so sure we'd find enlightenment in North Korea or Rwanda. And no matter who we bribed, we would forever be looking over our shoulder."

"Please tell me Option B is the *good* news."

"A clean slate." Hartzell smeared orange marmalade on the wheat toast. He'd been steering the conversation in this direction for the past half hour.

"A clean slate?"

"If we vanish without a trace, that is, assume new identities, say, somewhere in France or Spain, Italy or the West Indies, or even the Cayman Islands…well, it's a big world out there, Slim, with all sorts of nooks and crannies in which to fade away."

"How far down this road have you traveled, Papa?"

"There may be a villa and vineyard in Tuscany, all on the up and up, as the Yanks like to say, that's owned by a certain chap who's almost never there."

"Italy is nice."

"And there may be a string of five-star rental properties in Venice, Paris, and Madrid also owned by this same old fogy—all strictly obeying the tax laws of each home country, in both letter and spirit."

"And the new identities?"

"That needs to be handled in such a manner that there is no tie back to Drake or Lucy Hartzell," he explained, not admitting that he'd set her up months ago as part of Option B. He'd lifted a couple pictures of Lucy from her high school modeling portfolio—photographs that held only a passing resemblance to how Lucy currently appeared—and sent them on to a *documentation perfectionist* he'd come into contact with a dozen years back through a Chinese dissident he met at some long-forgotten fundraiser for Tibet. The documentation perfectionist, a Filipino forger-savant, knew Hartzell only through wire transfers and a bogus P.O. box.

"But if your face is plastered all over the news?"

"Best to be long gone before they start searching for us, Slim. Plus, *Andy* has short hair and a moustache, both dyed hideously black. I think the poor guy's sporting a midlife."

"Who's Andy?"

"*Andrew Pierson*, the Tuscany gentleman who owns the vineyard and rental properties."

"Well then, Andrew—when must we leave?"

"I'm afraid I must insist by the end of this month at the very latest. Drake and Lucy Hartzell will take a flight to Heathrow, pick up some accounting spreadsheets and a couple of keys from a safe deposit box at Barclays, and then father and daughter Pierson will Eurostar it to Paris, and from there to Tuscany."

"Too bad it has to be so soon."

"A damn shame, really, that we can't put it off for a few more months. It's just that I won't be able to keep the balls in the air that much longer."

"Why is that, Papa?"

"Like every other sucker, Drake Hartzell was taken aback at the suddenness of the crashing markets, stunned at the hemorrhaging stock prices as well as at the politicians' desire to repeat past mistakes. In other words, dear old dad got caught with his pants down. But over the decades Drake Hartzell has acquired several genuine endeavors, numerous real estate properties of substantial worth, a Bentley dealership and other tasty morsels here and there. Once Hartzell morphs away, the window will slam shut as the government steps in to seize all of Hartzell's remaining assets. Damn shame to forfeit the St. Leonards' estate—I've always loved that place—and the hut in Morocco, too. A damn shame." Hartzell looked at his daughter. "But we wouldn't want to get greedy now, Slim, would we?"

Lucy took a sip of her Earl Grey and then placed the cup down on its saucer. "What exactly do you need, Papa, to keep the *balls in the air* long enough to liquidate *Hartzell's remaining assets*?"

"You don't happen to have fifty million in loose change lying about your dresser, do you, Slim?"

Lucy smiled and shook her head.

"What I'd need would be a horde of new investors."

"What about Paul Crenna?"

Hartzell looked blank for a second. He knew Lucy's gentlemen callers more by the nicknames she'd assigned them. "Is that Metro or Hermes?"

"Paul Crenna is Metro, Papa, every hair on his head perfectly in place. Ridiculously GQ. He spends more time in front of the mirror than I do."

"Best to let Paul keep his lunch money."

"I'm serious, Papa." Lucy sounded frustrated at the slight. "You need time to work your pixie dust and I'd like to visit Mom a last time before we depart."

"Fifty million is a rather big fish, Slim. This is not anything you want to do to a friend."

"Paul's hardly a friend. He's a braggart and a bore."

Hartzell was surprised at the direction the conversation had turned. "In that case, tell me more about young Master Crenna."

"I met Paul at one of Caitlin's parties last fall. He's a friend of hers from NYU. He comes from money—a different convertible every time he picks me up. And you should be flattered, Papa—your reputation precedes you, even in Chicago. Paul mentioned that his father had heard of you, maybe even met you at one of your charity to-dos."

Hartzell thought of the events he'd held in the Windy City over the years. A zoo of faces, infinite handshakes. "Crenna doesn't ring a bell."

"Whenever we go out Paul prattles on and on about how he'd love to connect you with his father's investment group."

"What's Metro doing at NYU?"

"A business degree. I think he's being groomed to manage the family empire."

"What does Master Crenna's father do?"

"His dad leases buildings in cities throughout the Midwest. Something tedious to do with warehouse maintenance and some shipping interests on Lake Michigan."

Hartzell crunched numbers in his head. If this could buy him more time, diverting new investment funds to stave off earlier investors, Hartzell could cash out most of his remaining chips and he and Lucy would have a near bottomless pot of gold at the end of the rainbow.

"How soon can you set up a meeting?"

Chapter 20

Grand Rapids Police Chief Leigh Irwin listlessly stirred his house salad as though it were soup, eyeing Cady's cheeseburger and onion rings platter. "It's not fair. My wife and I eat the exact same food, yet her cholesterol test comes back with a thumbs up and coupons to Pizza Hut. My results come back with an urgent demand that I take a course in nutrition or buy a burial plot."

Cady had taken a bumpy puddle-jumper out of Minneapolis, grabbed an Avis—a red Saturn Astra—on Airport Road, and hustled it to the Grand Rapids Police Department on Pokegama Avenue. He had phoned Chief Irwin from Minneapolis that morning and bribed the head of the police department with lunch if he would be so kind as to dig up the police report on Bret Ingram as well as the autopsy findings. Irwin drove Cady in a squad car to the Forest Lake Restaurant and Tavern on Fourth Street—a rustic-looking lumberjack joint with bear skins on the wall.

"Want some onion rings?" Cady offered.

"Want some? I'd like to inhale all your onion rings and your cheeseburger, as well as gnaw on that gentleman's fried chicken," the chief said, nodding at another table. "But I best stick with the damned Bugs Bunny buffet."

"You try statins?"

"I'm sure that's next. It's hereditary—the Irwin bloodline is mostly Crisco oil. But I'm giving diet and exercise a first chance."

Leigh Irwin had round features, face, jowls, chest, and stomach—a defensive lineman gone to pot, the police chief looked like he could easily shed forty pounds. Rotund or not, though, Chief Irwin was an imposing figure.

"So are you here for the same reason that agent out of St. Paul was here a few years back?"

"Potentially," Cady said. "It's a preliminary investigation. Some friends of Bret Ingram's—his school-day associates, actually—were murdered several years back and we're still trying to figure out if there was any connection between Ingram's death and those other killings."

"Your guy in St. Paul—hey, I stuck him with the tab for a rib-eye right at this very table back when life was worth living—mentioned the killings in D.C. But there were no records of those murderers, the Zalentines or that Dane Schaeffer fellow, ever having traveled to Minnesota."

"I know."

"Bret Ingram may have owned that fancy resort out on Bass Lake," the police chief said, "but he himself was in the running for town drunk. Ingram had two DUIs before he figured out that it might make more sense if his wife or the local cab service chauffeured his intoxicated ass back home to the lake. When Terri finally saw the light and split, no one was there to watch out for him so Ingram pickled himself nightly and ultimately turned himself into Christmas roast while messing with gasoline."

"Terri's his wife, right? Terri Ingram?"

"Yup." Chief Irwin looked like he'd just bit into a lemon. "Wear a nut cup if you plan on talking to her."

"Why's that?"

"Terri Ingram is easy on the eyes, but she's a firecracker. She's got her teeth lockjawed on this notion that some imaginary Itasca County Mafioso or some such bullshit had her husband killed."

"That so?"

"I'll be honest, if I happen to see Terri Ingram on the street first, I'll make a fast turn around the corner because I'm sick of her harangues. Even your guy in St. Paul agreed with the evidence. At first I thought Bret Ingram had a meth lab going in that old barn of his when it went boom on him—that's the kind of shit we see day in and day out up here."

"What was he doing in the barn at that time of night?"

"Filling up about a dozen portable boat motor fuel tanks with gas. He rented outboards to some of the cabin folk who don't bring their own boats. Gouged them on the gas as well. Ingram had the barn completely closed off, probably didn't want any cabin renters to see how shitfaced he was. Terri really ran Sundown Point and I know she lived in fear of Bret interacting with the guests after, say, five at night, as that could negatively impact repeat business, if you know what I mean."

Cady nodded.

"Anyway, it was a hot night and the fire investigators felt that maybe with all the gas vapors, this old fan he'd been running could have kicked off a spark, but more likely he lit a cigarette…and that, my friend, was that. Half the barn burned down by the time the firemen arrived at the scene. Poor Ingram made it out of the barn and doused himself in the lake, but the poor bastard suffered major burns—over eighty percent of his body—mostly third-degree. They got him to Grand Itasca Hospital, but he only lasted an hour, which was for the best if you know anything about burns of this severity. It's all in there," Irwin said, pointing at the file on the table.

Cady lathered a remaining onion ring in ketchup and thought

about Bret Ingram's history of alcohol abuse. "Pathologist do a BAC that night?"

"Tests indicated Ingram's blood alcohol content at an even .2. Nothing earth-shattering for him, just another night."

"You got a desk or table I can steal for a few hours?"

"Anything to help."

"Excellent," Cady said. He began to fetch his wallet, and then stopped. "Would you like any dessert?"

"In my dreams."

"What in holy hell did you think you were doing?!"

Cady had to hold his cell away from his ear. He had answered his phone in the parking lot of the Forest Lake Restaurant while Chief Irwin stopped to talk to a table of Chamber of Commerce suits eating pancakes the size of Frisbees.

"Doing?"

"I just got off the horn with Steve Kellervick's pit bull. I had to grovel, Agent Cady—and you know how I despise groveling. If he follows through on his lawsuit threat, I'll have your butt in my briefcase."

"Steve Kellervick?" Cady squeezed a word in edgewise to the assistant director's tirade. "I have no clue what you're talking about."

"You demanded that Kellervick come clean because, quote, 'We know you gutted your wife. A squad is on the way over. Enjoy your new roommates in county lockup,' unquote."

"I have never spoken to Steve Kellervick in my life," Cady said, shaking his head. "I'm in northern Minnesota, for Christ's sake."

"His attorney said you called him on the phone."

"If I brace someone, I do it in person."

"Oh, shit!"

"It's him."

Cady heard voices in the background, but could not make out what was being said.

"I'm putting you on speakerphone," the AD said. "Liz is here."

"Hi, Drew," Agent Preston said. "I knew you would never have done anything that stupid."

"Thanks for the rousing vote of confidence." Cady saw Chief Irwin exit the restaurant and head his way. "Was that all the Chessman said to Kellervick? 'We know you gutted your wife'?"

"No," the AD answered. "Kellervick took the call from a male identifying himself as *Special Agent Drew Cady*. Evidently, the caller grilled Kellervick for ten minutes on what his wife did at Koye & Plagans, who she reported to, worked closely with, what projects she was on. Then faux Cady starts in with the stiff arm, accusing Kellervick of murder."

"Sounds like he was fishing. He rattled Kellervick to gauge his reaction."

"We'll trace the phone records," Preston said.

"Good idea," Cady replied. "But I guarantee he used a prepaid throwaway."

"At least this takes the heat off us. I'll call Kellervick's attorney back. Damn it, Drew, I don't know why, but he's dicking with you. Finish up in Minnesota and get back here ASAP."

"Nice to know I'm loved."

Chapter 21

"Of course Bret was murdered," Terri Ingram said. "That's what I've been telling Fife all these years."

Cady had called Mrs. Ingram late that afternoon from the Grand Rapids Police Department—Chief Irwin had made good on his word and found Cady a broom closet to work in. He introduced himself and asked if he could stop by her resort in Cohasset that evening and ask her some questions regarding her late husband. She responded in the affirmative. Cohasset was a small blip on Cady's highway map of Minnesota, a five-minute drive west of Grand Rapids. Grand Rapidians might get away with calling the little town a suburb but more than a few Cohassetians might take umbrage. Mrs. Ingram had sounded pleasant on the phone but as Cady's line of in-person questioning proceeded, she let her frustrations be known in no uncertain terms.

"Fife?" Cady asked.

"Police Chief Leigh Irwin. I call him *Fife*, like in *The Andy Griffith Show*, except lacking Barney's reassuring poise. Chief Irwin's IQ is lower than whale poop—please let him know I said that."

Cady tried not to gawk at Mrs. Ingram. The police chief had been correct on at least one point: Terri Ingram was easy on the eyes. She was short, maybe a hiccup or two over five feet tall, with dirty blond hair done up in an informal schoolgirl bun and white-cream skin that shouted Norwegian ancestry.

"The police report stated that Mr. Ingram had been filling the outboards with gasoline in order to prepare them for the next week's guests."

"Bret never fueled a boat tank in his life. Tommy Reckseidler from across the lake comes over every Saturday morning and takes care of all that mechanical stuff. Guests don't check in until noon and mostly they bring their own boats. There are only three or four boats that Tommy needs to rig up in a given week."

"But you weren't here the night of the fire?"

"I was living in town at that time. We were separated, but I still ran the day-to-day functions here at Sundown Point."

"The blood tests placed your husband's alcohol level at a .2."

Terri Ingram shrugged. "What else is new? Bret was an alcoholic. Hardcore. He drank every night of his life. That's why I lived in town."

"Any chance he was intoxicated and just messing around in the barn?"

"No way is Bret fartskulling with gas tanks in a closed barn at midnight. Bret would begin drinking at lunch, cheap beer and vodka. He'd be passed out no later than nine."

Cady scratched his temple, looked into Terri Ingram's blue eyes, and pushed. "Addictive personalities tend to have dependency issues that crop up in other avenues. You've probably heard of 'huffing'— inhalant abuse of chemical vapors to achieve some kind of euphoric rush. It's primarily adolescents huffing household products out of a plastic bag, but considering the gas vapors, could Mr. Ingram have—"

Terri burst out laughing. "No, Agent Cady, Bret had discovered his drug of choice years before I met him. And it had more to do with gulping than huffing."

"But he did smoke, right?"

"Yes." Mrs. Ingram suddenly seemed weary, as if she'd had this same conversation ad nauseam. "Bret was an alcoholic, not the village idiot. He would have passed out by nine o'clock, ten at the latest. Even in his most inebriated state he wouldn't be playing with gas and Marlboros. Bret didn't screw up and set himself aflame. And he didn't commit suicide, either, if that was the next item on your checklist."

Cady noticed a single tear swim down the side of Terri Ingram's nose. He swiveled in his plastic deck chair to watch two girls go ever higher on the swing set while a younger brother instead opted to smack the side of the miniature schoolhouse with a stick. Then Cady turned forward and squinted at the sun-specked water.

Sundown Point had a hundred yards of shoreline. A row of eight white cabins with red-shingled roofs were set about twenty feet back from the water with a tic-tac-toe board of wooden docks in front of them. Another row of eight cabins stood about thirty yards farther back, with a winding dirt road between the two rows, and a third row of eight sat a further thirty yards inland. Ingram's lake house stood apart from the rows of cabins, divided from them by the playground and a shed stuffed with inner tubes and life jackets. Across the way was a rec field with tetherball, horseshoes, and shuffleboard, but between that field and the road stood Sundown Point's equipment barn. The barn was brand new for all practical purposes, having been rebuilt in the years since the fire that claimed Bret Ingram's life.

Cady twisted back to face Terri Ingram. "Do you know of anyone who had a motive to harm your husband?"

"Of course," Terri answered. "Me. Bret and I were in the middle of a divorce proceeding. This way I wound up with Sundown Point and a quarter mil in life insurance. The whole kit and caboodle—everything came to me."

The two stared at each for several seconds.

"You have the right to remain silent. Anything you say can and will be used against you in a court of law. If you cannot afford an attorney...."

Terri Ingram slowly began to smile which then broke into a full grin. "So the G-Man has a sense of humor after all."

"Not really."

"Are you that agent from the Twin Cities? The one that phoned a few years back?"

"No."

"Good. I got the feeling he'd already been *Fifed* by the time he called me."

"What about your husband's life insurance policy? Any investigation there?"

"I screamed from the rooftops at ING, too, trying to get them to check into it. A couple of days later an investigator shows up—more Frank Cannon than Jim Rockford. I think after my phone call, ING was hoping to find a way to pin Bret's death on me. A couple days of *Fifing* and he left. I put the insurance money into modernizing most of the cabins." Ingram shrugged. "If you want to kill someone, Agent Cady, I'd highly recommend doing it in Itasca County. With that imbecile Irwin at the helm, it's the Bermuda Triangle of homicide."

She was a firecracker all right, Cady thought. A firecracker in a jean jacket.

"ING didn't try to point the finger at suicide?"

"Unless you're a Buddhist monk, suicide by fire is the road less traveled. Bret's burns were intensive, most of his skin layers destroyed. If he had survived, he'd still be in burn therapy treatment—and that's only if the skin grafts and plastic surgery took."

Terri shuddered and looked away. "Seeing Bret lying on that table at the hospital that night was the most horrifying thing I've ever seen in my life. The poor man. Skin all melted away. He didn't look... human."

"I'm sorry."

"I couldn't wish that on anyone." Her voice wavered.

The sun was almost down and Cady gave Terri another moment to compose herself. He turned and looked out across Bass Lake. It was calm at twilight. A couple fishing boats, a canoe, and a kayak were coming in to dock up for the night. Cady caught a quick movement in the sky.

"Is that an eagle?"

"Yes." Terri pointed across the lake. "She keeps a nest in that crop of elms. Do you see the slight V in that tree line?"

"Yes."

"It's right in there. Too bad it's getting dark otherwise I'd get the binocs out and you could watch her feed her two fledglings."

"Interesting," Cady said. "Are there many bass in Bass Lake?"

"Some bass, some rock bass, lot of pan fish and walleye. Northerns as long as your arm. Do you fish, Agent Cady?"

"Please call me Drew."

"Do you fish, Drew?"

"It's been years. My grandparents lived near Fayetteville in Ohio. In the summer my parents would dump me in their laps. Grandpa Paul and I did our best to empty Lake Lorelei."

"Good," Terri said, adding, "I don't trust a man who doesn't fish."

"Mr. Ingram go out quite a bit?"

"Never." Terri leaned back in her chair. "Bret hated the water."

"So why'd a guy from out east who hated the water buy a lake resort in northern Minnesota?"

"Life's an odd duck, Drew."

"Do you know who helped him with the financing?"

"At first I thought Bret was loaded, came from money—until I met his family. The resort is mine now. No liens. Bret may have had some financial backers in the early years, but he was the sole owner by the time I came into the picture."

"When did you come into the picture?"

"I met Bret about six years back in a—surprise, surprise—bar in Grand Rapids. I was a year out of college, teaching art to elementary schoolers during the day and bar-hopping at night. All very cringe-inducing in retrospect. I bumped into Bret one Ladies' Night at Rapids Tavern. We tied the knot three months later."

"A whirlwind romance, huh?"

"When I was young and foolish," Terri Ingram looked over Bass Lake and spoke more to the past than to Cady, "I was young and foolish. The first year of marriage I was your classic enabler to the point of getting lit with Bret. Second year I got him into detox. Repeatedly. Even forced him into AA and finally marriage counseling. I gave up teaching—not because Bret was paying this lame management company a gold mine to run Sundown Point, to do the basic stuff he should have been doing himself—but because I thought that my being around twenty-four-seven would keep him dry. Silly me. Year three was spent greasing the skids for the divorce. It was in the cards, I guess."

"But you did see something in Bret—at first, anyway, not just the drinking?"

"The only thing that came out of our year in counseling was my discovery that I have a serious rescue compulsion. Bret was inherently a good man, he really was. His heart was in the right place, but he couldn't get this monkey off his back, couldn't give up the firewater, and after all the bullshit we'd sludged through, it occurred to me that he wasn't really trying. That's when I finally left. Hardest thing I ever did."

"Did his family have a history of alcoholism?"

"Teetotalers stretching back to his great-grandparents."

"Did Bret ever talk to you about an incident at a party that occurred back east when he was in college, where a young woman he was with drowned in a lake?"

Terri Ingram looked as if she'd been stabbed with a hot fork, big eyes and dropped jaw. "He never once mentioned anything like that, Agent Cady. What happened?"

Cady gave her the Reader's Digest abridged version of the events that occurred at Dane Schaeffer's party that long-ago night. Cady stuck to the objective facts, kept any editorial comments to himself, and let Terri's own synapses click together and fill in any blanks.

"Bret never let me in on that. Not even in our counseling sessions, when the therapist had us brainstorming any trigger mechanisms that led to Bret's drinking. Perhaps that was the demon he couldn't exorcise."

The two sat quietly in thought. The sun finally ended its descent over the distant horizon. The kids had left the playground for the night. Moths bounced off the deck light.

Terri Ingram stood up, arms at her hips. "Why are you here? You're the second FBI agent to contact me regarding my husband's death. Aren't you guys too busy tracking terrorists or something to be poking around a small-town drunkard's *accidental* death? Don't you think it's about time you leveled with me, Agent Drew Cady, and told me what you're really doing at my door?"

Cady could have used a stiff drink himself at this moment—a moment he had known would come sooner or later. "Like you, I don't believe for one instant that Bret's death was an *accident*. Have a seat, Mrs. Ingram. I have some things to say that may be of interest to you."

Cady told her about the slayings that had followed her husband's death and the subsequent investigation. Uncomfortable discussing it, Cady left out his role at Farris's Woodley Park brownstone, and, after a half-dozen caveats, disclaimers, and other stipulations, Cady let her in on one or two of his less wild assumptions.

"Wow," Terri said when Cady had finished.

"Yes," Cady replied. "Wow."

"So you think that Bret was murdered by Dane Schaeffer as a vengeance killing for what occurred the night Marly Kelch drowned?"

Cady paused to parse his words delicately, stingily, in regard to the current investigation. "There were enough loose threads to gag a kitten, but it was wrapped up in a neat package that screamed closure. It should have been me who talked to you about this situation three years ago, but by then I was indisposed and, for better or worse, off the case. Recent events have caused us to question quite loudly whether Dane Schaeffer was the Chessman killer or yet another in a line of his victims."

"Bret never spoke about his Princeton years and he was already dead when the news about the two Zalentines came out." A pensive look washed over Terri Ingram's face. "Bret drank to escape his part in the cover-up of this girl's death? My God. Everything I've worked so hard for these past five years—this entire place—has been built on guilt and blood money."

"I didn't come here to shatter your world, Terri," Cady said, using her first name for the first time. "None of this is your fault. The wheels were set in motion years before you ever met Bret Ingram."

"If what you've told me is true, I should give Sundown Point Resort to Marly Kelch's family."

"I doubt her mother would take it. Look, Terri, that's not where the investigation is leading. You're not culpable in any of this."

"But it's the right thing to do."

"Seems to me your husband paid all outstanding debts with his life."

"I appreciate your honesty, Drew. It's...refreshing. You've certainly given me a bit to chew on."

Cady nodded.

"I want the man responsible for Bret's death to be brought to justice."

Cady nodded again. "Would you be willing to let one of our forensic auditors sift through Sundown Point's ownership records, deeds, title transfers, and sort out who your husband's financial backers may have been?"

"In a New York second."

"If some front company or subsidiary of a holding group that sugared the deal has ties to the Zalentines, it won't take our auditor long to find out."

"The important stuff is in a safety deposit box. Jim Sweeny is my tax guy. Jim's done the accounting for Sundown Point since long before Bret's death."

"I'll set it up, have our guy fly in and meet with you both."

"Do you travel a lot on these cases, Drew?"

"I used to all the time." Cady didn't want to muddy things up by getting into his current status at the bureau. "Wherever a case would lead, I'd find myself there."

"Does your wife enjoy that?"

"I'm not married."

"You're wearing a ring."

"So are you."

"Touché," Terri said. "Sundown Point is a family place. I don't want to get hit on by any of the men who pass through here. And I don't want any wives getting any wrong ideas. I apologize if I brought up a personal issue. I didn't mean to pry."

"No need to apologize. I'm the one who's spent the evening raking you over the hot coals." Cady said nothing for a second. "We got divorced a year ago. I imagine my being AWOL was a big part of it."

"You didn't want her to leave," Terri said quietly.

Cady shrugged. "We were…adrift. Then a pretty bad thing happened and I wasn't there for her. We both tried bailing out the boat, but then another bad thing happened…and we just stopped bailing."

"I'm sorry."

"She's remarried. I think she's happy."

Terri went into the screened porch, opened a fridge, and came back out with a couple of bottled waters. She handed one to Cady.

"Thank you."

Cady opened the bottle and downed half of it in a long swig before setting it down atop the hand railing.

"You were thirsty."

"Yes."

The two looked at each other from across the deck for several seconds before Cady looked down at his watch. "It's getting late."

"Where are you staying?"

"Any hotel in town you'd recommend?"

"You haven't checked in anywhere yet?"

"Busy day."

"Cabin eight is open."

"I think I've done enough damage here, Terri."

"I insist. You're the first law enforcement officer who doesn't think I'm a nutcase."

"You sure it's okay?"

"I might as well save the taxpayers some money."

"Thank you."

"Wait till you see cabin eight before you thank me. It's one of the few I didn't refurbish. I hope you like mosquitoes."

"I'm sure it'll be just fine."

"Let the shower run a minute or three if you want warm water."

The shower took five minutes to achieve lukewarm. By the time Cady dried himself off and brushed his teeth, he felt he could sleep a week. He had to walk to the front of the cabin to pull the string that turned off the overhead light. When all was dark Cady took a final peek outside and saw Terri—a solitary figure in the moonlight—standing on the dock and looking out over Bass Lake, likely pondering the curve ball he'd just tossed her way. Cady hoped he'd followed the Hippocratic Oath and done no harm, but she'd been living in the trenches and was owed some sort of explanation—even Cady's *through a glass darkly* version of the truth—at least the crumbs he could volunteer without compromising the current investigation.

Terri Ingram abruptly turned and stared at cabin eight. Cady almost jumped back, but knew she couldn't possibly see him in the darkness. Then Bret Ingram's widow walked up the steps of her deck and into the lake house.

Chapter 22

Albert Banning's head lifted as he fought the drowsiness. He opened his eyelids mere coin slits, and felt as though his eyeballs had been rolled across a sizzling iron. He laid his head back down on the cold cement and squeezed them shut.

"Stings at first," A voice across the room whispered.

This must be a nightmare, Banning told himself. As if his problems weren't already unpleasant enough, they now invaded his sleep.

"It's not a dream." The voice, low as a distant train rumbling on the edge of Banning's consciousness, seemed to read his mind.

Banning forced his eyes open. The piercing light from above like razors across his retinas. He blinked several times, struggling with the glare. Blurry, like staring through warm, oily water, the light slivering into his brain. Bright fluorescent lamps hung along the center of a long, gray room that had seen more pleasant days. He appeared to be on the floor of a cavernous old garage or abandoned warehouse that smelled more like a moldy cellar. Banning slumped lethargically on the bitter concrete, unable to move, feeling as though his hands were somehow glued to the ground.

"You'll feel better in a minute." Again, a quiet susurrus from the other side of the room.

Banning squinted toward the voice, but only made out a smear of white at the far end of the room, a tall figure in an open doorway, backlit by more piercing light. Banning tilted his head sideways for better viewing through the kaleidoscope of light and pain. He did his best to filter, to focus on the unknown voice.

Grandpa?

But Banning's grandfather was long dead, had in fact passed away half a century ago, back when Banning was a five-year-old boy. In fact, the only memory Banning had of his grandfather was from the old coot's funeral—Grandpa lying there in the black pine coffin, waxy, slightly bloated, and white. It had left an indelible impression on him at so young an age. Somehow that image, five decades buried, sprang to the forefront of Banning's thoughts as he strained to make out the figure from across the room.

"Where?" Banning's throat was sandpaper. He cleared it and tried again. "Where am I?"

"In a place of no secrets, Albert Banning," the voice replied slowly, heavily. "A place of no secrets."

He knows my name, Banning thought, fighting his way through the grogginess to piece together the last-known events. Banning remembered leaving work, of course. He remembered the commute home to Newton Friday evening, pulling into his driveway, thankful for a weekend reprieve from the living hell of the past week. Banning remembered a noise. Remembered the door to his 750i Sedan being torn open, remembered a frosty breeze across his face, a steel grip, an aborted scream…then darkness, then here.

An intense fatigue kept his mind grinding away in slow motion. Must be burning off whatever drug—Chloroform? Ether?—this old bastard had given him.

"You're next on the docket, Albert Banning. In a place of no secrets, you're next on the docket." With that the figure vanished, leaving an empty doorway of piercing white light.

Banning's lips were dry; an unquenchable thirst was forced to the backburner when Banning realized that he lay naked on the cold floor. Banning fought through the silent panic and gradually came to an epiphany. Banning's epiphany was a resounding *OH SHIT!*

Banning attempted to stand up, to make himself less vulnerable, but something caught and he got yanked back down to the concrete. He squinted back at his right ankle and saw what snared him. A handcuff tethered him to some kind of radiator pipe, round as a silver dollar, that jutted out from the floor and on up thirty feet, all the way to the high ceiling above. Banning wrenched at the handcuff for all he was worth. Firmly locked. He then pulled on the pipe. Immovable.

Albert Banning, Chief Investment Officer of Koye & Plagans Financials, had fancied himself a virtual Rock of Gibraltar in the face of the financial turbulence of recent years, but this situation tore at his sanity and the all-encompassing fear choked out rational thought. Banning looked around his newfound prison. The only thing within reach was a twenty-ounce bottle of Fixx, some type of highly caffeinated energy drink he'd never heard of before. It reminded him of his great thirst. Banning stretched forward and seized the blue plastic bottle. He paused a second, examined the plastic bottle top. The cap remained sealed to the collar, didn't appear to have been tampered with. Banning twisted the bottle top, broke the seal, and chugged down nearly the entire bottle before coming up for air. It was sickeningly sweet, and Banning almost gagged, but it tackled his dehydration in this *place of no secrets*. He took a second long swig, wiped a forefinger across his lips, licked at that, and then finished the remainder of the bottle. Having addressed his thirst, Banning returned to studying the room.

He saw his Joseph A. Bank's Signature three-button wool and silk blue tie, his Avanti white dress shirt, Madras silk boxer shorts, designer socks, and Gucci dress loafers in a heap about twenty steps away. Next to the pile of clothes, his Venezia calfskin briefcase had been flung wide open. His laptop sat open on the floor next to the briefcase, facing him. His Starfield screensaver stared back, mocking him, his RSA security token atop the keyboard. *Jesus Christ*, Banning grimaced and bit his lower lip. *I should be home asleep*—not in the middle of one of those horrid *Saw* movies he'd watched with his stepson last summer before the boy returned to UCLA.

That was precisely when Banning began hearing the noises from a neighboring room. Muffled voices. Banning leaned forward and closed his eyes. The dead-grandpa voice was asking some sort of question. Another voice in response—it was a short female sob in the negative. The dead-grandpa voice asked the question again, but this time Banning recognized one word. The single word that Banning recognized was *Kellervick*. As in Elaine Kellervick, his most thorough investment strategist, who had been murdered earlier that week, a victim of a random burglary that had rocked K&P to its very foundation. Good God. Banning's heart thundered faster. The man who'd killed Elaine had come for him. And he was...*next on the docket in a place of no secrets.* The panic sent him back to yanking on his tether, wiggling the cuff, doing everything he could to get loose from his hard steel snare.

Another question in the dead-grandpa voice, slowly asking something about Elaine Kellervick again. No responding sobs this time. Then a short phrase from the dead-grandpa voice. "Or neck?"

Banning was certain he'd heard the last part of what was asked, some sort of warped question—but it didn't make any sense. What would "*Or neck?*" have to do with anything? Before he could ponder its hidden significance, there followed pleas to stop, growing appeals for mercy. A pregnant silence stretched for eternity, and then another female howl rattled forth from the neighboring room.

The hair on the back of Banning's neck stood straight. A pause, then another scream. Banning unconsciously pushed his back against the radiator pipe, and then tried impossibly to squeeze himself into the four-inch gap between the pipe and the wall as the scream turned into a bloodcurdler of pain and terror. Through a pounding drum of fright, Banning recognized a noise, something familiar from the men who'd come to remove a storm-downed tree from his backyard last summer—a chainsaw.

Banning pressed down on the cuff, pushing with all his might, trying to smear it off his foot, not caring how many layers of skin it cost him—but to no avail. The scream gurgled on for another second, and then abruptly cut short. Banning saw a spray of blackness across the piercing light of the open door. The chainsaw continued its hideous adventure for several more seconds.

Banning forgot how to breathe. He didn't notice the steady stream of urine running down his leg. The chainsaw stopped as suddenly as it had begun. Banning shrank to the floor, a deflating balloon. *You're next on the docket* echoed through his mind.

The dead-grandpa creature again filled the doorway, staring back at Banning, a twenty-seven-inch chainsaw hanging from its left hand, dripping gore onto the dusty concrete. The dead-grandpa creature walked ten feet into the room, toward Banning, then knelt as though in prayer, chainsaw held upright, palm atop the handle— like some deranged priest out of the Spanish Inquisition.

The creature wore black work boots, a gray mechanic's jumpsuit now lathered in splotches of wet darkness. And the creature's face— Banning knew it had to be a rubber mask, the kind kids wore on Halloween, but he'd never swear to it. Banning knew now why he'd thought of his long-dead grandfather. The creature's face was that of an elderly man, ancient beyond years and the color of death, scraggly white hair at the side, waxen and bloated...definitely not smiling.

"What do you want from me?"

The figure stayed frozen in a dark sculpture of worship. "I'm here to wash away all sins, Albert Banning."

"Sins?"

"The flock has been diminished, Albert Banning." The dead-grandpa creature spoke low but with the ferocity of a Moses at Mount Sinai. "And in this place of no secrets, Albert Banning, I'm here to bear witness."

"Please," Banning's voice faltered.

"Quartered or beheaded, Albert Banning?"

"I don't want to die."

"Lady Tilden chose her neck, Albert Banning."

Dear God. Banning's eyes opened wider, his mind a throbbing block of ice. It was Mira Tilden this maniac had just decapitated. Mira was one of the front desk receptionists, the younger, unmarried one who always had a pleasant smile for him.

After Banning had passed through the initial astonishment over Elaine's death, and how Elaine had died, there rushed in an elevated sensation of anxiety—a heightened apprehension—over how all of Kellervick's projects and loose ends would spill over onto him, but after plotting how to clear his desk via clever delegation to his various subordinates, Banning found himself left with one emotion that he would never verbalize to another living soul: an overwhelming sense of relief.

Lately, the Kellervick woman had lived in Banning's face over one piddly work item after another, always acting so superior, and he often caught the woman glaring at him in meetings. It had gotten unbearably worse since his interview with *Fidelity Investor*. The damned Elaine Kellervick woman didn't have it in herself to be happy for him, for Banning bringing some much-needed positive attention toward K&P Financials. She'd gotten extremely snappish over some of his comments in the newsletter, felt that he didn't give her sufficient credit, making him feel guilty, when all he did was answer a few of that *FI* editor's questions. Sure, he'd solicited Kellervick's input, but those issues she'd brought up were issues that he'd already contemplated. Banning thought he'd switched up her wording a bit, but the editor had been under some kind of harsh deadline and had prodded Banning to rush his answers along.

He didn't know how the Kellervick woman's husband—Stewart, wasn't it?—would want to stay married to the frigid bitch-cake. Banning liked Stewie Kellervick. The two of them spent time together whenever the firm had a social event where family members were invited. He and Stewie would yuk it up at those events. Good old Stew Kellervick would pat Banning on the back and wave at his wife across the room as she stood there glowering back at them both.

Banning knew it was appallingly wrong to even contemplate certain thoughts about the Kellervick woman, and he'd been certain to *tsk-tsk-tsk* it when talking to the police and other investigators, and he did feel great sympathy for his good pal Stew, but, truth be told, Banning felt this overwhelming sense of relief that the frigid bitch-cake was dead.

But now, *in a place of no secrets*, this maniac thought he'd been involved with Kellervick's death…and Banning had to convince him otherwise.

"I loved Elaine. And Stew and I were best friends."

"Who is this Stew?" the creature growled at him.

Oh Christ, Banning thought as his bladder surrendered a final squirt to the stark terror of the situation—he'd messed up the Kellervick man's name. It wasn't Stew after all. It was Steve or Scott or some other damned thing that began with an S.

"Her husband." Banning shook his head and cried. "Everyone loved Elaine. She was by far my best analyst, incredibly meticulous.

I could trust her with any project; her market evaluations were full of insight."

The avalanche of Banning's random verbiage continued, for as long as he spoke to the creature kneeling in the middle of this dungeon, he remained alive.

"None of us know what happened, sir. It was a burglary gone terribly, terribly bad. This city—Jesus, it gets worse every year—Elaine probably interrupted some kids from Dorchester stealing her TV or something."

The creature stood slowly, towering like the grim reaper, and repeated his question. "Quartered or beheaded, Albert Banning?"

"I had nothing to do with Elaine's death. I've talked to the police. I talked to the FBI. I told them everything I know—which is nothing. The last time I saw Elaine, I wished her a good night. I swear I did. I said, 'Have a good night, Elaine.' That's exactly what I told her. You've got to believe me." Banning was weeping. Snot and tears saturated his white mustache. "Why would I want Elaine dead? It makes no sense. I've had to take over her projects, all of her work files."

"Files?" The dead-grandpa creature jolted forward. In three strides he was at Banning's pile of clothing and office materials. With a sturdy nudge of his work boot, the creature slid the laptop carrying Banning's RSA security token across the concrete toward him. "Show me, Albert Banning."

"But this is proprietary information—spreadsheets, strategies, e-mail records," Banning stuttered. "Client confidentiality."

The chainsaw still dripped crimson as the dead-grandpa figure reached for the starter rope. One swift pull and the saw clamored to life.

"No! God, no!" Albert Banning's fingers flew to work. He prayed this gray dungeon had access to a wireless network so he could log in to the VPN—the virtual private network. Banning tapped in his user login and password like a master pianist hammering on the ivory. He snatched his RSA token from where it had slid off the keyboard, and then hurriedly entered the numbers before they rotated. He sobbed with something akin to joy when the laptop made the connection and his personal and confidential desktop opened. Albert Banning slowly looked up.

The dead-grandpa creature stepped toward him, the clattering chainsaw held high in the air.

Chapter 23

"How the hell is your hand, Cady?" Allan Sears' low baritone came through the phone line much like the Cambridge detective himself in real life—loud and clear and demanding.

"About fifty percent. And I think rain is in the forecast," Cady said, then remembered something. "By the way, Detective, I never got a chance to thank you for the get well card and gift. Fortunately, they had me so morphined up I didn't turn red when the nurse opened the package."

Detective Sears laughed for several seconds, then the mirth petered out. "That nurse got something against *Penthouse?*"

"I couldn't move a muscle at that point so the poor woman gave me a pity laugh and then tossed it on the visitor table for everyone to see."

Sears chortled again.

"I've been reading the headlines and thinking of you, Cady. I thought you'd left the bureau after the...well, you know."

"I'm back short-term on this assignment."

"So it turns out it wasn't Dane Schaeffer after all, huh?"

"Not looking that way."

"That was the single thing that rubbed me wrong. Guys that plan shit out to the tenth degree like the Chessman aren't suicidal. They don't normally toss themselves into the volcano when all is said and done. Know what I mean?"

"That's pretty much what Detective Pearl said."

"Pearl, that D.C. homicide cop?"

"Yeah. Worked the Sanfield case. He's retired now in Boca Raton. I caught him between gin and tonics."

"I like the guy already. So, Cady, what was your gut check?"

"I wavered at the time. On the one hand the Chessman could have burnt out and gone Andrew Cunanan—if you remember him—killed himself rather than get caught and face the consequences. Plus, there was a certain symmetry. Schaeffer threw these drunken orgies, Schaeffer invited Marly—*he loved Marly*—and per his harsh standard, he was also guilty as hell, so he killed himself in the end. His own judge, jury, and executioner."

"I'm not that starry-eyed," Sears said. "Just ask my wife. But there is an old Native American custom that if your enemy has a knife at your throat, you push into it and rob them of the satisfaction of your fear. It's a control thing. Allows Schaeffer to give us the bird by denying us the catch."

"After the Farris debacle, Schaeffer was on our short list…and suddenly everything fell into place like dominoes. But Allan, I spent most of my time fixating on the other hand and losing sleep over this nightmare scenario, where the son of a bitch dances away scot-free. Which, unfortunately, turns out to be the case."

"And you've got a copycat in play as well?"

"Thank God that's not on my plate. I'm cold-casing the original, Allan, and wanted to pick your brain about what really went down back then."

"Them goddamned Zalentines turned Cambridge into some kind of Goth haven. Adrien and Alain must be giggling on the seventh ring of hell. Flakes in black leather and white makeup take pilgrimages to the Dorchester Towers, to peek at the Zalentines' old balconies or something. Dahmer never had such a fan base."

"I saw one of those Internet sites that glamorize them. Twisted stuff."

Cady gave the Cambridge detective five minutes on what he'd been up to this past week, his nighttime visitor, what he knew about the first victim—Bret Ingram in Minnesota—his false hunch about Eric Braun, and how the Chessman, by all practical appearances, was trying to track his own copycat.

"Why expose himself now?" Sears asked. "After all this time?"

"His was a highly personal vendetta. I don't think he's happy with an outsider messing up his magnum opus, his tapestry to Marly Kelch. Imagine if da Vinci caught you painting a moustache on the Mona Lisa."

"If you could figure out a way to use that fat ego of his against him, Cady, and use it to reel him in," Sears volunteered. "But I think you're on the right track. The Chessman stems from the Kelch girl— some kind of wrathful angel raining hell on her behalf. Keep shaking that tree and something might fall out. All you need to know is that you're after a smart-e...and that's a damned shame."

"A smart-e?"

"I know you've got those fancy profilers at your beck and call, the ones that'll tell you what kind of toilet paper the perp prefers— one ply or two—but I tend to follow a simpler, more pared-back methodology by, ironically, the man who invented profiling over two hundred years ago."

"Who?"

"Napoleon Bonaparte."

"What?"

"No shit. Bonaparte classified his soldiers into four basic categories and I stole the little emperor's philosophy and reapplied it to perps. Smart-energetic, smart-lazy, stupid-energetic, and stupid-lazy. Most of the ones I hunt, Cady, fall into the last category—the stupid-lazies. Just last week Cambridge PD picked up this young guy who tried carjacking a Mazda Miata. Thing of it was the Miata had a manual transmission, a five speed, and the dumbass didn't know how to stick shift. He made it half a block away in first gear by the time the squad car arrived."

"You've got some real doozies there in Cambridge, Detective."

"Tell me about it. The stupid-lazies make for great comic relief. Now the stupid-energetics, well, they fuck up everyone's good time, but that's because they're mostly politicians. The stupid-energetics were the ones Napoleon wanted to line up and shoot. Can't say I blame him." Sears took a long breath and continued, "But you, my friend, you're after a smart-energetic—a smart-e, that is. They're the worst."

"Lucky me."

"And your smart-e happens to be utilizing all three regions of his brain. Emotion is his motive. As for logic—well, he beat you Fibbies in a chess match. And clearly he's been exercising his reptilian side, for vengeance and survival."

"You do have a way of cheering me up, Allan."

"Watch your back, Cady," the detective said before hanging up. "This boy won't be bringing donuts to a gunfight."

"There was a chess piece in the ashtray."

Cady had seen Sundown Point Resort on his cell phone caller ID and was pleasantly surprised to hear from Terri Ingram. He was doubly surprised at what she'd just said.

"A chess piece in the ashtray?"

"Stay with me for a minute on this, G-Man," the resort owner said and hurriedly continued. "After I left him, Bret let the house go to pot big time. Every dish in the place was caked in crud and stacked in the sink, carpets all filthy, soiled clothes and empty Stoli bottles littered everywhere. You could write sonnets in the dust. And slimy critters evolving in his bathroom. I spent the funeral week literally sterilizing the place, fourteen-hour days of scrubbing it clean kept me moving. Whenever I stopped moving, I'd start sobbing uncontrollably."

"That's normal, Terri. You were grieving."

"I was in a bad state of mind for much of that time after his death, but I didn't want to take any prescription meds, Valium or anything else to dull the pain. As part of the endless cleaning I threw out all of Bret's ashtrays, but the one in the back office—right inside from the deck where you and I talked, where the guests come to settle their accounts—I remembered there being some kind of game piece sitting in it, right in the middle of Bret's spent cigarettes."

"Do you still have it?"

"That's what I checked on this morning. You see three years back—on my way to the big dumpster out by the charred remains of the barn—I stopped and tossed the game piece into the game box in the schoolhouse. Do you remember the schoolhouse?"

"Yes," Cady replied. The schoolhouse, made of plywood, was the size of an equipment shed that sat next to the playground. Little kids could spend the afternoon playing school.

"There's a wooden box the size of a Navy chest that's full of plastic toys and dolls and games for the smaller children to play with. Anyway, after our conversation I've been doing a lot of thinking and that came back to me early this morning, so I ran out to check. A single chess piece lay in the bottom of the box, even though there's no matching chess set or board to go with it and there never has been as far as I can tell. I even shouted 'Bingo!' and got some strange looks from the morning fishermen."

"Which chess piece is it, Terri?" Cady asked, feeling his enthusiasm well up from within.

"I've never played chess, but it's one of the small pieces, you know the ones that line the front row—the pawns," Terri Ingram said. "It's a single glass pawn."

"Excellent work, Terri. Excellent. Now listen, don't touch it and please keep the kids out of the game box. I'll have an agent there within—"

"I'm already at the airport in Minneapolis, Drew. I'm on the next flight out to D.C."

"What are you thinking, Terri?" Cady asked. "That chess piece is now part of a criminal investigation."

"Don't worry, G-Man. I picked it up with a tweezers and tossed it in a Ziploc—hey, I watch *CSI*. Besides, it's been in the grime at the bottom of a game box for three years, so I'm not sure what you'll be able to get off it. I'm bringing it with me. And I've also got photocopies of Bret's original purchase agreement of Sundown Point Resort—and all sorts of interesting paperwork. Turns out he did have a sugar daddy from out east—some entity called The SGL Group."

"The SGL Group?"

"I don't do this for a living but I'd hazard a guess that *SGL* stands for *Snow Goose Lake*," Terri answered. "By the way, Drew, I plan on seeing Dorsey Kelch when I'm out there."

Cady was disappointed in the direction the conversation had suddenly turned. "I'd strongly advise against doing that, Terri."

"Whether I get your help or not, Agent Cady," Terri Ingram responded firmly, "I plan on meeting Dorsey Kelch."

Chapter 24

"After saving the Kellervick files to a thumb drive," Agent Preston said while watching Cady, "he apologized profusely for 'any inconvenience' to the terrified Mr. Banning and, once again, introduced himself as Special Agent Drew Cady. He then told K&P's Chief Investment Officer that this was an 'enhanced interrogation technique' that the bureau had recently begun to implement."

Cady shook his head.

"Then he drugged Banning again and dumped the man back in the driveway of his Newton home. Banning awoke about three in the morning, still groggy, and almost had his fourth heart attack in as many hours before it occurred to him that he was inside a car trunk and not a coffin. Anyway, the UNSUB, ever the gentleman, had left the trunk unlatched for the CIO."

"After all, what's a little kidnapping, assault with a deadly weapon, and impersonating a federal officer when the bodies are stacking like cordwood?" Assistant Director Jund spoke slowly in a voice just above a whisper that all the federal agents around the conference table strained forward in their seats to hear. "The freak is taunting us now."

The room fell silent. Cady bit his lower lip and kept quiet. Preston was the SAC—the Special Agent in Charge—and he would show her due deference. Plus, Cady was thankful not to be sitting in Preston's chair, the hot seat, for this meeting where any new developments lagged far behind the eight ball.

"I had a discussion with Drew before the meeting and he and I are in agreement on three issues," Preston said, breaking the dead air. "First, the Chessman is alive. Dane Schaeffer and now Bret Ingram have been reclassified as murder victims. In fact, we now know that a glass chess pawn had originally been left at the Ingram murder scene in Cohasset, Minnesota. We're certain that Ingram ran cover for the Zalentine brothers and, quite likely, Congressman Farris, for their involvement in the death of Marly Kelch at Snow Goose Lake thirteen years ago."

"*Suggestio falsi.*" The assistant director said to the group as a whole. "*Suppressio veri.*"

"A statement of falsehood to conceal the real truth," Agent Preston translated aloud.

"A bogus account of events in order to bury the truth," Cady further translated, "to bury what happened that night at Snow Goose Lake."

"And for that Bret Ingram was the first in the series of the Chessman murders. The game opened with a pawn, Ingram, being taken out of play even before the queen, K. Barrett Sanfield, which we previously assumed was the first move. Secondly," Agent Preston continued her narrative, "Drew and I believe that a Chessman copycat is likely responsible for the Gottlieb and Kellervick killings."

"What's the intersection between Gottlieb and Kellervick?" the AD asked.

"The only connection we've been able to find was that Kellervick attended a conference five years back where Gottlieb was the keynote speaker," Agent Beth Schommer responded, reading from her legal pad. "But Kellervick's colleagues who attended the conference with her say they all blew off Gottlieb's speech and went out for a liquid lunch instead."

"How do the chess pieces correlate this go-round? Sanfield and Gottlieb both merit a queen, Ingram and Kellervick are pawns?"

"Copycat or not," said Agent Tom Hiraldi, the chess expert who had also been sucked back into the case, "it's a new game. Congressman Farris—the king—was lethally checkmated three years ago. Gottlieb starts a new match."

"What's your third item, Liz?"

"Drew and I believe the original Chessman has come out of the woodwork to hunt down his own copycat."

"So we've got the original Chessman chasing his own copycat from D.C. to Boston while posing as Special Agent Drew Cady in order to give the bureau the full extension of his middle finger. This is the career equivalent of getting my butt kicked in front of the girls at recess." Jund closed his eyes as though doing so would make it all go away. "People up the totem pole are monitoring this investigation—actually, excreting bricks would be a more accurate portrayal. I can assure you that the president has his eye on this investigation. I am personally taking a great deal of heat over this investigation. Daily. Volcanic-level heat. And it's looking more and more like something that fell out of a tall cow's ass."

Resounding silence. Any dropped pins went unheard.

Jund finally reopened his eyes. "What's he trying to achieve by gaining access to Elaine Kellervick's work files?"

"Still fishing, no doubt," Special Agent Fennell Evans said, picking up the ball. "We're compiling a list of clients that Kellervick had contact with over the past three years. However, Kellervick was more of a behind-the-scenes analyst. Not much direct client interaction. We're setting up to review Kellervick's work files. Albert Banning's not terribly pleased about that, but I've assured him our auditors will be on-site and that he can even sit in the room with them if he so desires. I've also assured Banning that all Koye & Plagans' client data will be kept in the strictest of confidence."

"Unless something breaks," Jund said.

"Unless something breaks," Evans repeated.

"On a similar note, our forensic auditors are combing through Ingram's original purchase agreement for Sundown Point Resort," Cady added. "The resort was purchased for Ingram with the help of a dummy front group—the SGL Group—that we're fairly certain will ultimately point back to the Zalentines. We've ruled out Eric Braun—an ex-Marine and old high school boyfriend of Marly Kelch. I'm meeting with Dorsey Kelch again in the morning." Cady didn't mention that he'd be taking a certain visitor along with him to the Kelch household. It ran against his every fiber, but Terri Ingram had been adamant about visiting Dorsey Kelch when Cady had picked her up at Ronald Reagan National and shuttled her to the Hoover Building, where she was currently providing her statement and meeting with the auditors.

"What about expanding the search to everyone in attendance at Schaeffer's party?" asked Agent Evans.

"Sheriff Littman out at Bergen County faxed me the list of partygoers from the old police report. He's done some sleuthing on this, but nothing has turned up. Mostly now-married yuppies with kids and alibis."

"Will no one rid me of this turbulent prick?" the AD said to the room, but glared at Agent Cady.

The room fell into silence a third time.

"Okay then," the AD said, looking down at his notes. "If the Chessman isn't completely yanking our chain, then what about this copycat in the woodpile? What's the copycat's motive in the Gottlieb and Kellervick murders?"

"Based on who they were, it's got to be something to do with the financial sector, an economic agenda of some kind, something with the markets. Honestly, sir," Cady said, broaching the topic he'd discussed briefly with Preston, "we may want to consider that the Chessman copycat is more than one UNSUB."

"A conspiracy?" The AD frowned. "But why the headache of stealing the Chessman's M.O.?"

"Easy," Cady answered. "To throw us off track."

Chapter 25

"Worst case scenario, Dorsey Kelch screams the F-word at me, you get to say, 'I told you so,' and I buy you a nice lunch on the drive back to Washington."

"She's too much of a class act to do that, but if there's an iota of awkwardness after you've said your piece, head out and grab a Starbucks. Give me an hour to compile an extensive list of the male figures that played a role in Marly's life."

"What if the guy was a Don Quixote, loving her chastely and from afar?"

"It'll be problematic if it's a nameless guy who changed the tires on the family station wagon two decades back. But there's more proximity than that. I can taste it." Cady hesitated. "There's just something along the line, some gap in the chain that I've missed."

It had been a quiet drive to Reading, Pennsylvania, likely to do with Terri collecting her thoughts and rehearsing in her mind exactly what she needed to tell Dorsey Kelch. The two had eaten overdone cheeseburgers and limp fries in the Embassy Suites bar last night before retiring, Ingram to her suite and Cady to a room now registered under the alias Eddie Hoover that Jund, always the kidder, had set up in order to minimize unwanted visitors.

Cady felt clumsy, put upon. They had discussed the best way

to place Dorsey Kelch at ease so Terri could say her piece, get her request for forgiveness off her chest, and then immediately vamoose if the chitchat went south. Cady had been against showing up and springing it on Mrs. Kelch, but Terri had been insistent, believing that if they called ahead, she would be turned away. By the time he pulled the unmarked, a Buick LaCrosse he'd been loaned, into Kelch's driveway, Cady had decided to play it Joe Friday—*just the facts, ma'am.* In the course of the current investigation, Bret Ingram's death has now been ruled a homicide and Ingram's widow, who has been devastated by the news of her husband's probable role in the events at Snow Goose Lake, would like to have a word or two with you, if that's okay, ma'am.

"I'm sorry to disturb you twice in one week."

Dorsey Kelch held the screen door and looked at Cady's automobile. "Wouldn't your partner like to come in?"

"Permit me to bend your ear, Mrs. Kelch."

An hour later, Cady was still trying to figure out how he'd lost control as he approached the rambler with the leash to Mother Kelch's dog, the hateful Rex, in his right hand and an empty plastic bag in his left.

Mrs. Kelch grimaced as he informed her how Bret Ingram's widow desired to have a word with her. Dorsey had reluctantly agreed, and Cady walked a visibly nervous Terri Ingram up the driveway and introduced the two. Terri looked like a million bucks, and some change if you counted her short sleeve cardigan and white linen trousers, but Cady could tell she was anxious—the have-a-last-meal-and-light-a-last-cigarette sort of anxiety.

Also, as prearranged, he asked Mrs. Kelch if he might use her restroom after drinking coffee on the long drive. In the bathroom Cady looked out the window into the backyard where Marly Kelch had played with her friends all those years ago. He noticed the toy dachshund still parked under the picnic table, as when he'd had last been there. Unfortunately, the dog noticed Cady at the same moment, stood up, and began yapping. Cady slowly backed away from the window until the dachshund ceased the racket. Evidently, Rex still harbored unpleasant feelings toward Cady. The feeling was mutual.

Cady could hear voices from the living room, but couldn't discern what was being said. Terri did the bulk of the talking, paragraphs at a time to Dorsey's brisk one or two word retorts. Cady heard Terri's voice begin to waver, so he opened the bathroom door, made fake hand-washing sounds, and joined the two in the other room.

"Is everything okay?" Cady had asked, expecting to escort Terri back to the sedan.

Dorsey Kelch gave him a slight nod. He turned to Terri and, while he was blocking Mrs. Kelch's view, Terri mumbled "ahuh" and pointed from him to the door, none too subtly requesting more time. He got the message.

"Excuse me while I make a phone call," he said and headed out to the Buick.

In the car Cady checked his voice mail. Just a message from Agent Evans asking if he could review the list of partygoers, suggesting that they might want to delve into the family and friends of Dane Schaeffer. Cady wondered if Jund had played a role in Agent Evans' offer to help.

Cady then dug through his briefcase until he found Agent Drommerhausen's old profile on the Chessman and flipped to the section that chess expert Agent Hiraldi had helped the profiler compose. He had read this section repeatedly in the past and ran through it again.

The UNSUB is playing at a championship level, several moves ahead of the competition. He's utilizing a hell-for-leather approach, brazenly taking out his opponents. Your run-of-the-mill chess players play the game cautiously, out of fear, because they don't know what will happen if they aggressively march their pieces down the chessboard, but experience tells them that the consequences will be rather dire. Great players understand exactly why it is that sheer aggression is usually punished. However, they also realize that if their opponent is not practiced enough to position his pieces strategically, an all out balls-to-the-walls attack thus makes perfectly good sense; vulnerable spots hidden to your average player are therefore mercilessly exploited.

Cady looked at his empty cup of gas station coffee and realized that now he truly needed to use the restroom. Upon returning to Kelch's house, Dorsey Kelch blocked his entrance, handing him Rex on a leash and a bag for any of the dog's exhaust and asking if Cady could take Rex for his morning walk. Dorsey's eyes were red-rimmed. He saw Terri across the room, tears slipping down her face. Cady took the leash, the barking dachshund, the special baggy, and left.

"Rex didn't go?" Mrs. Kelch asked upon Cady's return as she took the empty bag and undid the leash. "He's normally like clockwork this late in the morning."

Cady opened his mouth but said nothing.

"Oh my God, Dorsey," Terri said. "Look at his face. Rex went, all right, but the G-man didn't pick it up."

"Oh dear," Dorsey said. "I hope it was a block or two over. The immediate neighbors all know Rex."

"I'm going to use your restroom," Cady said.

He hurried down the hall, away from the duet of giggles, and wondered again exactly when he'd lost control.

"...and Marly continued to wait tables at the Sea Shack whenever she was home on breaks to make tip money," explained Mrs. Kelch.

"Mike Dean, the owner, is a family friend from church and Mike would let Marly work evening shifts whenever she was in town. The Sea Shack is always packed."

Cady scanned his list of names. "We've got Dean on the church list."

Dorsey smiled. "Mike's almost eighty."

"Any sons?"

"No."

"You said Marly gave private tennis lessons, but mostly to females, right?"

"She'd help out her old high school coach, Curt Wently, with some of the girls on the team that had potential but needed some additional one-on-one play. Mostly fifteen- and sixteen-year-olds trying to make the varsity cut. Once in a while Curt would have her play against one of his new tennis stars, just to gauge how good they were."

Cady added a checkmark next to Coach Wently's name and then went back to a timeline he'd developed. "You mentioned that Marly sometimes worked at the Pet Mart when in town?"

"She started helping them clean out the cages and fish tanks when she was fourteen. Loved animals. Marly worked there part time until she was seventeen, when she realized more college money could be made waiting tables. But right up to the end she'd stop by the pet shop and visit. If a manager was out sick, they'd sometimes call to see if she could watch the store. If she was free, she'd cover the shift."

"Your daughter was very pretty." Terri had been quietly paging through the family photo albums as Cady constructed his chart and discussed names with Mrs. Kelch and, upon closing the final album, had gotten up to look at the portraits lining the hallway. "Where was this picture taken?"

"Her father snapped that shot of Marly on our trip to Yellowstone. Peter liked that close-up so much he had it enlarged."

"Such a special person, Dorsey," Terri whispered, touching the frame lightly. "It's a heavier world without her."

"That's almost exactly what Jakey said on one of his last visits."

"Jakey?" Terri asked.

"Jake Westlow. Marly babysat him when they were kids." Cady thumbed through his notes. "Westlow took his own life after his mother passed away."

"Such sadness." Dorsey spoke more to herself than to her visitors. "It seems as if it were only yesterday that Jakey said that. He stopped by a week or so before Lorraine lost her battle with cancer. She was in hospice at that point. We were paging through pictures in some magazine and something reminded us of Marly, and Jakey said, 'The world is a much heavier place without her.' A decade later and it brought tears to my eyes."

The room sat in silence for several seconds.

"You must have seen a model in a fashion magazine that looked like Marly," Terri said.

"No." Dorsey pointed to a stack of magazines on her coffee table. "I get *Newsweek* and, come to think of it, they had this story on father and son Farris—the elder senator and his congressman son."

"The two were pictured together on the cover." Cady had read the human interest piece of fluff years back. Repeatedly. There was likely a photocopy of the Farris Dynasty *Newsweek* article in an old file in his cube at Hoover.

"You're right," Dorsey said, nodding. "We paged through *Newsweek* and I told Jakey that Marly had known Patrick Farris when they were students at Princeton, before he followed in his father's footsteps. Jakey hadn't heard that before and asked if he could borrow the magazine."

"When was the last time you saw Jake Westlow?" Cady asked.

"I was with him at his mother's funeral a couple weeks later. A small affair. Lorraine didn't have many friends. Jakey also stopped in a final time to say goodbye a week or so later. He'd made arrangements with a real estate agent to sell the house and had finished wrapping up his mother's…life…and was heading back to his place in San Diego, where he was living at that time. Jakey was pretty broken up." Dorsey shook her head. "If only I had known what was coming."

"Did you attend his funeral?"

"As fate would have it, Agent Cady, I found out too late. It happened in California. I heard about it a month after the fact from a neighbor of a neighbor. I looked up Jakey's obituary online. It was a short listing; the kind they have for young people where you get to thinking that it may have been a suicide. It broke my heart. There was no one from home there for him."

Terri did the math. "Jake couldn't have been that much younger than Marly. No more than five years."

"Jakey was three years younger. Marly was about ten and he was seven when they first met, you know, kids playing in the neighborhood. But Marly acted older and soon Lorraine would grab her whenever she went out on a date and needed someone to watch little Jake." A smile returned to Dorsey's face. "Marly was three years older, but as Jake used to joke, he caught up with her."

"He caught up with her?" Terri asked, confused.

"He took these tests they have, went through some special programs, and he wound up graduating from high school in Marly's class. Jakey was this boy genius. At his request, Peter and I pulled some strings to get him into Reading Central Catholic. We had to go a few rounds with Lorraine over the Catholic thing, but she knew her son was an extraordinary boy and feared he might get lost in the public school system. He was extremely bright in math and English, but a true prodigy in the sciences. Reading Central had never seen anything like him. Nor since. Aced any test you set in front of him without breaking a sweat."

"Very impressive."

"I did feel a little sorry for him back in high school, though, and not just because of, well, his family situation—having no father at home—but more from a *social acclimation* standpoint, not fitting in with the other kids. You see, he grew up so fast. Too fast, in retrospect, bearing in mind how it all turned out in the end. Jakey was this fifteen-year-old senior, a great athlete in his own right—a wrestler—but still a highly sensitive fifteen-year-old boy surrounded by these young men. He stood apart. Jakey was in twelfth grade but not of twelfth grade, if you know what I mean. I think Marly made that thorny transition a little easier for him."

"He loved her, didn't he?" Terri asked.

"I think Marly was the first friend Jakey ever had. Perhaps his only friend. This was Jakey's second home. We would cook extra dinner in case he showed up. Quite a pair those two goofballs made, lying in front of the TV playing all sorts of games—checkers, Battleship, Monopoly, that Ker Plunk marble game. They both got into tennis back then, played every night at the school courts. Marly had the knack and really took off. Jakey went to all her matches, her home matches anyway, to cheer her on. Yes, Terri, to your point—Jakey loved Marly with all his heart. At first and always."

Chapter 26

"But Jake Westlow is deceased," Terri repeated. "Wouldn't you call that the proverbial dead end?"

They were seated at a table on the lower level of Trattoria Nicola's, the hotel's Italian restaurant. The trip back to D.C. had been animated, more so than the grim trek out to Reading. Terri had heard Cady's side of the conversation as he read off the additional names and reported his findings back to Agent Preston.

"Think of the pattern we've witnessed so far, Terri. Your husband's death is made to appear an accident. Dane Schaeffer's death is sculpted a suicide. If Westlow were the Chessman, knowing the activity he was about to undertake—up to and including the slaying of a sitting United States congressman—faking his own demise would throw us off track, providing him maximum elbow room."

"But Jake committing suicide wouldn't be out of the question. Some people are too bright for their own damned good. The shooting star burns out quickest. Marly dies a tragic death. Jake's mother dies a slow and painful death. Suddenly, he's all alone in the universe." Terri took a slow sip from her glass of Pinot Nero. "Probably never got over the love of his life dying so young."

"That's the likeliest scenario. A quick peek at the autopsy report will settle everything. If that's cut-and-dry, we'll move on and see what Marly's tennis coach and those three other names have been up to in their free time." Cady pushed one of his remaining mushroom raviolis across his plate with his fork. "I'm proud of you, Terri. Meeting Dorsey Kelch today took a lot of gumption on your part. That's something I don't think I'd have it in me to do."

"Sure you would, G-Man. You'd just have done it in your own way."

"Did you offer her the resort?"

"Right before you brought Rex back. Dorsey laughed and told me she wouldn't have the foggiest idea what to do with a lake resort in Minnesota."

"Did you get what you were looking for?"

"I thought I'd feel better." Terri shrugged. "But I guess we're all open wounds in search of a Band-Aid."

"You think I'm an open wound?"

"You especially," Terri said, smiling. "By the way, I notice you're not wearing a ring anymore."

"Someone I recently met gave me pause to consider what ghost was haunting me…or what deluded statement I was trying to make. I see you're no longer wearing yours."

"Some fisherman is going to hit the jackpot when he cleans a largemouth bass. I tossed that ring as far into the lake as I possibly could."

"Why did you do that?"

"You shook up my world last week, G-Man. No way I go back to painting cabin walls after that bombshell. I haven't been able to think about anything else. What Bret did was unforgivable. What he did was vile and immoral—all those young women the Zalentines murdered would still be alive today if he hadn't covered up for them. Nobody deserves to die like Bret did, but it's hard to mourn now that I know his secret. Time wounds all heels, I guess, and Bret's past finally caught up with him. Anyway, I've cut all ties."

"I'm sorry, Terri."

"You're following the truth, Drew. The chips are falling where they may. I guess I'm falling where I may. You've got nothing to apologize for—well, except the dog thing."

Cady shook his head. "I hate Rex."

Terri broke out laughing and pushed her plate, now empty of chicken parmigiana, aside. It was good to hear, Cady thought. *What a difference a day makes.*

"So what do you do when you're not chasing bad guys and flabbergasting widows?"

"Ever hear of numismatics?"

"What's that?"

"It's the study of currency. In my case, I collect rare coins."

"So the G-Man is tall, dark, and geeky?"

"I know—a lot of people make fun of it."

"I wasn't making fun of it, Drew. I was making fun of you."

"Good one," Cady said. "Do you like studying history?"

"I catch the History channel now and again. Whenever I do I feel that I should watch it every day."

"I'm a history buff. Most of my collection contains rare American coins. Here's a major nerd alert for you: I'm an associate member of the American Numismatic Society."

"I bet the Holiday Inn gets awfully nervous when that bunch shows up for the annual banquet."

"We keep the joint rocking till almost nine o'clock at night."

"What coins do you have in your collection?"

"My stuff's pretty much nickel and dime. Literally. I scored an 1851 Silver Three Cents piece earlier this year, designed by a chief engraver named James Barton Longacre and made at the Philadelphia Mint." Cady grabbed his pen from the breast pocket of his sport jacket and sketched the coin on the back of his wine coaster, then slid it to Terri. "A giant 'C' with the Roman numeral III inside."

"A three-cent piece seems like an odd number."

"That's where the history comes into play. The California Gold Rush began in 1848 at Sutter's Mill. You remember the 'Forty-Niners'?"

"Sure."

"Well, as a result of the gold rush, the price of silver rose and people began to hoard and melt the silver coins since they were worth more as metal than as currency. Coins worth less than their face value back then were mostly rejected. At this same time, the United States postal system had reduced their basic rate to three cents. Congress came up with the idea to create a three-cent coin with just enough precious metal—silver—in it to avoid being worth less than the coin's face value, but not enough to make it worth melting. These coins were small and thin, but they served their purpose in the purchasing of postage stamps."

"Interesting. How big is your collection?"

"A few dozen coins. None of which cost me very much—I'm an amateur aficionado on a K-Mart budget."

Terri stared at Cady. He could tell something was on her mind, something eating away below the surface. She appeared hesitant, but after another moment, Terri made her decision.

"Speaking of history, Drew, after you left Grand Rapids I went online and read every newspaper account on the murders of the Zalentine twins, K. Barrett Sanfield, Dane Schaeffer, and Patrick Farris that Google came up with. The more-recent articles after Dane Schaeffer's death mentioned that an unnamed FBI agent had been with the congressman at the time of his…assassination…and that the agent had been brutally attacked by the killer." Terri's eyes danced briefly over the scars crisscrossing Cady's right hand. "I'm sorry, Drew."

Cady nodded. He felt himself begin to blush so he grabbed the bottle of Pinot Nero, refilled Terri's glass, and emptied the remaining wine into his own.

"Dessert?"

"What?"

"Here comes the waitress."

"Oh."

In a high-backed booth across the room, a man with black hair and John Lennon glasses signaled his waitress for another glass of ginger ale. His bruschetta lay off to the side, completely untouched. The man appeared to have been stood up. He checked his watch before glancing slowly around the dining room, eyes settling on Cady's table for a moment before returning to the *Washington Post*'s daily crossword laid out on his table.

Both stuffed, they'd split a Torta di Chocolate, with Terri allowing Cady to devour the lion's portion of the cake and ice cream. Both had a cappuccino to counterbalance the Pinot. Afterward, Cady walked Terri back to her room and waited as she dug her keycard from the bowels of her purse. Terri pulled out the card and looked at Cady.

The two stared at each other for several seconds.

"Sleep tight." Cady turned to go.

"G-Man?"

Cady turned back.

"Are you okay, G-Man?"

Cady gave her a quizzical look and nodded his head.

"I don't mean to be presumptive, Drew. It's been an intense week—and in a certain respect I feel as though I've gotten to know you quite well. You just seem so darned drawn, Drew," Terri said, taking a step toward him. "Are you sure you're okay?"

Cady paused. "I don't need rescuing, Terri. I'm not broken. And I'm not an open wound."

"Maybe so, Drew." Terri took a final step into Cady's immediate proximity and looked up at him. "Maybe so."

Cady stared down into Terri's eyes, suddenly wanting to fall deep into those marble-blues. He slid his hand beneath the small of her back and pulled her flush against himself. He leaned down into the kiss. Despite their embrace Terri somehow managed to swipe open the door with her keycard and the two tumbled backward into her room.

Chapter 27

Six Months Ago

"Papa," Lucy said, "you remember Paul Crenna?"

Hartzell tossed the *Wall Street Journal* onto the side table, dropped his bifocals on top of the newspaper, and stood up from the couch.

"Of course I do. NYU, right, Paul?" Hartzell shook the younger man's hand in a no-nonsense grip.

"Senior year, sir," Crenna replied. "Time to get serious."

"What's your area of study?"

"Business with a minor in Economics."

"I imagine Dr. Sladek keeps you hopping. Ty Sladek's a dear friend, Paul. A finer mensch you'll never meet."

"Who's Dr. Sladek?" Lucy asked.

"Tyson Sladek is the provost at New York University," her date answered.

"Ty's educational philosophy can be quite rigorous. To him the mind is a muscle in need of continual exercise, a strict regimen of aerobics, wind sprints, crunch-ups and power lifting for it to fully develop and remain finely tuned. The university as virtual boot camp for the intellect."

Lucy stifled a yawn and headed toward the kitchen. "Let me

get you boys some wine…a virtual guarantee of more stimulating conversation."

"Janice left a batch of those crab-stuffed mushrooms you love, Lucy, if you'd like to heat those up."

"Yummy—although I think we both know whose favorite those crab mushrooms truly are, Papa."

Hartzell grinned like the Cheshire Cat, placed a palm on Crenna's shoulder and led the business major to the wall of windows, far from the kitchen, so they could look out over the city at night.

"Million-dollar view, sir."

"Call me Drake, Paul. Besides, I owe you a debt of gratitude."

"What for?"

"If you hadn't gone tonight, Lucy would have dragged me along, and I can't do any more ballet. You took one for the team."

Crenna laughed and hushed his voice. "I thought about my Fantasy Football picks all through *Swan Lake*."

Hartzell chuckled. The kid wasn't half bad. Lucy had been correct about his appearance: every strand of dark hair was flawlessly in place, even the intentionally stray curl that comma-ed the center of the young man's forehead. Although the kid looked comfortably cosmopolitan, Hartzell disagreed with his daughter's assessment— he sensed the boy had more grit to him than the average metrosexual flotsam drifting aimlessly about the city.

"What's so funny?" Lucy appeared behind them holding two crystal glasses full of a dark ruby-colored wine.

"Paul's giving me some advice on whom to select for Fantasy Football."

Lucy looked as though someone had belched loudly in church.

"What have you got for us there, Slim?"

"Vina Alicia Cuarzo—a Petit Verdot blend from Argentina."

"Nicely done." Hartzell took his glass and inhaled the aroma. "A hint of blueberry."

"I'm putting the mushrooms in the oven, Papa."

Lucy returned to the kitchen and Hartzell steered the college senior back to the living room.

"That was a close one." Hartzell motioned for his guest to take a seat on the couch with his wine glass. "Lucy said that you wanted to talk to me, Paul."

"Yes, sir."

Hartzell sat on the edge of the couch, away from the young man. "You seem like a great kid, Paul, if I may speak openly. I must confess to a bit of a start when Lucy mentioned that you wanted to speak with me in private. It's very classy—quaint—but I must admit I think the two of you should date a while longer, get to know each other better. I'm sure your parents would agree there's no reason to rush things."

Paul Crenna stared at Hartzell for several seconds as a grin stretched across his face.

"I believe there's been a misunderstanding, sir. Lucy is aces in my book. Someday you and I may have *that* talk, but today—I was interested in discussing a business opportunity."

"You didn't come here to ask for my daughter's hand in marriage?"

Crenna shook his head.

"Oh, dear me." Hartzell leaned back and took a long sip of the Cuarzo. "I owe you an apology—though I think Lucy was having a bit of sport at my expense. Forgive me, Paul. When your only daughter informs you that her gentleman friend would like to have a private chat with you, the old mind starts to wander."

"No need to apologize. It was silly of me to approach you in this manner." Crenna scratched his cheek. "When my sister got married last fall, my father went to buy a new tux. My mother suggested he be fitted for a straitjacket at the same time."

Hartzell laughed. "Clearly I can relate to your father. Lucy's the only one I've got, Paul. I'll never be ready to stop being the most important man in her life."

"To be honest, sir, I'm never sure where I stand with Lucy."

"Nonsense. I only get to meet the cream of the crop." Hartzell finished his wine and set the glass on a walnut coaster. "Now, after making a complete ass of myself, what can I do for you?"

"My father met you at a charity event in Chicago some years back."

"Was that the restoration project for the Art Institute or the Breast Cancer Awareness at the Belden Stratford?"

"You shared a table at the Stratford. My aunt Nora is a cancer survivor. She likes to give back and lets my parents know whenever an occasion presents itself."

"Your aunt Nora is a saint, Paul. If I remember correctly, we raised a lot of money that evening." Hartzell peeked at Crenna. "Your father has the same dark hair, maybe a little gray on the temples, wears wire frames?"

"That's him."

"I do remember your father." Indeed, Lucy had described Crenna Senior to Hartzell from some family albums she had riffled through at Paul's apartment. "It was an enormous crowd that night and your father joked about us being packed in like so many sardines."

"Dad's a card, all right."

"Give your father my best, Paul, next time you talk to him."

"I will, sir. In fact, that's what I wanted to discuss with you. My father's investment group has been looking into market opportunities."

"Please have him let me know if he finds some good deals. It's been strange days, son, the likes of which I've never seen—and I'm as old as dirt. The monetary policy of this administration, if anything, has prolonged the suffering. Legislators on both sides of the aisle should be tried for economic treason. Everyone needs to calm down, be patient, and ride out the storm while confidence returns to the financial sector."

"That's exactly what Father's investment group is interested in, Mr. Hartzell. Safe places to ride out the storm."

"Give me a second, Paul. And you've got to start calling me Drake—I insist."

Hartzell grabbed his glasses and disappeared down the hallway for a minute and then came back holding a business card, which he handed to Crenna.

"Have your father give Ben Vetter a call. The number on the back will put him straight through. There are no miracles, Paul, but Ben will set your father's investment group up with a steady ROI and great positioning for when the Bull comes charging back, as it inevitably will. I cannot offer a higher recommendation than Ben Vetter."

"Thank you, Drake." Crenna looked a bit letdown, but placed the card in his wallet. "My hope was to connect you directly with my father's group."

"That's an endearing compliment, Paul. Very gracious of you. Lucy will wholeheartedly disagree about my awkwardness at tooting my own horn, but," Hartzell sat down and leaned forward, "certainly not through any god-given talent or genius, I find myself occupying a certain upper niche in the world of high finance. A certain niche that deals with an amount of funding required to initiate investments that is, quite frankly, highway robbery. It's shamefully elitist, Paul. The funding threshold is an amount of currency that I'm uncomfortable talking about in a pleasant social situation such as this. Let me assure you and your father that the investment firm I'm recommending is most trustworthy. You have my word."

"I didn't mean to cause you any discomfort, sir. My father and I have tremendous respect for your reputation and standing in the financial community. That's why I feel that connecting the two of you would turn into a win-win relationship. My father's group consists of several entities that pool their interests." The Business major with an Economics minor sipped from his glass of wine. "By all means, sir, tell me what this *threshold* amount is, and if it's out of our league, I'll toast you—I'll even hand-deliver my résumé—and then I'll bring this business card of Vetter's back to my father for consideration."

Hartzell cocked his head sideways and offered Paul Crenna an absurdly high number.

"You had me going there for a second, sir," Crenna said. "But I don't see that as being a showstopper."

Hartzell stared at the mark for several seconds.

"How about some more Petit Verdot, Paul?"

Chapter 28

"They never found his body," Cady told the conference room, focusing mainly on Assistant Director Jund. "Jake Westlow *is* the Chessman."

"Start at the beginning, Agent Cady, and walk us through your theory." A sullen Jund leaned back in his chair at the head of the table.

Cady knew what was coming. Jund was going to play devil's advocate and punch as many holes in Cady's *theory* as possible to see if it held up to the light of day before committing to additional steps. He respected the assistant director's strategy, knew his theory needed to be run through the wringer, but also knew this meeting had the potential to be a major pain in the ass.

"Jake Westlow had known Marly Kelch since he was a seven-year-old. Dorsey Kelch believes that Westlow deeply loved her daughter."

"We've been told repeatedly that everyone loved the Kelch girl. She was like…what's her name in that Ben Stiller movie? The one where he gets the gob stuck on his ear."

"*Something About Mary*," Agent Evans volunteered.

"That's the one. Evidently, Marly Kelch had that same girl-next-door thing going on that every guy falls in love with and the kind of face that 'launched a thousand ships.' But that in and of itself means nothing. When I grew up I fell in love with every pretty girl who smiled at me. I still do. Perhaps I'm the killer."

"Jake was a gifted child," Cady said, pressing on, "a brilliant mind, and he ultimately skipped three grades ahead to graduate in Marly's class."

"So what? My sister got moved ahead one grade and I've never heard the end of it. Perhaps she's the killer."

"Marly Kelch was a girl of endless energy. She worked nearly full time in high school, she was a phenomenal athlete—a tennis star, Homecoming Queen, played a mean clarinet, was lead in most of the plays, and, if not for Westlow, Marly would have been the class valedictorian. In fact, she gave the graduation speech as Westlow was too modest and opted out. But there was another endeavor, a smaller endeavor that the duo had cooked up at Reading Central Catholic High School, something that didn't snare many headlines. Turns out Marly had taught Boy Westlow how to play chess back when she first babysat for him. The two started the Reading Chess Club."

"The plot thickens, but most players learn at a young age. My nephew plays chess and he's eight. Perhaps he's the killer."

Cady knew the assistant director's sarcasm masked the incredible stress he'd been under the past ten days. The AD wanted the case presented to him from the very beginning, and Cady was going to give it to him—building block after building block.

"The Westlows were dirt poor. In Jake Westlow's single-parent household, Mom ran a consignment and sewing shop in order to make ends meet. There was no money, nothing for college tuition. Even though he was able to CLEP through most of freshman year, young Westlow wound up with a double major at the Massachusetts Institute of Technology—both Chemical and Mechanical Engineering. Now ask yourself, how could he afford this?"

"Scholarship."

Cady nodded his head. "The kid skated through MIT on a Navy ROTC scholarship."

"So he was a naval officer after MIT?"

"He was in the CEC, a Navy Civil Engineer Corps Officer. He was a lieutenant commander at the time of his *death*. Westlow ran civil engineering projects in Iraq back when it was a hot zone—bases, airfields, harbor facilities, that type of thing."

Agent Preston had Westlow's service record in front of her. "It fits the profile, sir. Military service would provide Westlow great know-how."

"His motive is vengeance over the murder of the person he considered his *soul mate*," Jund thought aloud. "As for means, he's got the skill set and brain cells necessary to plan and carry out these multiple homicides. But the opportunity is out of whack. Why the ten-year gap after the Kelch girl's death?"

"He didn't know."

"What?"

Cady offered a handful of photocopied sheets to Agent Schommer, who took one and passed them on. The page contained the timeline he'd scribbled down before the morning meeting. Cady waited until everyone in the room had a sheet in front of them.

"Westlow is devastated by Marly's death. He doesn't understand how a tremendous athlete like Marly can drown, even if she's had a couple glasses of wine. Let's say he's always been dubious. He makes it a point to stop in and visit Dorsey Kelch whenever he's in town, or, in this case, when he's on hardship leave over the impending death of his mother. He visits Mrs. Kelch. They page through the *Newsweek* issue that has both father and son Farris on the cover and Mrs. Kelch lets slip that Marly knew Patrick Farris at Princeton. This gets Westlow to thinking, to delving into his feeling that something wasn't quite right about Marly's death."

"What's this next mark, 'Funeral,' on your timeline mean?" asked Jund.

"That's the date of Lorraine Westlow's funeral. She died ten days after Jake Westlow's visit with Dorsey Kelch. However, please note that two nights after Westlow's visit with Kelch is when Bret Ingram dies in a fire at his lake resort. It's my belief that Westlow had a heart-to-heart with Ingram, used the threat of force or death to get Ingram's story about what really happened at Snow Goose Lake. Ingram confesses all he knows to Westlow, how the Zalentine twins woke him from his drunken stupor to have him mislead the police, how the purchase of Sundown Point and other things were handled by power attorney Barrett Sanfield. It may even have been a great relief to get this guilt off his chest, but in effect Bret Ingram signed his own death warrant. No way Westlow lets the man live after hearing of his complicity in the cover-up of Marly's death, so he improvises and the town drunkard dies in an apparent fire."

"What's this next date, marked 'Dorsey Kelch'?"

"That's a few days after his mother's funeral, now fourteen days after their initial meeting and the thumbing through of the *Newsweek* magazine that set everything in motion, when Jake Westlow stops by to bid a final farewell to Mrs. Kelch. Dorsey said he was still shaken up over his mother's death, but I posit that Westlow had made plans, knew the road ahead of him was turbulent, and stopped by because he knew he would never see Marly's mother again."

"And this next date, marked 'Westlow Suicide,' is a month later."

"Agent Preston has been digging into that," Cady responded. "Liz, can you walk us through Jake Westlow's *alleged* suicide?"

"At that time Lieutenant Commander Westlow was stationed out of the Naval Base in San Diego. Westlow had been UA from his 32nd Street Naval Station for four days—Unauthorized Absence or AWOL. This was highly unusual for someone at Westlow's level of command." Agent Preston shuffled the packet of papers in front of her, photocopies of which had been passed about at the meeting's start. "He then surfaced in San Francisco to rent a twenty-four-foot sailboat from the marina manager at Emeryville Marina, located in San Francisco Bay—a pretty idyllic place, fairly upscale. Westlow tossed twelve hundred plus a security deposit down on his American Express card for five days with the J/24 Presto, a boat commonly used for training or day-sailing in the bay. We will return to Westlow's intriguing utilization of credit cards in a minute," Preston looked about the table and continued, "but suffice it to say that the J/24 sailboat was far below the Lieutenant Commander's level of expertise. So in the early evening of August thirtieth, Jake Westlow was last seen motoring the small yacht out of Emeryville Marina—'a stunning figure in his service dress whites,' according to one witness. The Coast Guard received an SOS from the J/24 at exactly 10:30 p.m. Westlow radioed in an SOS on channel sixteen."

"What was his emergency?"

"The transcript of Westlow's SOS is included in Exhibit C." Agent Preston let a few seconds pass for pages to flutter. "Westlow followed standard procedure. He called 'U.S. Coast Guard' several times and then said, 'This is vessel Amber Waves, Amber Waves, Amber Waves,' which was the name of the rental J/24 that he was sailing. A minute later Westlow repeated the hailing procedure. At this point, as you can see in the transcript, the Coast Guard responded. They immediately sent him to a different frequency. On this new frequency, channel seventy-two, Westlow provided his name and the exact location of Amber Waves in longitude and latitude. When asked about his emergency, Westlow's answer was 'MOB.' MOB stands for man overboard. Then Westlow responded quietly, almost inaudibly, 'I'm sorry.' Even though the Coast Guard radioman repeatedly asked him to expand on his distress signal, Jake Westlow switched off the radio. He was never heard from again—not from the United States Coast Guard, anyway."

"What exactly did the Guard find on Amber Waves?" Jund asked.

"The officer I interviewed was on the Response Boat that night. He said it was like 'something out of The Bermuda Triangle.' The waters were calm. No other boats were in the vicinity. The Coast Guard found Westlow's shoes on the boat deck, his uniform folded neatly on top of them. Aside from that, the Amber Waves was completely deserted. The course Westlow set had been across the bay and then southward into the Pacific Ocean. The J/24 was about eight nautical miles off the coastline, north of Monterey. Westlow had dropped anchor, and the boat had moved only slightly in the twenty minutes it took for the HH-60 Jayhawk helicopter to spot the J/24. Evidently, Westlow had left the cabin light on for them. The Response Boat showed up ten minutes later." Agent Preston flipped another page. "Exhibit D is a copy of Westlow's short note to the rescuers, found next to the radio, that essentially apologized for wasting their time and stating that he 'did my best not to make any mess for you to clean up.' Our forensic handwriting analyst has verified it to be in the lieutenant commander's handwriting. In addition, there was an empty bottle of Valium on the floorboards, as well as a half-full bottle of Ambien rolling around next to it. They also noted some vomit along the starboard side of the craft." Preston took a breath and then continued, "The Coast Guard assumed that the hidden meaning in Westlow's distress signal signified that he was the man overboard—a suicide—and that the sea swallowed up Westlow's remains. Shark food. A body like that would be picked clean if it ever washed up at all."

"If he staged it, how in hell would Westlow have gotten ashore? An accomplice?"

"We'll certainly be looking into whether Westlow had an accomplice, but an inflatable dinghy, the kind you could pop a motor on, would serve quite nicely. Westlow could have set a waypoint on a GPS and followed that in. Easy as pie. He's long gone by the time the Jayhawk shows up."

Cady appreciated how Agent Preston didn't state the obvious to the assistant director, how she let him piece together that this same inflatable boat could also have been used in the killing of Adrien Zalentine in Chesapeake Bay.

"How would he sneak all that gear onboard?"

"Westlow's alleged suicide was on the night of his fourth rental day, so he had four days to get that stuff aboard and stowed in the cabin. He could have used a large box for the inflatable or he could have segmented it into several smaller boxes and whistled while carrying each aboard."

Cady thought of the boat motors Terri rented to guests at Sundown Point Resort. "No one at a marina is going to look twice at some guy carrying a five or six horsepower out to his boat, even if he doesn't have it boxed up. Remember, everything pointed to Westlow committing suicide, so the investigation never went down this path."

"This is all interesting conjecture," Jund said, tossing a hand in the air. "Have you got anything solid for me?"

"Let's talk about his financial trail," Preston said. "Beth, if you please."

Special Agent Schommer had done her homework and leapt at the opportunity to shine. "Jake Westlow siphoned off four credit cards before his so-called suicide. Two Visa Golds, an American Express, and a Discover Card. One of the Gold cards and the Discover he'd only recently received, and had applied for them immediately after his mother's funeral."

"So what?" Jund replied. "I find out I have terminal cancer, I'm off on a European tour compliments of AX."

"Westlow did not travel to Europe or anyplace else. His apartment wasn't stuffed full of ninety-inch HDTVs, gold-plated golf clubs, jewelry, none of that. The lieutenant commander tapped some sizeable cash advances on all four of those credit cards. All of these funds remain unaccounted for."

"Now we're talking my language. How much money is missing?"

"It's $110,000 in credit card advances. Another $42,000 left over from the sale of his mother's house. Add in another twenty-five grand from the sale of his nearly new Chevy Traverse so he could begin driving his mother's twenty-year-old Ford Tempo. That's $177,000 dollars."

"Somehow I don't picture the lieutenant commander going chitty-chitty bang-bang around his naval base," Jund said. "That's a pretty good nest egg for a start-over."

"And that's only the money we know about, sir," Schommer said. "Westlow did leave two grand in a savings account and about eight hundred in a checking account. I figure he did that for appearances' sake. In a cobbled-together last will and testament found in his motel room, he wanted that money and anything remaining in his estate to be given to his favorite charity—the Make-A-Wish Foundation."

"Misdirection for any superficial investigation into his death."

It was at that point that Cady knew they had Jund, that they'd convinced the assistant director. The AD's mood had lifted, his humor returning; he was seeing results. And the team of federal agents had left some of the best for last.

"They also found an envelope on the boat," Agent Preston said, resuming the narrative. "It contained a key to some sleaze-ball motel in Alvord Lake—near Golden Gate Park—where the junkies hang. Westlow had prepaid the room for a week and instructed the t-shirt manning the front desk that he wanted to be left alone—no house cleaning—not that this dive did much of that to begin with. A Do

Not Disturb sign had hung on his room door all week. Investigators found both a handwritten suicide note and the handwritten will that Beth mentioned on the unmade bed. There was an empty bottle of Ambien by the toilet, a picture of him and his mother from better days atop the TV, and not much else."

"This note is Exhibit E, right?" asked Jund.

"Correct," Preston replied, and gave the room a second to flip to that page. "Please forgive me in advance for butchering Shakespeare, but Westlow's short note reads as follows: O, here, Will I set up my everlasting rest, And Shake the yoke of inauspicious stars, from this world-wearied flesh. Eyes, look your last!"

"*Romeo and Juliet.* Act five, scene three," Special Agent Fennell Evans informed the room.

"You have that in your notes?" Jund asked, staring at Evans. "The act and scene number?"

Agent Evans shook his head.

"You've memorized Shakespeare's plays?"

"Just the more popular plays and sonnets, sir."

Jund continued staring at Agent Evans. "My wife is always showing up with tickets to theater—Shakespeare, Chekov, Ibsen—that sort of stuff. Any chance you'd like to attend some of these performances that I either can't or *won't* make?"

"Love to."

"All this time I've thought of you as that creepy blood-splatter guy who ate paint chips as a child. It turns out that you're a sensitive, poetic blood-splatter guy." Jund blinked and got back on task. "Romeo commits suicide. Westlow commits suicide. Any significance?"

"If he associates himself with Romeo, I don't think those lines refer to his mother," Evans responded.

"It's an interesting twist," Cady pointed out, "but remember how

Juliet's initial death is faked. She's not really dead. The Chessman has cornered the market on *faked* deaths—Ingram's and Schaeffer's—so it's no great stretch that he would have faked his own demise to throw us off track."

"It worked."

"He built in layers. His first tier was to pin everything on Schaeffer. But if that blew up in his face, a *living* Jake Westlow would be the frontrunner on our short list of suspects." Cady looked at the agents sitting around the table and knew it was time to unleash the clincher. "Tell them about Rochester, Liz."

"The day after he visits Dorsey Kelch and gets the *Newsweek* with the Farris article, Westlow catches an early morning flight to Rochester—as in Rochester, Minnesota. An hour after deboarding the plane, Jake has a half-hour meeting with one of the Mayo Clinic's top oncologists to review Lorraine Westlow's medical record in order to provide a second opinion, to see if anything was overlooked. Doctor Heidi Steicken, the cancer specialist, mentioned that Westlow wanted to be certain that his mother's providers had covered all possible bases. Doctor Steicken said she thought it was 'very late in the game for a second opinion,' but she knows how family members grasp at straws, often until the end. Steicken reviewed Ms. Westlow's file and informed Jake Westlow that it was exactly how she would have treated her for kidney cancer had Lorraine been her patient. Westlow thanked her profusely and left."

"And?" the AD asked.

"And he didn't fly back until the next afternoon," Agent Preston said. "Westlow rented a Hertz in Rochester. And even though he checked in to stay overnight at the Doubletree, he put on six hundred and fifty miles in a little over a day. Cohasset, Minnesota, is under a five-hour drive from Rochester. The night we've placed Jake Westlow in Minnesota is the night Bret Ingram died in the barn fire."

"Let me guess, the car mileage would more than cover it."

"It gets deeper," Cady continued. "Upon his return to Reading, Westlow gets a prescription for Ambien from his mother's physician due to 'having trouble sleeping.' Then he visits a grief counselor and scores some Valium to help him through his mother's final days, as well as the funeral week. He makes another appointment with this same grief counselor, but doesn't keep it. And once back in San Diego Westlow makes an appointment with a psychiatrist who specializes in grief counseling, but, again, stands that counselor up."

"Nice touch. The sly fucker mocked up a paper trail for suicide."

Agent Preston steered the investigators to the final page in their packets. "Exhibit F is an eight-by-ten copy of Westlow's picture taken from his military ID card—his CAC—which, of course, is now nearly four years old."

The room went quiet.

Cady had already spent no small amount of time examining Exhibit F, staring into the face of the man who had crippled him in the alleyway behind Farris's row house in Woodley Park. Not exactly the image Cady had conjured up of the man responsible for at least six deaths and possibly others. Westlow's blue eyes stared back at Cady, his hair a sandy blond, service cut above the ears; he was cleanly shaven, with a broad smile that reminded Cady of an old photograph Dorsey Kelch had shared with him of a long-ago birthday party and a little boy by the swing set caught smiling at Marly.

"One last item," Cady said, closing his packet. "Remember the time lag at the Sanfield slaying? The amount of time the killer was in the office with Sanfield?"

"Something like fifteen minutes."

"It doesn't take fifteen minutes to stab a person to death. As I previously mentioned, I suspect Westlow got all that Ingram knew about Snow Goose Lake, basically fingering the Zalentine twins and

Barrett Sanfield, but I believe Westlow got *the rest of the story* from Sanfield during that fifteen-minute gap. I could never figure out why Sanfield would put his ass on the line for a couple of freaks like the Zalentines, no matter what kind of money they could toss his way, but Barrett Sanfield would walk through fire for either Arlen Farris or his son Patrick. I'm sure that Sanfield provided Westlow the *unabridged* version of the events at Snow Goose while pleading for his life."

The table sat in silence for several seconds.

"I'll be goddamned. You pulled it off, Agent Cady. Motive. Means. Opportunity. The Chessman created this highly structured mirage, but damned if you didn't find him." Jund broke into a grin and slapped the tabletop. "I'd already acclimated myself to the fact I'd be greeting customers at Home Depot this time next month. Same-sex is legal in D.C., Drew—what say we tie the knot?"

"I say we've got a name and a face, sir. The hard part will be catching him."

"We'll plaster his name and face all over the news. It's a game-changer. By tomorrow night everyone will know this guy's mug. If Westlow tries to mail a postcard in Guam, he'll find an eight-by-ten glossy of himself on the post office wall. We'll leak some of the juicier tidbits to the press to turn up the heat on this joker. I want all of Jake Westlow's friends and fellow officers interviewed—haul them in here and make them know it's not funsie time. Drew, I need you to head up the manhunt."

"I'm sorry, sir." Cady held his palms out in front of him. "I've fulfilled my commitment—you got your *loose thread* to pull on, remember?"

"You know that was all bullshit to get you in the door," Jund protested. "You're not seriously going to bolt right now, as we're picking up a head full of steam?"

"Just as far and as fast as I can, sir. I've made some other plans."

"You have got to be shitting me."

"Believe it or not," Cady said, "I'm going fishing."

Chapter 29

Dennis Swann was in the process of committing suicide.

And it was turning out to be more time-consuming than he'd originally intended. It must be his work ethic right up to the very end that kept him from pulling the trigger. He sat at his laptop and retested the code, smiled, encrypted the compiled files, zipped it, pecked out a page full of paragraphs to his IT contact at St. Mary's Hospital in Richmond, Virginia, and clicked Send. Swann then forwarded the e-mail on to the project manager and her team of Oracle programmers, as well as the two physicians whose extraordinary vision had brought the project into existence in the first place. He was taking no chances, as any future bug testing would be completed sans Dennis Swann.

Swann's deliverable had been placed into Production late Saturday evening. His piece of the pie, the EDI code, worked swimmingly in the Test environment—in fact, the four databases interfaced seamlessly. But Swann didn't want to leave the gang high and dry at this juncture. The proof's in the Production environment, and he'd spent half the morning chasing a handful of minor bugs the end users had reported.

He could now resume killing himself.

Swann had already been compensated, and compensated quite

highly at that, for his consulting services. This final tidying up was strictly pro bono, more or less a matter of personal integrity on his part. So he told himself, anyway. His IT contact and the project manager wanted Swann to roll over to the next phase. They actually wanted him in a salaried rather than consulting role. Swann explained that he'd give that a great deal of serious thought, but first he needed to take two weeks in order to help move his sister's family from Austin, Texas, to Seattle, Washington. St. Mary's requested that Swann contact them as soon as he was back in town. That, of course, wouldn't be happening. For one thing, Swann had no sister, he wasn't from Austin, Texas, and he would never be contacting anyone from St. Mary's staff ever again.

Dying wouldn't be terribly hard on Dennis Swann. Second time's a charm, they say, and Dennis Jackson Swann had originally died thirty-odd years back of early childhood meningitis. A tombstone in a forgotten cemetery outside of Austin attested to that fact.

Swann took off his small round glasses and slowly bent the frames in half at the nose piece as he worked his way through his mental check list. His apartment was for all practical purposes empty. He'd sold off the few pieces of furniture he'd owned, as well as the television, and then Goodwilled most everything else. His work responsibilities had, of course, just been concluded. Swann had spent much of the previous day juggling the financial accounts. He looked at the warped glasses in his hands and then tossed them into the small garbage bag he'd be taking with him. The devil was in the details, but Swann was fairly certain he'd covered everything.

Dennis Swann snapped his laptop shut and tossed it inside its carrying case. He stuffed the plastic sack of throwaways inside his traveling bag, grabbed the bag and the laptop case and stood for a second by his door. As he left Dennis Swann to die, Lieutenant Commander Jake Westlow exited the little-utilized side entrance of his efficiency apartment and stepped out into the night.

The lieutenant commander hoped that Special Agent Drew Cady wouldn't get too upset with him over what he'd left behind in the freezer.

Book Three

♛

Endgame

Chapter 30

Five Weeks Ago

"Papa!" Lucy's scream intensified as the bald muscleman grabbed a fistful of her brown hair and forced her to her knees.

Hartzell took a step toward Lucy, toward killing the brute who'd somehow weaseled past the first-floor guards and broken into their condominium and was now accosting his daughter. He made two long strides, his heart pounding with rage, when an arm from out of nowhere tightened across his chest and some kind of straight-edge razor bit into his Adam's apple. He'd not sensed another's presence in the room, and now some damned ghost had snared him in a lethal grip. Hartzell's adrenaline deflated like a punctured tire.

"Papa?" Lucy said softly, staring up at him, terrified, a fist of granite with veins like power cords stemming up from her mop of curls. Light from the antique floor lamp glared off the brute's bald head and a tight gray t-shirt magnified muscles sculpted atop muscles. It appeared to Hartzell that this thug assaulting Lucy was in the early stages of reverse evolution—regressing back into an ape.

Hartzell heard footsteps and squinted across the living room, ever wary of the blade against his neck. A lone figure juggled an appropriated green apple as he stepped out from the kitchen and paced slowly along the window wall, his features hidden in the evening shadows. He took a bite, stared out across the Hudson for several seconds, then turned around and looked at the trapped Hartzells.

"Made it, Ma!" The figure stood silhouetted against the city lights. "Top of the world!"

"Cagney in *White Heat*," the bald ape man replied.

"A classic from the Golden Age," the figure said in a now laid-back, almost sedate voice. "I knew you'd tag it, Nick."

"Take whatever you want," Hartzell said against the knife at his throat, attempting to sound calm, in control. He thought fast, and foremost amongst Hartzell's fast thoughts had something to do with chickens coming home to roost. "There's no reason for anyone to get hurt."

The silhouette took another bite of the apple, chewed, and swallowed. "Actually, Mr. Hartzell, there are a hundred million reasons for someone to get hurt."

"You really stuck your dick in it, Hartzell," the ape man announced.

"No need for such language, St. Nick." Approaching Hartzell, the silhouette eased into the light—jet-black hair in a gray suit, medium height and wiry. Hartzell tagged him at mid-thirties. "There's a *pretty lady* present."

"Crenna?" Hartzell said. He'd received a hundred million dollar transfusion from Crenna Senior's AlPenny Group, which he'd been using to Ponzi out payments while converting his straight assets to currency and diverting those funds to numbered bank accounts in Switzerland, the Grand Caymans, and various other ports of call across the Caribbean. The Quarterly Reports had gone out early last week. He and Lucy were scheduled to jump aboard the Heathrow flight this Friday.

"Let's just say we received your materials and kicked it to some *accountants* that do certain work for us." The man doing all the talking began shaking his head. "I get this late-night phone call pulling

me out of bed. It's pretty frantic, so I double-time it into the city...
and they hand me a copy of this *fiction* of yours and—this'll absolutely slay you—guess what one of the number-crunchers hand
wrote across the cover page?"

Hartzell remained silent.

"They wrote 'WTF' right across the top." The talker tilted his
head toward Lucy. "I apologize for using such lowbrow language,
pretty lady, but I think we all know what 'WTF' stands for. You see
these bean counters are serious gents. They go over the prospectuses
with magnifying glasses, they read the fine print of every mutual
fund invested in, they do some kind of quantitative analysis that I
couldn't even begin to explain. And this report of yours, Mr. Hartzell, gave these serious gents a serious bug up their asses. And the next
thing I know, St. Nick and I and...well," he gestured at the ghost
anchoring Hartzell in place, "best for all involved if you're never
formally introduced to our *All-Star* employee, but damned if the
three of us aren't on the next flight to the Big Apple—and they didn't
spring for first class, so forgive me if I don't appear to be in the best
of moods. Anyway, Mr. Hartzell, I'm standing here before you now
to ask in person—WTF—what the fuck?!"

Hartzell talked slowly, intently aware that a sharp piece of steel
was at his throat. This had to be handled delicately. "I apologize if
your accountants noted an *error*. I'm more than willing to sit down
with your people and go over the investments line by line. But, quite
frankly," Hartzell glanced at Lucy pinned to the floor, tears sliding
down her colorless face, and continued, "I think we're beyond that.
Please allow me to return your original investment funds in their
entirety."

"Who is this dildo?" the ape man questioned. "Some fuckin'
maitre d' trying to placate me after the waitress spilled chili sauce
down my shirt?"

"Of course we're going to get *our* original investment funds back in their entirety. That's a no-brainer. But, *quite frankly*, Mr. Hartzell, I don't think you fully appreciate the *gravity* of your situation." The talker backed toward the kitchen, out of the way, and then spoke to the steroid called St. Nick. "Toss the pretty lady through the window."

"Grrflll," Hartzell said as the razor took another bite of his Adam's apple, the iron clamp across his chest pulling him backwards, up and off balance.

"That's fuckin' tempered glass, it's four times a car window," the ape man protested. "You remember Grand Plaza last year? Enstead? Took six tosses. That fuckin' banker was brain dead by the time he broke through—so he couldn't appreciate the nosedive. Tore my goddamned rotator cuff, had to see an orthopedic."

"Come on, Nick. I told you to watch the language."

"What the hell do you care? Bitch'll be splat in a minute."

"The pretty lady doesn't need the last seconds of her life to be littered with F-bombs. And I remember Enstead, but he was bigger than me, about a buck-ninety. The pretty lady is what, about one-ten dripping wet?"

"Papa!" Lucy's normally rosy face had albinoed. Her eyes wide open in panic as she tried to twist and squirm, a fish on a line. "Papa—"

The ape man called St. Nick yanked Lucy up by her hair roots, grabbed a fistful of belt buckle and skin, lifted her over his head and flung her at the wall-to-ceiling window. Lucy hurtled fifteen feet through the air, floundering ineffectively, managed to get her right arm up in front of her face but slammed hard, forehead smacking glass with a sickening thud, then a ragdoll plummet to the hardwood floor. The brutality took all of two seconds. Lucy lay in a limp pile on the floor, shoulders shuddering, one hand clutching her hairline, blood and snot pouring from her nose.

"If you hurt Lucy again," Hartzell spoke, no longer concerned about the probing knife tip, "you can kiss your hundred million goodbye. You lowlifes and Crenna can then go fuck yourselves."

"You don't know St. Nick very well, Mr. Hartzell. He has a rather unique expertise. You see, Nick pulls at things—pulls away at them with his bare hands—until they come off. In fact, before he gets started, you'll have to recommend a late-night diner because I'm a bit squeamish and can't watch. Last time I saw Nick in action, I couldn't sleep for a week. After your pinky finger comes off, Mr. Hartzell, I doubt you'll even remember you had a daughter." The talker motioned to St. Nick. "Give the pretty lady another toss. Let's break some glass this time."

The ape man walked over, grabbed another fistful of Lucy's hair, and dragged the dazed girl back across the floor.

"You bastards don't know me very well," Hartzell responded. "I'll chew my tongue off before you get the time of day out of me. You'll have a hundred years of shaking down pimps to recoup your losses."

"Shaking down pimps?" The talker laughed. "You've seen too much TV. But you've got me intrigued, Mr. Hartzell. I might stick around when old St. Nick applies his trade to see how that age-old paradox plays itself out. See what occurs when an unstoppable force meets an immovable object."

St. Nick lifted Lucy over his head.

"We never had the *intent*," Hartzell said quickly. "We didn't know who you were, so the intent—the mental desire to specifically screw *you* over—wasn't there. You understand that, right?"

The talker held up a hand, stopping the ape man from pitching Lucy Hartzell a second time. "Go on."

"Unlike what you're forced to *deal* with in *your* business—the Ensteads who knowingly screw you over—we had no idea. The intent was not there. That's an essential pillar in criminal law. Intent.

We didn't know about Crenna, and from everything I could tell, The AlPenny Group was squeaky clean."

"It had better be. The funds came out of the washer and were looking for a safe haven in these trying times. Paul made a tremendous case for going with your firm. After all, you had to be somebody or know somebody to be allowed to invest with the *great* Drake Hartzell. Nice work, by the way, if you can get it…but what we got instead was a Bernie Madoff with a better tan."

"There was no intent. Clearly, I don't run around in your circles. I had no clue who I was dealing with. Jesus, is Crenna even an Italian name?"

"It's Italian—that actor Richard Crenna was Italian."

"But I didn't know about Paul's father—what should I call him—Don Crenna?"

"Don Crenna." The talker laughed again. "No, Mr. Hartzell. You've pissed off the man behind Crenna."

"I hate to interrupt you two nattering hens, but the bitch is getting heavy. What do you want me to do?"

The talker looked at Hartzell. "Do you fully appreciate the gravity of your situation?"

Hartzell nodded his head.

"Put the pretty lady down, St. Nick. Very gently."

"What do you need from me?"

"For your daughter's sake, we want our money back with an appropriate amount of interest. I'm thinking twenty-five percent interest. That's non-negotiable."

Hartzell nodded. "What else?"

"You've got a great racket going on here. Once the bean counters figured out what you were doing, and talked it over with the boss, he became exceptionally curious. It's an avenue we've not explored. We'd like to know all about you, Mr. Hartzell. That's all. For the time being, consider your firm a wholly-owned subsidiary of The AlPenny Group."

Chapter 31

"But Minnesota?" Assistant Director Jund squinted from Cady to Agents Preston and Schommer, both of whom had been sitting quietly at the room's circular office table as the AD and the consulting agent lobbed volleys back and forth. "Help me out here, Liz."

"You broke the case, Drew, and the momentum is now on our side," Agent Preston said. "Don't you would want to see this through to the end?"

"Again, there's not much I can offer you at this point. Plaster his name and photo all over the media. He won't look like that anymore, obviously, but it'll put him in motion—smoke him out—and maybe you'll get lucky." Cady sat alone on the black office couch in the back of Jund's office. "I imagine Westlow's been living on the East Coast this entire time, although he's probably not into home ownership. An apartment or a shack somewhere that he can pick up and leave at a moment's notice. Probably a desolate part of whatever city he's nesting in, perhaps a warehouse district or someplace where the neighbors know better than to get nosy."

"Thanks," Jund said and leaned back in his chair. "I'll get right on the roadblocks."

Suddenly a commotion in the AD's outer office, a truncated

verbalization by Penny Decker, Jund's executive admin, and then the door burst open.

Senator Arlen Farris towered in the doorframe like a mother grizzly whose cub had just been kicked in the ass by a suicidal boy scout. A harried Decker peeked in around the side.

"Senator Farris," Jund said.

"My boy was a victim of the Chessman," the senator from Delaware said slowly, a gravelly focus on each and every syllable. "I'll not have you drag his name through the shit and the piss, Jund."

"I have no idea what you're talking about."

"Then you're a goddamned liar!" Farris lumbered past the female agents at the side table, ignoring them completely, leaned over the assistant director's desk and got in Jund's face. "You were in a tree house circle-jerking to *Playboy* when I came to this city. Thirty-five fucking years I've been here! So if someone farts twice, I damn sure hear about it."

"Now there's an ad for term limits if I ever heard one," Cady said, surprised by his own insolence. This was the second time he'd seen the senator without his *Aw-Shucks* mask on, the persona Farris used for public consumption, to get out the vote. The first glimpse had been that night in the hospital. At the time Cady had attributed it to a twisted sense grief over the death of his only son. Now he knew better.

The senator's head swiveled sideways, noticed Cady sitting in the back of the room for the first time, shot him a near-lethal glare, and then turned his attention back to Jund.

"I thought the *motherfucker* who got my boy killed had his incompetent ass tossed out of the FBI, Jund." Farris flung an arm in Cady's direction. "Is this the prick ripping off scabs, wasting time tying Patrick to those Zalentine wackjobs instead of figuring out who killed Ken Gottlieb?"

"If you had been straight with me from the get-go," Cady responded, "your son might still be alive."

Cady stood up as Farris marched toward him.

"How've you been, Master Fuck Up?" Farris said, poking Cady in the chest with his index finger. Hard. Repeatedly. "If I can't get you shit-canned, I'll have you in Alaska working out of a goddamned igloo this time next week."

"Don't touch me again," Cady replied, taking a step into the senator's proximity. "And if you'd come clean about Snow Goose—instead of burying it—none of this would ever have happened."

Farris's face burned deep red. Cady saw a heartbeat in the senator's temples.

"Patrick wasn't there, you one-trick-pony asshole." The finger poking began anew. "And I don't give two shits about what happened to that Goose Lake whore—"

Cady caught the senator's finger in mid-jab and twisted it upwards, forcing Farris to his knees.

"I told you not to touch me again," Cady said and spun his wrist, popping the senator's forefinger out of joint, leaving it pointing sideways and back toward the assistant director.

Farris, his face now white, cupped his shaking right hand with his left and slowly rose to his feet.

"You just fucked the pooch, Cady. You're done," Farris said in a notch above a whisper. He looked to Jund. "You're both through."

"Why ever would you attack *Citizen* Cady, Senator?" Agent Preston asked, tremor-voiced, while a visibly stunned Agent Schommer sat motionless next to her.

"Yes, Senator," Jund said, looking pink about the gills. "Why would you force Citizen Cady to defend himself in front of my staff?"

The assistant director and the senior senator from Delaware held each other's gaze. Cady wasn't certain if it was a trick of the light, but the look on the AD's face was indeed reminiscent of Stan Laurel.

"This isn't over," Farris said. "Not by a long shot."

"I suspect not."

Still cradling his disjointed finger, the senator strode out of the assistant director's office.

"I know I'm new to this office," Agent Schommer said after what seemed an eternity, "but does this happen often?"

Chapter 32

Two Weeks Ago

"Every time the door buzzes, I expect the Manhattan Prosecutor," Hartzell said. "What the bloody hell good am I to you in an orange jumpsuit?"

"You're not going to wind up in any orange jumpsuit, Drake." The man with the jet-black hair, who had yet to offer Hartzell his given name, sat at Hartzell's dining room table drinking Hartzell's Kopi Luwak blend.

Hartzell was red-faced. "The president's handpicked arse kicker is about to be the next Chairman of the SEC—the new marshal sent to clean up Dodge City—and some dime store market analyst in Boston is chomping at my ankles, but, hey…*no worries, dude.*"

"Look, Drake, you've made your fears abundantly clear these past weeks. Let me assure you that everything is under control. We've got eyes and ears in high places, my friend. High places. At the first hint that anything's coming down the pike, you and Lucy will get your *various* passports back and can hit the highway. I can even get the two of you into Canada with no record of it—if you'd like."

On the night that Hartzell's world had been flipped upside down, the men from Chicago had ransacked his condominium as though panning for gold. In short order they'd found the wall safe—hidden under the wet bar sink, behind a shelf of his hundred-year-old cognac. Hartzell had opened the safe immediately so as not to invoke the ape man's further mistreatment of his daughter. The two thugs—as the phantom that had held the razor against Hartzell's carotid artery instantly disappeared—cackled in delight at the hundred thousand dollars in stacks of hundred dollar bills and looked like they'd won the lottery when they opened the brown envelopes containing both Hartzell's and Lucy's authentic passports, as well as the forgeries from his man in Manila.

"Eyes and ears in high places? What's that mean?"

"Believe me, Drake, that's nothing you want to know." The man took another sip of the Kopi Luwak and shrugged his shoulders. "This is the best coffee I've ever had. Bar none. Even the knowledge that the beans pass through that critter's asshole doesn't diminish the taste."

"That *critter* is an Asian Palm Civet, about the size of a house cat. It eats the coffee berries, but the beans pass through its digestive track undigested," Hartzell responded. "The enzymes in the civet's stomach are what give the coffee its bitterness."

"Whether it's gaming the stock market or rodents shitting coffee beans, I learn something from you every day." The man set down his coffee mug. "Look, Drake, you've got to trust me on this and continue to do your job. We're not about to let anything happen to you. Hell—you're our cash cow. We love you."

Hartzell's job of the past two plus weeks was to train a couple of money-laundering accountants from Chicago on the ins and outs of every aspect of his operation, walk them specifically through the inside dope on the financial investment scheme he'd been running these many years. Show the bean counters the dos and don'ts, the tips and tricks, his best practices. In return, Hartzell and Lucy were promised, first and foremost, survival, and, after a bit more squeezing and bleeding of Hartzell's considerable nest egg, the father and daughter duo would eventually be allowed to fade into the woodwork, debt to Chicago paid in full.

The two green eyeshades had been introduced to Hartzell, with a few chuckles from the no-named guest who was now running his life, as Smith and Jones. Smith and Jones stayed in his guest room, shared meals with him, came to work with him and, in other words, were on Hartzell like a fourth layer of skin. The three made the best of a bad situation and the two bean counters were plainly in awe of what Hartzell had accomplished.

"Just think of me as the Coordinator," the talking man with no name had told Hartzell that night of their arrival. Now, he stopped by every day or two, like today, and had a private chat with Hartzell, made sure all the gears were properly lubricated and that everything was running friction free. The Hartzells had been informed at the end of that first night that St. Nick's project would be Lucy. That sometimes the pretty lady would see St. Nick, perhaps on a street corner or by the escalator at, say, Macy's, or in the hallway at Juilliard. And although he'd always be around, most of the time she wouldn't spot him. And as long as Lucy's father played ball, St. Nick would never lay a hand on her. As for the phantom with the razor, Hartzell would never see him again unless Hartzell did something to *displease* the Coordinator, and then it'd be the last time Hartzell would ever see the phantom…or anything else, for that matter.

As for Lucy on that night of utter bleakness, St. Nick's demeanor had turned on a dime from arch tormentor to that of a clinging nursemaid. He'd gotten an ice pack for her forehead and mouth, made a quick call from his cell phone, and ten minutes later a short man with raccoon eyes and a doctor's bag right out of a late 1950s *Naked City* episode was buzzed up to their high-rise unit. Raccoon Eyes shined a light in Lucy's eyes for a minute, checked and cleaned her other wounds and bruises, gave her enough Vicodin for five days, told her to get a lot of rest and that even though there'd be pain for several days, as if she'd been bumped about in a car accident, there was nothing life-threatening or permanent. She'd be fine in a week.

Hartzell bent heaven and earth to return The AlPenny Group's original investment in its entirety, along with the strongly advised twenty-five mil in interest—a *shenanigans'* fee, per the unnamed Coordinator sitting at Hartzell's dining room table and reading the *New York Times* as if he owned the place. And, quite literally, The AlPenny Group did indeed now own Hartzell's Manhattan condo. That sale had closed at the beginning of week two; they got it at a steal. The deed for Andrew Pierson's Tuscany villa and vineyard had been transferred earlier this week. The Coordinator had been the perfect gentleman since the incident between Lucy and the tempered glass, but certain *requests* for additional nourishment with which to feed the insatiable beast were periodically delivered with a sly smile indicating that there'd be no negotiations. All closing transactions had gone smoothly—that is, except for the seller's remorse on Hartzell's part—largely due to the fact that no actual funds had changed hands.

So Hartzell fought a rear-guard strategy, relinquishing the Tuscany assets as that property had already been tainted by the Chicagoans' knowledge of his forged Pierson passport. Uncle Sam would have eventually seized Hartzell's Manhattan throne in any case, so losing it wasn't that bitter a pill for him to swallow. In fact, his unnamed companion, currently perusing the Sports section, had informed him that Hartzell morally and psychologically owed the penthouse apartment to Young Master Crenna, as it would help the kid get past his deep *heartache* over Lucy's betrayal. *The kid must have had one hell of a broken heart,* Hartzell thought as he signed off on the paperwork in triplicate.

Hartzell grumbled loudly, mostly for the benefit of Smith and Jones, over every shiny bauble he was forced to relinquish to the hungry Chicago swine, doing his damndest to make the trio believe the shakedown had done infinitely more than scratch the surface of the Drake Hartzell Empire. However, inroads with the Coordinator were all dead ends, as the more Hartzell groused about his losses the more the Coordinator would grin sheepishly and shake his head. The Coordinator wasn't buying it.

It became apparent to Hartzell early on that Smith and Jones—Vince and David, as they eventually shared their possibly authentic first names with him over breakfast bagels, what with living with him and all—weren't merely mining his great knowledge of the financial markets, but also attempting to gauge how big a stack of gold old King Drake was perched upon. Hartzell felt like Penelope staving off the suitors in Homer's *Odyssey*. Only in his case he didn't undo the weave of a burial shroud each night, but rather used every sleight of hand in his arsenal to convince his particular *suitors* that more—much more—had been paid out to investors over the years and that he truly was a softy when it came to charity, with a great deal of currency being distributed to a wide-ranging list of worthwhile causes.

And it was in filtering through his past charity work that Hartzell came across the name of that endlessly ravenous beast in Chicago, the man behind the curtain. He remembered Boy Crenna mentioning something about his dear cancer-surviving auntie, whom Hartzell may or may not have met at that now regrettable event he'd attended in the Windy City a few years back. Boy Crenna had referenced her as "Aunt Nora." Amazing what a person could find on Google, right at your fingertips, truly an information superhighway. Hartzell was quickly able to find a most pleasant puff piece on the cancer event that night at the Belden Stratford. There was only one woman on the planning board for that fundraiser named Nora: Nora Fiorella.

Hartzell next Googled Nora Fiorella's name crossed with breast cancer awareness. His Internet search resulted in numerous hits of both her and her husband as sponsors-slash-donors for a variety of cancer research and fundraising to-dos. Her last name sounded slightly familiar and, peering at her online picture in one of the articles, he had a vague recollection of not only meeting Mrs. Nora Fiorella that night but also pressing flesh with her stocky barrel-chest of a husband. Hartzell didn't recall the conversation from that evening and knew that on his end he would have mumbled the established template, perfected for such events, with a twinkle in his eye and a smile on his lips and a heavy dose of ersatz empathy for the cause-du-jour.

In fact, something about the Fiorella name had sounded hazily familiar at the time of the event, even though he'd not done any work directly with Boy Crenna's dear auntie. Hartzell recalled pausing during the introductions, sifting through his memory as though trying to summon up the name of a forgotten stage actor or long-retired senator. The moment had been fleeting and then Hartzell moved on to meet and greet the next set of deep pockets with his prefab template.

With mounting trepidation Hartzell cut and pasted the husband's name into the search engine and smacked the Enter key. Crenna Sr. was a front, the Coordinator had admitted as much. Within five minutes of reading articles from his search results Hartzell discovered the true depth of what he was up against, and he now had a face as well as the identity of the starving creature he'd been feeding his assets to these past few weeks.

Duilio "Leo" Fiorella.

There wasn't much meat in any of the Googled newspaper articles, but there were enough "alleged" this and "flimsy indictment" that and a federal witness's testimony "recanted" over there and another "missing" witness here for Hartzell to read between the lines. What Hartzell found there sent a chill through to his bone marrow. One *Sun-Times* article provided great insight into a *civil rights* PR group that Duilio Fiorella had created to specifically apply pressure via political coercion, slap lawsuits, or in some cases even transporting a parade of union goons to picket and intimidate the offending party whenever anything besmirching regarding the Fiorella family appeared in the local media. All under the politically correct guise of these minor slights being *discriminatory* or *anti-Italian* in nature.

Brilliant, Hartzell thought; Duilio "Leo" Fiorella was one cagey son of a bitch, likely a job necessity if one was seeking to direct organized crime in the most corrupt city in the nation. No wonder Boy Crenna was so cocksure of himself. It worked wonders for your self-esteem if your uncle happened to oversee the Midwest branch of La Cosa Nostra. Evidently, the Mack truck known as St. Nick had been dead right—Hartzell had really stuck his dick in it.

Hartzell didn't trust the phones at home or in his office anymore, figured the lines were tapped and frankly assumed everything he said above the lowest of murmurs was heard by whatever technical miscreants the Coordinator had working New York with him. He also assumed they had some kind of tracking software on his computers, the kind that reveals anything typed, as well as monitoring incoming and outgoing e-mails. They were probably able to review his browsing history in real time, but Hartzell figured this minor Googling would indicate that he was not an oblivious dunce cap—in fact, it would be expected, and make them feel they had him exactly where they wanted, which the bastards did—but he spent another half hour surfing cricket scorecards in order to bore any observing hired guns stiff.

Children are often cautioned never to threaten animals, no

backing a raccoon into a corner or tossing a rock at a hornet's nest, which then forces the creatures to defend itself with everything in its god-given arsenal. Nothing good can come of that, children are warned. The same holds true for con men. Best to quickly fleece them or have them jailed and hopscotch down the boulevard. Caging Hartzell, forcing him to submit as though he were a *common thief*, stripping him, little by little, of the fruits of his labor not only rubbed against every fiber in Hartzell's soul, but gave him time to pause, and think, and get a mental second wind.

Remarkably, Lucy had been miles ahead of him in pursuing this line of thought. That very first morning after the Coordinator's arrival, she had the gumption and grit in her to head off to her morning Juilliard classes, more to get away from these demented freaks than concern over any missed assignments. So with her locks combed over the bandage covering half of her forehead, one arm wrapped in a sling, a medicated look about her eyes, and the bald Hercules as her shadow, she stopped to give Hartzell a long and soulful hug. They draped across each other a full minute so that even the Coordinator turned to stare out the window in order to give them a brief moment of privacy. Hartzell was dead on his feet, having spent a nerve-wracking night making *arrangements* with the nameless gentleman from Chicago who would be *coordinating* his life into the foreseeable future, but her hushed words pierced through his foreboding. "Turn the tables, Papa," Lucy had whispered, like a ghost in his ear that very first morning. "Turn the tables."

Blind with greed, that was Duilio "Leo" Fiorella's critical character flaw, Hartzell had calculated. Having much the same defect, he considered himself an expert in this arena. To keep with St. Nick's carnal metaphor, what if the tables could be turned and if, blinded by a burning greed, it was Duilio "Leo" Fiorella who had really stuck his dick in it?

Hartzell knew the Coordinator wouldn't budge one iota, but Vince and David, they were white collars from The AlPenny Group, that alchemist outfit charged with turning Fiorella's common metals—steel, iron, nickel, and platinum, tainted black by racketeering, drug-dealing, narcotics, gambling, prostitution and god knew what else—into legal gold. These two were guys that Hartzell could deal with, worm his way in, wine and dine them into giving him some wiggle room in which he could maneuver.

So Hartzell went on the charm offensive with a baker's dozen of specialties catered from H&H Bagels every a.m. to be washed down with the Coordinator's now-favorite coffee, Kopi Luwak—and for lunch, perhaps some French grub at Daniel or double-cut lamb rib chops at The Palm or, if you're in the mood, off to Gramercy Tavern for some fish croquette, and, in case they were feeling homesick, end the long day with a feast at Da Nico. He even scored box seats at the new Yankee Stadium for the trio to attend an evening ball game—and all on Hartzell's dime. He enthusiastically answered all of their questions, even the awkward admissions of his fraudulent activities, with about seventy-five percent truthfulness, a high-water mark for Hartzell.

By the beginning of the second week, the three were best mates, three blokes in pretty much the same line of work sharing secrets between shits and grins. Hartzell would become energized in explaining to them in detail the twists and turns of the scams he'd perpetrated and who he'd stung. And for how much. The three would laugh endlessly about Hartzell's genius tax evasions, accounting frauds, equity leveraging, layers of fees amassed at every level, capital kiting, and the psychological profiling of his rich victims.

Hartzell set them up behind the solid African mahogany table in the large conference room on the thirtieth floor of his Park Avenue office building, Hartzell Investment, Inc.—an expensive front that filled his wealthy clients with an aura of Hartzell's gravitas as they rushed to open their checkbooks for him. He gave Vince and David a tour of the building, buying them café lattes at the kiosk on the second floor lobby, and showed them the best nooks and crannies in which to inconspicuously people watch. He told the two how he'd determined the times when some of the office building's knockouts in skirts came to the kiosk to refuel, which Hartzell had truly done for his own amusement some time back.

So by the middle of the second week, when he pointed two fingers at the accountants and asked, "Normal and extra leaded?" to their nods of approval, he was able to disappear for twenty minutes. Of course it would only take a determined fellow ten minutes to grab three cups of java at the coffee kiosk and return, but, in Hartzell's case, he grabbed Stephanie's cell phone from the top of her purse on his way out, raised a finger to his lips to hush her and shake his head as he pointed back down the hallway and grinned mischievously, and slipped out to the elevator bank. Stephanie, his front desk receptionist, had been surprised by the two visitors, who had soon become regular fixtures at the firm. Although Steph knew nothing of Hartzell's financial scam, she knew him to be a private person and performed her assigned tasks, for which she was highly compensated, with committed discretion. Hartzell didn't know if they'd done anything to his cell phone, but he knew there were ways in which his cell phone signal could be monitored. Even in the days B.C.—Before the Coordinator—Hartzell only utilized clean phones, unconnected to him, to make certain calls.

Hartzell took the elevator down two floors, making sure to press Lobby and a handful of other stops as he stepped off onto the lower floor. He swiveled his head left and right as he crossed the elevator bank, turned a corner, and quickly stepped inside the stairwell. He leaned his back against the door, shut his eyes, and counted slowly to sixty, listening for any suspicious noises or accompanying footsteps. He started swiftly down the stairs, taking them two at a time, while flipping open Stephanie's cell phone. Speaking in the stairwell was nothing new to Hartzell, as he'd moved mountains in the privacy of the stairwell over the years on throwaway phones in conversations that would be meaningless to any potential eavesdroppers.

He hurried down the staircase, making all sorts of blusterous phone noises—scoring additional box seats for yet another Yankees game for his visitors and himself to attend. When that call ended, he came to a sudden halt and listened in silence for another sixty seconds. Hartzell didn't sweat the two accountants reviewing spreadsheets in his conference room several flights above; he knew those two would have to be directed to where the staircases were situated in case of an inferno. Instead, Hartzell's excessive caution was due to that unknown third man, the goddamned phantom who had come out of nowhere and caught Hartzell in a death grip that first night. That was who Hartzell feared most, Fiorella's number-one weapon. Assuaged of his concern that Fiorella's trained killer had omnipotently hidden inside a potted plant on the floor Hartzell had randomly chosen to depart on and then transmutated into the east staircase as a dust bunny, Hartzell punched in a number he'd long ago memorized and spoke in a quiet tone for no longer than sixty seconds. Twelve minutes later, Hartzell returned to his office with three hot coffees and drank his cup while bullshitting with the bean counters.

By the end of the second week, he dropped down to the twentieth floor, to the office of a patent law firm where both senior partners had hefty investments with Hartzell's firm, gave them a song and dance about changing computer systems and asked if they had a PC for him to use to log in to his Internet e-mail for a few minutes now and again until the IT gents buggered off. After a quick *No Problemo* and *Anytime, Drake,* they let Hartzell utilize a computer in a private conference room. Hartzell made a mental note to send both partners a handful of tickets to a comic musical that was soon to open at the Bernard B. Jacobs Theatre for them and their wives, or mistresses, to attend.

Five minutes here and there with a clean phone or unmonitored PC, away from any prying green eyeshades, was all Hartzell needed to set events in motion. He had new passports to obtain, numbered accounts to shift, tables to turn, and one last mountain to move— and this particular Everest Hartzell was planning to move straight up one Duilio "Leo" Fiorella's ass.

The bastards should never have touched Lucy.

Chapter 33

"Are you sure you can walk away?"

"It could take months to find him, Terri. Westlow planned for this day, so he'll have a change of ID and looks. In the end, he'll be burned by a friend or an astute motel clerk."

The two were in a couple of bench chairs at their boarding gate at Ronald Reagan National, sucking down Starbucks and waiting for the mid-afternoon flight into Minneapolis.

"I'm torn."

"What do you mean?" Cady asked.

"After looking through Dorsey's photo albums, and knowing how her daughter's death shattered that sweet, wonderful woman's life, and how the Chessman's victims were complicit in Marly's murder. I'm torn."

"Is this the same girl I met in Cohasset? The one screaming for justice?"

"It's not black and white anymore."

"It never is."

"The only reason I want him caught, Drew, is for what he did to you."

"The man methodically plotted and carried out a string of murders, including the assassination of a sitting congressman."

"We both know Patrick Farris was at the lake that night, right there in the thick of things."

"Look at what Westlow did to the secondaries, Terri, the victims not directly responsible for Marly's death. Barrett Sanfield was stabbed in the heart over his part in the cover-up, right up close and personal. Bret was the patsy they sucked in for concealment, but he didn't deserve to be burned alive."

"They used to hang horse thieves. Bret and the lawyer were involved in something a bit more than snatching a pony."

"They used to do a lot of things, Terri, but what about Dane Schaeffer? The kid threw a party, a stupid drunken bash at the family lake home. Did that merit the death penalty? When Schaeffer heard Marly was missing, he jumped in a boat and took off searching for her. Yet Westlow killed him just the same, drowned the young man—again, up close and personal." Cady shrugged. "I guess what I'm getting at is that Jake Westlow's not some modern-day knight-errant on a quest to save the kingdom."

"He's not the one I've been thinking of as a modern-day knight-errant on a quest to save the kingdom."

Cady shook his head. "Right."

A cell phone buzzed. Terri dug through her purse and flicked it on.

"This is Terri."

Cady had decided to build a career out of gawking at Terri; he studied her profile as she answered the call. He watched her mouth suddenly drop, the humor fall from her eyes as she held the cell phone toward him.

"What?"

"I think it's him," Terri said slowly. "And he wants to talk to you."

Cady took the phone and held it to his ear. "This is Cady."

"Did Simon say you could jump on a plane?"

Cady recognized the voice of his late-night hotel visitor and was already on his feet, spinning three hundred and sixty degrees in the pre-boarding area, scanning the faces of all male passengers, searching for anyone with a phone to their ear.

"How'd you get this number, you son of a bitch?"

Cady stepped out into the walkway, sweeping dozens of faces in the two neighboring wait areas. Traffic was thick; a recent flight had deplaned. Cady's head swiveled left to right and back again as he filtered men of Westlow's height. He began walking toward the terminal, assuming the Chessman wouldn't allow himself to get caged in at the far-away gates.

"It's one of the contact numbers listed on Sundown Point's web site. I thought I might need a rental cabin."

"You leave Terri the hell out of this," Cady spoke into the phone as if it were a separate being. "You understand me?"

"You're calling her *Terri* now?"

"She gets one prank call, Westlow, or a car drives by her place she doesn't recognize and you'll spend each day finding a new rock to sleep under because I'll never stop looking for you. Never."

"Understood."

"Good. Any chance of telling me where you're calling from?"

"Was your Café Au Lait as weak as mine?"

Cady felt ill. Had the bastard actually been in line with them? He began to jog, sweeping faces and heights, looking for men over six feet tall, men holding cell phones or wearing earpieces, perhaps with a cup of Starbucks in tow.

"I was disappointed. I mean I can make lousy coffee at home for practically free, but I suppose they've got a captive market here."

Cady neared the security lines. Westlow had either passed through security or had merely followed them to the airport and was now trying to get in his mind.

"So where do you call home these days, Westlow?"

"Thanks to you, Agent Cady, I find myself out on the streets. Truly homeless."

"Good to hear, but you can cut the Agent Cady crap. I'm no longer working with the bureau."

"Oh my—I'm afraid that won't do. Not yet, anyway."

"What?" Cady's voice dripped sarcasm. "Now I'm working for you?"

"I wouldn't say that, but what with the FBI being *compromised* in the Gottlieb investigation, I suppose others might phrase it that way."

"Compromised," Cady replied. "Bullshit."

"Did I catch you at a bad time, Agent Cady? I sense hostility."

Cady gave up scanning the hordes of travelers. The Chessman could be three restrooms away, in the airport parking lot, or ten miles down the road. He turned to information gathering mode.

"If Gottlieb's not on you, then why do you care? Why come out of the woodwork?"

"I'm being framed to steer you in the wrong direction."

"We'd have seen through the copycat, Westlow. You know that. So I'm curious, why tip your cards? Now we know for fact you're in the weeds."

"The night at the hotel—you were well on the way to that conclusion."

"I could have pressed a case, but there would always be lingering doubt and no small amount of disbelief. But you've removed all uncertainty. That's not only a poor chess move, it's a blunder. And you don't blunder, so again—why do you care?"

Silence ensued.

"For Christ's sake, Westlow, Marly's been in the grave for thirteen years," Cady said, hoping to pinch a nerve. "That's a mighty long stretch to keep at this."

More silence ensued. Cady slowed his pace, his focus now on the phone and not the endless parade of air travelers.

"You still there, Westlow?"

"Love doesn't carry an expiration date, Agent Cady…as though it were a carton of milk."

Cady stepped out of the flowing traffic to chew that one over. He wasn't sure what to think and next went after the red flag Westlow had raised.

"Why do you say the FBI is compromised?"

"Have you got a pen?"

"Yes."

"You need to take down an address."

Cady scribbled on the palm of his hand. He began to ask Westlow about the address, but received a dial tone in response.

Cady walked back to his boarding gate. Terri stood waiting for him. Passengers had begun boarding the airliner.

The two stared at each other for several seconds.

"I know," Terri said finally. "Go get him, Galahad."

Cady smiled dryly, without amusement. "Good one."

Chapter 34

One Week Ago

"My God—you killed them."

"I have no clue what you're rattling on about, Drake."

"Why Elaine Kellervick?" Hartzell's face had emptied of all color. Legs like rubber bands, he slumped into the dining room chair on the opposite end of the table from the Coordinator. "I had her stalled out. I'm sure you *listened in* on our phone call."

"Are we talking about the tragic victims of that serial killer again…the one they call the Chessman?"

Hartzell was exhausted, running on fumes since the news broke last week of C. Kenneth Gottlieb's assassination in his Georgetown domicile. They couldn't have, Hartzell thought, not even with all his whining about the soon-to-be SEC Chairman to this gangster sitting across the table from him. It was too insane to contemplate and would only buy them—what?—a month at best before the president installed a new pit bull. Then, as the story unfolded in the press, it appeared to have been done by a copycat of that killer who had terrorized the Eastern Seaboard some years earlier. Then came hints that the original Chessman had never died, had merely passed into remission, and that the authorities had been cuckolded with smoke and mirrors.

Hartzell had a discomforting chat with the Coordinator when he next checked in; a full day after the Gottlieb story exploded onto the headlines and became the primary sustenance of all the cable channels twenty-four-seven. After some awkward verbal fencing as Hartzell hemmed and hawed and tried to feel him out on the matter, the man from Chicago squinted at Hartzell in bewilderment.

"What are you driving at, Drake? You think I had Gottlieb killed?" The Coordinator slapped the table and began laughing hysterically. "That's rich. You're the one who's been bitching about the son of a bitch for weeks, not me. Maybe I should be asking where you were the other night."

After another round of cackling, the Coordinator informed Hartzell that, in his humble opinion, Gottlieb's death was a coincidence, an odd twist of fate, and that the Chessman in all likelihood deeply missed sponging up all of the bullshit media attention after his self-imposed sabbatical, and that he almost surely yearned to mark his reemergence with a tsunami-sized splash, and by killing Gottlieb who, as the soon-to-be SEC Chairman, had garnered a significant amount of air time on the alphabet channels in the past month, the Chessman would accomplish exactly that.

Yet Hartzell continued to lie awake at night, turning that notion over in his mind, dissecting it, holding it up to the light and looking at it from every possible angle. It did make a certain degree of sense; however, Hartzell knew that the Coordinator would want to give him something to hang his hat on in order for him to continue his *work* with their accountants. Hartzell also knew that his belly-aching about Gottlieb and the woman was meant to hurry Fiorella's extortion along, to force a timeframe, to create a light at the end of the tunnel before he'd been bled dry. On the surface, anyway. But below the surface, Hartzell had voiced those issues to the Coordinator so they would believe that these were the concerns that were first and foremost in Hartzell's mind. They would believe these to be the issues on which he spun his tires, so they would be looking off in one direction and never notice how he had placed the pea under a different shell.

The Coordinator was a skilled liar and an even better manipulator. No way the man was going to confess to having ordered a hit on a sitting SEC Commissioner in order to buy them more time to squeeze Hartzell. But killing Gottlieb and pinning it on the Chessman was so absurdly over the top as to be sheer madness. Of course, the flip side of madness is genius, and Hartzell knew Fiorella had some end goal in mind. Plus, Fiorella had a certain employee stealthy enough to make the unthinkable happen without so much as a single bark from a neighborhood dog. Hartzell kept thinking that there was something he was missing, something out of focus.

And so it went for Hartzell through sleepless night after sleepless night.

But now, the news of the Elaine Kellervick killing left no room for doubt.

"You're barking mad." Hartzell stared at the table and whispered, "You're all barking mad."

"Let me give you a little friendly advice in return for everything that you've done for us. One must be most careful in both words and deeds, Drake. From everything I've heard about the Chessman, he's one sharp thumbtack. Imagine if he lifted a little something from each of the crime scenes, some trinket or small piece of property that could easily be traced back to the victim. It could be most damning if these trinkets appeared at inopportune times in inopportune places. Yes, Drake," the Coordinator enunciated slowly in a hushed tone and penetrating stare that spoke volumes about the delicate balancing act necessary for survival, "one must be most careful in both words and deeds."

Chapter 35

Assistant Director Jund got a no-knock on the Richmond address that the Chessman had provided Cady. The apartment was rented to one Dennis Swann, but the picture from the Virginia DMV was certainly Jake Westlow—Cady could tell, even with the mid-length black hair and round John Lennon glasses. It was sure as hell Westlow.

The address proved to be a cheap and lonely efficiency, one of one that sat above a cut-rate furniture shop in a depressed and dusty business district on the city's ever-deteriorating north side. Cady understood immediately why Westlow chose to rent this place. First, the side entrance was inconspicuous; no one would assume an apartment was there to begin with. Second, although the businesses in this part of town appeared to be doing everything they could to eke out a meager living, everything shut down at five and the place was a ghost town by seven at night. Third, Westlow's main window and corner bathroom window covered both intersections. Fourth, Cady discovered that Westlow had jerry-rigged both windows to pop out at a moment's notice and there were no pesky screens to fiddle with were one in a hurry. Five, although invisible from the street, Cady could tell that Westlow had chipped out minor crevices in the brickwork above both windows. The pattern of the crevices would allow an athlete to rock climb to the rooftop of the furniture building in seconds. And once up on the second-story roof, he'd be a block away moments later.

All in all a nice hidey-hole, nondescript, secluded, with an excellent view of any potential outside activities...and an escape hatch.

The door to Westlow's most recent abode was new, must have been replaced, as it certainly didn't blend with the rest of the surroundings. With a galvanized steel frame over two inches thick, the twelve-gauge steel door included a six-point locking system plus latch with security bolts on the hinge side of the door. The security door had been a bitch for his team to breach, even with the hydraulic spreader-cutter—a bit overkill for your garden-variety crack head seeking plasma TVs and cheap jewelry to pawn off in order to afford the next fix. The security door had in all likelihood cost more than anything Westlow had stuffed away inside the dank and shabby efficiency.

In Westlow's world as Dennis Swann, Cady thought to himself, every second counted.

The apartment had been emptied of most furniture. A twin mattress with no coverings lay in front of the window. A card table and folding chair sat flush against the bathroom wall, above the room's only electrical outlet. Cady figured it served as both desk and dining table.

The only other two items that the federal agents discovered in the nearly vacant apartment were in the kitchen. An empty bottle of mustard sat by itself on the top rack of the refrigerator. In the ice box, however, the agents hit pay dirt.

A severed hand in a freezer bag.

"The prints off your frostbitten hand belong to a Marco Palma," Jund said in a voice above a whisper to Agents Cady and Preston, sitting in guest chairs across his desk. The door was closed. "After perusing young Palma's altogether riveting rap sheet, I made a call to an old friend in OCTF."

OCTF was the New York State Organized Crime Task Force.

"Turns out that Marco 'Polo' Palma is, or suffice it to say was, a sgarrista, that is, a suspected foot soldier for the capo de tutti capi—Fedele Moretti—the boss of all bosses in New York City. I think we've all heard of him."

"My God," Agent Preston said. "The Chessman is now killing members of the New York underground?"

"It appears that way. Although I do wonder where the rest of Palma wound up."

"We'll probably never know," Cady said. "But Westlow left the hand to tell us something."

"Tell us what?"

"Remember his warning about the FBI being compromised?"

"That's more of his smoke and mirrors, Agent Cady. Westlow wants us to chase our tails and give him time to make his next move."

"Maybe so. But he gave up Dennis Swann, turned in his own false identity because he wanted us to find *that hand*, identify it… and realize what we may be up against."

"That the Moretti family used a copycat to kill Gottlieb?" Preston asked. "What possible motive could they have?"

The three exchanged looks of confusion.

"Congrats, you two," the AD said. "I wish the signpost up ahead read *The Twilight Zone*; unfortunately, we've just crossed over into the city limits of clusterfuck. Turns out I will be greeting shoppers at The Home Depot after all."

"If the FBI has been instrumental in bringing down organized crime via infiltration," Cady said, "why wouldn't that concept work in reverse?"

Agent Preston agreed. "All it would take is one person with mid-level security clearance to find and feed data on a multitude of investigations."

"We've been pretty tight-lipped on this case from the get-go, more out of media concerns. And we've got to consider that it's more of Westlow's misdirection." Jund shrugged. "However, outside of the tech running the print, only the three of us know the identity of the victim in Westlow's apartment, and it's going to goddamn well stay that way until we can untangle this knot. Nothing leaves this room unless I say so. Understood?"

"Yes, sir," the special agents agreed.

Jund shrugged again. "I'll talk further with OCTF, gingerly pick their brains; see if they've heard any chatter or know what Moretti's been up to lately. If there are dots to be connected, they'll know about them."

"What about the phone, Agent Cady?"

"I'm keeping Terri's cell on me at all times in case Westlow calls again, but the trace back was a dead end. He used a throwaway."

"Westlow's been Dennis Swann for almost three years. That's an interesting development. Put everyone on Swann. There might be something there, something he left behind, that we can use to nail his ass."

Chapter 36

"Vince and David are on a red-eye to Chicago next Wednesday and they insist on taking us out to celebrate that evening. They've already made a dinner reservation for the lot of us at Seppi's."

"Pity to ruin Seppi's by dining with those swine," said Lucy.

"Best to sit back and eat to your heart's content on account of it being your last meal. Vince and Dave will hop a cab to the airport. I did them one last favor and upgraded their tickets to first class. Nice chaps, actually, and quite taken with me, but a tad despondent of late. I doubt they're in the know—after all, they're only the accountants—but they follow the news and I suspect they see what's coming."

"What's coming, Papa?"

"I imagine that you and I and St. Nick and the Coordinator will take a limo ride, chartered of course, for the night's celebration, only I expect the chauffer will turn out to be the quiet charmer with the straight edge we met that first night. And I imagine we'll be shuttled off to a safe house, somewhere out of the city, a place with a PC, an Internet connection, no nosy neighbors, and thick walls. And I imagine that I'll have to make a mammoth down payment out of our remaining nest egg in order for them to kill you quickly...then they'll find out how many pennies I have left while your personal caveman starts prying off a finger or two."

"He's not my personal caveman."

"Speaking of cavemen, I'll be right back." Hartzell slid out of the booth nearest the kitchen at the Carnegie Deli and headed toward the entrance. It was the height of the dinner hour and the restaurant bustled with servers and those waiting to be served, but Hartzell, with his back against the wall, had either spotted the bald man or been allowed to spot the living steroid as he peered into the restaurant portion of the deli from behind a rack of pickle-scented candles and designer mustards.

"Nick," Hartzell said, reaching out his hand, "please join us for dinner."

St. Nick shook Hartzell's hand in a vice-like alpha male grip. "I can't impose on your evening out, Mr. Hartzell. I've been too big a nuisance already, but I've heard about this place and as long as I was in the neighborhood I thought I'd pop in and see what all the fuss was about."

Hartzell looked at the hanging salami in the window display. "You can't come all the way to New York and not grab a Carnegie sandwich, Nick. Do you like Pastrami Hash?"

"I'd kill for a Pastrami Hash."

"I'll have the waitress bag that up with a slice of their famous cheesecake and a Pepsi."

"Why thank you, Mr. Hartzell. That would be a helluva treat for me. Can I get that with a Diet Pepsi instead?"

"Diet Pepsi?" Hartzell said. "That's not living up to your image, Nick."

"I need to watch my girlish figure."

Hartzell marched to the counter, whispered to a clerk, pointed across the restaurant at St. Nick, and slipped the server a fifty dollar bill. He then dodged a flurry of customers on his way back to Lucy.

"Is he always poking about like that?" Hartzell asked his daughter.

"A lot more visible this past week."

"Time is getting short. They're tightening the leash."

The food had arrived and Hartzell made a big production out of cutting up his baked meatloaf, but he wasn't hungry. He got the sense that Lucy didn't have much of an appetite either.

"What are we going to do, Papa?"

Hartzell had become increasingly paranoid. He'd gotten up early that morning, tossed in a load of wash, and then run the load through the dryer. After dressing in his freshly washed and dried Polo shirt and dress pants—which was a vast understatement in his world of style, but he mumbled some mush about Casual Friday in the two bean counters' general direction—he woke Lucy and informed his daughter that he'd washed some stuff for her to wear. She took the hint and dressed accordingly. Hartzell figured he was going overboard and that the Chicagoans didn't have his or Lucy's clothes somehow bugged, but he knew these men played for keeps and today would be the only chance he and Lucy would get to discuss strategy before they made their break. He'd been having his dry cleaning delivered to work for a quick change on the days of his stairwell chats.

Hartzell had called Lucy a little over an hour ago and *spontaneously* suggested they meet for dinner at the deli. He now leaned forward over his food and spoke softly. "Fiorella has us in a classic Morton's Fork."

"What's a Morton's Fork?"

"A hell of a dilemma. What to do when faced with two equally horseshit options, you know, choosing between a rock and a hard place. The concept was derived from the confiscatory tax policies of a fellow limey named John Morton, who was a Lord Chancellor in olden times. If you were living the life of Riley, Morton knew you had money for the king. If you lived in squalor, Morton knew you had money for the king squirreled away somewhere."

"Rich or poor, you were still screwed."

"Our particular Morton's Fork is that we either get in bed with Fiorella or face a painful death or lengthy imprisonment." Hartzell looked at his daughter. "Remember that first morning, Slim? When you told me to turn the tables?"

"I didn't know if you heard me."

"I did and set about doing just that, and compounded by these senseless killings, Fiorella has handed me enough dynamite to blow our Morton's Fork to bloody hell."

Lucy's face lit like a Klieg light. "What have you been doing, Papa?"

"I've been working damned hard for our Chicago friends. Did more than was asked of me, above and beyond the call—one hundred and fifty percent. But while I showed them some of mine, Vince and David slowly showed me some of theirs. Had to for the purpose of our new *business venture*. And, ultimately, the two couldn't hold back—they felt some psychological need to boast about what they'd accomplished in order to earn my admiration, which of course I dolloped out in spades. Shell companies, front organizations to hide Fiorella's DNA, set up overseas. Phantom accounts. Their shipping lanes, if you will, bouncing assets from Brazil to Tobago into a half-dozen other buckets. The biggest bucket of all, The AlPenny Group, is spick and span. All quite ingenious. They gave me more than enough to get the Feds off on the right foot. Anyway, whenever I printed out a data model for them to review or a spreadsheet or flowchart or anything else of substance, I photocopied an extra set, along with bountiful copies of cricket scores in case anyone was counting sheets."

"You don't like cricket."

Hartzell gave a hollow chuckle. "They think I'm nuts for the sport and whenever I'm asked about it I prattle on until all eyes glaze over. So a copy goes to Vince, a copy to David, and I leave my original printout with them after we've walked through the data points, but the pilfered copy here and there winds up in the filing cabinet, folded in half in the middle of some old prospectuses."

"You're tracing your financial deals back to Fiorella?"

"A trail of illicit breadcrumbs, Slim. Who'd have thought that all these years I've been here in New York working for Chicago. That documentation along with a heart-wrenching handwritten confession detailing my long-term relationship with Fiorella, my advising Fiorella that it was time for us to get out, my being stunned cross-eyed at Fiorella's subsequent actions, his ordering of Gottlieb's death along with this financial analyst who had our firm in her crosshairs... and how at that point I began to desperately fear for my own life as well as the safety of my daughter and, in case I wind up mysteriously deceased or *missing*, this is what led to my demise. With these Chessman killings fingering him, the Feds will rain down shit on all things Fiorella. I don't see bail in his tarot cards."

It was Lucy's turn to lean forward. "Why did he have those two killed?"

"Three reasons as far as I can tell," Hartzell whispered back. "One, to buy them more time to understand my operation, so they can turn around in a year and set up a few bite-sized Drake Hartzells. The second reason is fairly obvious. These bastards are all psychotic. And sewage, like water, seeks its own level. Three is the tricky one. After we become missing persons, two things occur in quick succession. The first is that the dike breaks wide open and it's Madoff time as the Street begins peeling back layer after financial layer. Secondly, the authorities will discover certain *trinkets* in our home tying me to

Gottlieb and Kellervick."

A Boston investigator had already contacted Hartzell about Elaine Kellervick, regarding a scheduled meeting with him in New York City that she'd had in her appointment book. Hartzell told the detective how he was physically ill over the news of Elaine's death, and that Elaine was coming to town to discuss a potential job offer. Although he didn't know any specifics, he informed the man that Elaine didn't sound happy in her current position and that, knowing the high quality of Elaine's work, he was in the process of moving heaven and earth to create a spot for her before some other investment firm snarfed her up.

"Hell," Hartzell continued, "they'll probably toss the weapons used in the murders inside my wall safe for good measure. Essentially, not only am I Bernard Madoff, I'm also the Chessman."

"The authorities search for us; meanwhile, Fiorella waltzes away with all the marbles."

"Only we'll never be found on account of our being at the bottom of Lake Michigan."

"So we beat them to the punch."

Hartzell nodded. "It's imperative that we beat them to the punch. By the way, Slim, one of those shell companies I told you about now owns all of Andrew Pierson's rental properties and vineyard, as well as our penthouse, where young Crenna is under the distinct impression he'll be redecorating in a few months."

"Paul's face when his uncle gets frog-marched into a squad car," Lucy replied. "Priceless."

"I'm afraid all sorts of trials and tribulations lie on the road ahead for Boy Crenna, my dear."

Lucy's face turned somber. "How do we beat them to the punch, Papa?"

"For one thing, neither of us is getting within spitting distance of Seppi's on Wednesday night. Friday evening we're all taking in the White Sox-Yankees game. As it's Chicago versus New York, we've been playing grab-ass all week and have a few hundred in side bets on the outcome. I'll be sure to keep the drinks flowing all evening for Vince and David. We'll come home, have a night cap, then pour the two middle-agers into bed. They'll be out before their heads hit the pillows. I'll run the shower while giving myself a passable buzz cut, give them enough time to achieve some solid REM sleep."

"What an interesting new look you'll have."

"Something to go with my Buddy Holly glasses. I'll have to wear my Yankees cap so Kerry won't notice."

"Kerry," Lucy said, realizing what her father was driving at. "You're a mastermind."

"We'll sneak up to the roof where he's been instructed to meet us on the helipad with the JetRanger."

When the Coordinator audited Hartzell's key drawer in his home office that first night, he'd held a key card up to Hartzell and asked him what that one was for.

"Roof access in case of a fire. They passed those out to all tenants after 911 in case of another attack." It had been Hartzell's first lie in their new relationship.

"I suppose if the sand niggers blow out a floor that cuts off the down stairwell," the Coordinator thought aloud as he tossed the card back into the drawer, "you go up and hope for the best."

"Never been up there. Dread heights. I hear it's windy enough to blow you over the edge."

When in fact Hartzell had, eight years earlier, sprung for the helicopter pad on top of the skyscraper. Only he and a fellow resident and real estate billionaire had key cards to the building's rooftop. Chartering Kerry's JetRanger had come in handy navigating above New York City's traffic jams over the years, as well as blowing the socks off of potential clients. Friday night, it would come in handy one final time.

"A package containing our new identities has been delivered to Kerry's office. Kerry thinks it's a box of Cubans, a surprise gift for a most special client we're meeting later that evening, and has been reminded, repeatedly, that he must bring it along. I told Kerry we'll be on the roof by midnight and that it's of utmost importance for us to get to LaGuardia in order to meet this most special client of mine from *Chicago*, someone we dare not be late for. I told him that he won't be flying us back, so once he's out of sight, we'll hop a cab to Newark International Airport."

"Newark Airport? Being extra cautious, Papa?"

"The more head feints the better, Slim, in case Vince or David get up to vomit and notice we're AWOL—in which case the alarm bells go off." Hartzell shrugged. "Remember, no cell phones or laptops. Most of the new stuff has GPS built in, so, conceivably, they could track us, which would put a hell of a damper on the best-laid plans. No credit cards, either. I'll have a pocket of cash to get us where we're going. Our flight's at eight o'clock in the morning, so we loaf in the lounge until then."

"Where are we going?"

"Cambodia to start."

"Won't they come after us?" Lucy asked. "He does run Chicago."

"Our new identifications come from a savant in Manila and he's all but impossible to find," Hartzell continued in a whisper. "But I have a little something in mind for our friend in Chicago to speed things along, an insurance policy to detonate events, so the fucker will never know what hit him. Thugs like Nick and the Coordinator will shuffle along to pleasing their new master—that is, whoever wins King of the Hill in a post-Fiorella Chicago."

"What's the insurance policy?"

"All that incriminating documentation I told you about, along with my handwritten confession itemizing my tenure with Duilio Fiorella, will be sent off to a couple of attorney contacts I have in high government positions. They'll discover how Fiorella has directed the financial Ponzi scheme out of New York City all of these years, how Fiorella had Gottlieb and that poor Kellervick woman murdered, and then Fiorella had both of us silenced. They will see this as manna from heaven, windfall from God above, and there'll be a fistfight to see which attorney gets to play Eliot Ness against Fiorella. And for the coup de grace I plan to place a brief but frantic phone call to one of them from my stairwell late Friday afternoon, before the game, begging a meeting first thing Monday, that it's Richter scale time, I need his help, I can't discuss it over the phone, but his boss's boss should be present. Then, when I don't appear for this most-urgent meeting, he'll begin nosing about, and then he'll receive this gift-wrapped bombshell of evidence as an early Christmas gift and… well, Slim, stick a fork in Fiorella, he's a goner. He should have never picked on someone his own size."

"Who are these attorney friends of yours?"

"One works out of the Governor's Office. The other pit bull—the one I'll call to set up Monday's meeting with—he's in the New York State Attorney General's Office."

Chapter 37

"No more crap about killing for love." Cady answered the call a split second into Terri's first ringtone as he exited the rail station, scanning commuter faces while he picked up his pace, knowing full well there would be a handful of agents tossed into the mix and fluttering about him at all times—a businessman here, a tourist there, the haggard-looking nurse over there—on the off chance that his encounter with the Chessman turned face to face. "With a hand in the freezer, Westlow, you've gone full Dahmer."

"That was self-defense, Agent Cady." Westlow sounded hurt. "And I didn't eat the rest of him for dinner, if that's what you're implying."

"Self-defense? You cut the man's hand off."

Cady had received a five a.m. wakeup call on Terri's cellular. The wakeup call consisted of two sentences. Those sentences being: "It would behoove you, Agent Cady, to be outside Penn Station at noon today. There's something you need to see."

Cady scrambled. Called Agent Preston for two minutes. Skipped a shave and spent another two minutes in the shower. Five minutes later he was picked up in a Mercury and on the way to Union Station. In the back seat he spent another ten minutes on the phone with Assistant Director Jund. This was going to call for massive coordination with Federal Plaza—the New York Field Office.

"I'm the first to admit it went awry," Westlow replied. "Palma was one tough hombre. I'll spot him that much. It got real ugly real fast after the enhanced interrogation."

"Enhanced interrogation?"

"Well, he hadn't been terribly forthcoming, not at first. A Greek Chorus of 'Cock Off' and 'Fuck You.' After I'd gotten all I could out of him, I unsecured his hands from the table, one at a time, and then played nice and put the cuffs on in front. My bad."

"Table? You waterboarded him?"

"It was a god-awful mess, Agent Cady; an inch of water on the floor, Palma's soaking wet, seemingly exhausted, which made perfect sense considering what he'd been through. Before I leaned him upright, I explained that I was going to let him go—that he meant nothing to me, he was catch-and-release material. Evidently, Palma didn't buy it. Not a lot of catch and release goes on in his world, I suspect."

"He fought back?"

"Tell me about it. In a flash he's got his cuffed hands around my throat. He jerks me in for a quick headbutt, but everything's slippery at that point. If he'd tagged me good, that would have been all she wrote. So Palma's got my neck in this iron grip—chubby fingers cutting off my oxygen. I'm feeling a bit woozy but it breaks through the haze that I'm still clutching the water hose I had hooked to the sink. I grab the back of his head with my left hand. Took me two tries and some shattered incisors as I jammed the hose down his throat. It was all I could do to twist the water back on before I passed out."

"You *drowned* Palma in your kitchen?"

"Turns out filling lungs trumps old-fashioned strangling."

"You're not right in the head, Westlow."

"Perhaps, Agent Cady, but we digress. You need to jump on the tube. Stat!"

"You're kidding," Cady said, wanting to draw out the conversation. "I just stepped off the train."

"We're on a tight schedule, my friend. Time is of the essence and you've only got twelve minutes."

"To go where?"

"You decide. But I'm going to call back in twelve with more instructions and the reception's shit in the tunnels. If you don't answer, Agent Cady, enjoy letting the Gottlieb and Kellervick families know why you didn't catch their killer. Best to hurry. And remember…I'll be watching you at all times."

"Bullshit."

"I know, but I heard it in a movie once and have always wanted to say it."

The line disconnected.

Cady switched phones as he jogged toward the steps of the subway station. "You get all that?"

"Yes," Agent Preston replied immediately. They'd rigged up Terri's phone so she and Jund could both listen in. "Go north to Times Square. We'll have some people in the car with you, but keep your eyes wide. If you spot him, grab his hands. You will have immediate backup."

"Anything on the phone?"

"Triangulation is tricky in the city, but from what I'm overhearing they think he's by the UN."

"Him and about two hundred thousand other people."

"They're trying to trace his mobile phone through the roaming signal. Possibly get a more accurate bead if they can track his phone's GPS through the satellite. The techs here talk in a foreign language."

Cady took the down steps three at a time. "He'll be constantly on the move and switching phones. Or flipping his cell off until he calls again."

"We'll flood the zones with agents and NYPD. Keep Westlow on the line as long as possible to slow him down and we might catch a break."

"He's too smart for that."

"Try to puncture that façade he's got going, Drew. That may stall him up."

Cady took the subway uptown one stop to Times Square, the busiest of all of the NYC subway facilities. He darted up the stairway, dodging in and out of passenger traffic, cut out through a 42nd Street exit right as Terri's cell began ringing.

"So the New York mob killed Kenneth Gottlieb?" Cady said into the phone.

"Did I say that?"

"You left DNA pointing us in that direction."

"Tangentially," Westlow said. "I was staking out a lead, snapping pics of a man I suspected of having daily meetings with my lead. On the beginning of the third day I noticed Palma following this man. People who tail others tend to be founts of information, so I figured he'd be the one to talk to."

"What did your *torture* session tell you, Westlow?"

"Torture? They waterboarded us in officer training. It was scary as hell, but a couple of hours later we were at a tavern and most of the guys were hitting on the cocktail waitress. Tell me, Agent Cady, can it be considered *torture* if you're hitting on a cocktail waitress two hours later?"

"Doesn't sound like there'll be more cocktail waitresses in Palma's future."

"Who are you rooting for, anyway? That mob enforcer damn near killed me."

Cady switched tacks. "Did Patrick Farris rape and murder Marly

Kelch that night at the lake?"

A dead silence descended.

"I'll have to save that for another phone call, Agent Cady. Time for another jaunt. I need you to get to the 72nd Street stop along Central Park West. You've got twelve minutes and counting."

"You're wasting my time," Cady said to a dial tone, then turned back inside the station. He hustled down the steps, scanning heights and faces on autopilot, grateful that Agent Preston had a double-dozen federal agents shadowing his trajectory, each armed with a couple pictures of Westlow's mug from his navy days. If the Chessman did attempt direct contact, they'd have him in a net. Of course, Cady knew in his gut it would never be that easy.

"How's your field trip to the Big Apple so far, Agent Cady?"

"Peachy." Cady stood on the corner of West 72nd Street and Central Park West, outside the Dakota apartment building. "You were going to tell me about Marly Kelch?"

"You ever see *King Kong*?"

"The giant ape?"

"You're missing some of the finer subtleties. Let's see, there's the classic from the '30s and the last remake by that Hobbit guy is pretty good."

"You got me here to talk movies?"

"They did a film in the '70s, too, but best to skip that one."

"What the hell are you going on about, Westlow?"

"Bear with me, Agent Cady. You see, Kong's a busy fellow, eating dinosaurs, flinging natives—all sorts of crazy shit to do on Skull Island. But once Kong sees Ann Darrow, that's all she wrote. He must be with her. He will do anything to protect her. He loves her. In the end, to borrow a line from Lincoln, Kong gives Ann Darrow his *last full measure of devotion*."

"You've got some eccentric musings on love, Westlow, but if I remember correctly, the ape spent most of the movie on a murderous rampage."

"There are, of course, those drawbacks," Westlow responded. "Say, have you ever gotten a chance to visit the John Lennon memorial?"

"Nope."

"Guy can't come all the way to New York City without stopping by Strawberry Fields and paying his proper respects. You're at the entrance. Can you *imagine* a better day for a quiet stroll and meditation on a nice pathway? Yup, Agent Cady, I'd highly recommend that you stick to the path."

"Enough of the bullshit, Westlow." Cady crossed into Central Park. "It's another phone call, already."

"As you wish."

"What made you get involved ten years after Marly's death?"

"The *drowning* made no sense. Marly was an incredible athlete. And just as unbearably painful as her loss, there was this silent river of uncertainty—running deep, forever cutting. Then one day Dorsey Kelch mentioned that Marly had known Patrick Farris at Princeton."

"The *Newsweek* article on the Farrises."

"Marly was loved by anyone who met her. The funeral was standing room only. Except a certain someone didn't make an appearance. Care to hazard a guess, Agent Cady?"

"Patrick Farris," Cady responded, slowly stepping along the Strawberry Fields pathway. "So you went to have a chat with Bret Ingram."

"Ingram didn't know diddly-squat, but the broken little man shared a common belief with me—that it was anything but an accident that had occurred."

"He didn't know about the senator's son?"

"Like I said...diddly-squat about what truly went down. Swore he was shaken awake by the Zalentines and, after he barfed out more of his guts, he was promised shiny objects to say that Marly had been fooling about with him that night, that she didn't get out of the water when he did, that the poor girl drowned while he was passed out on shore. The Zalentines told Ingram that it was all an unfortunate accident, but that any bad PR, however unfounded, could devastate the family business, and cause them financial ruin. It was later, after he'd already done his piece and gone on record, that Ingram began believing otherwise."

"Then how did you connect it to Farris?"

"Ingram told me about the bribe—Sundown Point Resort—and about Sanfield, the Magician, who had arranged it all for him. I'd done my homework, Agent Cady. I knew Sanfield was Senator Farris's right-hand man. That was all the connection I needed."

"What did Sanfield tell you in the last fifteen minutes of his life?"

"Everything I needed to know."

"What happened at Snow Goose Lake, Westlow?"

"I'm afraid the operator is insisting on another two bits and I'm all out of coins. Enjoy the memorial, Agent Cady."

"Westlow!"

He'd been cut off. Cady dropped Terri's cell into his front pocket and continued onward. Seconds later the phone in his breast pocket began vibrating.

"Did you catch all that, Liz?"

"More than that, Drew. He's in Central Park."

Cady stepped to the side of the pathway and did a three-sixty. He scanned the grove of elms, glanced across the black-and-white mosaic with the word IMAGINE in the center, looked at Rose Hill and then down the pathway toward the bronze plaque. People were milling about everywhere—tourists, school kids, people watchers crowding the benches, picnickers with homemade sandwiches, and other lunch dawdlers in no hurry to return to the grind. An army of humanoids. Cady studied faces.

"Do they know exactly where?" Central Park was over two miles long and a half mile wide.

"Yes," said Agent Preston. "And after he hung up, he left his cell on. We've got the coordinates on the phone."

Cady listened as Preston talked to someone in the background.

"He's not moving, Drew. We have him at a hundred yards southeast of you."

"Get a team ready, but send a jogger by for a visual. He probably ditched the phone in a trash bin or behind a tree to play more games."

"Already happening. I'm also flooding the entrances and exits with our people."

"Good move, Liz, but he might already be out of the park."

"He's not done with you yet."

"I've been instructed to stick to the path, which loops back around. I'm getting the feeling that something's been left for me."

Less than a minute after Cady clicked off, Terri's ringtone sounded.

"What did Sanfield tell you?"

"No time for small talk, Agent Cady?"

"It was Patrick Farris, right? He raped Marly?"

"Farris had done a dozen lines of cocaine by the time Marly arrived at Schaeffer's party. He'd been washing that down with whiskey sours. He'd had a thing for Marly, all right, and the twins took the two of them out on Schaeffer's pontoon, some kind of *booze cruise*, Farris had called it. Marly sipped wine, Farris kept sucking down sours out of a Princeton Tigers football mug. This led to some light necking. Then some untoward and not-so-light necking, Agent Cady. Marly kept telling Farris to stop it, but Farris was beyond hearing. He shoved his hand down the front of her pants." Westlow's voice had gone cold. "Marly slapped Farris across the mouth to make him stop. Stunned, he put the offending hand to his lip and came back with blood. He called Marly a 'whore cunt' and spit a mouthful of blood into the water. Then, like the ghosts from hell they were, the Zalentine twins were on Marly like a burial shroud, clutching at her arms, a sticky palm across her mouth as she tried to scream, pressing Marly slowly to the floor of the pontoon, ripping her shirt off, then her bra—then pants, then panties—spreading her legs as an offering for Patrick Farris to have his way…and Patrick Farris had his way, Agent Cady. He raped Marly on the floor of Schaeffer's pontoon while the Zalentines held her still and watched. And afterwards, a decision was made by Adrien and Alain. Farris, Sanfield tried to justify, was a worthless lump by that point, not involved in the murder as he lay fetal himself in shock, knowledge of what had just occurred seeping in through a fog of whiskey and cocaine. The Zalentines then tossed the only girl I've ever loved in my entire life, Agent Cady, into the center of that dark fucking lake."

"Jesus Christ."

"They cranked Def Leppard from the boat's boom box and revved the outboard to cover the sounds of Marly's struggle and screams for help. You've been to Snow Goose, haven't you?"

"Yes."

"Then you know how big the lake is. No matter how hard Marly tried, the twins didn't allow her to swim to safety. There was a pool net on board that they used to dunk her whenever she screamed or broke for the distant shore. Farris told Sanfield how it seemed to go on forever, but was likely no more than ten minutes before Marly fought her way back to the surface after a final dunking with lungs full of lake water. It went quickly after that, but Farris shared with Sanfield how even in the black shadows of that deadly night, he could see that Adrien and Alain had erections, obvious in their swim trunks, the entire time they ran around the boat killing Marly."

"Farris got Daddy and Sanfield to clean up for him." Cady could visualize how it went down in his mind's eye, had suspected the generalities, but the heartbreaking truth was no easier to absorb.

"A sobbing Farris spilled his guts to Sanfield, telling him every detail so the Magician could best work his sleight of hand to fix the situation. Smart move, frankly, to get Farris and his fattening lip off the scene. As though he were never there."

"All that bloodletting, Westlow," Cady said, squinting against the afternoon sun, "but it was never enough to bring Marly back."

"So much for playing God, huh, Agent Cady?" Westlow responded. "Funny thing, though. When I blew Alain's brains out in the rest stop and then Adrien's out on his boat, I mentioned Marly's name before I pulled the trigger. Both times I got the same demented smile from each twin right before I sent them back to hell."

Nothing was said for several seconds.

Westlow finally spoke. "As much as I'd enjoy hobnobbing with your colleagues, Agent Cady, I'm afraid I have to leave now. There's a bouquet of red roses on the Imagine mosaic. Do you see it?"

Cady looked at the memorial to John Lennon. "It's littered with flowers."

"There's a freshly wrapped bouquet sitting dead center."

"I see it."

"You're a kindred soul, Agent Cady. I'll certainly miss our little chats, but it's time for me to fade away. I suspect you may be too smart for my own good."

And with that, Westlow was gone.

Cady let the stares bounce off his back as he walked across the mosaic, making certain to step nimbly around the flowers that had been left in memory of the murdered Beatle. At the center he picked up the fresh bouquet of roses. He held it in his arms like a newborn and then peeled back the light blue wrapping with his left hand. The first thing he saw were three five-by-sevens, medium-range shots of two men he'd never seen before, talking together on a busy street—perhaps near Times Square. A yellow Post-It note on the bottom of one read: "I would advise keeping these in your utmost confidence. Marco, as I came to call him toward the end, told me that your mole would know these men. If warned, they'll disappear like cockroaches under the fridge."

He peered in the bottom of the wrapped bouquet, down by the stems, and saw the second item. An item marked specifically for Cady and Cady alone. It was a cell phone with another Post-It attached. The note read: "I'll use this to reach you if you ever decide to lose your entourage." Cady thought for a half second, then palmed the phone into his suit pocket as he turned around and stepped off the mosaic. Agent Preston stood on the path waiting for him.

"How did the bead on his phone shake out?"

"You were right about that; we found it dropped in a bush. His last call points at 81st Street, but we'd already pulled everyone in to cover the park." Agent Preston looked like she could sleep a year. "What have you got there?"

"Pictures, Liz. And a major problem."

Chapter 38

The dark-haired man known to Hartzell as the Coordinator was secretly delighted that the Yankees had won a 5–4 victory over the Sox, secretly delighted to grudgingly peel a hundred-dollar bill off his money clip, shake his head in faux displeasure, slap it into Hartzell's hand, and watch as the two blottoed accountants followed suit. It was hard not to be partial toward the smooth-talking flim-flam man, and the Coordinator knew that people were, on some unconscious level, seduced into *wanting*—or more accurately *needing*—Hartzell to like them back. But the Coordinator also knew the fate that was coming swiftly down the pike, so he was delighted to let the New York Investor Extraordinaire savor his winning night at the ballpark.

He wondered if Loni's flight had been on time, if she would be waiting for him in the Star Lounge at the Ritz-Carlton where he'd been living these past weeks. The level of his anticipation amazed him; he missed her and couldn't wait to give the stewardess a bear hug as though years, not merely days, had passed. He'd take a long sip of her Shining Star served up with the Ketel One Citron, order a bottle of Dom and the two of them would head up to his room. If only the cabbie could make quicker time as they skirted Central Park. Duilio Fiorella had told him not to get too accustomed to living the high life, but Hartzell was booming business, so the Coordinator had been spoiling himself rotten. Central Park across the street, Broadway and Park Avenue a few Frisbee tosses away. Damn, he was going to hate leaving the Big Apple and returning to the Windy City.

The assignment, for the most part, had been cushy. Vince and David on Hartzell twenty-four-seven, St. Nick had the girl under his thumb, and after his pop-bys with the investment scammer were done, he had free days...and nights. And this stewardess—good God—Loni knew more about what made him tick after one night than Gina back in Chicago could possibly fathom after six years. Sure, Gina was a ten, no doubt about that, and she'd be the perfect mother to any potential sons or daughters, but the thrill had dwindled and now she just lay on her back while he did all the heavy lifting. He'd spot Loni an easy eight and a half, a strong nine in low light, but the flight attendant had titties out to Montana and enjoyed reverse cowgirl as much as he did. And she'd been screwing him dry near nightly.

The Coordinator still felt the occasional pang of guilt, especially when Gina called during one of their trysts one evening and the stewardess, dominatrix-like, demanded he answer his cell phone. He pressed the green button, did his best to sound normal, but Loni slid his right hand, gripping the phone, slowly down their moist torsos toward the wet sounds of their lovemaking. After several thrusts of heightened exhilaration he jerked the phone back up to his mouth.

"What's that noise?" Gina asked.

"It's coming down cats and dogs, honey. Cats and dogs. I'm at the window sneaking a smoke."

And Gina bought it. Told him he'd better be careful about getting in trouble with the hotel. After he clicked off Loni rolled on top and brought him to the greatest orgasm of his life.

Though not for a lack of living space, Fiorella had barred the

Coordinator from living with the subject in the Midtown Manhattan penthouse, like the bean counters were.

"He's charismatic. A snake charmer, a pied-fucking-piper," Fiorella had warned him. "That's how he's made it this far. If you're around Hartzell for more than the daily check-in, it could prove unhealthy—a person might fall into the man's orbit, go native, and start thinking the wrong thoughts. It's axiomatic, but it would break my heart if St. Nick or our quiet friend had to pay someone I'm fond of a visit."

"No worries, Boss," the Coordinator had responded. He and St. Nick were friends, even shared season tickets at Soldier Field, but if Fiorella pointed St. Nick his way, well, Nick would feel awfully sorry as he ripped out the Coordinator's liver. "When have I ever let you down?"

"Have some fun, see the sights, but no other business besides handling Hartzell. Stay off the radar, too. The last thing I want to do in life is to kiss Moretti's ring. That fat Long Island fuck will demand half."

"I'll be a light touch," he told Fiorella. "New York will never know I was there."

So the Coordinator found himself in the Big Apple with copious free time on his hands. After his morning touch-base with Hartzell, he hit the tourist spots—the Statue of Liberty, the Empire State Building, a forgettable sprint through the Museum of Modern Art, a tour of the NBC Studio—and then prowling the after-hour spots come nightfall. That's how he'd bumped into Loni that first week in the city that never sleeps, at a nightclub on 11th called Webster Hall. Sappy as it sounds, and no way would he waste time trying to explain this feeling to St. Nick—*lust at first sight*, the big man would call it— but their eyes met from across the room as he leaned against the bar and she worked her way slowly toward him, neither one breaking the gaze. Fifteen minutes of loaded chitchat later, they could barely keep their hands off each other. An hour after that they were back in his Ritz-Carlton suite for a marathon humpathon, the first of many, on or against every possible surface the room provided. They'd even momentarily studied the chandeliers, but the Coordinator figured it would never support their weight.

Loni had the JFK-Heathrow route and had taken to staying with him between flights. He'd flown Gina out one weekend while Loni was in the UK. Alas, the sex had been unsatisfying. He found himself closing his eyes and fantasizing about what he and Loni had done nights earlier. Not a good situation at all since Gina wore his engagement ring and was planning some grandiose pain-in-the-ass seashore nuptials for next summer. Gina was also the daughter of Duilio Fiorella's cousin, which meant…fuck.

But it was no use to think about any of that now. The Coordinator couldn't wait until he and Loni got back to his suite, to see what the stewardess had in store for him this evening. And he longed for the following weekend, because he was booked, first class, on Loni's flight to London and had been promised that, after the meal had been served and the passengers had settled in for the night, Loni would fetch him and soon after that he would become a proud new member of the mile high club. That rite of passage would help take the sting off of how the Hartzell matter was going to end…and end badly. The bean counters had grudgingly conceded what he already knew: that after all the give and take of the past weeks, Hartzell remained a vastly untapped oil well.

Fiorella had given him a courtesy heads-up that Hartzell's concerns regarding Gottlieb and that pesky Kellervick woman were indeed about to be addressed in full. The Coordinator pondered the wisdom of making such brazen moves; he played mental gymnastics, evaluating both pros and cons, but ultimately kept any trepidation to himself. It was ballsy. He did chuckle at the twisted brilliance of Fiorella's plan and realized again why it was that his mentor ruled Chicago: two parts genius and one part iron fist. Fiorella had even instructed him to play dumb with Hartzell on Gottlieb and that Boston analyst bitch, but to provide a not-so-veiled threat if pressed.

He had also been instructed to glean any news about the ongoing investigation from that maggot in the New York Attorney General's Office, but mostly get the lowdown from their trump card at the FBI. In fact, his bureau source had tipped him as to how the real Chessman had been poking about the hornet's nest, hadn't been happy at all with their borrowing his greatest hits, had even fucked with that Elaine Kellervick woman's boss, and had recently killed again, dismembered some poor anonymous schmuck who'd evidently been in the wrong place at the right time…real sicko shit. Serial killers—whattaya gonna do? At least having that motherfucker in play, Fiorella pointed out, would keep the Fibbies marching sideways.

The Coordinator tossed a couple bills at the cabbie, pressed a fiver into the doorman's palm after he opened the cab door and sprinted into the lobby, then walked over to the Star Lounge. He saw Loni immediately. Her back was to him; she sat alone at a high top table, sipping her Ketel One Citron and waiting on him. She'd yet to spot him, but he was able to watch her in the wall-length mirror spanning the far end of the hotel's watering hole. He also caught sight of a few businessmen at a neighboring table sneaking peeks in her general direction. He was a lucky bastard. And what in hell had he been thinking? An eight and a half? On a scale of one to ten, Loni was a goddamned fifteen. Suddenly an errant thought struck the Coordinator. The thought being that he mighy just be head-over-heels for this woman, truly in love with her—he'd never felt this way before, about anyone. It was absolutely terrifying, and he wondered what the fuck he was going to do.

Shit.

The Coordinator suddenly back-stepped toward the coat check and pulled out his cell phone. Stouder had called him during the baseball game, right at the moment when the only home run of the game had occurred, with New York sending in two runs. The crowd roared in good cheer as he had brought the cell to his ear.

"Fuck is it?"

"What's all that noise?" Stouder asked. "I can barely hear you."

"I'm at the game. Anything up?"

"The usual daily chatter." Stouder still spoke with that grating aura of self-righteousness. "You know, it might help if you could specify what it is that you're after."

"Anything. Everything," the Coordinator said dismissively. "I'll call you after the game."

The Coordinator's least favorite part of his assignment in the Big Apple was dealing with this Peter Lorre motherfucker. He'd lied to Hartzell that first night; his crew hadn't just arrived in the city that day. No, that would have been rushed and stupid. He and St. Nick had already been in New York City close to a week getting their ducks in a row. Chief among the ducks was this sad sack of child-abusing shit named Stouder. Fiorella's web guru—a pimple named Gordy Hoyt—had been cracking into the private e-mail and Internet trafficking of several key staff members in the New York Attorney General's Office and hit pay dirt with this fucking scumbag. The perv made his skin crawl. The Coordinator wanted to shower after every time he spoke with Stouder. He'd have Loni scrub his back tonight.

Duilio was going to owe him big time when this venture was over. He knew that the leveraged-against-Stouder boy would be returned safely and, after a short amount of time had passed, Stouder would be wrapped up by Fiorella's stealthy exterminator as the final loose end of their New York adventure. But he would lobby hard that it should really be St. Nick paying Stouder that last late-night visit, and that it should be drawn out, highly painful, all culminating in one particular organ being torn asunder at the root. Just having to talk to this budding pedophile made the Coordinator queasy. He punched in the number for the cell phone he'd given Stouder.

"Hello."

"So nothing major to report?"

"Pretty much status quo," Stouder replied.

The Coordinator was tempted to hit the red button to end the call and then help Loni finish off her Shining Star, but thought better of it. Another thirty seconds to complete the daily debriefing with the scumslime wouldn't kill him. "Walk me through it."

"The mayor stopped by. We're all placing bets on who the president is going to name to head the SEC."

"Any frontrunners?"

"Everyone's got an inkling, but nobody knows for sure."

"Other news for me?"

"The only other news I can think of is that a colleague of mine— Mark Kolar, the Chief of Staff—mentioned some big-shot investor called him to set up a meeting first thing Monday morning. Wouldn't tell him what it's about, though."

The Coordinator felt the hair on the back of his neck begin to prickle. "What's the motherfucker's name?"

"Heavy hitter by the name of Drake Hartzell. You know of him?"

"Why the fuck didn't you tell me that earlier?!" The Coordinator felt his chest constrict.

A long pause hung over the conversation.

"I called at the scheduled time, but you were at the game."

He hung up on Stouder, and then hit St. Nick's phone number on speed dial. He dreaded the phone call he'd have to make after telling Nick to haul ass over to Hartzell's penthouse condominium. But as much as Fiorella's predator made him nervous, Fiorella would want him to be there as well. Tonight was going to get fuck ugly and his services would be called upon. Evidently, Hartzell thought it was all bullshit about their having eyes and ears in high places, and it was good that Hartzell had enjoyed the evening at the ballpark because his actions had just hastened his fate a full five days ahead of schedule.

The Coordinator glanced again at Loni sitting alone in the lounge, then turned and ran toward the lobby exit, where the cabs lined up.

Chapter 39

"It's gone Chernobyl, Agent Cady."

"Stop jerking me around, Westlow!" Cady barked back into the phone.

It was half past eleven, but Cady was wide awake. He'd been sitting there feeling guilty about saying zip, zero, and zilch to either Jund or Preston about the cell phone Westlow had passed him at the John Lennon Memorial. His silence on that transaction cut against both the grain and spirit of any chain of custody protocol the bureau had put to paper since 1908, when Attorney General Charles Bonaparte had created the agency out of his Department of Justice. But so far, following the proper protocol had gotten them zip, zero, and zilch.

So Cady had sat alone in his Midtown hotel room, in an upright chair, staring at Westlow's cell on the table in front of him. He knew it was only a matter of time before the phone rang, and Cady had acclimated himself to sitting in the upright ordering cold room service until hell froze over or Westlow's cell phone buzzed. If anything, Cady was surprised at how soon the Chessman's call came in.

"A young woman will die badly if you're not outside your hotel in one minute."

"Why don't you tell me what the hell is going on?"

"I'll explain everything in the cab," Westlow replied. "What hotel are you at?"

"You don't know?"

"The clock is ticking."

"Holiday Inn Express, Fifth Avenue."

"See you in thirty or not at all. If you're playing phone games with the posse, I'll drive on past, Agent Cady, and you can play catch-up by reading the *New York Times* headlines tomorrow."

Cady was out the door a second later, heading toward the elevator bank. He felt a jolt of apprehension as he jogged past Agent Preston's room.

Cady stood curbside, studying the night owl traffic in the city that never sleeps, making himself seen a half block up 45th Street—well away from the hotel's main entrance. He'd already waved away two empty taxis and shook his head at a third. Cady glanced at his wristwatch, then back to 45th. It had rained lightly an hour earlier and the street shone in the warm moonlight. Cady's crippled right hand was stuffed in his jacket pocket. The Glock 22 felt heavy in his grip.

In Cady's other hand, Westlow's cell phone began to vibrate.

"Who were you on the phone with?"

"What are you talking about?"

"Never mind. I need you to go right on Fifth and just keep walking." Westlow clicked off.

Though it was far too late for shopping, Cady headed toward Fifth Avenue. It had taken several minutes for Westlow to call him back instead of the threatened thirty seconds. Now Westlow had tried to rattle him about being on the phone, trying to ascertain whether Cady was calling in the cavalry. He got the sense that Westlow was improvising on the fly.

Cady turned onto Fifth and hit the green button as soon as he felt the phone vibrate.

"Cut left on 44th," Westlow commanded. "A little hustle, Agent Cady."

Cady dodged cars as he jaywalked across Fifth. He crossed 44th and headed toward a single double-parked cab halfway down the street.

Westlow's final call was the essence of brevity.

"Get in the cab."

Cady scrutinized the taxi for a second and made eye contact with the driver—a thirty-something man of Middle-Eastern descent stared curiously back at him. Cady opened the back door and slid across the back seat.

"Is he with you?" the driver asked, looking at the still open door.

"Yes." Jake Westlow appeared curbside, right hand on the cab door as he peered inside at the special agent, and then he slipped quietly into the back seat beside Cady and gave the driver a Manhattan address.

"That a real tattoo?"

Westlow wore pointy-toed cowboy boots, blue jeans, and a white wifebeater. He sported a red crew cut, a silver barbell piercing in his left eyebrow, and a serpent tattoo slithering up his right forearm, across his bicep, and swerving around his neck.

"No," Westlow replied. "But thanks to you, Agent Cady, I look like a groupie for the Village People."

Cady held the Glock on his lap, aimed dead center at Westlow's chest.

"Let the record show I caught you."

"I saw that bulge a mile away. Almost said screw it and left."

The two men sat unbuckled in their seats, twisted toward each other, unblinking—boxers in their respective corners, awaiting the bell. Neither inclined to speak, the discomfort between them palpable, thick as putty and threatening to suck the oxygen from the cab. Cady felt like a stubborn child, but he'd burn in hell before he broke the silence.

"So," Westlow said finally, "how ya been?"

"How've I been? It's taking extraordinary willpower not to shoot out your kidneys. That's how I've been."

"They've got anger management for that."

"Cut the shit, Westlow. Why are you and I playing patty-cake?"

The amusement dropped from Westlow's features.

"Fair enough, I owe you an explanation. It's a given that the best-laid plans tend to get tossed out the window upon implementation because of unknown factors that *inevitably* crop up. Three years ago I did you great bodily harm. The others deserved everything I meted out in spades, but—"

"You killed the Schaeffer kid for throwing a party."

"And the booze flowed. And the drugs passed hands. And the sociopaths were unleashed. One could make a case that Dane Schaeffer was the catalyst that set this all in motion. He didn't die for throwing a party. He died for inviting Marly."

"You're insane."

"I could live with a hundred Dane Schaeffers and not lose a wink. But then there's you—the unknown factor that inevitably cropped up. I ruined your life, Agent Cady. As far as I'm concerned, you were my only victim."

"That's what this is all about?" Cady laughed out loud. "I'm your bullshit charity case? Something to be pitied?"

"Nothing I've done has been out of pity. When Gottlieb was killed and the press dropped hints about the Chessman returning, that kind of caught my eye. I started digging. I started thinking. And you know what I thought, Agent Cady?"

"What?"

"That you and I had been granted a mulligan."

"A mulligan?"

"Yes."

"Fuck you, Westlow." Cady was at a loss for words, but that response seemed as good as any and better than most.

He slid his handgun into his shoulder holster, glanced at the back of the driver's head, wondering what the cabbie made of anything he may have heard through the partition. Cady then turned and stared out his side window.

"Tell me about the girl who's in danger."

Chapter 40

The cab was speeding toward the high rise where the Hartzells lived. Westlow gave Cady a thumbnail sketch of what he knew.

"So Drake Hartzell's a scam artist being run out of Chicago—by Duilio Fiorella—and New York—meaning Fedele Moretti—has his people all over Hartzell's Chicago keeper?"

"Moretti's man, Palma, told me they've got a security cracker with access to the train and airport databases. Moretti feeds this guy a list of names. If any of these *people of interest* arrive in New York City, Moretti's to be notified immediately. That's how he knew that Rudy Ciolino was in town. Ciolino is Fiorella's right hand—his protégé. Palma was assigned to trail Ciolino—remember, that's how I tripped over him. Moretti's been trying to noodle out what Fiorella's been up to in *his* city. The plan was, if they couldn't piece it together beforehand, they were going to break Ciolino next week and find out what Chicago is up to. Of course, with Palma going dark, Moretti is likely to move that date up."

"They kill Gottlieb and throw it on...*you*...in order to buy Hartzell time to liquidate a billion in assets. But why kill Elaine Kellervick?"

"Kellervick's most recent work files included some kind of financial analysis of Hartzell's firm. She had three separate analyses created in the week before her death, each analysis completed on a different day. This raises flags because Hartzell's firm is neither a client nor partnered with Koye & Plagans. And Kellervick's Outlook calendar indicated an upcoming meeting scheduled with Hartzell himself."

"They checked with Hartzell about that appointment," Cady filled in, almost without thinking. "He downplayed it as a touch-base job interview, which, without context, appears benign." Cady had spent time with Agent Preston reviewing the Kellervick investigation. "You get anything else from the Kellervick files?"

"I doubt Albert Banning was terribly upfront with you regarding Kellervick's recent work. Might be considered bad PR or bring about allegations of corporate espionage, maybe even a lawsuit. Anyway, what was odd about Kellervick's spreadsheets is that they all appeared to track the same numbers; that is, the versions were pretty much identical as far as I could tell. I couldn't make heads or tails out of the Excel numbers, and Kellervick had no summary page to lay out her findings. It was Swahili. Remember, Gottlieb was set to take the reins at the SEC when he was murdered. From everything I read, the man was going to hit the ground running, taking names and kicking ass. I suspect Gottlieb put the fear of God into Drake Hartzell. And I imagine it was poking around Hartzell's investment strategies that got Kellervick in the crosshairs."

"If Hartzell has the Midas Touch, why are Fiorella's men coming for him?"

"The last thing Palma told me—before it got ugly—was that Moretti had someone on the inside, someone chummy with Hartzell's keeper, Rudy Ciolino. Anyway, Moretti's certain someone was able to sneak a bug on Ciolino's phone." Westlow held up a cell. "I got this from Palma. It allows me to listen in on Ciolino's phone calls. The guy's a tight-lipped bastard, but after a phone call from a contact in the New York Attorney General's Office, there was a flurry of panicked calls from Ciolino that painted a bleak picture. That's when I called you."

"The New York Attorney General's Office?"

Westlow nodded. "The contact informed Ciolino that Drake Hartzell was coming in first thing Monday morning. You can guess what that means. Ciolino just about popped a blood vessel."

"You got me a name on who's inside the Attorney General's Office?"

Westlow shrugged. "Ciolino doesn't use names on the phone."

"Nothing on the leak in the Bureau?"

Westlow shrugged again. "Ciolino made three short calls in rapid succession. Like I said, he doesn't use names, but there was a common theme—theme being, quote, 'Hartzell's fucking us! Get to his penthouse!' unquote."

The cab pulled up to the skyscraper. Both men climbed out of the passenger door and stepped over the curb.

"Any idea who Moretti has on the inside with Ciolino?"

"Not a name per se," Westlow replied. "Just someone Palma referred to as *the stewardess.*"

Cady badged the red-suited guard behind the security counter in the main lobby at Drake Hartzell's high rise.

"Are the Hartzells in?"

"They got back from the ball game an hour ago. With their guests."

"Guests?"

"A couple of businessmen have been staying with Mr. Hartzell," the guard answered, a what-the-hell-is-this-all-about expression on his face. "More of Mr. Hartzell's business associates were buzzed up maybe ten minutes ago."

"We've got a situation here." Cady pointed at the security guard after getting Hartzell's top-floor suite number. He read the guard's nametag. "No one can leave the building until the FBI arrives or I come back down. You understand that, Derek?"

"What's going on?"

"I'll tell you about it over a beer sometime, Derek. You need to call 911 and then alert your other security guards. Make sure the police cordon off this building. No one leaves, right?"

"Yes, sir."

The two men sprinted toward the elevators.

"Not very sporting putting Derek on lockdown, Agent Cady," Westlow commented. "At least when it comes time for me to dance my way out of here, Derek here will think I'm a Fibbie."

Cady ignored Westlow. He flipped his cell phone open and speed-dialed Agent Preston.

Cady selected the floor two flights below Hartzell's penthouse. They would take the north stairwell up the rest of the way to maintain whatever element of surprise they could use to their advantage. Both men watched the numbers fly past on the digital display above the sliding doors.

"It's the girl, right?"

Westlow glanced at Cady but said nothing.

"You think the rest of them deserve each other," Cady said. "But we're here to save Hartzell's daughter."

Westlow looked back up at the floor display. "Don't leap over a terrace this high up, Agent Cady."

Chapter 41

Rudy Ciolino—aka the Coordinator—was knee-deep in blotted accountants.

Codename Smith had already darted to the bathroom for a second sweaty purge into the shitter, and Jones was draped over Hartzell's settee as though he had no vertebrae, unfocused eyes hidden behind drooping lids. Ciolino thought they'd have to shoot the security guard. The guard had phoned Hartzell's suite a half-dozen times to no avail before shaking his head. St. Nick took over on his own cell phone, pressing redial through five attempts flipping over to voicemail. He hit pay dirt on the sixth ring. Nick cut through Smith's drunken fog by ordering him to buzz them up or face the fact that he'd be swallowing his own dick long before the night was over.

"'Zin there." Jones sloshed an arm in the general direction of the hallway. "Ta bed."

"No, they're not *zin* there, you drunk fuck!"

Ciolino remembered Hartzell buying drinks all night in their private box at the ball game. He now realized why Hartzell had the bartender vary up the cocktails: to cause the alcohol to take its maximum toll on the bean counters. Ciolino was lucky he'd turned down a lion's share of the mixed drinks himself. He'd not wanted to spoil an Olympic-level performance with Loni later in the evening. But Hartzell had intended to get the two live-ins fully soused so he and his daughter could give them the slip and then rat-fuck Fiorella and company at the NY AG first thing Monday morning.

"They must've snuck out one of the side entrances downstairs," Nick offered.

"Those are alarmed, used for emergencies."

Ciolino squinted from the accountant on the couch to St. Nick to the tall man who stood motionless, waiting, his back to the window. It began to sink in how truly fucked he was. St. Nick was one of Fiorella's top enforcers. He bent adversaries to Fiorella's will. But the tall man, he was Fiorella's assassin—and among other assignments, he dealt with the hard-cores who refused to bend. The tall man had been flawless with Gottlieb and Kellervick. Drake Hartzell wasn't the tall man's "shit," so he leaned quietly against the glass window, arms folded across his chest, taking in the show. However, the thought sparked through Ciolino's brain like a bolt of lightning that if the tall man made a phone call to apprise Fiorella of their current dilemma, Hartzell seeking out the authorities and his subsequent disappearing act, it would instantaneously become the tall man's "shit."

Fiorella would want all tie-backs swiftly eliminated. Fiorella would be immoveable on that issue. If Ciolino himself was not the one in the pinch, that would be the word-for-word advice that he'd offer the man who ran Chicago. For starters, everyone in the apartment would have to die, and probably that buck-toothed security guard who had been at the front desk when the tall man brought in a removal team.

They say a man can shine at any given task if he devotes ten thousand hours to it. The tall man had logged the hours and was exceptionally good at *his* given task. Or, more explicitly, his calling. *I'll only have one chance*, Ciolino thought to himself. If the tall man took out his phone to contact Fiorella, Ciolino would draw his Heckler & Koch and shoot the man right in the face. Twice. Without hesitation. He wouldn't have time to lobby St. Nick ahead of this action, but Nick would understand if Ciolino walked him through his rationale after the fact.

"Then they left through the basement garage," Nick said, drawing Ciolino back into the present debacle.

Something nibbled at the back of Ciolino's mind. He looked at Nick as the thought sank in. Ciolino turned and dashed into the den and tore open Hartzell's key drawer. He ran his hand over the items, then through them, and then yanked the drawer out of the desk, spilled the contents onto the floor, and raked through the bits and pieces with a dress shoe. He thought back to the helicopter tour of Manhattan that he and Loni had taken the previous week.

"Not the garage," Ciolino said to St. Nick and the tall man who stood inside the office doorway, silently watching him. "The roof."

Chapter 42

Like candy from a baby.

Hartzell was fully aware of his shit-eating grin as he pumped
Kerry Evans' hand and stared at the JetRanger atop the helicopter
pad with unconditional love. Not until this evening had he realized
how beautiful a bird the JetRanger was—a truly remarkable piece of
equipment—an extraordinary deus ex machina.

"LaGuardia, huh, Drake?"

"And don't spare the horses."

"Hey, Lucy," the pilot said, winking at Hartzell's daughter. "The
rain stopped. Almost no wind. A beautiful night for a flight."

"A splendid night for a flight, Kerry."

Kerry Evans stood about six-three with a face like a ruggedly
aging Ken doll; a hint of gray dusted the brown hair at his temples.
Evans was central casting's version of a helicopter pilot and he knew
it. The flyboy was on his third divorce and hit on anything in a skirt.

"So when do I get to take you for a personal spin above Manhattan, Lucy?"

"You free next Saturday?"

"I am now."

"It's a date."

Like candy from a baby, Hartzell thought again as he helped Lucy up into the passenger area of the JetRanger helicopter, delighted to discover a package in the shape of a cigar box sitting atop his seat. His and Lucy's new identities. It just kept getting better and better.

Vince and David were going to be deep in the tank all day Saturday with killer hangovers. The coup de grace had been the several Long Island Iced Teas he'd pushed on the two men. Those shots of vodka, gin, tequila, and rum could really sneak up on you if you weren't counting. Hartzell had left a note for the accountants stuck on the refrigerator, informing them that he and Lucy were busy helping a painter friend of hers set up a gallery showing. He wrote that they'd be back by eight that evening and, if the two weren't still a tad green behind the gills, he'd love to bring them to Le Cirque or perhaps even Sarabeth's for a late dinner. Hartzell buckled his shoulder harness in place, checked that Lucy did the same, and did his best to wipe the absurd smile off his face. He figured that by ten o'clock Saturday evening Vince or David would place an awkward call to the Coordinator. By midnight, the Coordinator's knickers would be in such a hellacious twist his balls would turn bright blue.

In a few days, and from an ocean away, Hartzell would monitor the news via the Internet and the cable channels as Duilio "Leo" Fiorella began on his heretofore unforeseen trek through the bowels of the United States' criminal justice system. And once Fiorella's permanent residence had been firmly established by the courts, Hartzell would unearth a means for something simple like, say, an anonymous card to worm its way through the various tiers of concrete and steel to reach the new abode of the imprisoned mob boss. Nothing incriminating, of course. Hartzell would give it immense thought on his and Lucy's upcoming flight across the pond; perhaps an unsigned postcard from the Mediterranean coastline would suffice. Fiorella would know exactly who had sent it.

Hartzell watched as Evans, meticulous as ever, walked through his pre-takeoff sweep of the controls—a range check of the transmitter, a visual peek at the blades, a verification that all throttle functions were properly working. And even though Evans had recently landed, he proceeded through his mental checklist of these and a half-dozen other items. The rugged Ken doll was a first-class helicopter pilot. Hartzell would never have feared a crash should Kerry truly have taken his daughter for a *personal spin* above Manhattan in the JetRanger. Simply terrible of Lucy to tease poor Kerry regarding a date she'd never keep. However, when the time came, as it inevitably would, that meager detail would make the pilot's testimony all the more believable.

Evans turned back toward the Hartzells and shot them his signature thumbs-up, indicating all systems go, when a thunderclap burst the night. Dark crimson splashed across the windshield. Evans convulsed forward, shoulders shaking, only the belt keeping him slumped upright in his seat. The poor man's face, now shattered, a dripping pulp—never again to be compared with that of a Ken doll.

Hartzell jumped in his seat. Lucy climbed his arm in panic, her fingernails piercing his flesh. He looked across the body of the dead pilot. A tall man in black stood ten feet from the helipad. The end of his right arm extended into a pistol as though it were a natural appendage. The pistol now aimed at them, Hartzell and Lucy. Beyond the tall man, just outside the door to the roof of the skyscraper, stood St. Nick and the Coordinator.

The Coordinator was now the one sporting the shit-eating grin.

Chapter 43

They hit Hartzell's master suite hard.

Cady and Westlow had come out of the north stairwell, and they slid noiselessly along the wall until they reached the door to Hartzell's penthouse. Cady slipped beneath the peephole and back up the other side of the door. They stood still a moment, listening. Cady reached across and touched the handle, was surprised to find it unlocked. He looked to Westlow, and was equally surprised to find a Beretta 92FS in his right hand, pointed down at the carpeting. Westlow sent him a *don't ask* shrug.

Cady had committed to memory the images of the two men in the pictures Westlow had left for him at Strawberry Fields. Jund had earlier checked with his OCTF contact, but had come back with no hits linking them to the New York families, or to New Jersey. The dark-haired man, Westlow informed him, was Rudy Ciolino—Fiorella's chief advisor. He also told Cady that Ciolino called the other man in the pictures—the bald guy who looked as though he'd been carved out of block by a deranged stonemason—St. Nick, no last name. Drake Hartzell was near the half-century mark, and tall. With a little luck, Hartzell's daughter Lucy would be the only female inside the suite.

With that cast list in mind, Cady would force them all down on

the floor. Fast. And cuff them. Let Jund make sense of it later. If Ciolino or the bald man resisted, or drew down, Cady had no qualms
about dropping them on their asses. In an odd sense he was relieved
that Westlow had pulled the Beretta out of thin air.

Cady swung in low with Westlow on his heels. They swept Hartzell's living room—the size of a regulation tennis court, but empty.
Cady veered right into the kitchen, jutted around a jungle of hanging pots and pans, and then rushed through another twenty yards
of dining room. Both empty. He shot a quick glance out the dark
windows before looking back across the suite at Westlow. Westlow
had the Beretta aimed down the hallway and was quietly closing the
door with his free hand. He tilted his head from Cady toward the
foyer. Cady made it halfway across the living room before he heard
the raucous splashing noise.

Inside the second guest bathroom they found a man in boxer
shorts hobbled over the toilet, both seats up, a limp hand hanging
onto the flusher. The man's face gleamed with sweat; his blond hair
looked like it had been combed with a pork chop. Cady could smell
the alcohol as he stooped next to him. The man squinted up and
bumbled incoherently. Worthless.

"Someone's in the bedroom," Westlow whispered from the
doorframe.

Cady flushed the toilet and then turned on the sink faucet to
cover his sounds. Although it was likely for naught—the blond man
wasn't going anywhere—Cady had the drunk flex-cuffed and on his
side in the neighboring Jacuzzi in less than ten seconds, possibly
shattering a rodeo record. He thought about shoving a washcloth in
his mouth to keep him quiet, but feared the man would drown on
his next wave of puke.

In the last room of Hartzell's seventy-second-floor penthouse
estate they found a second man rolling up clothing as if making

giant snowballs and stuffing the handfuls into a leather suitcase that sat atop a king-sized bed. Cady had him in cuffs in another ten seconds while Westlow hung in the doorframe, guarding the hallway.

"Where did they go?"

The second man sat on the king-sized and said nothing. He too was intoxicated—easy to infer even though the man had stuffed his mouth with a tinful of Altoids. Cady looked at his face and noted the dilated pupils.

"Where are they?"

The second man remained silent. Cady shook his head, walked toward the bedroom window, and took out his phone to call Agent Preston.

Westlow looked back down the hallway, marched across the room, and then stuck four fingers deep into the flesh under the man's jawbone and jerked him upward as though pulling a fish from the water by its gill. Loud farting sounds erupted as the man rose to his feet.

"Where are they?" Westlow repeated Cady's question.

"The roof," the man said, stretching on his tiptoes in hopes of freeing himself from Westlow's grip. "They went to the roof."

Chapter 44

The blue door blocking the ascension to the peak of the sky-scraper looked as if it'd lost three rounds with Mike Tyson. It warped inward around the lock, never to shut properly again. Cady and Westlow stood on either side of the busted door, listening for sounds emanating from the stairwell. Cady gave the door a shove with two fingers and both men peered up the final stairway.

Two flights of steps, wide enough to accommodate an elephant, zigzagged upward to a double door leading onto the building's top. The men crept upward, backs pressed against the black railing and guns held high until they reached the middle level. There they noticed how one of the doors had been propped open, made ready for any swift entrance or exit. Roof Access was lettered in black on the door facing them, the one that remained shut. Both men contin-ued to slide slowly alongside the gray cement walls. A dull fluorescent light off the high wall kept the little-utilized access path to the roof dimly lit.

Cady pointed to a metal ladder fixed in place at the side of the access doors, which rose straight up to some kind of hatchway in the top of the enclosed stairwell. The idea of taking the high ground and coming out above the killers from Chicago flickered through his mind, but was dismissed at the sight of a padlock set in the hatch handle. Poking around up there trying to pop that lock could leave a guy completely exposed. Vulnerable. Dead.

Then they heard the gunshot.

Cady's first inclination was to run like a madman in the opposite direction. His second inclination was to double-time it out onto the roof and throw himself into the middle of an unknown O.K. Corral scenario. Both inclinations could prove fatal, for someone. Cady and Westlow hugged the wall, Glock and Beretta aimed at the doorway as they climbed the cement steps. They held their breath as they slunk up the final flight, embraced the doorframe, and peeked out at the drama unfolding on the roof.

Six paces outside the doorway stood Rudy Ciolino. Opposite Ciolino stood the bald man from the pictures. Cady put two and two together as he pegged Drake Hartzell, financial wizard and felon extraordinaire, on his knees before the two thugs, Yankees cap askew, with a thick line of blood slipping down a recently malformed nose. Lucy Hartzell stood next to her father, quaking in her high-heeled shoes.

"Nobody move a goddamn inch!" Cady yelled in his no-shit tone, stepping out from the doorway, his Glock leveled at Ciolino's torso.

Ciolino and St. Nick glared at the figure who'd materialized out of nowhere, now threatening to spoil their party.

Cady noted the mess in the helicopter. "You two, on the ground right now! Hands on your heads!"

Ciolino had made three calls for help, but there were only the Hartzells and the two unarmed men in front of him. Where were Fiorella's other men? Where the hell was the shooter? Neither man showed any indication of obeying Cady's command. Ciolino's eyes shot to Cady's left. Drake Hartzell leapt to his feet. And in a flash Cady knew exactly where the shooter had been positioned, hugging the shadows of the outer wall…and in his periphery, Cady glimpsed death.

Westlow had seen Cady step forward, shot out a hand to pull him back but was too late. He remained inside the doorframe, gun centered on the monster called St. Nick. He was the main threat to be removed if the two men continued to ignore Agent Cady's commands. He heard movement first, and then saw the flash of an arm as an unseen third man stepped from the outside wall, pistol pointing into Cady's ear. Westlow leapt forward, his own gun flying upward as though fencing with a short blade; he nudged the third man's pistol up a sneeze before it exploded.

Westlow latched onto the pistol barrel with his free hand, twisting it up and backwards, breaking the shooter's grip. Westlow moved left, sweeping the Beretta with him, planning to put four into the third man, when a blow from nowhere smashed into his ribcage right as the shooter's gun popped free in his hand. Westlow tossed the pistol behind him into the stairwell and brought the Beretta full to his left. A stitch jabbed into his side and caused him to gasp.

Then he and Cady fired simultaneously as the shooter—a tall man dressed in black—darted around the corner of the access building. They heard receding footsteps as the tall man escaped to the south side of the rooftop. Westlow gritted his teeth against the twinge in his left side, shot Cady a look, and took off after the tall man, chasing him into the darkness.

Drake Hartzell had dropped to his knees after being clubbed across the face by a horribly irate St. Nick. A precursor of things to come, no doubt. Shards of pain spread across both temples and he feared a broken nose. Hartzell was stunned to look up and witness a stranger emerging from the rooftop doorway, his gun centered on the Coordinator, commanding him and the ape man to get on the ground. Hartzell also saw the tall man emerge from the shadows at the side of the building, his pistol aimed at their would-be savior.

That was all he needed. Hartzell sprang to his feet in an instant and had Lucy by the hand, pulling her away from the fray, away from certain death. They both ran fast and hard cross the flat-top roof, Lucy kicking both heels off on the fly, in a frenzied exodus to the north side of the high rise.

Cady's heart was in his throat, a deafening ring inside his head. He swept the Glock back as Westlow took off after the tall man. He'd seen Hartzell and the girl make tracks as his eardrum burst. But now the bald man had turned, taking off after the Hartzells.

"Stop!" Cady screamed—or thought he'd screamed, as he couldn't hear a goddamned thing besides the incessant ringing. He put one into the air but the bald man was out of range and lost in the gloom.

Ciolino made a move, his arm shooting inside his jacket. Cady was on him immediately, smashing the barrel of the Glock against the man's ear, splitting it open and taking all fight out of Ciolino as he slammed him down hard on the roof tarmac. He had Ciolino flex-cuffed, hands behind his back, in seconds. Cady dragged him to the far side of the JetRanger, into the darkness opposite the doorway, and popped another flex-cuff to tether Ciolino's bound hands to a leg of the helicopter. He found Ciolino's Heckler & Koch Parabellum holstered under his suit jacket and was glad he'd pistol-whipped the son of a bitch. He shoved the 9mm into the back of his belt.

As a parting thought, in order to make rescue an extra thorny task, Cady grabbed Ciolino's suit jacket by the front lapels and wrenched it over Ciolino's shoulders and as far down as possible, cementing the man's torso in place. Ciolino mouthed off the entire time. Cady couldn't hear word one screamed in his direction, but he didn't need to read lips to understand the man's intent.

Then Cady took off on a sprint northward, after the Hartzells—and after the bald man.

Chapter 45

There was nowhere left to run.

Hartzell glanced over the three-foot safety wall that kept maintenance workers from an accidental misstep and a seventy-flight plunge to an unforgiving walkway below. A wave of vertigo splashed through him and Hartzell jerked back. He and Lucy had skirted a metal shed housing electrical equipment, bolted past a briar patch of satellite disks with the odd antenna tossed in the mix, dodged a minefield of round pipes that jutted up indiscriminately from the flat top of the roof itself, and now stood—barring both of them miraculously sprouting a pair of wings—at journey's end.

Hartzell had heard three shots ring out in rapid succession. Likely from the same gun. He got an inkling that it didn't bode well for them.

In the moonlight they watched as the bulky shadow steadily advancing toward them turned into the beast they knew as St. Nick. They didn't need the moonlight to recognize the crooked smile of a psychopath.

Hartzell stepped in front of Lucy, brought his fists up in front of himself in a classic boxer stance, and then danced out to slay the beast. St. Nick showed no inclination to defend himself, but marched onward, full-speed ahead. Hartzell prayed for a glass jaw and threw all his weight behind a roundhouse aimed at the bald man's chin. Nick tipped his head at the last second and Hartzell's blow crashed against an iron cheekbone. Then Nick was on him. A shocking head-butt to the brow dropped Hartzell like a sack of wet cement. Hartzell groped blindly at Nick's feet, trying to slow the big man down, keep the bastard away from Lucy, give her another chance to flee, but he failed miserably and the caveman paused only long enough to give Hartzell a breath-stealing jab in the guts with the metal toe of his work boot.

Lucy raced diagonally, but St. Nick read her movements like a billboard and had her by the throat in an instant. He lifted her high into the air with his right hand, turned, and began walking back to the skyscraper's edge.

"You were fucking warned, Hartzell!" St. Nick screamed at the night as Lucy gasped for air, her legs kicking at the emptiness beneath her. "And goddammit—we were fucking serious!"

Cady's lungs were aflame from the mad dash across the roof when he caught sight of Hartzell laid out on the deck with the bald slab of granite carrying Lucy in a choke hold toward the side of the building, his intention crystal clear: to send the girl into orbit. Cady dropped into overdrive, came in hard and slammed into Fiorella's enforcer hockey-style, his shoulder knocking into ribs on the left side of the big man's spine, spinning the giant around and forcing him to release the girl. St. Nick tossed Lucy to the ground hard and then focused his full attention on the federal agent.

Cady swept the Glock upward but St. Nick latched onto his gun hand, effortlessly shoving it sideways, wrapping his bratwurst-sized fingers around Cady's right hand—his crippled hand—and crush-ing it into the 9mm. Cady swiped an elbow into the bald man's chin. The blow did nothing. He squeezed the trigger, hoping that would free him from the ever-tightening vice grip. Two shots rang out. St. Nick barely blinked. Cady withered to his knees in excruciating pain and realized his hearing had returned as he heard the bones in his hand begin to snap. Cady knew he'd never reach the Heckler & Koch in the back of his waistband, so he shot a south paw upward, hammering his fist into the big man's testicles—finding the creature's Achilles' heel.

St. Nick released Cady's broken wing and dropped a hand between his legs, but thundered down his own right fist across Cady's eye and cheekbone. Feeling as if he'd been hit by a meteor shower, Cady found himself on his back, stunned like a bird that had ricocheted off a window, gazing philosophically up at this leviathan that clung to his nuts like a kid holding candy, a look of murderous rage smeared across his reddening face.

And as if the situation couldn't get more surreal, Cady noted, a shadow suddenly flew over him.

Air crept back into Hartzell's lungs as he watched the stranger from the rooftop doorway—the man who was miraculously not dead—crash into St. Nick, freeing Lucy. He got to his feet as the stranger sunk to his knees before the living steroid. Hartzell nearly cheered as their rescuer pounded the cold-blooded bastard smack between the legs. His heart sank as he watched St. Nick club the man with his free hand, hatred engraved across the behemoth's brow, his back now against the ledge... *his back now against the ledge.*

Hartzell leapt over the man who had saved Lucy's life, pushing St. Nick backward with all his might, pushing him over the edge. Fiorella's enforcer's attention had been focused on his balls, first and foremost, and then the man spread-eagled before him, so Hartzell's sneak attack began to pay dividends as Nick stumbled backward against the short wall. But the big man had lightning speed even as he lost his battle with equilibrium. A right hand snaked out and clenched Hartzell's left forearm to stop himself before he plummeted into the void.

Lucy—God bless his beautiful daughter—joined the fray. With a rush of adrenaline the girl performed a masterful stroke, attacking St. Nick's legs while Hartzell's continued shoving and the big man's momentum forced him backward. Lucy cupped the back of his ankles, and like raising a wheelbarrow filled with blocks, she pulled up for all she was worth, and lifted and flung Nick's legs over the side of the ledge in a flurry of pure adrenaline.

St. Nick's eyes were now the size of saucers, but he clung to Hartzell's forearm and pawed at the ledge top with his other hand. And slowly the monster began to pull himself back up. Hartzell shot forward and down against the short wall, trying to keep the giant off balance. He rained blows on the bald man's free hand, which clutched the ledge urgently. Lucy suddenly appeared on Hartzell's left side, her face stretching down as she opened her mouth as wide as possible and sunk her teeth deep into St. Nick's wrist where he gripped her father's arm. Her jaw squeezed tighter and Hartzell saw blood begin to flow. The killer's mouth opened into an ever-widening ring to match his saucer eyes as he relinquished his grip on Hartzell's forearm.

Everything hung in the air for an endless moment, but Nick's other palm on the ledge wasn't nearly enough to save him. A second later the threat was over. The mob enforcer screeched bloody murder all the way down the side of the high rise—until the sidewalk far below cut him short.

Hartzell and Lucy slid down to the rooftop, backs against the ledge wall. Combat weary. Excited to be alive.

Chapter 46

Some *Chessman* he had turned out to be.

Jesus, Marly, Westlow thought, *I'm traipsing along the pinnacle of a Manhattan skyscraper, nearly a thousand feet above street level, in hot pursuit of a professional hit man from Chicago—the man I'm positive is my own copycat—while wearing a white muscle shirt, which means—even though this absurd get-up makes me look like the anti-Jake Westlow—that for the task at hand, I'm lit up like a Christmas tree. What a fustercluck this is turning out to be, huh, Marly? You can stop your giggling at any time now.*

But Westlow had one last arrow in his quiver. A final move that would keep him from eating prison chow for a decade before a lethal injection worked its way down the pike. Turned out he wouldn't have to break into a room on much lower floor and go out the window. No, something much easier had presented itself, and Westlow only hoped he wouldn't have to go through Agent Cady. He'd already hurt the man enough. His very last chess move was simplicity itself. He couldn't believe his eyes when he saw it sitting there on the helipad. Westlow knew how to fly that bird.

And all he had to do was survive the task at hand. If not for Hartzell's daughter being snared in this deadly mix, he'd have FedExed Agent Cady all of the materials from the *discovery* phase of his investigation. Of course, speaking of Agent Cady, he did owe the man a hand. Literally.

Westlow ignored the throbbing in his side. The son of a bitch in black had been savvy enough to break one of Westlow's ribs once he realized he was on the losing end in the dispute over his handgun. The tall man hadn't panicked, not in the least. Like a snake he'd struck a blow to keep Westlow from getting off a shot and bringing tonight's extracurricular activities to a resounding halt.

The silhouette darting thirty yards ahead of him made for an all-but-impossible shot. By the time Westlow took the proper stance and aimed, the tall man would be further along in the murkiness of the night—out of range. The tall man cut right in front of some type of air-handling unit sheathed in metal. Westlow paused long enough to place three shots through the tin to usher the killer onward, give the tall man no time to regroup, and keep on offense. Westlow made a wide arc around the rectangular unit, slowly, in case the killer pulled another gun from his arsenal. The front of the housing unit was grated shut, no escape there. Westlow crouched down to limit himself as a target and swept the Beretta left to right and back again, searching the shadows.

Thin air.

The southeastern corner of the high rise lay before him. Two short walls converged as one. The hair rising on his neck, Westlow checked his back. Between him and the building side were two industrial turbine ventilators, each nearing four feet in height and wide as a box spring. A dozen or so circular pipes shot up from the roof, but nothing even the puniest of anorexics could take cover behind. He looked left and spotted some kind of facility shed off to the west. No way the tall man had made tracks for that destination without Westlow hearing him. He crouched still and listened. *The tall man is either keeping this housing unit between us like bad Vaudeville or he's hunkered down behind one of the industrial ventilators. If he's playing possum, he likely has another gun and is waiting for me to saunter into view.*

Westlow cut sideways, used his left hand to vault up onto the housing unit he'd recently put three holes in, rolled across it, flattened out, and peered over the corner edge, left and right.

More thin air.

Westlow jumped off the unit, made a hell of a ruckus as he jogged in place, Beretta aimed in the direction of the two turbine ventilators. Nothing. He put a bullet through the center of each one.

More nothing.

The son of a bitch has nerves of steel or he's not there, Westlow thought. He crept wide, toward the building side, knowing he'd have to clear out the industrial turbine ventilators like spider holes on Iwo Jima before he could move on. Westlow concentrated on the moonlit shadows as he curved around the first one, looking for any indeterminate shapes or sizes indicating someone lying in wait.

A thought pierced Westlow's mind. If pursued, do the unexpected. He thought about his escape route from Dennis Swann's north-side apartment up to the roof back in Richmond. If a guy had remarkable upper-body strength and a pair of rubber-soled shoes, it wouldn't take much more effort than climbing rope in gym class. He could hang over the side of Hartzell's tower, focus on anything and everything but the view down, wait a minute or two for the threat to pass by, flip quietly back over and then attack from the flank—from prey to predator in a single instant.

Oh shit!

Westlow twisted about-face. What seemed a flapping of raven wings was upon him. The tall man flung sideways as Westlow aimed the Beretta, a straight-edge razor slicing down through Westlow's forearm, cutting deep. The 9mm fell to the rooftop. Westlow lashed out with his left palm, throwing the tall man off balance, buying

Westlow a moment as the shadowy figure realigned himself for the kill. Westlow leaned back on his left side, and then snapped a side-kick at the tall man's kneecap, hoping to hobble the stealthy fucker. It missed his knee but the heel of Westlow's cowboy boot caught the tall man's fibula, enough to smart and put him momentarily on defense.

Westlow knew he'd been tagged bad, blood flowing freely down his right arm, and knew that time was not his ally. He couldn't imagine the tall man being one to follow the Marquess of Queens-berry rules on this rooftop, spot him a minute to tourniquet up before they continued. In a knife fight it was best to get in close, make it hard for the opponent to maneuver, so Westlow went in like Mohammed Ali, quick uppercuts connecting with air. The tall man feigned and swiveled, somehow knowing each of Westlow's swings ahead of time. Westlow backed up, breathing deep, and the tall man flashed forward. Westlow's right leg went up to block and the tall man's knife flashed again, cutting through jeans, skin, and nicking Westlow's own fibula.

Westlow bounced back to the building corner, fists in front of him, a game face hiding the fact that his rib was broken, that his forearm was gushing blood, that his right leg felt as though it had been gnawed by a pit bull. Westlow stared into the killer's face, the tall man's features sinewy and focused, narrow eyes radiating an intensity seen in athletes at the top of their game, an ice-pick nose, thin lips bent in a smirk. A lethal Ichabod Crane, the tall man was going to carve Westlow up like a prize turkey at Thanksgiving din-ner and love every second of it. The tall man was playing matador to Westlow's bull—and he knew that Westlow knew it.

The tall man is familiar with my boxing skills and leg kicks, West-low calculated. *Suicidal to sludge forward with the same futile bag of tricks*. Westlow figured he could stomach dying, but one thing he couldn't stomach would be losing to this sinister prick. Time to switch it up, change tactics. Westlow danced a counter-clockwise arc around the killer, circling the arena as though stalling, making the tall man pivot, his back now to the building corner. Fiorella's assassin held the straight-edge out in front of him, shoulder level, adopting a *wait and see* posture, taking great pleasure in Westlow's predicament, knowing that with each passing second his opponent was weakening.

Westlow peeked down as though looking for the dropped Beretta, knowing full well he'd be dead long before he could pull the trigger, but wanting to flip diversions at the tall man in real time—steer him in other directions, keep him busy processing alternate scenarios. Have him prepare for the obvious, and then attack from left field.

Westlow tossed a glance backwards, make the tall man think that he might be getting ready to turn and flee, however one-sidedly lethal that footrace would be. Westlow feigned a short step left, and then charged inside the tall man, broadcasting a right hook. Once inside, Westlow dropped to a crouch, switching from boxing to wrestling. Both arms circling inside the tall man's right knee, Westlow shot up like a rocket launch.

The tall man slashed at empty air where his opponent had been. He realized a split second too late what move the man in the white muscle shirt had made, knew he'd committed a fatal error, and brought the straight-edge downward even as he felt himself begin to rise. The razor sliced at the back of his opponent's neck and then deep into his shoulder blade before the tall man was spun hopelessly backwards over the edge of the high rise, airborne, and out into the midnight air.

Westlow slid to the ground, breathing heavily.

I think I'll just sit here and rest a moment. Westlow's thoughts ebbed in slow motion. *Take a quick coffee break.* He stuck a palm to the back of his neck. It came back covered in blood. He felt like a fish fillet. Nothing that a couple thousand stitches and a quart of O negative couldn't cure. *Just a little siesta before I commandeer that JetRanger and head for parts unknown.*

Just a little siesta is all I need.

"What do you think, Marly?" Westlow didn't know if he'd spoken aloud or simply imagined that he had. A dense fog wrapped his thoughts. "Agent Cady can take it from here, can't he?"

It was nap time, like in elementary school, but floating through the haziness and shade, Westlow felt a familiar presence. As suddenly as the feeling appeared, it was gone. She was gone. And Westlow was left with the singular notion that Agent Cady was indeed in deep trouble.

"No, I didn't think so, either."

Somehow Westlow pushed himself to his feet.

Chapter 47

Cady's right eye was swollen shut. He'd need an ENT to determine what percentage of hearing loss he'd have to live with. Right now life sounded as though he lived in a vacuum cleaner. Worst of all, his right hand looked like something the cat had screwed. Cady couldn't bear to look at the mangled mess and dropped a flap of his suit jacket over it as he marched the Hartzells back to the helicopter pad.

Clutching the Glock in his one good hand, Cady had identified himself as a federal agent to father and daughter Hartzell, and then tossed his last flex-cuff at Lucy. "I don't feel safe on this building top," Cady had informed the duo in perhaps the understatement of the decade. "You need to place these cuffs on your father or I'll be forced to do *something else* in order to feel safe again."

The hint of something else—possibly an impromptu kneecapping—hurried the young lady along.

Ciolino remained exactly as Cady had left him minutes earlier, tethered to the far side of the copter. Never having heard St. Nick scream before, the mobster's jaw dropped as the realization sunk in that it was his friend who had made that horrible shrieking noise, that it was his friend who would not be joining them tonight or any other night.

There was no sign of Jake Westlow. Or the tall man in black. Cady considered digging out his cell phone to contact Agent Preston, but with only one hand, he didn't dare put down the 9mm in case the tall man re-emerged from the shadows. He hung near the front of the JetRanger, back to the mess in the cockpit, and constantly swept the darkness on both sides of the stairwell enclosure, playing mental gymnastics as to when Agent Preston and the team from Federal Plaza would ferret their way to the rooftop. Cady had a bad feeling about prancing the Hartzells headfirst into the stairway. If the tall man had returned, that would be the perfect spot to set an ambush from a hidden corner or even pick them off from the mid-level where the final flight of steps banked upward.

He hoped he was still recognizable, as it would be a damn shame to go down in a hail of friendly fire after all he'd been through that evening. Liz Preston had not been happy with him at all—another major-league understatement. He'd dumped a ton onto her shoulders in two abbreviated phone calls, leaving Agent Preston holding the bag to roust a team of agents and consult with the AD as well as coordinate with NYPD at the scene.

"You're not looking too hot, Agent Cady," Drake Hartzell said. He and Lucy stood together a few feet back from Cady, adjacent to the tail of the helicopter. A certain phobia hung thick in the air as they kept enough distance between themselves and the man called Ciolino. "Are paramedics on the way?"

Cady shot him a glance, then raised his Glock at the figure now standing in the roof access doorframe.

"Agent Schommer," Cady said, breathing a sigh of relief and lowering his weapon.

However, Special Agent Beth Schommer did not reciprocate in kind as she stepped out into the night, her weapon never wavering from Cady's chest—and suddenly it became clear. Their first conversation flickered through his mind.

Go Bears.

They're not going anywhere with that quarterback.

"So you're Fiorella's *man* on the inside."

"Drop your weapon, Agent Cady," Schommer instructed. "Don't force me to kill you."

Cady dropped the Glock. He noticed what Schommer gripped in her hand was far from Bureau-issue. It looked to be some kind of Saturday night special, a junk gun like a Jennings 22 or a Raven 25. Something clean that she could toss.

Cady shook his head. "Why?"

"Sticks and carrots in an insane world." Schommer took in the Hartzells and then looked beyond Cady at Ciolino, who squirmed on the other side of the helicopter, his neck twisting as far backward as possible without snapping.

"Federal Plaza's going to be here any second now."

"Stop fucking around, Beth!" Ciolino shouted over his shoulder. "Blow this cocksucker's head off and get me out of this goddamned straitjacket!"

"The *stewardess* works for Moretti," Cady said, his eyes never leaving Schommer.

"Moretti's in this?"

"That's fucking bullshit!" Ciolino screamed back. "Kill this motherfucker right now!"

"If the stewardess is planning your trip, don't blow money on a return ticket."

As though flicking an off button, Ciolino deflated without another word. The man known to the Hartzells as the Coordinator ceased lobbying for Cady's immediate extinction, his head slumped forward, chin to chest, adrift amongst his own private demons. Cady could not have hoped for better.

"Moretti's been tracking them since they arrived in New York."

"That's not good." Evidently, Agent Schommer was a master of understatements herself.

"It gets worse. We got tipped about a leak. Jund's held all the cards to his chest this past week. We know about Fiorella and Hartzell."

At that point Cady could not believe his eyes—or, his one eye not swollen shut. Westlow, steeped in the shadows as though dipped in black ink, stepped from the side of the stairwell enclosure, yards behind Agent Schommer. And if Westlow looked like hell warmed over, that had to mean that the tall man was out of the picture. Cady was momentarily grateful that his face looked like a used piñata. It helped him give nothing away to Schommer. And he prayed that any looks on the Hartzells' mugs would follow suit.

"Turn and walk," Cady continued, wanting to keep her attention focused solely on him as Westlow crept forward. "Badge your way out of the building and just keep walking."

Westlow was a dozen feet behind the agent from Chicago. Now ten.

"You'll call."

"Take my phone." Cady pointed at his jacket pocket. "Take all our phones and jam the door shut. That's a hell of a head start."

Then Cady, a lifelong student of human nature, read Special Agent Beth Schommer's eyes. Her eyes read simply: dead men tell no tales. Four shots with the non-traceable. A couple more in the back of the head to take care of any medical marvels, wipe off, and then a quick toss under the seat in the helicopter or over the side of the building before sneaking back down to the security desk on the first floor with a bullshit story for Agent Preston. By the time Liz or Jund got suspicious, it'd be too late to test her for gunshot residue and by then she'd be wrapped tight in attorneys.

Westlow was now six feet and edging forward.

"Don't do it, Beth," Cady interjected, playing for time. "You run to Fiorella, you'll have the life expectancy of a housefly."

Westlow, a look of fierce determination on his brow, must have come to the same conclusion as Cady, that Schommer was ginning herself up for the wet work that lay in front of her. He stepped hard, planting a boot on the rooftop before him, distracting her. Schommer turned simultaneously with Westlow's swing, a mammoth left hook to her jaw. The junk gun went off as Westlow's blow connected, point blank, and both flew backward and down as if they were bowling pins.

Cady kicked at what turned out to be a Jennings J-22, sent it spinning into the stairwell. Unlike the bald monster, Schommer had a glass jaw. She'd gone down hard, a smash to the face and then another blow to the back of her head on impact with the roof asphalt.

"If she moves," Cady screamed at Hartzell while running toward Westlow, "kick her in the head."

"What?"

"She comes to, she'll kill your daughter."

Nothing more needed saying, as Hartzell rushed over and stood above the fallen agent like a placekicker.

Cady knelt over Westlow.

"Let the record show...you caught me."

"Don't try to talk, Jake."

The bullet had entered Westlow's lower ribcage and done its damage. Cady pressed down on the wound with his good left hand and tried to ascertain the depths of Westlow's other wounds. He was badly cut up. Cady was astonished that the man had been able to make it back here at all.

"Where's..." Westlow coughed. "Where's—"

Cady read his mind, knew he was referring to the threat they called St. Nick. He tilted his head toward the Hartzells. "They threw him off the side of the building."

Westlow took a string of short gasps.

"Forecast…didn't call…raining Mafia."

"You need to save your breath, Jake." Cady continued to apply pressure to the wound, his hand now covered in Westlow's blood. Westlow's eyes dropped out of focus and Cady knew he was losing him. He placed his crippled hand on Westlow's shoulder.

"Marly!" Westlow lifted his head, staring forward.

Cady, startled, twisted around to see what Westlow was seeing. Nothing but the night sky in front of them.

"She's here, Jake," Cady said. "Marly's here."

Westlow's head sank slowly back down to the ground.

"Marly," he whispered.

And died.

Epilogue

"The forensic auditors are already analyzing the—"

Cady stopped in midsentence when he spotted Terri Ingram standing in the doorway of his room at St. Vincent's Hospital. The two agents at the guest table, stellar intellects that they were, mumbled inanities about grabbing a late breakfast long enough to snap shut a laptop, then left to give the couple some privacy.

Terry arched her back and did a skillful impersonation of Special Agent Drew Cady. "Just a couple of scratches, Terri. The doctors are all over it. Makes no sense for you to fly out right now—Jund and the attorneys won't let me up for air until next week."

"I didn't want you to see me like this, Terri."

The swelling had decreased dramatically, but the area encircling his right eye was still a palette of yellows, blues, and dark black. His right hand was elevated, propped up and enmeshed in a sling. Cady was being prepped for a third operation in as many days.

Terri walked across the room, held his free hand in both her palms, leaned forward and kissed him full on the mouth. "Roland said you've got this *stoic-dipshit* thing going and flew me out."

"I'm surprised you caught hold of him between TV interviews."

"He called me back." Terri scootched Cady over so she could sit up next to him on the hospital bed. "He let me know how you're really doing."

"I didn't want you to worry."

"So my G-Man thought he'd show up in Cohasset looking like the Frankenstein monster and this small-town gal would be none the wiser."

Cady opened his mouth, but then decided to cut his losses and shut it.

"I saw your colleagues drag Fiorella out of his house while he was still in his jammies. They're looping that footage on CNN."

"I suspect a certain AD made damn sure the press would be there."

"I suspect a certain AD is going to fight me for you."

"My money's on the small-town gal."

"Good answer," Terri said. "Anything new, G-Man?"

"The accountants are going into Witness Protection. Schommer's trying to cut deals, but that may not be in the crystal ball."

"I see they got that poor boy back from Guatemala."

"They used the kid to twist a New York Deputy AG, some drip named Stouder, into providing Fiorella with daily updates. Stouder's talking. Drake Hartzell is talking. The only person not talking is Rudy Ciolino—Hartzell's Coordinator. He hasn't said one word since we had our chat on the rooftop."

"Cat got his tongue?"

"Something's got his tongue, all right."

"What about the daughter? Is she tied up in any of this?"

"Hartzell claims not. Claims Lucy never knew what he did with investor finances, and that she only came into play as Fiorella's tool to extort Hartzell into playing along."

"Do you believe him?"

Cady thought some more. "Lucy's only twenty. Any involvement in Hartzell's scam would have been a recent development. Jund will watch her, though, see if she leads him to any hidden treasure."

They sat together, holding hands for several minutes.

"Can I come with you to see Dorsey?"

"I'd like that."

"What are you going to tell her?"

"Everything."

They sat for several more minutes.

"I think you need some serious R&R, G-Man. And I happen to know just the place where you can sit back, rest your dogs, and cast a line in the water."

Cady glanced at his elevated hand. "I won't be able to reel anything in for quite a while."

"Well, if that's the case, I know something we can do instead."

Cady smiled. "Good one."